# Claiming the Heart of Vraithe

## A Vraitheian Alien Romance

### Book One

### Kelly Washington

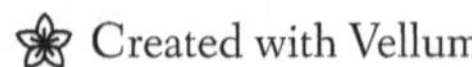 Created with Vellum

# CLAIMING THE HEART OF VRAITHE

## A VRAITHEIAN ALIEN ROMANCE

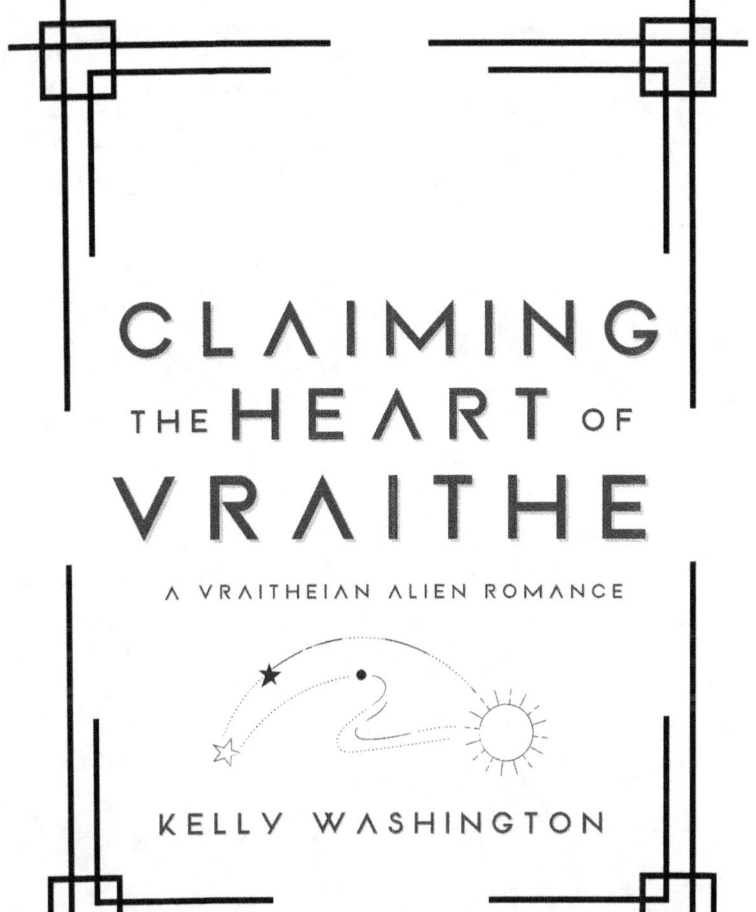

## KELLY WASHINGTON

# SYNOPSIS

*Can an army combat veteran find new love with an alien prince from another planet, or will the machinations of her ex-husband lead to disaster for both worlds?*

What happens when an ebook in cyberspace ends up in outer space?

It turns a failed author into a bestselling one. On another planet.

Wounded army vet turned English teacher Mara Eldress figures her flop of a memoir has sentenced her to the classroom...until she discovers her book is massively popular with space aliens.

Who knew a book signing tour would take an author to a distant planet?

Enter Vikk Stravdas. Sexy. Smoldering. And an alien prince who claims to be in love with her book, and offers to transport her to his home planet of Vraithe where she's a famous celebrity.

Yeah, sure.

But once Mara calls his bluff and is beamed away by this hunky extraterrestrial, her life turns into a whirlwind romance.

Talk about close encounters of a *kinky* kind.

One small step for a writer, one giant leap into an alien's sexual paradise, boldly going where no woman has gone before.

Mara wonders if she should ditch her anonymous life and remain on Vraithe...until her evil ex-husband stirs the pot back on Earth, causing a series of unfortunate events that require Mara's return, which triggers consequences that affect both planets.

With lives on the line, will Mara be able to write her own happily-ever-after with Vikk?

Find out in *Claiming the Heart of Vraithe.*

*I dedicate this novel to those readers who would not push a sexy
alien out of their bed*

# ONE

If she'd known that teaching ninth grade English would cause the local school board to launch a battle against her, Mara Eldress would have stayed in the military.

It had more tools at the ready.

Sitting at her desk in a just-vacated classroom, Mara was hate-reading the superintendent's email for the tenth time, when the principal, Dr. Eliza Brady stepped inside.

"I'm glad I caught you before you left for the two-week winter break," Dr. Brady said. The principal was a forty-year educator with a steady, stoic voice that carried weight and authority.

As a fifteen-year military veteran who'd reached the rank of Master Sergeant, Mara appreciated hierarchal order and predictability. She'd still be wearing an army uniform if it hadn't been for two concurrent IED blasts.

The resulting traumatic brain injury cut her military career short, but after regular therapy and early medical intervention, Mara was in a much better state. Her mood swings were less pronounced, the debilitating headaches less severe, and her sense of self-worth and achievement had skyrocketed after she'd completed her English degree two years ago and established a new career.

She was only a few months into her first year of teaching. She'd lived through the foster care system, she could coach screaming generals off a ledge, and she could dismantle an explosives ordnance with her eyes closed. But as a newcomer to academia, Mara did not have a lot of experience with *academic* obstacles.

In short, Mara's life had trained her to deal with conflict, but it hadn't prepared her for an overzealous school board.

"Good evening, Dr. Brady."

Dr. Brady leaned against one of the student desks across from her and crossed her legs. Her long gray hair was twisted in a tight bun and her tiny eyeglasses were perched precariously at the tip of her nose. It was a mystery to Mara how the wiry frames stayed put.

In the principal's hand was a slim novella and the object that had caused the school board's nuclear meltdown.

*The Curse of Mathilda's Sorrow* was a recently published manuscript that had been found in the estate of a rare books dealer who'd died a few years before. Its authorship was highly debated, though every famous author from the 1970s—which was when scholars believed it had been written—made the tale of an orchid that could grant near-immortal life all the more intriguing. That it had been tucked within the pages of a first edition of *The Picture of Dorian Gray* only added to its mystique.

"Given the way your eyes are cursing the screen, Mara, I surmise you received the superintendent's message?"

"What I surmise, Dr. Brady, is that they have not read *The Curse of Mathilda's Sorrow*. They claim the orchid is a hidden message of overt female sexuality." She glowered again at the open email. "How very convenient to issue the ban after the last class on the Friday before a two-week break. Can I challenge them?"

The principal moved to the frosted, icicle-laced windows and looked out over the gray twilight sky. Mara shivered as she followed her gaze, taking in the mounds of snow in the parking lot. Last week, Boston and the surrounding areas, which included Riley Township, woke up to two feet of snow. New to Boston, Mara had yet to find a way to warm her blood once winter set in, though she had to admit her blood was boiling at the moment.

With a neutral voice, Dr. Brady said, "Perhaps, Mara, though I am loathe to place impediments in your path. Tell me more about the English assignment."

Dr. Brady reminded Mara of a prim 1800s English governess. She'd overheard other teachers say the principal was intimidating, but Mara found formidable personalities relatable.

She'd worked tirelessly for demanding army generals, navigated the military's complicated medical system and, for the last two years, she'd fought tooth and nail to get her daughter's mysterious symptoms diagnosed.

She wasn't asking for a miracle cure; she and Finley just wanted to know what was wrong.

Mara had even written about her experiences. Part memoir, part self-help book, *Fighting for Her: A Soldier's Struggle* had barely made a blip in the publishing world. Mara didn't blame her literary agent for dropping her. His note said that their "interests no longer aligned but he wished her continued success in the future."

Mara hoped that Dr. Brady's interests would align with hers about the school board.

"My students are exploring the differences in how the English language is used between two stories of similar theme that are at least fifty years apart. *The Curse of Mathilda's Sorrow* is one of five options. All selections were pre-approved by the school board with the understanding that students, or their parents, could opt out, provided they suggested a proper alternative. Four students chose *The Curse of Mathilda's Sorrow*, fourteen students chose one of the other offered choices and two students opted out. They owe me their selections by tonight. They have the two-week winter break to do the reading."

Mara figured Dr. Brady must not have expected such a precise response because, as she slowly pirouetted to face Mara, her delicately arched eyebrows went into super-arch mode.

Then, almost as quickly, she dropped that expression, clasped her hands behind her back, and sighed. "I can tell you've put careful planning into the assignment, Mara, which I admire. However, the school board received multiple complaints about this book in particular and have voted to remove *The Curse of Mathilda's Sorrow* from the curriculum until it has undergone a content review. You will—"

"How many parents?" Mara interrupted. She figured one or two might object to the book, but to prevent *everyone* from reading it was in poor spirit.

Dr. Brady's mouth snapped shut. Her steel-gray eyes turned cold and reprimanding. Mara chastised herself. She'd gone and pissed off Dr. Brady.

"You will instruct your students to select a different book. The superintendent has already emailed their parents."

"Will you support me if I submit a rebuttal?"

Eliza Brady softened toward Mara. She fiddled with the colorful silk scarf that hung loosely about her throat as she thought through things. Mara was beautiful but also a willowy thing, tall and thin, with brittle edges that might snap under duress. She knew her history, her military career, her combat experience. The school system was a different beast. It could chew up and spit out the best. She didn't want that for Mara.

"I admire your dedication to literature, Mara," Dr. Brady said. "But my hands—and yours—are tied until the school board makes a final determination."

She paused in front Mara's busy desk, her hand hovering above a precarious stack of books that needed returning to the library. It was an assortment of young adult dystopian novels her students must have read for a previous assignment.

A hopeful expression bloomed on Mara's face. "I sense a 'but' in your statement."

Dr. Brady smiled. "Yes, you have my support in submitting a rebuttal. While I have not yet read *The Curse of Mathilda's Sorrow*, I will say this: after a short amount of research, I am of the opinion the school board is overreacting."

"Thank you."

"Don't thank me yet. Send me a draft email tonight and I will review it." Her gaze flicked over to the stack of books. "Best get these to Ms. Stravdas before she locks the library. I believe she is leaving early. Something about her brother being in town."

Mara groaned, practically feeling the color drain from her face as she glared at the books stacked on her desk. They taunted her. She could have avoided this fate if she'd returned them earlier in the day.

Dessa Stravdas, the school's librarian, would not shut up about her older brother, Vikk Stravdas. Every conversation somehow veered into Dessa suggesting they meet. The librarian failed to understand that Mara just wasn't interested.

Mara was not in the right frame of mind for romance, not a

casual date or two, not even an erotic daydream. So why bother?

As Mara left her classroom, a flood of injustice filled her veins, the delayed emotional reaction not unexpected even as it threatened to drown her.

She wanted to run, to scream, to punch the school's boring beige brick walls, but of course she would do none of those things, at least not while carrying a dozen books in her arms. It wasn't lost on her that everyone seemed to want to protect impressionable teenagers from reading controversial novels, yet had no qualms with eighteen-year-olds joining the military to bear arms and fight—and often die.

Mara stopped walking. She was shaking. Then a wave of nausea hit and her ears started to ring.

Negative thoughts did this to her. She hated looking or feeling weak, even if no one was around to witness it. It was almost ingrained into her soul. Mara had been one of those eighteen-year-olds. As soon as she'd aged out of the foster system, she'd joined the military. With average grades and no money to attend college, she had no other prospects.

Truth was, it wasn't all bad. She'd traveled the world, made amazing friends, and true to the military recruiter's word, she was finally able to go to college—even if it was well after the fact.

*Think positive thoughts, Mara.*

For several long moments she practiced a series of breathing exercises to keep her stress level from rising and prevent a debilitating migraine from sneaking up on her. Elevated stress levels made everything a thousand times worse. Mara could not afford to have a breakdown, not when things were finally starting to go well, not when she had to be strong for her daughter.

After a short time, she felt steady enough to continue, grateful that the hallways were quiet as she made her way to the library. Up ahead, a petite figure in a puffy purple coat carrying two large canvas bags stood at the library's double doors.

Mara, sighing with relief, didn't see signs of anyone else with the librarian. Perhaps Dr. Brady was incorrect.

"Please wait, Ms. Stravdas," Mara called out. Ms. Stravdas turned in surprise before a large smile spread across her heavily bronzed face. The blond hair piled atop her head was so bright, it was almost white, and shone like a lighthouse beacon. As soon as Mara closed the distance, she added, "I apologize for my tardiness."

The librarian pushed open the doors with animated flare. She was as tiny as a pixy and as energetic as a sparkler. She assessed the pile of books in Mara's hands.

"For that many books, Mara, your late fee will cost you a pretty penny." She let out a tinkle of a laugh that made her seem so young compared to Mara's own thirty-nine. Ms. Stravdas had a masters in library science, but she looked all of twenty-two.

"Yeah, sorry about that, Ms. Stravdas."

Mara hadn't been able to place Dessa's accent. It seemed a cross between Australian and Russian. Some words were light, with a lilted pronunciation whereas other words were rough, even choppy.

Over her shoulder, the librarian said, "Mara, I really wish you'd call me Dessa. I've only asked you like a million times."

Mara's arms had begun to ache, and she took a deep breath as she placed the books on the counter. The pleasant scent of a thousand books restored calm to her nerves. Books had gotten her through a rough childhood, heartbreak, and even combat. Late fee or no, a library would always be a safe haven for her.

"Right. Dessa."

Mara was formal with everyone because, well, as a new teacher, she never wanted to overstep bounds. She was extra formal with Dessa Stravdas because she didn't want to open any informal channels where the librarian might find an opening to casually mention her brother, Vikk Stravdas, a successful filmmaker who was supposedly single *and* handsome *and* funny.

Mara didn't have time to be set up on a blind date.

As Mara zipped up her winter coat and dug deep in a pocket to retrieve her keys, Dessa made no secret of studying the books' spines while also stealthily observing the new English teacher.

"Lots of dystopian novels in that stack," Dessa said conversationally. She liked Mara, but she retreated easily. "My brother Vikk"—Dessa said with an innocent smile—"he's a film director, in case I haven't mentioned it—likes to say that art imitates life."

Dessa swiveled and directed up her full gaze at Mara, who was easily five or six or ten inches taller. *Wow, what an Amazon. Tall and statuesque. Beautiful, with a touch of hardship tucked in the dark circles beneath her eyes.*

At the mention of Vikk's name, Dessa watched Mara's face tense up. It made Dessa want to laugh. She had to wonder if Mara was worried she'd recite Vikk's stellar qualities again. She wouldn't. Not tonight. Not after what she'd heard about the school board's decision.

Dessa took a deep breath and opened her mind's eye to Mara's essence. Her azure aura contained a tinge of red at the edges. Stress was trying to push in, but Mara was actively combatting it. *A fighter. I wish she'd let someone take care of her for once.*

To lighten the mood, Dessa said, "I can tell from your expression that you've been chatting with Dr. Brady."

"Am I that easily read?" Mara asked.

"Your face is etched with bewilderment and agitation. Hallmark Dr. Brady reaction. Plus, I heard about the school board's decision. What a bunch of assholes deciding that, and right before the two-week break. Never forget: it is always a strategic decision to drop negative news on a Friday night." Together they stepped out of the library. Dessa turned off the lights and locked the door. "For what it's worth, *The Curse of Mathilda's Sorrow* is a huge hit with the Vraitheians."

*Vraitheians?* Mara frowned, her eyebrows bunching. She'd never heard of such a word. "Who are the Vraitheians?"

"Uh..." Dessa froze for a second, stumbling to respond.

Just then, the janitor came toward them pushing a giant microfiber broom. She and Dessa made their way to the main exit lest they get swept up in crumpled paper, bubble gum wrappers, and chewed-up pencils. Mr. Jones, the high school's long-serving janitor, didn't care who or what got swept up.

"If you'd rather not discuss it, I'll totally mind my own business," Mara said with full understanding given how private she was about her own life.

"Oh no, it's okay," Dessa said quickly, an instant smile brightening her face. Donning her fuzzy gloves, she added, "Vraitheians are what I call my extended family."

"I see." Mara didn't see. She had this weird idea that Dessa lived in a cult called the Vraitheians.

Once outside, winter's cold air slapped Mara in the face

and she had to blink back icy tears. The ground was crunchy with snow and laden with salt crystals to keep everyone from slipping.

Mara eyed the distance she'd need to cover to get to her truck and knew she would need to tread carefully. She'd bought the used Ford F-150 truck after the school district hired her and now, having experienced a New England winter where twenty inches of snow falling in two hours wasn't unheard of, Mara knew she'd made a smart decision in purchasing the heavy-duty vehicle.

Her small two-bedroom, one-bathroom house was only a few blocks away. She eagerly looked forward to a warm fire, a hearty dinner with her daughter, and then a glass of wine after Finley fell asleep. Mara had a ton of work to do, namely drafting the school board rebuttal email, grading assignments, and sending notes to several students on alternate book selections.

However, she was mostly looking forward to spending time with Finley as well as her best friend from the military, Command Sergeant Major Hannah Atholms. Hannah, who was stationed at Fort Drum, New York, was coming to visit them next week. They'd been through so much together, it would be nice to see a friendly face.

"Earth to Mara," Dessa said with a wry grin.

"Ah, sorry about that. My mind was a million miles away." As Mara's gaze fell on Dessa's tangerine-colored Mini Cooper, a sense of worry filled her. "Can I offer you a ride home, Dessa? I have four-wheel drive."

Dessa shook her head and pointed toward a running SUV parked next to the Mini Cooper.

"Vikk is picking me up." With a twinkle in her eye, she added, "Come meet him."

"I need to get home to Finley. Perhaps some other t—"

Before Mara could finish the sentence, the driver's door

opened and a man stepped out of the SUV and strode toward them. Even on a slippery parking lot, his steps were confident.

As Mara took him in, her ability to think straight evaporated into a thousand snowflakes.

He was incredibly tall with a chiseled jaw and a rugged five o'clock shadow. He was as tan as Dessa but instead of blond locks, he was blessed with a thick crown of curling chestnut hair. His lips, which were red with the cold, were full and sensual and very much deserving of being the subject of poetry. Mara was reminded of Byron's poem, "She Walks in Beauty."

Even through his black wool coat, she could tell that he was an Adonis. *Why did he have to go and be an Adonis?*

Mara did not blink as he approached.

*Don't gawk, Mara. Keep your mouth closed. No gaping.*

The man was definitely hot enough to melt the polar ice caps. That said, Mara was shivering. While her Texas upbringing may have prepared her for encountering good-looking men, it had not prepared her for standing still in below-freezing weather.

"Good evening," he said simply. His eyes were dark, almost black. Sinful. Sexy. A hypnotic grin grew on his face. She had an instant thought that he could read minds, but shook it off. *How absurd.*

"Hello." Mara's voice was calm though she had to fight to keep it that way. Dessa's brother's voice, which held the same confusing accent, was a deep baritone that could easily turn disinterested listeners into sudden admirers.

She reminded herself that she was not usually attracted to extremely good-looking men. They were like shooting stars; nice to look upon but never obtainable. What would she do with a shooting star?

Beside her, Dessa bounced into action. "Vikk, allow me to introduce you to my friend, Mara Eldress."

*Friend?* Vikk projected the thought into his sister's RMO. The RMO—short for receptive mind orbit—was the Vraitheian channel for familial telepathic communication. *That's generous,* he added.

Dessa widened her eyes and threw him a reply of, *Knock-it-off, Vikk,* along with, *Not in front of the human.*

While Dessa had talked almost nonstop about Mara Eldress for several months, he knew that they were not exactly friends. In fact, just reading Mara's current body language, not to mention the red and gold rings encircling her aura, it was clear that Mara actively avoided his baby sister.

Vikk grinned. Mara looked ready to bolt. As Dessa made the introductions, she gestured up at Mara, as if she needed to distinguish whom exactly she was referring to. His sister was too energetic by half. No wonder the gorgeously tall woman was standoffish.

"Hello, Mara Eldress," he said with a smile. Little puffs of white air escaped his lips.

Extending a gloved hand, he felt Mara accept it with her own gloved fingers.

"Hello, Vikk Stravdas," Mara said.

There was something like reassurance, even comfort, in his handshake. Something she didn't know she needed until that moment. Vikk held her hand for a beat longer than normal, and Mara surprised herself by not pulling away.

*Before* the handshake, she'd been wishing she had ice skates so she could glide far, far away. *Now,* however...

She noted his facial expression, the interest written there, how he seemed to capture all of her with just one look. All at once, he lifted a masculine eyebrow, which accentuated his dark, sparkling eyes. *How could dark eyes sparkle so much?* Mara wondered. Then, biting down her tongue, she asked herself, *How could his dark eyes enthrall me so quickly?*

When Mara glanced away and spotted Dessa, the little librarian was grinning like a maniac. That was enough to zap Mara out of her dazed feeling.

Her chest felt like it had come loose and that something was unspooling out of her. She couldn't deal with this right now. She needed to leave.

Even without any movement, Dessa sensed Mara's emotional withdrawal. She'd figured it might happen but she could not miss an opportunity for the Vikk and Mara to meet.

"Here." Dessa shoved the canvas bags at Vikk. "They're getting heavy."

He took them without missing a beat.

"It was nice to meet you, Mara," Vikk said as he shifted the canvas bags in his hands.

Every few months Dessa loaded him up with the newest bestsellers. Her brother was on the hunt for books that could be translated into Vraitheian that might also be turned into a feature film on their home planet, Vraithe.

Dessa, who had lived on Earth for several years now, started translating many of the novels herself, though she usually translated only young adult dystopian novels or erotic romance novels. After meeting Mara and discovering she wrote a military memoir, Dessa thought she would take a stab at translating a work of nonfiction.

*Fighting for Her: A Soldier's Struggle,* became a surprise hit on Vraithe. Everyone was reading it, even at Taloncourt, the seat of the royal family. Dessa just wished she could tell Mara about it.

Vikk watched as Mara carefully descended the steps.

"I'll see you in two weeks, Dessa," Mara said. "It was a pleasure to meet you, Vikk. Goodnight to you both."

As Mara walked to her truck, got in, and started it up, Vikk could tell she'd briefly been under his spell but that it was now broken. He wasn't disappointed. He'd rather she decide that she wanted to get to know him on her own accord versus it being the Vraitheian appeal. It was easy enough to attract human women, but he never let it grow into anything more than a light flirtation.

From the moment he laid eyes on her, he knew Mara Eldress could never be a light flirtation.

There was a solid connection, even on his side, which was rare between a Vraitheian and an Earthling. He could feel the strings within his Vraitheian heartstrings tether outward, searching for her essence, seeking acceptance, permission, love. He called it back. *Not yet,* he told his lonely heart. *Soon, and only if she agrees.* Had Mara felt anything? Was there a tingle in her chest? Was that why she fled?

"I think that's enough matchmaking for one evening, Dessa," he said in their native language as they entered the warm SUV. He cranked up the heat.

He felt Dessa's eyes on him as she pointedly asked, "Are you wearing the locket, Vikk?"

A Vraitheian locket helped block false heartstring connections. Without consciously thinking about it, he reached into his shirt to feel the warm locket pressed against his chest.

"You know I never take it off," he said as he carefully drove out of the school's parking lot, "but it isn't foolproof, either."

"Ah, so you felt a heartstring stirring? I thought you might," Dessa said in a bubbly way. "Mara Eldress will come around." She paused, then added, "Eventually. She'll come around eventually."

Vikk rolled his eyes as he steered the SUV onto a mostly snow-free highway. "You can't force these things, Dessa."

"I know," Dessa said with a pout. "But, Mara has been through so much. I want to punch her ex in the face, and that's saying a lot."

*True,* Vikk thought as Dessa talked on. *Vraitheians are not violent by nature.*

"How is the movie version of her memoir coming along?" she asked.

Unbeknownst to Mara, her memoir was being made into a feature film on Vraithe. The hype surrounding it was off the charts, which meant the studio had given him carte blanche to produce and direct it, but things were not going as well as expected.

"Badly," Vikk said with a slight groan. "Filming has commenced, but I think I need to redraft certain parts of the script. There are not enough who have had a meaningful experience with humans to do it justice."

"Hmm," Dessa mumbled under her breath. "I wish I had the capacity to help you. Too bad we can't just ask for Mara's help."

His sister's casual remark took hold and Vikk found himself contemplating it. Naturally, he wanted to produce a well-received feature film. Additionally, he needed to please the queen or she'd cut his portal privileges.

But now that he'd met Mara Eldress, he wanted nothing more than to do justice to her story.

*Why* not *ask Mara directly?*

As Vikk exited the highway, he drove slowly through a

showy, holiday-lights-blaring neighborhood and let his mind wonder for a minute. His brain latched on something.

"Earlier, while we were standing on the doorsteps, did I hear correctly?" Vikk asked as he turned down Dessa's street and navigated fresh mounds of plowed snow. "Everyone who works at the school is on a two-week break?"

Dessa smiled a knowing smile as they pulled into her driveway. "Your hearing is as impeccable on Earth as it is on Vraithe, dear brother."

Vikk nodded as he contemplated his options. He knew what he had to do.

His chest squeezed and fingers flew back to his locket.

There was only one solution—and he had a strong feeling that the human woman who had activated his long-dormant Vraitheian heartstring was not going to like it one bit.

# Two

Tucked under a thick blanket, fifteen-year-old Finley Eldress was lounging on the living room couch, reading a text from her dad, when the front door opened and closed in a flurry of clatter.

A huge gust of icy wind blew into the house, something fell to the floor, and she heard her mom mutter a *Dammit!* under her breath. Finley's thin frame shivered. Her eyes glanced at the clock on the cable box just as her stomach grumbled. *Dinner time*, she thought with a smile as the scent of cheesy goodness filled the room.

Anything that distracted her from Dad's text was welcome. A few moments ago, Dad texted, "Abigail and I are getting married on Christmas Eve." *Poor Abigail.*

Finley locked her phone and placed it in her pocket. Mom must have grabbed pizza on the way home from school. Finley shuffled to her feet with the intent to assist.

"I'm coming to help," Finley said in a loud voice as she walked into the hallway.

There, on the floor, was an upside-down box of pizza. Finley let out a short laugh as she bent over to pick it up.

"Careful," Mom said in her mom-voice, "don't give me that look, unless you want to eat *floor* pizza." Then, after a soft sigh, Mom added, "I'm doing the mom-voice thing again, aren't I?"

"When don't you?" Finley rolled her eyes in exaggerated fashion but her voice wasn't tart. As it so happened, *everything* Mom said was said in mom-voice. It kind of came with the territory.

"Sorry," Mom said. "It's been one of those days."

*Tell me about it.*

At fifteen, Finley had recently been diagnosed with chronic fatigue syndrome, but she'd been suffering for close to two years before doctors finally took her and her mom seriously enough to pursue tests.

While there were some days Finley could barely manage to open her eyelids, today she felt pretty decent.

"I think I can manage picking up a box of pizza without blacking out, Mom."

Of course, as soon as she stood back up with the hot box in hand, Finley saw the blinking stars in her vision. *Floaties.* Nothing to worry about, but still, she casually leaned against the wall and quietly took a restoring breath. The weight of the box was imbalanced, which meant the pizza had slid to one side.

"I'm sure I'd manage to slip on it, like some bumbling idiotic cartoon character," Mom said with a bemused laugh. She hung up her winter coat and scarf.

Finley scoffed. "Says the woman with four combat tours under her belt who can expertly dismantle military bombs with her eyes closed."

Mom grinned when she said, "Well, my enemy these days are members of the school board, and their metaphorical bombs are much harder to dismantle than anything I ever did for the military."

"Sorry you had a crappy day." *I wish Mom wouldn't worry so much,* Finley thought. It killed Finley that she was a huge reason for Mom's stress.

It certainly didn't help that Dad bailed the moment Mom got injured by that IED blast, shirking every ounce of responsibility. Oh, he helped in the beginning, but things changed when he started to complain about it interfering with *his* life—how he couldn't focus on his newly started nutrition business. He didn't like taking Mom to her appointments, driving her everywhere, picking up her medicine. Toddlers were better behaved.

Finley had only been ten at the time, but she wasn't stupid. Plus, Dad wasn't very smart at hiding the fact that he was seeing someone else—or maybe he wanted to get caught. It all came to light when he forgot to pick her up from school one day. Finley had been left out in the cold because he was with his girlfriend. Mom had positively flipped out and had to ask a neighbor to pick her up.

Finley knew she needed to change the subject and fast. "Half cheese, half pepperoni?"

Unaware of her daughter's dour thoughts, a smile bloomed on Mara's face as she thought, *The kid worries about me too much.* "Well," Mara said as they made their way to the kitchen, "it *was* half cheese, half pepperoni."

Finley, who was wearing thick socks, slid her feet against the hardwood floor. It made a shush-shush sound that Mara found endearing. *Finley must be having one of her better days.* She placed her oversized backpack full of papers to grade on a dinette chair while Finley did her best to flip the pizza box right side up.

Mara held her breath as Finley placed it on the counter.

"Shall we see?" Finley asked, adding in a "ta-da!" once the lid was up.

"Yikes." Mara let out a low whistle. Stringy cheese was stuck to the top of the box while the pizza itself was an oblong lump shoved to one side. "What a messy mess."

"Metaphor for my life," Finley added sarcastically as she plucked pepperoni from the cardboard and popped it in her mouth, then abruptly spit it into the sink, her face going ashen.

Mara knew that look. Finley was about to shut down.

"Hey, don't say that." Mara took a few steps in her daughter's direction before pulling her into a gentle hug. "We're going to figure this out. I promise." She had to be careful since even regular hugs could restrict Finley's lung function. At first Finley was stiff in her arms but after a few seconds she relaxed in Mara's embrace. In the chaos of her former military injuries and her divorce from Calix, Mara's small pockets of contentment were in moments like this, when Finley melted into her arms and accepted comfort. "I know things are rough now, but we Eldress girls persevere. This is a new town and we have a fresh start."

When Finley pulled away, a tear slowly made its way down her pale cheek. "I'm too tired to eat anything. I'm going to go lie down for a while."

*What was Finley truly worried about?* Mara wondered. She felt sure there was something else troubling her daughter tonight.

It took everything within Mara's willpower not to wipe the tear away. She never wanted to minimize her daughter's emotions, but sometimes she felt like crying herself. Instead, she smoothed down Finley's long, brown, static-prone hair. It was on the stringy side, but at least it wasn't falling out in clumps like it was two years ago. That had been such a terrifying time.

"Okay, sweetie. If you get hungry later, I'll make you soup, if you want, or I can heat up the pizza. Do you want me to help you to your room?"

Teenage defiance flashed in Finley's dark brown eyes. "No," she said weakly before shuffling to the end of the hall. Her bedroom door closed with a soft snick.

This had been their standard evening routine for a few weeks now. Perhaps in a few months Finley would want to attend school in person. It was her choice. Until then, however, she was taking self-paced online high school classes while also receiving virtual tutoring for her Latin language coursework. Mara provided one-on-one English tutoring.

Overall, the extra tutoring was pricey but Mara refused to let her daughter fall behind academically. Her teacher's salary and military medical retirement check barely covered their monthly expenses. Thankfully, Mara's status as a one-hundred-percent medically retired soldier gave them access to the doctors at the nearby Veterans Affairs hospital, which covered medical expenses.

If they were lucky, Calix sent a few hundred dollars their way, but it wasn't something he did regularly. He had his own life now, with a successful business and a model girlfriend. He had his own interests and had used their moving out of state to his financial advantage.

Calix had been a shitty husband and an even crappier father, but Mara didn't talk bad about him because at some point Calix might surprise them both and own up to his mistakes. It was Finley she was worried about; worried that she'd try to reach out and get rejected by a father who had shown very little interest in his daughter's well-being. As much as Mara hated Calix's guts, she would always be civil for Finley's sake.

As Mara bit into a tasty, though oddly-shaped slice, of

pizza, she couldn't stop herself from comparing the attentive Vikk Stravdas to her absent ex-husband.

Dessa had not been lying. Vikk belonged in a cologne commercial. As his image materialized in her mind, a tingle entered her chest. It felt like her heart had shifted into a nest of threads ready to reach out and grab hold of what it desired.

*Stop!* she told herself.

Instead of analyzing it further, Mara poured herself a glass of wine, sent a venting text to Hannah about the school board's decision, and started drafting her rebuttal email.

Vikk had never made an overt decision to kidnap anyone before. Vraitheians avoided violence at almost all costs with the exception of self-defense, and even then they would try to talk it out first.

*How exactly does one go about kidnapping a human?*

He parked his SUV on the street across from Mara's house and shut off the engine. It was very dark out, but her lights were on. He knew she was up because every few minutes he'd see movement at one of the lit windows.

He was a filmmaker, not a kidnapper. Perhaps he should just tell Mara the truth. Clearing his throat, he practiced the conversation in the SUV: "I look human but I am not human. My image is a mirage. I'm an alien from the planet Vraithe and I need your help. Will you walk through the Vraithe portal with me?"

She would think him insane.

He had never before invited a human to return with him through the Vraithe portal. That thought alone made his heart skip a heavy beat.

The two main portals back to his home planet were in North America and South Africa, with a few lesser portals throughout the globe that would transport a Vraitheian to one of the two main portals. The best Earth comparison Vikk could come up with was that it was like regional airports that flew passengers to and from main airport hubs.

In the beginning, it was all quite accidental. A young Vraitheian, tinkering with portal tools, found herself teleported to New England in North America in the Earth year of 1870 with no way back. Young Burbur worked tirelessly to build a portal that would let her return home and found her niche within the Bell Telephone Company working alongside Alexander Graham Bell and Thomas Watson. Shortly after humans invented the telephone, Burbur succeeded in creating a two-way portal. Ever since, Vraitheians, who could assume human characteristics via a glamour veil, had been visiting Earth. Several Vraitheians, like Dessa, had even made Earth their home.

A wry smile touched his lips as he thought about Earth's obsession with alien abduction. If only they knew how wrong they were. Little green men! Ha! Vikk recalled his amazement at learning humans had multiple entertainment channels solely devoted to solving alien mysteries. Granted, Vraitheians had done everything possible to steer humans away from the truth.

Though, it could not be denied that the Vraitheians were much more advanced in both technology and medicine. Vikk did not own a flying saucer, nor could he conduct medical experiments. Contractually, when they signed the portal's end user agreement, Vraitheians agreed to not interfere in human civilization—although sometimes that could not be helped, such as when Earth-bound Vraitheians founded prestigious tech companies or helmed scientific research labs. Smartphones and incredibly powerful vaccines did not just magically appear.

No, what Earth had over Vraithe was *entertainment*. Droves of precious, delicious, juicy, drama-filled entertainment.

Vraitheians lived and breathed for Earth-found novels, television shows, and feature films. The more dramatic, the better. Their never-ending demand was almost insatiable, and made worse because very few Vraitheians could translate the various Earth languages into Vraitheian. Dessa was doing her best by simultaneously translating several books at once, and Vikk trusted her judgement, but Taloncourt was demanding more. More. More. More.

As of late, the queen had become enthralled with Earth's military stories. The Earth film *Saving Private Ryan* had been translated into Vraitheian as *Stalking the Fourth Son*. Queen Uska hailed it as a masterpiece and all but ordered her royal filmmaker to produce more...or else.

Since Vraitheians were not violent, the "or else" mostly meant Vikk would lose his chosen profession, he'd be banned from Taloncourt, and his portal privileges would most likely be revoked for an extended amount of time. This was ironic considering the queen was his aunt and he her heir.

Vikk wanted to keep his queen happy, but he also wanted to keep his job, his home, and his travel privileges, which was why he was parked outside of Mara Eldress's house trying to decide on how to go about politely absconding with her person.

It had only been a few hours since he'd met her and his heartstrings still ached to reach out to her. He could feel her heartstrings unraveling, too, though he doubt that Mara Eldress understood it. Truthfully, this had never happened to him before. It was a helpless feeling. If Dessa were here, she'd be both pleased and amused.

In something of a nervous fit, his heartstrings wove themselves into knots. "Calm down," he told his chest.

It was as if his connection to Mara was getting stronger. Worry consumed him. What if Mara agreed to travel to Vraithe and something went terribly wrong? Vikk had to remind himself that humans *had* successfully traveled through the Vraitheian portal. He had to think positively.

Granted, there was that one ill-fated human, who had inadvertently stumbled into the portal center, accidentally passed through the portal and had, as a result, become liquidated. The portal was shut down for more than a week to clean up the biological contamination.

"It has been many years since a human was liquidated as they passed through the portal," he said out loud to himself.

Mara would *not* be liquidated. Vikk was playing several scenarios in his mind when he heard a crisp *tap-tap-tap* on the passenger window.

"What the hell do you think you're doing?"

Vikk recognized Mara's voice. Gone was that polite, professional voice from this afternoon. This was an angry Mara. However, before he could respond, he was momentarily paralyzed by an incredibly bright beam of light.

No one had ever accused Mara of being an easy target and she wasn't about to start now. She was almost finished writing her rebuttal email when she heard the approaching vehicle. When a few moments passed and no one rang her doorbell, Mara looked outside and immediately recognized Vikk Stravdas's SUV parked on the street. *How does he know where I live?*

Her pulse jumped and she felt a throb in her head. Instinctively, she knew that Dessa was not with him. She was more annoyed than scared.

Mara donned her winter coat and pocketed pepper spray and a self-defense flashlight that could temporarily blind someone. She slipped outside through the kitchen door.

In the darkness, she kept to the thick row of hedges that separated her property from her neighbor's driveway and ducked behind his vehicle before crouching beneath the passenger window.

Even though it was below freezing and snow was coming down in fat flakes, the man's sheer audacity made her blood boil. She felt hot and itchy inside her thick winter coat.

In the hum of the night, Mara listened for a long moment. He seemed to be talking to himself. She overheard words like *portal* and *liquidation*. Mara decided that just because Vikk was a good-looking man, it did not eliminate the possibility that he was bonkers in the head. Or, she thought, perhaps he was reciting lines from a film he was producing.

*Listen to your gut, Mara. A man does not park outside a woman's house just to recite film lines.*

She jumped up, tapped on the window, and demanded, "What the hell do you think you're doing?" When she flicked on the flashlight and aimed it at his face, she expected Vikk to flinch or duck or throw his arm over his eyes. Instead, he looked straight at her, through the extremely bright lumens.

For several long seconds the man did not move. Mara thought, *It's like he's carved out of stone.* His eyes were glowing like silver orbs, which was something she'd never seen before. Then, he blinked, and Mara gasped.

He didn't blink in the normal way. His eyelids fluttered *in* from the sides several times before his arm finally came up to block the light.

Mara scrambled back and barely kept herself from falling on the slippery road. She was steady with the flashlight—it was still aimed at him.

*What the hell just happened?*

Mara was not tired. She was not drunk. She did not have vision problems. Somewhere in the distance a dog barked and, with startling precision, Mara heard the clean crunching as she stepped in fresh snow. It was oddly mesmerizing in a slow-motion sort of way. Her nose was frozen and she could taste the cold air on her tongue.

And yet she could not deny that Vikk Stravdas's eyes blinked *sideways*.

*Sideways* while staring directly into a retina-destroying flashlight.

As casual as could be, he rolled down the passenger window and said, "Hi."

"*Hi?*" Mara let out a murderous hiss. Her brain could not process all the questions flooding her mind. "That's what you got? Hi?"

"Seemed like the appropriate thing to say. I didn't mean to startle you."

"Do I look *startled*? I am *angry*. There is a vast difference. Why are you—"

"Sitting outside your house? I wanted to ask you a question."

Mara was on the verge of laughing hysterically. His eyes had blinked sideways.

"Oh, *you* have a question for *me?*" She switched off the flashlight. She didn't want to draw attention from her neighbors. "How about this: What the hell are *you?*" It came out as a whisper.

"Mara, please," Vikk said hoarsely, "let me explain."

Vikk observed her startled expression, the way she huddled into her coat like she was more confused than cold. His chest ached. He desperately wanted to comfort her, to tell her everything was all right, that he would never harm a single hair on her beautiful head.

"Your eyes..." she said in a faltering voice. "They..." He could tell she wanted to say more but he knew she probably felt crazy. Humans tended to feel that way when presented with something from out of this world.

From above, muted yellow light cast down from nearby streetlamps and a few front porch lights flicked on. Most of her neighbors' holidays lights were turned off. It was like a scene from a noir film the way she stood in the middle of the icy road. Snow floated around her, landing on her hair, her coat. Even with the small distance, he could hear her perfectly. It was as if he was already in tune with her.

Vikk could almost see the thoughts brewing in her mind. Her aura was copper tinged with black, which meant she was contemplating violence.

She had no way of knowing that Vraitheians could withstand incredibly bright light, that they went into something of a paralysis to protect their nervous system before their inner defense mechanisms took over. That's why his inner eyelids shut the way they did. He tried to prevent it from happening but perhaps it was for the best that Mara witnessed it. It might make his business proposal somewhat easier to swallow, easier to believe.

"I know, weird, right?" Vikk said with a soft chuckle. He decided to just go for it. "Has Dessa told you about the Vraitheians? About our quirks?"

He smiled when Mara's head tilted sideways just as her aura shifted back to her natural shade of azure. So Dessa must have let *something* slip. Vikk wondered what.

Of course Mara knew that Dessa displayed quirks—many of them, in fact. However, sideways-shutting eyelids had never come up as a topic of discussion with the Riley High School librarian. Why would it?

Mara wasn't ignorant. She'd witnessed anomalies while on

active duty. Several soldiers, to include high-ranking generals, displayed extraordinary skills and abilities that seemed to defy human conventions. She remembered once talking about it with Hannah. However, at the time, they'd chalked it up to super intelligence or athletic prowess usually found in Olympic candidates. Mara never once thought them otherworldly or paranormal.

While standing here, she'd kept one hand in a deep pocket, ready to pull out the pepper spray if need be. Now, however, it felt like overkill. Instinctively, she knew that Vikk Stravdas was harmless. Mara had no idea how she knew this, she just did.

"You said you had a question for me?" she asked flatly.

"I have an early departure tomorrow, so I have limited time." Vikk lifted an object in his hand and, in the dim light, it took her a second to recognize it. It was her book, *Fighting for Her: A Soldier's Struggle*. "I have a business proposal for you."

Mara scrunched her eyebrows, her mind racing. Vikk was a film director. Was it possible he wanted to turn her book into a film or a documentary? If so, her story might reach a wider audience. Her literary agent and publisher might start talking to her again, maybe even ask her to write another book. Hadn't that always been her goal?

Vikk was struck by the various aura shades that morphed around Mara as she contemplated what his business proposal might be. Then, out of nowhere, the atmosphere shifted when he heard someone weakly say, "Mom?"

At the front door of Mara Eldress's house stood a smaller, thinner version of Mara Eldress. Did Mara have a child? He thought through the ramifications. This changed everything. His chances of convincing Mara to come with him to Vraithe dwindled by the second.

"I'll be right there, Finley," Mara called out in a reassuring tone.

He watched as Mara's contemplation aura returned with a vengeance. She had to be debating between convincing her daughter that everything was perfectly fine while also making it clear that he should get lost.

"Vikk," she said, surprising him, "why don't you come inside so we can discuss the specifics."

# THREE

After napping for a few hours, Finley woke up famished but was quickly distracted when she couldn't find Mom. Worry squeezed her insides. She tasted blood before realizing she was biting her inner cheek, and forced herself to calm down. Sometimes, when Dad called Mom, she'd take the phone call outside. Was he calling her now, with the news?

Finley peeked out a window and noticed an SUV parked out front. Whoever they were, Mom was talking to them. Dad drove a sports car so it wasn't him, not that she thought it would be. She looked at her phone to read Dad's text again. *"Abigail and I are getting married on Christmas Eve. We want you to be a part of the ceremony. I'll be there Monday to pick you up. Don't tell your mom. I'll call her in the morning."*

Finley didn't care that Dad was getting remarried. Good for him. She'd had zero illusions that her parents would get back together, and too much respect for her mom to even suggest it. The truth was that Dad didn't deserve Mom. But, they were her parents and Finley had to make the best of it. Still, Dad suggesting that he was just going to pick her up without coordinating it with Mom was an epically bad move. He hadn't even asked if she *wanted* to attend the wedding. Baltimore was hours away and Finley didn't do well in long car rides.

Putting that worry aside, if Mom wasn't talking to Dad outside, then who was she talking to at ten o'clock on a Friday night?

Finley wasn't one to sit around and wait for answers. Opening the front door, she yelled, "Mom?" and watched in amazement when Mom invited the stranger inside. Mom never acted irrationally, so Finley knew that whoever he was, he was either a friend or someone Mom trusted. Probably another teacher.

The closer he got to the front door, the taller he became. Stepping back, Finley practically had to crane her neck to look up at him. He didn't look like a teacher; however, something about him seemed calm and familiar, like a family doctor or a favorite uncle.

Finley was at ease almost instantly. Mom always said to listen to your gut. She didn't know this man, but she felt that she could trust him.

Mom led them into the living room. "Finley, this is Vikk Stravdas. I work with his sister, Dessa."

Finley nodded, recognizing his unique last name. The high school librarian's last name was Stravdas.

"I'd shake your hand," Finley said in as strong a voice as she could muster, "but I have this strange notion you might crush my bones."

Mr. Stravdas looked downright horrified at the suggestion. He glanced briefly at Mom before saying, "I assure you I would do no such thing." *What an interesting accent*, Finley thought. He lifted an eyebrow. "How about a fist bump, instead?" he suggested.

Mara wanted to smile as Finley gently tapped her pale knuckles against Vikk's massive fist, but she managed to keep her face neutral. It surprised her just how comfortable Finley appeared to be around Vikk. Kids usually made their thoughts known pretty quickly through their actions.

"It is kind of late for a visit, Mr. Stravdas," Finley said as she sat down in her favorite chair. Mara sat next to the fireplace while Vikk sat in the middle of the couch, leaning in, facing them. He wore a cream-colored business shirt and dark charcoal-colored slacks. In a comical way it seemed like Vikk was under their inspection. Around his neck, an onyx locket that was connected to a thick cord toppled out from beneath his collar before he quickly tucked it back in his shirt.

*He looks nervous*, Mara thought. He had her book in his hands.

"I see that you're holding my mom's memoir," Finley said. "Is that what you wanted to talk about?"

Feeling like a giant on their normal human-sized couch, Vikk looked back and forth between the two Eldress women and realized he'd probably bit off more than he could chew. Convincing one woman to go with him through the Vraithe portal was going to be extremely difficult. Two of them? Nearly impossible. Mara would never leave her child behind.

Their house was warmly furnished with thick rugs and burgundy-hued furniture. Prints and replicas of famous paintings lined the walls. Hanging pots of ivy vines cascaded from each corner, while side tables held framed photos from when the already small Finley Eldress was an even smaller human. Dessa once explained to him that these particular objects were called "yearbook photos" and that human parents and grandparents prized them above all other human artifacts.

It didn't escape Vikk's notice that there were books *everywhere*. On shelves. Piled in stacks under tables. On the mantlepiece. Atop the coffee table. There was even a slim novel tucked between the couch cushion and the armrest. Vikk read the title. Angela Carter's *The Bloody Chamber*. He wondered which of them was reading it.

Finley's aura was much like Mara's, though there was a bit more purple in her azure aura. There were several rings around Finley's aura, though, that worried Vikk. Rose gold was a concerning ring, signifying medical distress. Her bright silver ring meant she was pushing out a form of bravado. The girl was the size of a whisper, but Vikk admired her strength. Kindness toward the young girl washed over him. He found it reassuring that she didn't seem nervous or frightful of him.

While Vikk could never be too sure, Finley did not look very healthy. An idea formed.

Finley arched an eyebrow, watching their tall guest take in the room while waiting for his answer. She was pleasantly surprised when he said, "I hope to turn your mom's memoir into a film. I'm here to ask for her help."

She then understood why he was holding a copy of Mom's book.

"And you're, what, from Hollywood or something?" Finley asked just as she felt her mom's pointed glare. Finley chanced a glance at her. "What? I have a right to ask. It could be a scam— or a front for an international crime syndicate."

Finley knew just how important Mom's memoir was to her. She'd spent countless hours writing and rewriting it to meet her agent's expectations only to be let down after publication. Everyone and everything had let down her mother—the foster system, the military, Dad, and the literary world.

Finley would be damned if she'd let it happen again. *Mom deserves to be happy.*

"I appreciate your questions, Finley," Mr. Stravdas said. "No, I'm not from Hollywood. I'm from a place called Vraithe. International, yes." He smiled warmly and added, "Crime syndicate, no."

As Mara watched their exchange, she couldn't help but feel excitement bubble up within her. Finally! Someone who took notice of her work, her military story, her experience. That's all Mara had ever hoped for—to inspire, to educate. She didn't know who or what Vikk Stravdas was, but she was willing to listen to what he had to say.

However, when Finley asked, "Where exactly is Vraithe?" things took an unexpected turn.

Mara watched as Vikk swallowed several times before answering. "Well, Vraithe is somewhat difficult to explain. It's not exactly on any map you would have seen. In fact, some might say it's, ah..." He paused and his eyes crinkled when he finished with, "out of this world."

*Does he mean what I think he means?* Mara wondered as her mind traveled back to his sideways blinking eyes. What about Dessa? Did her eyelids blink that way, too?

Finley let out a huff of air as she stood. "He's wasting our time, Mom."

The words were barely out of her mouth before Finley wobbled. Mara's stomach dropped. In a flash, she was at her daughter's side, catching her before she crashed to the floor.

Finley's eyelids fluttered open and closed. "I'm fine," she whispered, trying to bat her away. "I should have eaten something first."

Vikk crouched beside them. Mara saw the depth of concern in his eyes when he asked, "May I assist in some way?"

"In the fridge, you'll find a bottle of cranberry apple juice," Mara said. "Bring it here."

Vikk sprinted down the hallway to perform the task and returned in a matter of seconds. He was not considered an athlete by Vraithe's standards, but here on Earth his movements were swift and effortless. He was not too concerned if Finley or Mara noticed. If they decided to return with him to Vraithe, they would hardly remember his physical movements here, not after they witnessed just how different Vraithe was from Earth.

He could tell, however, that Mara noticed his speed and precision.

"Thank you," Mara said as she helped Finley into a sitting position. They were still sitting on the floor with a petite Finley leaning against Mara's chest. "Tiny sips," she instructed Finley.

Finley grumbled. "I know how to drink, Mom."

Vikk assumed that this outburst would anger Mara but instead it made her smile. "Teenage rebellion," Mara said by way of explanation. "She'll be fine in a minute. Finley didn't eat dinner. She needs the electrolytes. It's not a cure-all, but I used to drink it in the military all the time, especially after physical exercise. That, followed by a can of plain tuna with a sprinkle of lemon juice seems to work well in a pinch for Finley."

With a flush spreading across her face, Finley felt warm all over and elbowed her way out of her mom's embrace. She didn't need them both to baby her. She leaned against the chair while finishing the drink.

"Next you'll tell him this sort of thing happens all the time." Finley threw a haughty glare at Mr. Stravdas, daring him to feel sorry for her. When she didn't read any pity in his expression, she relaxed a bit. Maybe he wasn't so bad. "Well, let me tell you, sir, it *doesn't* happen all the time." She put the glass down. The room was no longer spinning and her pulse was not as erratic. "Just *sometimes*."

"Do you need more juice?" Mr. Stravdas asked. His voice was baritone-deep yet melodic. It was like he was speaking English through a Russian-Australian voice converter.

Where the hell was he from? How could Vraithe not be on any map? Next he was going to them he was from another planet.

Finley felt a smile tugging on her lips. "No." She handed him the empty glass. "Please put it in the sink for me."

"Happy to," he said before doing that very thing for her.

While he was in the kitchen she said to her mom, "He's kind of weird but in a sweet way. He doesn't give off bad vibes. I hope he's legit, you know, about the movie thing."

Mara's focus was solely on her daughter's health—Vikk and his business proposition could go to the devil for all she cared. In her mind, she was already scheduling the necessary appointments with the right doctors in Boston. It was always an uphill battle just to see the right specialists when every doctor shrugged and said, "Give it time" when what the assholes really meant was, "We think it's all in your daughter's head."

From the doorframe, Vikk observed Finley's closed eyes, her orange hue aura of pain, while Mara displayed her typical azure aura with her own version of a bright silver ring. She was trying to be brave and strong for her daughter. In reality, she seemed very worried. Worried beyond measure.

It was almost as if they'd forgotten he was even in the house. He was proven right when he cleared his throat and Mara jerked her head in his direction, startled.

She got up and helped Finley to her bedroom. He overheard her say, "I'll leave your bedroom door open and be right back with some tuna. Call if you need anything else."

Once back in the living room, Mara began to straighten up the papers on the coffee table. She was ready for him to leave while at the same time she wanted to get lost in his dark, sparking eyes. "It's getting late, Vikk. Perhaps you can stop by the next time you're in town."

Something tugged at her chest, some invisible string that seemed to urge her into his arms. Instead of listening to that urge, she stood behind an armchair and studied his strong, steady figure in the doorframe. *Why do I get the sense that he'd do everything in his power to help us?* Mara wanted to laugh. Vikk Stravdas was a film director, not a miracle worker.

"When I leave in the morning, I won't be returning to Earth for some time, Mara. That's why I'd like to invite you and Finley to join me on Vraithe."

Mara blinked. *Returning to Earth?* She could not have heard correctly. Then she remembered what she'd overheard him say in the SUV. *Portal. Liquification.*

"I'm sorry, but what did you just say?"

Finley left her bedroom and tiptoed down the hallway. The juice and tuna fish had given her just enough energy to eavesdrop on the conversation in the living room. Though, just to be careful, instead of standing the entire time, she sat on the floor near the end of the hall, just out of sight, to listen.

"Vraithe is a small, Earth-like planet about ten thousand light years away," Mr. Stravdas was explaining in a low voice. It did not sound like he was joking. "There is a portal nearby that will take the three of us to Vraithe in under one Earth hour. While you and I work on the script for your memoir, Finley can receive medical screenings for her symptoms at a Vraitheian premiere medical facility."

Finley could not believe her ears. Was she dreaming or hallucinating? One thing she could ascertain was that Mr. Stravdas sounded pleased with himself, as if he'd come up with some grand solution to all their problems.

"Slow down," her mom said, in something of a stressed-out voice. "On an individual level, I understand each word you're saying, but when I put them all together, you sound delusional. I'm willing to accept that Vraithe is a small island I've never heard of, but another *planet?* I know you did that eye thing in the car, which I'll admit was nonhuman-like, and you moved way faster than a normal human when getting Finley her juice, but did you honestly believe that coercing a concerned parent into traveling with you under the pretext of medical treatment for their child would work?"

"Until I saw Finley tonight, I didn't even know you had a child, Mara."

There was dead silence in the living room and Finley was very worried about Mr. Stravdas's survivability.

"Let me get this straight, Vikk. You want to turn my memoir into a movie, correct?"

*Don't answer it, Mr. Stravdas. You're walking into a trap.*

"Correct."

*Dumbass.*

"And you did not know I had a daughter?"

*Seriously, do not respond.*

"No, I was not aware."

Finley shook her head. *He's a dead man.*

In a seething voice, her mom whispered, "Get out. Get out now."

More silence but then it sounded like he was gathering his things.

"I apologize for whatever mistake I have made, Mara." He actually sounded sorry. "On Queen Uska's honor, it was unintentionally done."

From the living room doorway, Finley stood up, entered the living room, and said, "Half of Mom's memoir is about me, Mr. Stravdas." She leaned against the couch. Mom was behind the armchair, a grim expression in her face that said, "You should be in bed" while Mr. Stravdas was standing near the window, holding his coat, scarf, and gloves. "Which suggests," Finley continued, "that you have not read it, nor are you serious in your effort to turn it into a movie."

Mr. Stravdas had an "Oh shit, so that's what I did wrong" expression.

He turned to Mom. "Mara, I must admit that I read the *Vraitheian* translated version of your memoir, not the Earth version." He cursed under his breath in some other language. "Dessa tends to, ah, take liberties with her translations."

Mom closed her eyes briefly. "Dessa translates them?" Mr. Stravdas nodded. "The books tonight, the two bags she gave you, were they also all translated versions?"

"No. I'm taking them to a group of translators in Taloncourt. There's only so many translations Dessa can do at a time."

"What is Taloncourt?" Finley asked.

Mr. Stravdas smiled at the question. Whatever it was, Finley surmised that it was important to him.

"Taloncourt is the Vraitheian royal palace. Under the patronage of Queen Uska, that is where I live and work. I run the royal filmography center."

"Enough." Mom was rubbing her temples. "Vikk, I'd like you to leave now."

"Where is the portal is located?" Finley asked at the same time.

Vikk saw the hopeful look in Finley's eyes as he dug into his coat pocket.

"Here." He handed Finley a business card that simply listed an address. "If you and your mom change your mind, meet me there at eight tomorrow morning." Mara had begun to crowd him, which he knew was a way to corral him. Without the slightest hesitation, she fastened a hand around his forearm and led him to the front door.

"Time to go," she told him as she opened the door. Her grip was firm, determined.

His skin sizzled beneath her touch. Sparks flowed through his veins and into his heartstrings. He could barely breathe.

There was no doubt in his mind: he belonged to her, and would move mountains to make Mara Eldress happy.

"I apologize for barging in on you like this and for surprising you with otherworldly information," he said. "My goal was to be upfront and honest from the start. I hope you will reconsider. Vraithe is more medically advanced than Earth, and I have every belief that we can help Finley. For me, the movie is an afterthought."

With that, Vikk cast a long look at Mara, hoping to see something other than confusion and distrust. Her aura was a strong copper with a black ring—she was considering violence. It was clear to him that she was not experiencing the same heartstring charge toward him. His heartstrings vibrated with a sting of sadness as he bid Mara goodnight and quietly left the Eldress house.

Mara sank in the chair after locking up the front door and checking all the other doors. She needed hard liquor.

"You okay, Mom?" Finley asked, nibbling on a cold slice of pizza as she sat on the couch.

It was late, after eleven, and Mara had a massive headache. The throbbing was thick in her skull. Did he think her gullible? That she'd cave at the promise of some magical hospital curing her daughter? Part of her desperately wished it were true. Her very soul begged for it to be a real, concrete, viable option.

"I'm sorry I let him in," Mara said. "I had no way of knowing he was bonkers. Dessa, his sister, seems...well, I was going to say she seems so *normal*, but she isn't. She's quirky and energetic, like a bag full of bumblebees, but I never would have guessed the family was, well, insane."

"In a way he seemed sweet, even if he hadn't actually read your memoir."

Mara looked up and watched Finley pick up the copy he'd left behind on the couch. "Even the part about the portal to a planet named Vraithe?"

Finley let out a giggle. "Yes, even that par—" She stopped suddenly after flipping through the pages. She dropped the half-eaten pizza slice right on top of Mara's ungraded papers.

"Finley," she groaned, "That's going to leave a greasy stain on my students' essays."

"Um, Mom," Finley said in a tone that made Mara take notice. "You should take a look at this." Finley waved her over.

Mara picked up the pizza and moved over next to Finley. "What?"

Finley placed the open memoir on Mara's lap. Except, it wasn't her memoir. Oh, it had her cover, her title, and her name was on every evenly numbered page, but the words were not hers. Mara wasn't sure if the writing *was* words.

Instead of English, a series of lines, slashes, long dashes, multiple-sized dots, and wiggles filled each page. She didn't know if it was read left to right, up to down, or right to left.

"Is it a translated version?" Finley asked in a quiet voice. "Do you think it's a prop or the real thing? Like, is this the Vraitheian language?"

Mara shut the book. A tiny puff of air wafted into her face and the gentlest scent of hazelnut hit her senses. "We will never know, Finley."

Finley turned to her. She seemed on the cusp of blurting something crazy. Finley was like that.

"I think we should show up tomorrow morning."

Finley watched as her mom's eyes went wide. Not much surprised Mom, but tonight had not been a normal night. It would be a night neither of them would forget for the rest of their lives—the day Mom invited the crazy alien inside.

"Give me one reason why we should, Finley."

She grinned. She wanted to say, *If it's true, then I won't be here on Monday when Dad shows up to drive me to his wedding.*

Her phone buzzed. Dad texted *again*. She angled it so Mom wouldn't see Dad's newest message: *"Finley, can you at least acknowledge my message?"*

She ignored the phone as she continued her conversation with Mom. "Well, for starters, we'd be calling his bluff. Let him show us this 'portal' so we can laugh in his face. No one dupes a

Eldress girl. But," she continued with something of a conspiratorial flair, "if it's *true*, if we're transported to a planet that's ten thousand light years away, how cool would that be?"

Mara wanted to laugh. Oh, to be a fifteen-year-old with no grown-up worries.

"All I can imagine is that we'd be stuck on another planet, with no way back," Mara said. "Which means I wouldn't be able to give the school board a piece of my mind."

"Then how'd he get here if he's from Vraithe?" Finley's eyes crinkled with delightful mischief. "It has to be a two-way portal."

"If it's true."

Finley nodded enthusiastically. "Right, if it's true."

She gave her daughter a kiss on the forehead.

"Time for bed, kiddo. When we wake up, I'm sure we'll both think this has been a crazy dream."

As she watched her daughter shuffle down the hallway to her bedroom, Mara could not ignore Finley's enthusiasm...or forget Vikk's strange eyes.

*What if it is true?* Mara pulled out her phone and set an alarm for 6 a.m. Just in case.

From inside his SUV, Vikk reserved his portal timeslot through a unique Vraitheian device. He wasn't convinced Mara and Finley would show up, but he couldn't leave it to chance in the event they did.

His confirmation code came through moments later. In the Vraitheian language it read: *Departure 08:01:01, Earth Eastern*

*Daylight-Saving Time, Stravdas, V., + 2 Non-Vraitheian Passengers. Eldress, M., adult, Eldress, F., minor.*

Then he did something he'd never done before: he removed his heartstring blocker locket.

It was heavy in his hands as he inspected the Vraitheian meteorite jewel encapsulated in black Vraitheian metal. Once it was no longer touching his chest, the locket deactivated, its inner swirling metal transforming from a bright, gleaming liquid essence into a static, matte gray rock. There was nothing to prevent his true feelings from developing.

He couldn't remember the last time he had removed it. *Had he ever?* He slipped it his coat pocket.

Deep in his soul, Vikk knew he wasn't wrong about Mara Eldress.

That done, he drove back to his sister's house. All he could do now was wait. And hope.

# FOUR

A beeping alarm woke Mara, and it wasn't her own.

"Finley," she grumbled sleepily as she pawed at her phone to check the time. They were on a two-week winter break and her daughter set an alarm for five forty-five in the morning. Mara was going to disown her, but first she planned to go right back to sleep. It was way too cozy under the thick blankets.

But then the events of last night crash-landed into her waking consciousness.

*Vikk.*

*His sideways closing eyelids.*

*A portal to a planet ten thousand light years away.*

It hadn't been a dream.

Then she remembered that she'd even set her own alarm for six. Okay, so maybe she'd had a fanciful moment last night when she'd dreamily hoped that everything Vikk said was true. That Vraitheian doctors could diagnose Finley. That she could help write the script for her memoir.

Hmmm, she thought. That might prove difficult. Mara did not know how to speak or read Vraitheian. How on Earth was she going to assist with that? Would she be working side by side with Vikk? She thought about that for a second.

*There were far worse scenarios.*

Then she considered the fact that no compensation had been discussed. Her US publisher owned the film rights to her memoir. "Well," she said out loud. "*Earth's* film rights. If these Vraitheian doctors help Finley, I'll consider that as more than fair payment. I'll help them with a thousand scripts if that turns out to be true."

From her bedroom doorway Mara heard, "What's this about a thousand scripts, Mom?"

Mara focused her eyes and found a fully dressed Finley munching on a blueberry muffin they'd bought from a local baker. Crumbs were dropping on the floor and Mara decided she was not awake enough to make a stink about it. They'd both had an interesting night.

"By the looks of you, I'm guessing you're still game to call Vikk's bluff?" Mara asked as she took note of the fact that Finley was wearing snow boots, sweatpants, and a long-sleeved thermal top. A recent edition to Finley's wardrobe was wearing Mara's military dog tags as a fashion accessory.

Finley liked to joke that if she ever got lost, the authorities would take one look at the dog tags and know who to bring her back to. Mara laughed the first time Finley said it, but it warmed her heart that her daughter was proud of her military service. At least someone was.

The metal tags made a clattering of tinny sounds as Finley crouched down to pick up the muffin crumbs. Straightening, she said, "The roads have been cleared and traffic into the city isn't terrible." There was a twinkle in her daughter's sparkling brown eyes that worried her.

"Good lord," Mara said as she got out of bed and threw on a robe, "did you *actually* watch the weather and traffic report?"

When the kid made up her mind, she made up her mind.

"On the threes!" Finley answered in a faux-anchor's voice, following her into the kitchen.

Mara started a pot of coffee. She inhaled the delicious aroma of roasted arabica beans and wondered if Vikk's home planet had coffee.

Mara leaned back against the counter to look at Finley. "Who are you and what have you done with my daughter?"

"See, the thing is...I've been thinking." Finley was absently tinkering with the salt and pepper shakers. "We haven't been to the city since we moved here." She was moving the shakers around like little dancers. "Perhaps we can make a day of it?"

"In the city?"

Finley saw the exact moment when reality entered the room. Mom's shoulders went tight as she reached into the cabinet for a coffee mug. When she turned, there was a grimace on her face.

"Yes." Finley knew from experience she shouldn't overdo it. It would set her back days, maybe even to the point where she couldn't even leave her bed.

"I don't know if that's such a good idea, sweetie. I have a lot of grading to do today, I'm expecting Dr. Brady's reply to my email, and I need to check in with my students about their novel selections. Plus, we need to get ready for Hannah's visit. She'll be here next week."

Finley tried not to pout, even though she was looking forward to seeing Mom's best friend again, a woman she'd called "Hant Anna" because, as a toddler, Finley had a difficult time enunciating *Aunt Hannah*.

"Hant Anna won't be here for days." It came out more like a whine than she had intended because Mom made a face at her.

The thing was, Finley felt good—*better* than good—today, and she didn't wait to waste moments like this. *Seize the day*, and all that. And she sensed that Mr. Stravdas was being honest with them last night. She pressed a fingertip against the edge of the business card in her pocket. *It* was real. *He* was real.

*Vraithe has to be real.*

Finley was going to get them to the portal by eight this morning, no matter what. Even if it wiped her out for days.

She'd been sick for two years straight. What if she never got well?

What if what he said was true and they missed their shot?

Finley would regret it forever.

She wanted to live.

Mara watched a series of emotions pirouette across Finley's beautifully freckled face. It was heartbreaking. All Mara wanted to do was protect her daughter from the world's harshest realities, but in doing so, it meant she also prevented Finley from experiencing life at her fullest.

What harm would it be to go into the city, confront Vikk, and call his bluff? Was there any wrongdoing in encountering a handsome man who told them a tall tale? They could eat breakfast at a diner, visit the Museum of Fine Arts, and be home by dinnertime.

While Finley's health wasn't getting any better, she wasn't getting any worse, either, which counted for something.

"All right," Mara said after pouring herself a cup of coffee and blowing on the hot liquid. "Pack a day bag with snacks and water in case we get stuck in the snow." The truck already had several thick blankets for that very reason.

For several long moments Mara leaned against the counter and sipped her coffee as Finley made happy noises all through the house. Mara smiled. She had Vikk Stravdas to thank for this. But, as the nature of her thoughts turned dour, when Finley discovered he was a fraud, Mara would be the one to carry her daughter home and mend a newly broken spirit.

Vikk paced up and down the terminal's dimly lit walkway, occasionally saying hello or giving a quick head nod when he saw someone he knew.

The Vraitheian portal was located in a secret basement next to the East Boston Tunnel station in the Old State House. The clanky sounds and vibrations of the bustling subway station next door could be heard and felt all around him. Sharp whistles and tinny dings of the human's subway cars grated on his nerves.

It felt like he'd already ground his teeth down into stumps. It was pretty clear he looked preoccupied because no one stopped to chat, not even one of his primary cousins who sauntered in for her 07:51:01 portal appointment. CeCe, who worked as a sitcom actress and part-time Broadway star in New York City, arched a delicate eyebrow at him, offered a casual wave, and stepped into a portalpod after a steward scanned her reservation code.

That was five minutes ago.

If Mara and Finley did not appear in the next four minutes, he would have to leave without them. He did not want to think about how this made him feel. It was obvious he felt a stirring with Mara and she, in some fashion, perhaps faintly, felt that same stirring. His heartstrings would not have behaved that way otherwise. And he dearly wanted Finley's health to improve.

Dessa would call him a sap—and she would not be wrong.

"Hey, you over there in the black suit, are you Stravdas?" one of the stewards called out from the terminal's entrance.

"Yes."

Into an earpiece, the steward responded to someone. "Found him." He turned back to Vikk. "Are two non-Vraitheians travelling with you today?"

An avalanche of relief bloomed in Vikk's chest. "Yes, they are."

The steward studied him for several long seconds before speaking into an earpiece. "You can send them in." The steward checked something on a travel log device. "The group appears to be traveling on Queen Uska's royal passport visa. No, I know," the steward said, chuckling into their earpiece, "that doesn't happen very often, does it? Recommend a gray suit escort for these visitors."

Queen Uska must have amended his reservation.

A moment later Mara and Finley appeared inside the terminal. Three stewards, all clad in gray suits, escorted them to him. Vikk would have wished for less fanfare, but he was so pleased to see them that he let the feeling slide.

As Mara took stock of the "terminal," which was what the three women—the stewards—called the room, she had a distinct feeling of being closed in. Something feral bubbled up from her core and she wanted to lash out at everyone nearby, Finley excluded.

The space was dark and noisy, like a sports stadium—if the stadium happened to be in a low-ceilinged basement with poor lighting. She could barely see a thing, though she could discern colorful graffiti on all the walls. What she didn't see was a big round circle or a portal or some hackneyed version of a British phone box resembling a Tardis.

Vikk stood before her impeccably dressed in a suit so dark it resembled the color of the night sky. It looked good on him. Very good, in fact.

She and Finley, on the other hand, wore cold weather attire —snow boots, thick coats and mittens, and chunky knit scarves. Mara carried their backpack.

The shocked look on his face was worth all the embarrassment of them having to ask multiple times where the entrance to 199 Washington Street was only to be told 199 Washington Street didn't exist. Did she mean The Old State House? Were they looking for the Blue Line?

It didn't matter how many times Finley had showed someone the crisp white business card with the address clearly printed on it, the answers were all the same—until a random person asked, "First time headed to Vraithe?" to which Finley cried real tears of joy. "Yes, we are," she'd said, barely able to conceal her excitement. "Told you it was real, Mom! Mr. Stravdas was *not* lying."

The man's eyebrows shot up as he said, "Stravdas, huh?" before leading them through a maze-like corridor that ended in a door that did not look like a door.

All Mara could do now was try not to visibly show just how stressed out she felt.

When the stewards did not immediately leave, Finley felt a little worried, so she asked Mr. Stravdas, "Are we, like, in trouble?"

Sure, the "terminal" was seriously a dump, but it was staffed with nicely dressed, professional stewards who escorted them inside. It seemed natural to her that the portal to an alien planet wouldn't just be in *any* old location. It needed to be a *secret* location, and what a better place than some dank basement that no one even remembered existed.

Mr. Stravdas smiled. "Not in the least," he said kindly. Finley liked that he was being nice. "I think the gray suits intend to escort our group. We're traveling under the royal visa of Queen Uska. It affords us an extra layer of security."

He checked his watch just as an overhead announcement came through. The first announcement was not something she could understand. If Finley had to guess, it was spoken in Vraitheian.

Then she heard, "First call for Stravdas party of three for a zero-eight, zero-one, zero-one departure with an arrival time of zero-eight, fifty-five, fifty-five. Please enter the transport dais."

"Suppose that's us," Mom said in a high-pitched voice. Finley knew that Mom was so surprised that she might be in shock. She was so sure that they'd call Mr. Stravdas' bluff. "Where exactly is this portal of yours, Vikk?"

Like Mom, Finley had been inspecting the space. Other than the stewards and several individuals loitering around, presumably waiting their turn, not much was happening within the secret lair.

Mr. Stravdas pointed toward the far wall, the one covered in graphic graffiti. "Please tell me we are not traveling through a neon-green penis," Finley said. She felt her mom's arm stiffen at her back.

"A what?" Mr. Stravdas asked. "Oh, that's right, I forgot. Until a human has transported through the portal and back, you cannot *see* the actual portalpod, only what's behind it. Our scientists call it an ocular mind block." He turned to Mara. "I'm sorry about the graffiti. If I had known what it looked like, I would have warned you."

Smiling, he handed them each a lanyard to wear around their necks. "You'll need these before you enter the dais. The steward will scan it. Think of it as a boarding pass. Don't lose it —it's your return ticket."

Finley elbowed her mom. "See," she said with glee, "I told you it would be a two-way portal."

To Mara, it felt like all the air was being sucked out of the room.

*This can't be happening. How is this happening? It must be some kind of joke. He's a film producer, right? And these people are all actors....*

Without singular awareness, she found herself moving with the group toward the neon-green penis. She did *not* want to go near a large cartoon penis the size of the steward standing in front of it.

She had things to do.

Still, they moved forward. Vikk cradled one of her arms while Finley clutched the other. Mara had errands to run. She wanted to re-read the school board's email even though she had memorized it.

"Ready Mara?" Vikk asked.

*My God, he is so tall*, she thought. And steady. And handsome. One of his eyebrows was slightly higher than the other.

"No," she muttered. It sounded like she was talking in an echo chamber. She heard him chuckle. He sounded so far away, yet he was right beside her. Any second now she was going to pass out.

Her heart was beating so hard she wondered if it was going to unravel into a million fibrous threads and cling to the first solid object in its path.

"You won't see the ledge, but you'll need to take a step," Vikk instructed them at certain points. The steward scanned Vikk's ticket, then hers, then Finley's.

There was a step, then another step, and soon she was face-to-face with a male organ that should never be that size or that color. They were, apparently, inside an invisible portalpod.

"Enjoy your visit," the steward said with placid professionalism. She wondered how many times a day the steward said that.

"I feel like we're being punked." Mara looked at the neon-green penis and then at the steward. "What's to enjoy about it? It would never fit."

"Mom," Finley groaned in embarrassment.

"Sorry, kiddo." Mara then remembered she needed to assist those four students in selecting a new piece of literature. "Listen," she said, turning to Vikk, "can we take a raincheck? I have a stack of papers to grade and I didn't bring my laptop. I cannot leave at this critical moment in my students' academic careers."

Finley grinned at her. "Rest easy, Mom. I packed everything we might need. It's in the backpack."

Her daughter had left nothing to chance.

"All we have to do it take one last step," Vikk said. "The portal takes care of the rest."

Mara didn't move, she swore she didn't take a step, and yet still she moved with the group. With Vikk on her right and Finley chomping at the bit on her left, Mara really didn't stand a chance.

Then a silver and black glimmer, almost like liquid silk, rippled around her legs, her hips, her arms, before it covered her face.

It wasn't anything like water and yet it was. It coated her, warmed her, soothed her, and her first thought was that it smelled like black licorice, a flavor she detested. Whorls of dark lights shot out in front of her, like a twisting lane that got smaller and went on forever.

Instinctively, Mara knew there could be no talking. Sound didn't exist, either. She wasn't even sure if she was a fully formed human being right now. For all she knew, she'd been broken up into a thousand pulses of light waves moving through the Milky Way galaxy like shooting stars, and she wondered if that's what shooting stars really were.

But Mara could not finish the mental image. Within seconds, even thoughts disappeared. Worry evaporated. And the intimate knowledge of who she was, was given up to the universe, trusting it to deliver them to where the boarding passes hanging around their necks said they were supposed to go.

For the first time in years, Finley's pain melted away like ancient history. As the cloudy, static-filled mist engulfed her, she held her breath for as long as possible, her heart pounding furiously. If she could have pinched herself, she would have.

*This is really happening.*

Everything was dark with flickering pulses of light darting out before her eyes. It reminded her of a long, straight race-track, and Finley could only surmise that in any second now they were going to be hurtling forward through space at the speed of light.

When she could not hold her breath any longer, she took a panicked breath and discovered her lungs worked just fine. Seconds later she felt the sensation of being lifted before floating upright, like a hovering ghost.

*Very cool,* she thought just as Mom gave her arm a squeeze of reassurance. She couldn't ignore Mom's very visible panic from a few moments ago. If Finley hadn't been so awestruck, she would have tried to comfort Mom.

Squinting, Finley saw what looked like Vraitheian signs—at least the images resembled the types of symbols, lines, dots, and dashes she'd seen in Mom's translated memoir. There was movement, and Mr. Stravdas reached up and pressed one of the signs. If Finley had to guess, it meant their group was ready to proceed with takeoff.

Then a wave of drowsiness hit her. *No!* she wanted to scream. *I want to experience this! I want to stay awake for the entire transport.* But it was not to be. Deep down she knew she wouldn't be able to process most of it; her damn brain might shut off for good and then where'd that leave her? Space coma? Yeah, no thanks.

She fought like hell to keep her eyes open but in the end she lost the battle. Lights blurred. She felt warm and toasty, as if she'd been swaddled in a blanket. Sounds wafted in and out like someone opening and closing a door to a movie theater. She even imagined she smelled popcorn, which led into wondering what kind of food they had on Vraithe.

In a brief second of clarity, Finley seemed to understand some of what was being said. She could have sworn someone said, "Relax. Keep calm and mind the gap when exiting."

Sitting in his own chair, Vikk waited for Mara and Finley to succumb to the portal's numbing effects. He wasn't exactly a fan of this process, but he had been assured through several transport officials that they would absolutely, most definitely wake up when they entered Vraithe's atmosphere.

Until then, as the round portalpod powered up for light-rail travel, Mara and Finley's forms were secured within the portal's turbulence avoidance system—a static, transparent cloud that locked them into place. For one long moment, they kind of hung there like inanimate objects, heads drooping, mouths open, arms akimbo, before their forms were gently guided into two empty chairs within the pod.

He didn't want to laugh but they were pretty funny-looking. Several years ago, after Vraitheians discovered that humans found enjoyment in photographing their extremely scared expressions while on rollercoasters, the portalpod technicians had installed cameras to capture the moment humans fought to stay conscious. He'd have to remember to show them their transport photos once they arrived Vraithe's main terminal.

There was a slight jerk, and then the pod shot forward. Vikk, used to such travel, absently watched the blur of stars streaking past the small portholes on either side of the pod. Every few minutes the portalpod would lurch ever so slightly as it entered a different warp tunnel, each transition shortening the distance by five hundred percent.

A trip that used to take days now took less than one Earth hour.

The three gray-suited stewards escorting them sat quietly in the front of the portalpod. Since the portalpod was on automatic pilot, their inclusion was purely due to Mara and Finley's royal passport visas. One gray suit was reading Mara's translated memoir while the other two appeared to nap.

Vikk was still embarrassed that Dessa failed to include any mention of Finley in her translation. He wanted to ask her about it last night, after returning from Mara's house, but Dessa had already been asleep.

As it was, it was too late to make such drastic changes at this point in the film's production schedule, to include hiring a young actress to play Finley.

Given the fact that Finley was nowhere in the translation, adding her character into the movie version might not go over so well with Vraitheian readers. *Mara will understand*, Vikk thought. Most feature films rarely mirrored the novels they were based on.

*No, Mara will not understand because the translation is the least of her worries.* He knew that she didn't believe a single word he'd said about the portal. She'd come only to prove him wrong. For all intents and purposes, he'd just kidnapped Mara and Finley Eldress.

Which meant he had to make good on the medical promises he'd made.

Vikk groaned, which caused the reading gray suit to look up. The steward appeared to be at the end the book.

"I have been meaning to ask, Stravdas," the steward named Werlaun said in their native language. Vikk noticed that she'd been casting secret looks at Mara for several long moments. "Is that *the* Good-General Mara Eldress?"

Werlaun knew that she was violating *all* sorts of professional rules. As a gray suit, she was supposed to be quiet and nonintrusive. Asking questions was very much out of the norm.

"It is." Even though Stravdas's smile felt forced, it still gave Werlaun an extra boost of joy.

Werlaun let out a little squeak and steadied her breathing.

It wasn't very often that Earth authors traveled to Vraithe. In the past, Werlaun, during moments of boredom, had reviewed the transport manifest roster and saw that Ursula K. Le Guin, Susan Cooper, and Sarah McLean had all visited Vraithe. She hadn't yet been assigned her role as a gray suit for the North American Vraitheian portal when they came through, so the fact that she was in the same portalpod as Good-General Mara Eldress caused her oxygen air flow to dip.

"Do you think she'll sign my copy?" Werlaun held up the book.

"She might," Stravdas said in a tone that told Werlaun to cut things short.

Werlaun snorted. While a brooding Stravdas stared out the porthole—it wasn't like the cloudy, black warp tunnels were interesting to look at—Werlaun pulled out her Vraitheian device to post all the particulars of Good-General Mara Eldress's arrival. She doubted any young Vraitheian could keep something this big a secret. Within minutes her post had thousands of jubilations.

Vikk didn't usually sweat during a portal transport, but his suit was beginning to cling to his skin. He had an inkling that Werlaun was letting everyone on Vraithe know of their arrival. He hadn't planned for this.

Double apprehension began to fill Vikk's mind. First, he was worried that Dessa botched other parts of the translation and now he had to worry about Mara's groupies showing up at the terminal, which would cause all sorts of issues.

"Excellent," he heard the steward say as she slipped her device into her pocket. "My absolute favorite part is when Good-General Eldress and Enemy-General Calix swap bodies and she cuts off his twatsizzle. The writing is so good I could feel the dismemberment and I don't even *own* a twatsizzle," she added with a laugh.

Vikk laughed with her and some of his nervousness went away. There was no denying that *everyone* loved the twatsizzle scene.

# FIVE

One moment Mara felt like she was being mummified in a cloudy curtain and the next she was wide awake, inside a sphere, and trying not to hyperventilate while a very chilled-out version of Finley sat beside her. Mara's goal in life, for however much of it remained, was to be like Finley—calm and composed and less mad and murderous.

Vikk had called the sphere a "portalpod." It reminded her of an old-school science fiction arcade chair, just bigger with smooth, round edges. It was also much more advanced, with floating holographic buttons and screens that displayed Vraitheian words.

One of the three gray suit stewards pressed a green floating button. A hissing noise emerged from the front of the pod, then a doorframe-sized section of the material popped out, up, and away.

The stewards then exited the pod, waiting on a raised landing just outside the door. Beyond them Mara could see neon lights. She could even hear muted conversations and soft music.

She'd had the taste of black licorice on her tongue after they'd stepped inside the portal. Now she smelled coffee and fresh-baked pretzels. Whether or not they were on another planet, she wasn't willing to speculate, but Mara knew they were not anywhere near that dank basement. For one thing, she was positively sweating in her winter weather attire.

"How do you feel?" Vikk leaned forward. He displayed both hands and wiggled his fingers. In a loud voice he asked, "How many fingers am I holding up?"

Mara wiped beads of sweat from her brow. "Please tell me that's not your voice's normal volume."

He grinned. While her aura had morphed ever so slightly into a coppery color with a black ring, it wasn't very solid, which meant her thoughts of violence directed at him were not serious. He could accept that.

Now all he had to do was get them out of the portalport terminal without anyone seeing them.

"Mom's fine," Finley said with a laugh. "So, did we travel across the galaxy, Mr. Stravdas? Like, for real?"

"Ten thousand light years, for real," Vikk said.

It was nice to see it from Finley's perspective; she was so starry-eyed and full of wonder. Had he ever been like that? Probably not, he thought, though his first portal trip to Earth had been a memorable experience. He remembered thinking it was strange that Earth was one solid planet and not a fragmented one, like Vraithe.

One of the stewards cleared their throat in a meaningful way. Vikk nodded at them and then said to Mara and Finley, "We can't stay in the portalpod much longer. The gate is needed for the next arrival, three minutes from now."

*The next arrival?* Mara wondered. Would their portalpod get hit like a marble and career across a futuristic landscape? She didn't like the image.

Mara stood and was surprised when her legs didn't buckle. Strangely, she felt fine. Oh, she hated Vikk's guts and couldn't believe that any of this was real, but physically she felt fine. It was probably for the best that they'd slept through the trip—though *forced unconsciousness* seemed more accurate.

Turning, she helped Finley stand, but the grimace marring her daughter's face spoke volumes. Finley plopped back to the seat. Until she got her bearings, Finley would not be able to walk for any distance.

"Do you think you can stand long enough for me to pick you up?" Mara asked Finley.

Finley crossed her arms and assumed the finely crafted look of teenage rebellion. "I refuse to be carried like an infant during my first outing to an alien planet."

The portalpod started to beep just as a multitude of red lights began to flash. The signs for impending danger seemed to be universal.

"Stravdas," one of the stewards said in gravelly English, "we kindly request that you and your passengers exit the pod."

Finley gawked at them and thought, *Wow, they are so polite even as the threat of an oncoming portalpod might kill them all.* Okay, so she didn't have time to be combative with Mom and argue that she could walk out by herself.

So she attempted to do just that and swore when she crumpled. The portalpod's grate flooring dug into her knees and palms. "Ouch."

"Here, let me," Mr. Stravdas said, leaning down to her. "Climb on my back and I'll give you a back of a pig ride." Within seconds Finley's arms were clutching his neck as he brought the both of them out of the portalpod. "Be sure to duck," he said just as they passed under the pod's exit point.

Finley laughed the entire time. "I think you meant *piggy-back ride*, Mr. Stravdas." She laughed again, muttering "back of a pig ride" under her breath. This exchange was totally going in her journal.

"My English is not always accurate," he said with laughter in his voice.

They turned to wait for Mom, and Finley got a good look at the portalpod from the outside. It was a very large sphere that could comfortably fit a few more bodies. Black and shiny, its surface looked to be metal, though what type she couldn't guess. It had to be very strong to withstand lightspeed travel. Finley waved at her Mom.

Mara waved back. The scene in front of her made her heart melt. She literally had to turn away to hide the tears gathering in her eyes. Not even the urgent wailing of the portalpod's alarms, which had gone up about two octaves, could distract her from such a tender moment.

"Good-General Mara Eldress," one of the stewards said to her, arms out, urging her forward.

*Who the hell was Good-General Mara Eldress?*

"Please do not delay in exiting the portalpod."

Right, the incoming portalpod. It was just that Mara was discombobulated. She didn't know where she was or how she felt about Vikk's kindness toward Finley. She'd never seen Finley grinning from ear to ear like that.

Mara took a few steps just as Vikk said, "Oh, Mara, can you grab the books?"

Did she want to growl at him? *Yes.* Instead, she picked up the heavy canvas bags Dessa had given him the night before. Arms straining, she looked down. There had to be thirty books in each bag.

She stepped out of the portalpod and onto the landing just as a strong gust of wind pushed her forward. Mara's hair flew about wildly. Twirling to look behind her, Mara saw that their portalpod was gone and in its place was an identical version whose door was beginning to hiss open.

She faced the nearest steward. "That was close," Mara said. The steward possessed a shocked expression. Poor thing was traumatized by their near brush with death. When the steward didn't reply, Mara asked, "What is your name?"

"Werlaun." Mara heard the trepidation in her voice. "I am one of your escorts. May I assist you in carrying your luggage?"

Vikk and Finley had already descended the landing when Mara gladly handed over a bag. "Thanks, Werlaun," she said as she pivoted to get a better look of her surroundings.

What she saw wiped all doubt from her mind  they were not on Earth.

"Your mouth is hanging open, Mom." Finley said it like she was having a blast. She was still on Vikk's back as he and their three gray suit stewards escorted the group away from the portalpod.

Mara was astounded. The Vraitheian portalport resembled a futuristic airport. Lots of silver arched beams and sleek architecture. Large windows showing bright sunlight, puffy pink clouds, and a large purple moon.

She took a calming breath. *You are not dreaming, Mara.*

The portalport's silvery floors gleamed. Restaurants and bars were decked out in gemstone-laden dark wood paneling. Vraithe had their own versions of fast-food joints, though everything seemed to be liquid or plant-based versus junk foods or burger and chicken eateries. Some businesses appeared to be a form of "duty-free" shopping with liquor, upscale purses, perfume, and jewelry.

The portalport was not very busy, but everyone she saw looked like them, just better dressed. The fabric was drapery in fashion. Suits appeared to be well-tailored, and casual-looking outfits, the equivalent of jeans and T-shirts on earth, looked really comfortable.

It occurred to Mara they would need a change of clothes. She'd have to ask Vikk about that, once they made it to wherever he was taking them.

They passed gift shops chock full of magnets, sweatshirts, and translated bestsellers—Quinn's Bridgerton series, Carr's Virgin River books, and even every volume of *Diary of a Wimpy Kid* ever published, not to mention a few knockoffs. However, for the most part, the rest were clearly Vraitheian-written novels and not translations.

There was even a store called Earth Found Treasures. Big sellers were dusty rocks, bags of dirt and seashells, bathrobes, caulking guns, panini grills, and statues of a very creepy Easter Bunny holding a basket full of teeth.

Mara shuddered. *Not all translations worked out so well.*

She bumped into Vikk, who had stopped in front of a large display of her memoir. The cover and title remained the same but inside everything resembled the translated version he'd left behind on their couch. A round sticker with Vraitheian words had been affixed to all the copies.

Vikk pointed at the sticker. "It reads, 'Soon to be a Taloncourt Feature Film.'"

"It's so strange to see this," Mara admitted as she returned the copy she'd been perusing. Years ago, when she'd confided to Calix that she wanted to be a writer, he all but laughed in her face. She told Vikk, "I might have sold fifty copies of my memoir back home, yet it resonates for readers on an alien planet. Goes to show you that you never know what will strike gold." She gave him an arched look. "You know, I don't recall signing a translation contract or agreeing to sign over the film rights to you."

"Mom, don't be weird about it." Finley was chewing on something that looked like fruit. Vikk must have bought her a snack.

"Why don't *you* spend four years putting together a nonfiction book proposal, securing an agent, fighting your naysayers, and then writing the damn thing and then let me know if you want to get paid for it or not."

"It's just that I don't think they have a form of currency here, Mom."

Vikk listened to Mara and Finley's conversation with interest. The concept of having to "pay" for something was intriguing. Here, on Vraithe, if he wanted to take a book, a fruit poppel, or a drink, he merely retrieved it from the shelf and continued on his merry way, like he'd done for Finley's tazmil fruit, which was like a pear.

All Vraitheians contributed to society to the best of their abilities during prime years. After that, unless they wanted to offer their services, it was not required. Housing was provided. Education was offered throughout a Vraitheian's life. The idea of having to pay someone—*who?* he wondered—for nourishment, or anything else, seemed odd to him.

However, he was not one to judge if that was how humans did business.

"If you wish to draft a contract, Mara, I'd be very happy to sign it." They moved away from most of the portalport's businesses. Ahead of them was a set of double doors that led to the general public. If someone wanted to meet a traveler, they'd usually wait on the other side of those doors, but there was nothing preventing someone from coming inside.

In the same vein, if a group of fans happened to be waiting for Mara Eldress, that's where they would be. He'd watched Werlaun during their walk. The steward was incredibly honored to be carrying the bag of books Mara had handed her. She'd been trying to sneak looks at the books on top. No doubt she'd be telling her friends, online and in-person, all about it as soon as the escort duty was completed.

"Just like that?" Mara asked. "I could put anything in the contract and you'd sign it?"

Vikk shrugged, which made Finley reclasp her arms around his neck. She wasn't heavy or anything. "I have no reason to distrust you. If you wrote it into a contract, then I would believe it is something you wish to be there."

Mara just stared at him and for a long moment he couldn't read her aura. Perhaps not even she knew how she felt in that moment, but then her aura changed and he wasn't disappointed in the least.

Mara nodded and saw the wisdom in his words. Just by bringing them here, it was obvious he trusted the both of them. At any rate, there was no reason to keep the topic alive. Even if Vraitheians paid her, it wasn't like she could use their money on Earth.

Finley said, "Does everyone on Vraithe look human?"

Mara thought it a valid question. Was there a way to distinguish humans from Vraitheians? She studied Vikk carefully, from his tall stature to his dark eyes, thick eyebrows, his full mouth, his chiseled jaw, to the way he filled out his impeccable suit.

*Maybe what lay beneath the suit was the difference.*

"What if..." Vikk said after a slight hesitation. He'd been starring at her as if he'd been reading her mind. He cleared his throat. "Humans resemble Vraitheians? From our calculations, our species came into existence approximately one hundred thousand years ahead of human civilization. How's that for an answer?"

"Makes sense," Finley said. "It's not like humans are traveling to distant stars."

Vikk chuckled. "That you know of."

Then, for a brief moment, Vikk stopped walking. There was concern written on his face, which confused Mara. He was staring at the large set of double doors. To her, it seemed like that was the portalport's only exit.

Even the three gray suits were talking amongst themselves, with two of them gesturing with accusatory fingers at Werlaun.

The group ahead of them walked through the double doors, and it looked like there was a commotion happening on the other side, like a group of teens waiting for their favorite band to walk out.

From her perch on Mr. Stravdas's back, Finley was able to get a very good look at the crowd on the other side of the portalport's exit. They were holding signs. Most of them were in Vraitheian, which of course she couldn't read, but a few of them were in English.

Unless there were other humans arriving today, which was

very possible, Finley had an inclination that the group waiting outside was here for Mom.

One sign read, "Team Enemy-General Calix" while other signs read, "Team Good-General Eldress." Finley literally had no clue what any of it meant, other than recognizing her dad's name—Calix—and the Eldress part.

"Um, Mr. Stravdas," Finley started, "who are Enemy-General Calix and Good-General Eldress?"

Mom's head jerked up. "That's what Werlaun called me earlier, the Good-General Mara Eldress. I found it strange, but the portalpod was on high alert and it didn't feel like the best time to ask."

"Well?" Finley prompted when Mr. Stravdas did not answer right away.

With her arms around his neck, she felt Mr. Stravdas take a very large breath. *Was he preparing to make a run for it?* She tightened her grip.

"You see, the thing is..." He stumbled over his words while swallowing a few times. "There is a possibility, however small, that we've made a translation mishap or two."

It shouldn't have surprised Mara that Vraitheians would own camera phones. One second after the other, someone was happily saying her name and a bright light flashed. In terms of crowd size, Mara couldn't be sure, but there was somewhere between one to two hundred Vraitheians waiting outside the portalport exit.

She was thankful that the stewards had come up with a quick solution. They'd ordered her fans to congregate behind a specific line on the gleaming floor. *Fans.* She, Mara Eldress, had fans. How crazy was that?

They consisted of all ages, from the very young to the very

old, and each and every one of them looked human to her. There was nothing to stare at, precisely, as she, Vikk and Finley walked by, except that they were very orderly and very polite. No one was shoving or pushing their way forward. Their voices where not overly loud or jarring. Her students could learn a thing or two from this group.

"What do they want?" she asked Vikk. Mara could not understand what the group was saying since it was mostly said in Vraitheian with a smattering of English thrown in there. The signs were interesting to look with bright colors and metallic stenciling.

Vikk pointed at a colorful sign. "He wants to tangle heart-strings with you."

"What does that mean?" Mara asked.

Finley giggled. "Isn't it obvious, Mom?" In a whisper-voice she added, "*Sex*, Mom. It means *sex*."

"Lovely," Mara said dryly.

Mara noticed that Vikk, suddenly silent, was struggling to keep a straight face. He pointed at another sign in the back. "She wants your autograph." Finley was still on Vikk's back. She was smiling for the cameras and waving at everyone. "Others are asking if Enemy-General Calix deserved his fate."

Mara furrowed her eyebrows as they walked through the exit corridor. Up ahead she saw what looked like a train station.

"Do they mean the divorce? Of course, Calix deserved it." Vikk gave her a horrified look and she offered a gentle smile. "Divorces are very common on Earth, though perhaps they are not as common here on Vraithe."

"It's called a *divorce* on Earth?"

"Yes, first there's a separation and then, if the courts agree, a final divorce is granted and both parties agree to the split."

Vikk looked visibly pained at the explanation. Maybe Vraitheians mated for life, she thought. Not that it was really any of her business. She didn't plan to stick around to learn the ins and outs of life on Vraithe. All that mattered was that they helped Finley.

Someone produced a marker and Mara autographed a few books before they made quick work of the walk. The recipients were very happy with her scribble.

Once they were outside, Mara stopped in her tracks. The scene before her was truly one of science fiction movies.

The sky was a brilliant purplish pink. A large moon covered most of the sky. It was a rich amethyst hue and resembled a gorgeous celestial gemstone. High in the sky, on the opposite side, was a fiery sun, a red dwarf star if her former science classes taught her anything. The air temperature was comfortable, not too hot, or too cold.

Far off in the distance she saw the outlines of dark buildings and even farther away, she spotted snowcapped mountains.

But that wasn't what stunned her.

The planet was not one solid surface. Sections of land appeared to hover or float. Large, empty voids filled the distance between each section, and she had to wonder what happened if someone fell over the edge. Perhaps Vraithe was a planet without vast oceans.

Mara pondered: how did they get from one section of land to the other, because she did not see bridges. Vraithe, or at least *this* part of Vraithe, did not have transport vehicles. Without fumes or exhaust, the atmosphere was clean and quiet.

The rest of the scene had a dream-like quality to it. Vibrant emerald trees filled the sectional landscape. Fairy-like glowing creatures fluttered about, while smaller metallic critters that resembled a cross between a spider and a scorpion skittered up trees and into flowery bushes. Citizens of all shapes and sizes traversed to and fro, some on foot, others seated in what Mara might call a single-occupant hover-chair, which hovered only a few inches off the ground. Nothing was alarming, just dissimilar to Earth.

"It's so pretty here," Finley said in a tone of awe. "The colors are different, though, like a video game. It's brighter, sparkly, like I'm looking at Vraithe through gemstone glasses."

Vikk chuckled. "Thanks. The top layers of Vraithe are filled with various gems and jewels."

"That's cool," Finley said.

"Without cars and the like"—Mara pointed toward the gaping black trenches that reminded her of the Grand Canyon—"how do you get around?"

"Inner-planetary portals," Vikk said. "As you can see, Vraithe is a fragmented planet. Gravitational pull keeps everything from spreading apart, though sometimes a land spherule might rise higher or sink lower. It is nothing to be concerned about, though. We have no need for cars or trains or airplanes, such as those on Earth, because the makeup of our metal alloys forms portals. Eons ago our engineers connected all the land spherules. As long as you step into the right portal, you'll end up where you planned to go."

The large portico structure head of them had Romanesque architecture with stately columns and multiple rounded arches. Vikk explained that it was an inner-planetary portal terminal.

As they got closer, Mara saw the portal maps. They resembled the line diagrams of a metro system. She guessed that because this was the portal station right outside the portalport, that there might be hundreds of portal paths. The large building was very busy. Throngs of individuals were coming and going. She felt the stares from some of them but for the most part everyone was minding their own business.

"Where exactly are we going?" Mara asked as they followed the three gray suit stewards. She'd removed her coat, and now carried it over her arm. She'd thought she could keep it on until they got to wherever they were going, but had soon found herself sweltering, her shirt plastered to her skin. She was dressed for below-zero weather, not a comfortable, sixty-five-degree day on Vraithe.

"There." Vikk pointed toward the dark building two land spherules away. From their vantage point, that particular land spherule was higher in the sky. The building towering into the clouds looked like a gothic castle. "The black palace of Taloncourt. A portal will take us to the outer entrance in under a second. Queen Uska has secured a set of chambers for your use."

*Chambers*, Finley thought. How fancy. It was their first day on an alien planet and the queen was letting them stay in the palace. On Earth they'd be lucky if their hotel had hot water.

"That is very gracious of your queen," Mom said in a guarded voice. Finley wondered if Mom was worried about being in debt to someone they had never met. Mom rarely let her guard down.

"Queen Uska is rather invested in the movie getting made," he said. "She's a big fan."

Finley laid her head on his shoulder. She was beginning to feel tired. "Will the portal feel like the one we just took?"

"No, it's different. It sort of feels like falling for a split second. By the time you correct yourself, you're already there."

The three gray suit stewards walked under a specific rounded arch with a castle-shaped symbol above it and disappeared almost as quickly. Inside the portal it was all black, with shimmery ribbons floating about within.

"Hold on tight, Finley," Mr. Stravdas told her, and she squeezed his neck to the point he was probably unable to breathe. He gestured toward Mom. "After you, please, Mara."

She gave him a look but did not argue. She seemed determined to see this through as she stepped into the glimmery portal. Finley heard the start of Mom's scream just as it was cut off.

"Ready?" Mr. Stravdas asked Finley.

"Yes."

He stepped in front of the portal and the next thing she knew all was darkness, with the exception of swirling lights, and her stomach was turning inside out. Years ago, before she was chronically sick, Finley had been a cheerleader. Because she was one of the smallest on the cheer team, she used to get tossed in the air to perform quick flips.

The portal felt like that, a quick flip in the air before landing solidly on your feet two seconds later.

One second she was staring into a liquid portal, and the next she was looking up at a sparkling black building that was supposed to represent Taloncourt. Or, as Mr. Stravdas called it, Vraithe's royal seat.

Taloncourt's portal, a smaller version of the portal terminal at the portalport, was located just outside the court-yard. Mr. Stravdas collected Mom, who was standing there looking slightly dazed, and together they followed the stewards.

Still on Mr. Stravdas's back, Finley turned to get a good look behind them. There were dozens of land spherules in every direction, each with houses and lakes and trees. In between each was a dark gulf that made her shudder. Though, before she returned her attention to what lay ahead of her, she thought she saw staircases and lights on the visible parts of the dark gulfs.

Finley then studied the stewards. She wasn't entirely sure what their role was. Were they going to escort them their entire stay? She hoped not. She didn't want too many adults watching her. Not that she planned to do anything wrong.

That was the problem, Finley thought. She never had

anywhere to go to get into trouble. It'd be nice if she found a friend while here.

Vikk always enjoyed coming home. The water fountain in the courtyard was a joy to listen to. Children played in the shrubbery pathways while Taloncourt's youth spent time running about, completing archery lessons, or painting watercolors Taloncourt's hilly landscape. He, Dessa, and their cousins had all taken part in these youthful rites of passage.

The large lake out back was a year-round cool repast for sweltering days. With Finley on his back, he'd been sweating for the better part of an hour, so the idea of jumping into cool water was rather appealing at the moment.

But first he needed to get Mara and Finley established. Finley was either asleep or nearly close to it and Mara was drenched in her winter clothing. Her light brown hair was plastered to her head and he'd caught her looking longingly at the water fountain. She had to be hot and thirsty.

At the palace's entrance, they parted ways with the gray suits. "Thank you for your service today," Vikk said. All three bowed to him. "The banquet hall is to the right if you would like a small meal before returning to the North American Vraithe Portal to reassume your daily duties."

The stewards took him up on his offer. "Oh, Werlaun," Vikk said. "The books?" Werlaun handed over the bag. As she turned to go, Vikk added, "And, kindly refrain from posting details about the queen's guests."

Mara watched this exchange with some puzzlement. It was as if Vikk held some sort of authority here.

Werlaun ducked her head and had the grace to look ashamed. "My apologies, Stravdas." She turned to Mara. "My apologies, Good-General Mara Eldress."

Mara figured Werlaun was the reason the crowd was waiting for her at the portalport. "Thank you," she said.

"You may go, Werlaun," Vikk said. To Mara, with her daughter fast asleep on his back and the gentlest of smiles aimed her way, her insides did a little summersault when he said, "Let's get you both taken care of."

# Six

Finley was just lucid enough to follow the conversation between Mom and Mr. Stravdas. She was no longer on his back, but tucked in his arms as he carried her into a crystal elevator where the button for each floor—and there were twelve of them—was a sparkling gemstone.

Rubies, diamonds, emeralds.

Mr. Stravdas leaned forward and pushed the black onyx button. The twelfth floor.

She heard Mom say, "Taloncourt is beautiful. From the outside I expected stainless steel, black jade, and dark paneling. Instead, I find it bedazzled with precious gemstones, gold, and silver. I'm afraid to touch anything."

Finley felt Mr. Stravdas's chest rumble as he chuckled.

"It is not precious to us, I assure you. Most homes are designed this way. These gemstones are as plentiful as rocks are on Earth. Those of us who travel to Earth for business, like I do, are authorized to trade in a gemstone or two as a form of currency conversion." The elevator came to a stop and they exited. "Money is a meaningless concept for Vraitheians, but we play by the rules on Earth." He said the last part as a whisper and Finley had the impression they were walking down a long hallway.

With half-opened eyes, she saw dark tapestries, ornate mirrors, and framed portraits. Light appeared to be coming from the end of the hallway. Moments later, Finley was jostled about a bit when Mr. Stravdas opened a door to a brightly lit chamber.

"This is the royal guest quarters and where you and Finley will be staying."

As Mr. Stravdas placed her on a very soft bed, an unknown voice further in the room said, "I am Areola, the queen's chief attendant. Queen Uska sends her compliments and hopes you find the space to your liking."

Mom said, "Everything is breathta—" before suddenly stopping. "I'm sorry, did you say your name is *Areola?*"

"Yes. For Earth's stiff mountain peaks." The attendant's voice did not convey irritation.

Clearly, they didn't understand what that word meant on Earth.

There was a pause. Finley figured Mom was looking at Mr. Stravdas for an explanation. Thankfully, Finley was too tired to laugh. She didn't want to insult anyone three seconds into their visit.

"The story goes," Mr. Stravdas said with a gentle touch of humor in his voice, "that Areola's parents visited Earth before her birth. Apparently, they liked the word so much, they bestowed it upon their only child."

"Of course," Mom said good-naturedly. She'd never make fun of someone's name. "As I was saying, Areola, the suite is breathtaking. I don't know if I've ever seen a more lovely set of rooms in my life."

"Very good, Good-General Eldress," Areola said. She

sounded relieved by Mom's response. "You will find a meal laid out for you in the next chamber. Our technicians used the pictures from a human cookbook as their guide. The refreshing chamber is behind that door."

There was a pause and Finley suspected they were pointing at the discussed door.

"And here, near the door," Areola continued, "is our control panel. There is one next to each bed, too. We have converted the buttons to human words. We hope you will forgive any little mistake. Our normal technician accidentally got stuck in the elevator shaft this morning. Oh—do not be alarmed. He is going to be perfectly fine after Dr. Smindle mends all thirteen bones. And the elevators are all in excellent working order, too. Anyway, as I was saying, from the control panel, press the corresponding button for your needs, such as the need for grooming, fireworks, or the day's entertainment schedule. Should you need emergency assistance, kindly press the *red* distress button and the royal physician will come right away."

"That was all very thorough, Areola," Mr. Stravdas said. Finley was pleased to discover that she could tell he was amused just by the tone of his voice. "Thank you."

"Thank you, Areola," Mom said as the queen's chief attendant departed.

From the doorway, Finley could hear the two of them talking in low tones. She overheard Mom say, "Finley needs to rest for a few hours..." before she drifted off to sleep.

"I hate to ask," Mara said to Vikk as she tucked the blankets around Finley, "but we will need suitable attire. And...I don't know if I trust the control panel. Every button is red. I'm sure by now that you realize we did not pack for such an excursion."

"Meaning you didn't believe me?" Vikk asked with playful inflection.

Mara glanced at her sleeping daughter before responding. She was like a tiny kitten nestled in a gigantic four-poster bed. "Finley believed you."

"Fifty percent is good odds in my book. She's a really good kid, Mara. I've only known her a few hours but I already know she's great. I wasn't lying about Vraithe's medical advancements over Earth. Tomorrow, if she's up for it, do you think you'd be willing to let the royal physician attend to her? If at any time either of you are uncomfortable, I'll take you back to the main portal. I'll take you home, no questions asked."

Was he always this kind? Did men like him really exist? Alien men, apparently.

"And the script?" Mara asked.

They stood less than a foot apart. His suit had wilted and she could smell the day on him. Granted, it wasn't bad, but he could use a shower. So could she.

"Queen Uska will not be very happy with me." He ran his hands through his damp, curly hair. He was still sweating from carrying Finley. "But as a nonviolent species, she'll mostly pout at me until I promise to make her another movie she's been talking about lately, the one where the kids kill each other in a gaming arena."

"Good god! Does your queen like violent movies?"

"Oh, the more violent the better. It's a little unsettling if you ask me. She likes to translate the titles herself."

"I'm not one to throw stones. After all, I served in the military as an explosives ordnance technician and saw combat. We Earthlings"—*Did she just call herself an Earthling?*—"like our violent entertainment."

Vikk seemed to perk up. "Queen Uska was very impressed with the violence displayed in your memoir."

Mara frowned. That seemed callous. "I guess that's one way to look at my getting blown up by two IEDs."

"And the sex," he continued as if she hadn't said anything. "That's why it's been flying off the bookshelves."

"Vikk." Her voice was whisper-quiet. Deadly quiet. Somewhere in the room she could hear the ticking of a clock. If Finley were awake, Mara thought, she'd know to get up and start running away. "What? Sex?"

His expression was comical. It was like he'd been caught by surprise, but he also looked guilty. How could one person's expression convey both surprise and guilt?

"Between Good-General Eldress and Enemy-General Calix?"

"Was that a question, Vikk? Furthermore, *who* are Good-General Eldress and Enemy-General Calix? Because those two people are *not* in my memoir. It's like...it's like..." She couldn't think straight. "Well, I don't know what it's *like*, but what little I've heard about it, doesn't sound anything like my book."

"I apologize in advance for the mistranslations. It's a good thing you're here. The script just isn't working and now, with your input, we'll get it right."

Mara crossed her arms.

"Think about it," he suggested as he backed away.

Mara was amused at his retreat. He was practically ten feet down the hallway when she said, "I'll think about it *after* the medical team looks at Finley's case tomorrow."

"Excellent," he said as he nodded. He looked tired but he also looked earnest. Vikk didn't seem like he was blowing smoke up her ass. "I will see you in a few hours."

"With attire?"

"Yes."

Mara shut the massive gemstone-laden door and sighed. What a zany day, she thought.

She took one look at the bed and decided the best thing to

do was to close the curtains and climb in next to Finley. Mara hoped to drown out the world for a few hours. Maybe things would make more sense when she woke up.

"Who," Queen Uska said, extending the *ooooo* with her throaty, booming voice Vikk had known his whole life, "was that adorable urchin clinging to your back like a lawnfrog? I saw *all* the pictures, Vikkolo."

*Vikkolo* was his proper Vraitheian name, though only the older members of his immediate family called him that. Vikk paced the front of the queen's room of business. Pink light, which slanted in at an angle from several wide windows, cast colorful spots of light on the carpet at his feet.

In a way, as he stole a glance at his questioner, Vikk felt like he was on a stage. Queen Uska sat behind her stone desk, peering at him with intense eyes the way aunts were famous for doing. She was very tall, taller than he was, with a golden-hued complexion, a narrow face, silver-gray hair, onyx-colored eyes, and a firm grimace.

It was just the two of them in the room, though at any moment the wall-sized holographic screen behind him could come to life and he'd have to answer to the fourteen prefect council members who governed Vraithe. Queen Uska, the figurehead, was a tiebreaker.

He knew that at some point he'd get asked about Finley— he just hoped he'd be able to clean up and change clothes first. Vikk hadn't yet worked out how to reveal that everyone's favorite character—Good-General Mara Eldress—had an Earthling daughter. He didn't think it would change things, but he also hadn't thought about how it had looked when Finley, an unknown human by everyone's standards, was plastered to the back of the queen's prime relative.

Or, as he would be known on Earth, the queen's chosen heir.

Werlaun had really done him a disservice. Vraitheians did not consider the royals celebrities the way Earthlings did. The gray suit stewards were not escorting them because of *his* status —there had to be at least twenty Stravdas relatives the queen could tap on the shoulder to succeed her.

In most cases, Queen Uska's own offspring would have been her heir. Qoral, the queen's only daughter, had traveled to Earth thirty years ago and never returned. The queen could have chosen any prime relative in her place, and yet she chose him. Vikk was fifteen at the time. He'd spent his life trying to be worthy of the distinction. It was a duty he took seriously. He well knew Queen Uska could change her mind at any point and select one of his prime cousins for the role.

No, the gray suits had escorted them because of *Mara's* celebrity status upon Vraithe.

Uska kept her gaze locked on her prime relative as he paced the thread off her carpet. He seemed distracted, worried, an emotion she did not wish upon Vikkolo. He was always so easy-going, calm, and collected.

To be blunt, she'd never seen him this disheveled.

It was downright unusual.

"The urchin is a human girl named Finley Eldress," he said.

*Finley.* Uska lifted one of her gold eyebrows. She needed to know more. "A prime relative of Good-General Eldress or Enemy-General Calix?" Uska had read the human's memoir two times through. She did not recall any mention of a young prime relative, but for such a violent book with several erotic scenes, it made sense.

"Both. Mara is her mother. Calix her father. And just address her as Mara. She's no longer in the Earthling military."

*Good to know.* Uska made a few mental notes, one of which was to make a few adjustments to today's parade and firework display. The existence of a child changed things. She tried to keep her expression neutral, but by the looks of things, Vikkolo was too exhausted to pick up on her senses.

"And what of Enemy-General Calix? How shall we address him?"

Uska watched his lips quirk into a quick smile. *Did her prime relative have feelings for this human, Mara Eldress?* Matters of the heart were rarely discussed aloud. She pushed the question to him using their receptive mind orbit channel but he ignored it.

"Around Mara?" Vikkolo asked. "Don't mention him at all."

She nodded. "Good thinking. After what he did in the snake scene, I wouldn't trust him either. That must be why he is her enemy."

"It's such a pivotal scene in the third act of the book," Vikk added, hoping to change the direction of his aunt's thoughts. The question she sent him using RMO was effectively blocked as soon as he realized where she was headed with it. He was not ready to think too deeply on how his heartstrings ached to be near Mara.

Queen Uska merely smiled at him.

He continued, "Mara has agreed to assist me with the script. In exchange, I offered our medical services to Finley. The child is ill. I believe Vraitheian medicine can help."

His aunt gave him a reassuring nod. Vikk knew she'd be pleased with his decision. It was diplomatic, kind, and service-oriented—principles of every Vraitheian. He wasn't so sure

Mara saw it that way. By Earth's standards, was this considered a bribe? He wondered she would have come if it wasn't for his promise to help Finley.

But that's what mattered, right?

"Was there anything else, Aunt?" Vikk asked. He was hungry, dirty, and tired. And he needed to locate his primary cousin, CeCe. She'd be able to assist him in finding suitable attire for Mara and Finley.

"No, be off with you." Queen Uska offered him a magnanimous smile. "I sense you have things to do. At sunset, bring our guests to my balcony. It will have the best view of tonight's entertainment."

"Aunt," he said, letting out a frazzled sigh. "What kind of entertainment?"

"Just a little something we threw together to honor our guests. We began working on it after you submitted your portal request last night."

*Think positive*, Vikk thought as he left his aunt's room of business. *She's had only a few hours to plan something. How bad could it be?*

Vikk took the stairs to the fourth floor and tapped on CeCe's door.

CeCe opened her door with a flourish. When she saw him, she frowned. She was young and fashionable and lived in New York City, working as an actress on a popular sitcom. CeCe closed her door behind her with a quick snap but Vikk saw enough to make him concerned. A half dozen of his younger cousins were sorting stacks of fabrics and larger-than-life costume ensembles.

He looked down at her and narrowed his eyes. "Did our aunt summon you?"

"Worried, Cousin Vikk?" CeCe tilted her head and gave him a bored smile. Most of his younger cousins called him Vikk, which he preferred, but he wasn't thrilled that she used her human expressions on him. Her long, sleek hair was pulled up in a high ponytail, and her eyelashes were so tall they cast shadows on her cheeks. "I'm on a deadline. What do you want?"

"Clothes."

Looking up at her *very* disheveled cousin, CeCe leaned against the door's sturdy frame and wrinkled her nose. There was a long mirror hanging on the wall behind him. All of his hair was plastered to one side of his head and the back of the suit looked damp with sweat.

"That suit has seen better days," she said.

"Not for me," he said with a loud sigh. *He's agitated, too,* she thought. "For the queen's guests. They are..." he trailed off. He used his hands to indicate how tall and wide they were.

"Do you mean the pretty human lady and her adorable daughter?" she asked innocently, even though she knew precisely who he was referring to.

"How do you know she's pretty?"

She smiled. "I saw the pictures, dummy."

"Oh. Right."

"Just so you know, your measurements were way off. It's a good thing you came to me. I'll help you under one condition."

Vikk expected this. CeCe was nothing if not predictable, but he had no choice. Mara and Finley would dehydrate and wither into human jerky if they continued to wear Earthling winter clothing.

"What's your condition?" he asked. She looked so pleased with herself that he laughed.

"Give me a good part in the film."

He snorted. In all actuality, he was going to do that anyway. No lie, CeCe was a good actress, not that he'd ever tell her that.

"Done."

"Right answer. I'll find a few outfits to bring them. Which guest suite did our aunt give them?"

Vikk hesitated before saying, "The corner suites on the twelfth floor."

CeCe blinked hard several times.

"Qoral's old rooms?" There was astonishment in her voice. "How very interesting, Vikk." Before she went back into her room and closed her door, she said, "Certainly makes you wonder."

Vikk had been wondering that very thing ever since he was told to escort them there. Queen Uska never let *anyone* use Qoral's suite.

Vikk made quick work of showering, getting dressed, and taking the prescribed tonic the royal physician had left on his vanity along with a note that read, "Your electrotones and phlindophomes were low this morning when the portal sent in your scan. I've brewed this concoction to replenish your stores."

His suite, which consisted of a sitting room, a room of business, a bedroom, and a refreshing chamber, was also located on the twelfth floor but in the Swest Wing near the storage rooms. Because he was often away on Earth, several years ago Queen Uska had offered him this simple suite, which was perfectly acceptable to him. It was quiet in this wing, and no one bothered him.

Granted, by Earth's standards, the rooms were still palatial, but compared to the rest of Taloncourt's luxurious apartments, some considered it an insult, given that he was his aunt's heir.

"Perhaps she means to change her mind," an older relative once remarked.

Vikk wasn't picky. Well, he *was* picky about certain things, just not about his apartment, though he had to admit that he enjoyed the wall-to-wall bookshelves in his room of business. Many, many years from now, when he finally took the throne, he'd be sad to leave the suite behind.

Sitting in his favorite chair near the window that over-looked the lake, he sent a text to Dessa using his Vraitheian device. He wrote, "Mara and Finley are with me on Vraithe. You never mentioned that Mara had a daughter. Why not?"

Taking alternate warp tunnel paths, electronic packets did not take as long as transporting individuals, so it would take only a few minutes for the message to reach Dessa's device.

While he waited, Vikk sorted through and read the notes for the novels she'd left with him. He was always on the hunt for Vraithe's next literary smash hit. Earth-Alien romances were always popular as were coming of age stories. He'd pulled aside several promising titles when his device dinged. He opened Dessa's message and laughed until there were tears in his eyes.

Dr. Smindle entered the Swest Wing, intending to discuss the young Earthling's portal scans with Vikk. She was raising her hand to tap at the door when the physician was stopped short by Vikk's outburst of laughter.

"She thought Finley was a cat. A cat!" Vikk said, along with more laughter. "A cat!"

Dr. Smindle was an excellent judge of when to intrude and when to back off. She would come back another time even though the outburst was of slight concern.

*Perhaps his phlindophomes levels were lower than the*

*portal's scans indicated*, she thought after returning to the elevator that would take her to the infirmary. The portal scans were not always perfectly accurate, which would explain the Earthling's scans. Still, with her mind replaying Vikk's unexpected outburst, she decided to update his tonic, just in case.

# SEVEN

Finley woke feeling refreshed. Pleasant rays of sunshine slipped in through a gap in the curtains. It was dim, but not too dark, in the room. Mom, snoring softly and buried under a mound of blankets, was sound asleep. Her long brown hair was strewn about in tangled locks.

Finley touched her own stringy hair. Knots everywhere.

Because she'd been barely awake when Mr. Stravdas carried her inside, she didn't get an initial view of the room, but from what she could see in the shadows, it was like living in a palace. The suite smelled fresh and graceful, like the gentle hints of an expensive perfume. The walls were covered in a dark green brocade fabric. Oval mirrors, framed alien-esque landscapes, and stained-glass sconces hung about the suite.

The curtains were also a dark green color. Various wooden tables and lamps butted up against every wall. Delicate vases filled with delightful turquoise blooms topped those tables, and in one corner Finley spotted a marble bust of an elegant-looking woman who wasn't quite human in appearance. Finley squinted to get a better look. The forehead of the marble face contained bumps in the shape of teardrops above the eyebrows.

Sliding out of bed, she tested her balance before padding across the room. The carpet was thick and soft against her bare feet. She glanced outside and gasped. They were in the clouds, but she could easily discern the edge of their land spherule, where the blue grass ended at the shadowed edge.

Finley saw what she thought was a garden maze on the far left part of the grounds. In the distance, the surface of the water reflected the red sun and the purple moon. The water went right to the edge, and she had to wonder if it fell over, like a waterfall.

She wasn't afraid of heights but she felt somewhat dizzy, so she left the window and explored a chamber so glorious it didn't seem to be meant for mortals.

In the connected chamber, she found and used the bath-room—everything pretty much resembled a human bathroom, just way more glamorous. Every knob was an enormous gemstone. It wasn't every day you flushed with a toilet handle made of amethyst.

After that, Finley discovered a table full of food in what looked like a formal dining room. Burgers, chicken fingers, a fully dressed turkey, French fries, bowls of soup with bread-sticks. She found steaks and crab cakes, now room-temperature, along with multiple pitchers of tea, water, and coffee. There was a sideboard with a stack of clean plates, bowls, cups, and cutlery next to trays of little cakes, cookies, fruit, and pastries drizzled with chocolate.

Not only was it enough to feed a dozen softball teams, but everything also appeared to be homemade. Someone had gone to a lot of work for them. Finley was just biting into a delicious-tasting fruit-filled pastry when she heard a knock on the main door. Mom was still in bed and hadn't moved. Finley's stomach twisted. She didn't want anyone to think they were being rude, but she didn't want to open the door while Mom was still asleep.

"Mom." Finley went back into the bedroom and nudged her shoulder. "Someone's at the door." Mom merely turned over and snuggled back into the blankets while mumbling something about the school board. Mom would never wake up if she were dreaming about getting her revenge on the school board.

"Yoo-hoo, anybody home?" a female voice said on the other side of the door. They knocked again.

Finley opened it on the third round of knocking. A petite woman, carrying a garment bag, stood in the hallway. She looked like and sounded like the nineteen-year-old actress CeCe Banks, except for one difference: her skin was a shimmery cerulean color.

"So you're awake!" the visitor said in a bubbly voice as she slipped into the room. "You must be Finley and I bet the lump in the bed is your mom, Mara."

The woman flitted about the room, turning on a few lamps. She darted into one of the other rooms and whistled.

"Nice spread they fixed for you," she said, coming back into the main suite. She was stylishly dressed in dark leggings, a shiny sleeveless tunic, and tall boots.

Swirls of tattoos snaked up her arms and over her shoulders before disappearing into her shirt. Her long black hair was up in a high ponytail, just like CeCe wore it, and her eye makeup and arched silver eyebrows were expertly done. Finley couldn't believe her eyes. It *had* to be CeCe Banks, or if not, then the Vraitheian version of the singer, songwriter, and popular actress.

"Are you...?" Finley asked a little breathlessly. Sadly, she did not have the energy to fangirl.

"CeCe Banks?" She smiled. "I am. It's nice to meet you, Finley. Thanks for not going bananas about it. Nobody cares about that kind of thing here." Her New York accent made her sound human and not Vraitheian.

"But you're..." Finley stopped short. She was about to blurt out that CeCe Banks looked nothing like she did on Earth, that she was sparkly. But that might be offensive. "You look different."

CeCe's smile deepened as she struck a pose. "It's called a glamour veil. Think of it as a *vision tuner* that makes you see what you expect to see. Once on Vraithe, it takes a few hours to wear off."

Finley was confused. "Everyone at the portalport looked human."

"Exactly. The glamour veil isn't on me. It's on *you*. They looked human because you expected them to. But it appears you are beginning to see the real us. We are fabulous, by the way." CeCe winked and Finley couldn't help but giggle.

CeCe pointed toward the dining room. "Our technicians have *never* been to Earth. They assume humans eat a *ton* of food in a single sitting. Doesn't matter how many times I tell them." Her bracelets jangled as she moved about the room. "You'll have to let me know if it tastes like the real thing."

Finley gave an uneasy look at the half-eaten pastry in her hand. "It's not real food?"

"Not in the way you think. It's made in our nutrition labs. We don't have cows or chickens or fish on Vraithe. We mostly consume vegetables, fruits, legumes, and nuts."

"It tastes just like a fruit pastry." She took another bite. "Are you related to Mr. Stravdas?"

CeCe decided that she liked the little Earthling. The kid looked a little sick, but a few days of fresh air, healthy nutrients, and a custom tonic from the royal physician would do her good. She always looked forward to Dr. Smindle's tonic and personalized note. Today she was high on wrigglezomes. Who even knew what that meant?

"We're cousins." CeCe hung the garment bag on the back of the door and unzipped it to reveal several outfits. "Figured you and your mom needed clothes. I live in New York City when I'm on Earth, so I know how cold it can get there. But"— she looked Finley up and down—"you're going to pass out if you keep wearing snow pants."

"Yeah, you have a point." Finley looked down at her clothes.

It might as well be sweat clothes, CeCe thought.

"Listen, run a bath so you can wash off the portal junk while I pull out ensemble choices for you for tonight's activities. I'll do that in the other bedroom so I don't wake up your mom."

Finley shuffled into the cleaning chamber and asked, "What activities?"

"Queen Uska likes to entertain." *Understatement of the year.* "I've not been briefed on everything, but I think there will be fireworks and a jousting ceremony. Is there soap and shampoo in there?"

There was a pause, then Finley said, "Yes. It smells good, too, like oranges. I've never seen a jousting ceremony." CeCe heard the water faucet start up. "Is that where knights on horses run at each other with really big sticks?"

CeCe stopped in her tracks. She'd completely forgotten that jousting meant something different on Earth than it did here on Vraithe. They'd have to change tonight's program.

"Yup," CeCe called back. "That's exactly what it means. Hey, you're pretty good at describing things. Do you think you want to help out with the royal announcements tonight? Areola, the queen's chief attendant, adopts a monotone when talking to a crowd."

"Maybe," Finley said from the cleaning chamber.

CeCe was laying out the clothing when a shadow appeared in the doorway.

With hair sticking out every which way like she'd been electrocuted, the approaching figure of Good-General Mara Eldress looked dazed and confused. She looked nothing like the photos from earlier. She wore a tank top, boxer briefs, one sock, and a deep scowl. "Who are you and where is my daughter?"

The familiar-looking young woman was holding back laughter. She couldn't have been more than twenty, if that. Mara turned, found a mirror, and discovered that she looked like a knockoff Barbie doll who'd just been spit out of a dog's mouth. Laughter seemed a reasonable reaction.

"I'm CeCe, Vikk's cousin. You must be Mara." She was sorting through shirts. "Finley's in the cleaning chamber."

"Don't move," Mara ordered. She walked back through the dining room, picking up a cold chicken strip as she passed the table and nibbling at it as she walked to the cleaning chamber. Tapping on the door, she called out, "Finley, honey, you in there?"

"Yeah, Mom." Mara heard the telltale sounds of splashing water. "Did you meet CeCe Banks, the actress?"

*Ah, so that's why she looked familiar.*

"She brought us clothes," Finley continued. "None of the food is real. I'm going to announce the joust. How cool is that?"

Mara looked at the half-eaten chicken strip in her hand, shrugged, and ate the rest of it.

"Very cool," she said instead of asking Finley to clarify what she meant. She wasn't a fan of talking through doors, especially ones with inlaid jewels that kept reflecting pink light in her eyes. "See you when you get out."

Mara returned to the second bedroom where CeCe was

laying out clothes, some of which, if she was not mistaken, were meant for her.

"I guessed your sizes," CeCe said. "You're a high school teacher, right? I brought what I thought a fashionable teacher might wear. All my teachers dressed pretty casual, but you seem like you'd be more stylish. For Finley, when I was her age, I was totally into tunics and leggings." She looked down at her own clothing, which consisted of a tunic and leggings. "I suppose I never grew out of that phase."

"That's very kind of you." Mara glanced at the articles of clothing and surmised all were of good quality and would probably fit. Finley was going to love the rose-gold top. "I take it you lived on Earth for a number of years?"

"Thanks, and yeah, since middle school. I make Earth my home. New York City, in fact. Queen Uska sent me a missive last night, ordering my return for the foreseeable future. Thankfully, my sitcom is on winter hiatus or auntie dearest would be out of luck."

"The queen is your aunt?" *Did she say she and Vikk were cousins?*

"Yeah, but it's no big deal here on Vraithe. I know that on Earth we'd be followed night and day. I get a little bit of that just by being an actress, but in New York City being an actress is like being a hot dog vender—we're everywhere. *You, though...*"

Mara jerked her head in surprise. "Me?"

"Oh, yeah. You're like a Big Deal here. Everyone has read your memoir—and of course, you must know that Vikk is making it into a film."

Mara heard Finley humming a tune in the bathroom. She was almost finished. Mara couldn't wait to clean up. She felt grimy.

"Did you read the English version," she asked CeCe. "Or the translated version?"

CeCe appeared to consider the question thoughtfully. "The translated version, now that I think of it. I don't recall ever seeing it on Earth. Wait"—she stopped all of a sudden and her jeweled brown eyes enlarged—"I didn't mean to make it sound like it was a dud on Earth."

It was Mara's turn to laugh.

"No, it *was* a dud on Earth, through and through. I might have sold fifty copies. Even my agent was ashamed to be associated with me."

"Rough." CeCe was waving her hands all about, which made her bracelets clink like musical notes.

"Exactly. So learning that my memoir is famous on Vraithe is both thrilling and terrifying because..."

"Because?"

"I have a very strange feeling that there have been a few significant mistranslations."

CeCe took her in as Mara was voicing her concerns about the film. CeCe brought a top and a bottom up to Mara's body to visualize the effect. No. Not that combination, she thought. It was also pretty obvious that Mara's glamour veil hadn't yet worn off. She'd been waiting for the woman to flip out.

"Oh, with translations," CeCe said with authority, "that's bound to happen. I acted on a few films when I was a child and one thing that I remember is that a movie adaptation is not an exact replica of the book. That goes double for a piece of translated work."

"How do you mean?" Mara asked.

CeCe could tell she was actually interested in the answer and not just asking for conversational sake. Just then, Finley emerged from the refreshing chamber. Her long, light brown hair was dripping wet, and she clutched a towel about her thin body.

"Here." CeCe handed Finley a handful of clothes. "Go into the main bedroom and try these on."

"Oh my gosh, thank you!" A happy Finley all but shuffle-danced into the next room.

"She loves clothes," Mara said in a proud-mom voice. "I haven't seen her this excited in a while."

"I love Earth, Mara, but Vraithe has superior fashion and fabrics," CeCe said. She looked Mara up and down. Even though Good-General Mara Eldress was disheveled, she had a very nice figure and would clean up nicely. "She seems like a great kid. Now, as I was saying about translations. Your Earth memoir was first translated into Vraitheian, and from *that* version it is being given a script treatment. A group of writers and the producer—that's Vikk—are using the translated material to further convert it into a movie."

"That's a lot of layers."

"Yeah, like thrice-heated leftovers. Doesn't taste as good as the first night."

Mara smiled at that. "Thank you for describing the process to me. I know a little bit about the publishing industry but virtually nothing about Vraithe or the film world. I feel better about everything now."

CeCe beamed at her.

"You'll feel a thousand times better after taking a shower and donning clean clothes. Here." Mara reached out for the clothes. "See if these don't meet the mark. You get cleaned up and I'll check on Finley once she's dressed. Trust me, we do not want to be late for the queen's balcony get-together."

At eight o'clock sharp, Areola was sent to collect the

queen's guests. She knocked on the queen's royal chambers. *Qoral's suite*, she thought with a tear in her eye. How could Queen Uska let guests use *this* apartment? She found no fault with the guests themselves. Good-General Mara Eldress and her daughter, Finley, were the loveliest of Earthlings.

Yet, Areola recalled Qoral's birth. She had been a squab of a baby, all teal and vocal, as if she was determined to make known her displeasure of Vraithe life from the start. Poor thing had always looked toward the horizon, wanting something different, something more. Vraithe's peaceful life, fragmented land spherules, pink skies, and blush lakes and rivers could never hold sway over the queen's only child.

It was during a mandatory school field trip through the portal to North America that Qoral decided she wanted that life more than anything.

"Doing what, though?" Queen Uska had asked.

"To join the military" was Qoral's answer one day after completing an Earth history and anthropology assignment. Queen Uska breathed the word "anarchy" under her breath, a word so foreign that Areola had to research it.

Yet upon her maturing age, when she was free to secure a portal reservation, Qoral and her Vraitheian beau, Boheerim, had departed without so much as a parting wave. And now, after all this time, after her suite had been kept ready for so long in the event Qoral decided to return, someone *else* was opening the door from the inside.

"Hello, Areola," Finley said after letting in the queen's chief assistant. Finley wasn't sure if she'd ever get used to addressing someone as *Areola*. For a brief moment, Finley thought the older Vraitheian looked mournful, as if she were remembering someone who had passed away, which made her wonder how long Vraitheians typically lived. She'd have to remember to ask Mr. Stravdas. "I heard that there is to be a joust tonight."

The queen's chief assistant smiled a toothy smile. Now that Finley understood the mechanics of the glamour veil, she began to see Areola's true form. For an adult, she was short and wide with shiny white hair styled like a Lego brick. She was pink, like the color of the sky, with silver eyes, silver eyelashes, and silver eyebrows. Her forehead displayed five bumps the size of acorns.

Finley decided it would be best to not let on that she could see it. It seemed like Mom's glamour veil hadn't yet dissipated.

In choppy English, Areola said, "Yes, you heard correctly, Finley. We will perform Earth's version of a joust." Areola's eyes darted around the room. Finley mirrored her movements. The suite was empty. Mom was in the other room getting dressed. "Is Good-General Eldress ready?"

"You mean my mom? She and CeCe are in the other bedroom. Did you know CeCe is an actress on Earth?"

Areola grumbled a non-answer.

"She's pretty famous in my world so it's cool to get to meet her here," Finley went on. "She said I might get to do the jousting announcements."

"Did she, now?" The older woman's lips flattened. Perhaps Finley shouldn't have said anything. For all she knew, it was not a done deal and maybe CeCe said it to be nice. CeCe might be the queen's niece, but Areola appeared to have a great deal of authority.

"The rooms are nice. After my parents' divorce, one time my Dad stayed at the Ritz when visiting me. I thought those were the nicest rooms I'd ever seen."

"What is the Ritz?"

"A super expensive hotel." Finley watched as Areola tried but failed to understand. She tried again. "Nice guest suites, but not as nice as here. No one at the Ritz ever made me a special tonic. I didn't see it until CeCe pointed out the note, but apparently my aura is a putrid color and my klugarsturn count might be low. Do you know what that word means?"

"Child," Areola clucked, showing tiny teeth, "no one knows what Dr. Smindle's words mean."

Finley laughed. "I guess it is a good thing. I feel a lot better after taking the tonic than I did before."

CeCe entered the room. "I thought I heard voices. Oh, hello, Areola. We're almost ready. When do they need to be on the balcony?"

Finley knew that CeCe spoke in English so that she could follow the conversation.

"You're not coming with us?" Finley asked.

"I'm involved in the queen's planned activities, but I'll catch up with you later, I promise," CeCe said with a smile.

"What exactly are you promising Finley?" a deep voice asked from the open doorway. Finley swirled and found Mr. Stravdas leaning against the frame. She took a little step back. He was always tall but now, with the glamour veil fading, he seemed broad shouldered and ginormous. He had a blue complexion, like CeCe, but it was more of a steel-blue hue, and didn't glimmer. His eyes were like black pearls, and a small row of bumps pebbled out above his thick black eyebrows.

Vikk found the scene before him comical. Areola was probably crying over the fact that his aunt put her guests in these rooms. CeCe was up to some mischief, though he doubted it was aimed at Mara or Finley. If he had to guess, CeCe was involved in some shenanigans that their aunt authorized— something to do with the color fabrics and costume heads he glimpsed in her room earlier, though what, he could not fathom.

And Finley...she was looking at him with fresh eyes. He had been wondering when the glamour veil might evaporate. He watched as her mouth moved. She was counting the bumps above his eyebrows. Five on each side.

It didn't escape his notice that Mara was nowhere in sight. His heartstrings, however, told him she was nearby. Perhaps in the second bedroom. Would she see him, the *real* him, when she emerged?

"I promised that she could make the jousting announcements if she wanted," CeCe said with a sly smile. So she wanted to take the job away from Areola?

Using RMO, Vikk asked her, *"A Vraitheian joust or an Earthing joust? Because I do not think Mara will appreciate her daughter witnessing a Vraitheian sex party."*

CeCe replied, *"No, it will be Earth's version of a joust. I want Finley to have a good time, not be traumatized."*

Vikk determined that he liked her answer. He peered down at Finley. She looked bright and fresh in a sparkly rose-gold top, black leggings, and flats. Her light brown hair was clean and shiny. She smelled like oranges.

"Is that something you'd like to do?" he asked her. "Make announcements?"

"I might," she said shyly. He could tell she was trying not to stare at him. He recalled that humans found that to be insulting. "I think it will depend on how many people might hear me speak."

"Not many," he answered. "I have a feeling most of Talon-court's occupants will be directly involved in the entertainment versus being spectators."

"In that case, yes, I'd like to. I've never done that before."

"I will help you," Areola offered, her tone gruff but genuine.

Suddenly, the air in the room changed for Vikk.

His heartstrings vibrated and wound themselves into a big knot seconds before Mara appeared, wearing a blue slouchy top that showcased toned arms, and snug black jeans. She'd pulled her hair up in bun just messy enough that several locks of hair framed her face.

"I'm almost ready," she announced to the room.

Her eyes met his and it felt like they were the only two souls to exist in the entire universe for that small second. Vikk was desperate to know what she saw, what she felt. He sensed the confusion in her heartstrings, how they reciprocated a fraction of his feelings. He could never be sure since she was human and it wasn't always a perfect transmission. Honestly, it might all be in his head.

He'd always found her beautiful, even when she was stunning him with that incredibly bright light. Her radiance echoed that same paralyzation in him, however briefly, and he stopped breathing for a solid minute.

It was quite audible when he finally inhaled.

Everyone was staring at him, even the stoic Areola, whose mouth needed to be collected from the floor.

"*I cannot deny how I feel,*" he said through an RMO channel to Areola, feeling a brief need to explain himself to his aunt's dearest friend.

"*How does the beige human lady feel?*" Areola responded.

Vikk wished he could answer out loud. Thankfully, CeCe was distracting Mara with a collection of shoes to select from. He hadn't fooled Finley, though. She was squinting at him. His answer to Areola was, "*At the moment, I think Mara is indifferent toward me.*"

Areola shook her head. "*You are headed for heartbreak, Vikkolo Stravdas.*"

As the group made their way to the queen's balcony, Vikk worried that Areola's words might come true.

# Eight

*There are no words*, Mara thought as they left the chamber and made their way down the hallway and into the elevator that would take them to the fourth floor.

No words to describe the way Vikk's gaze heated every cell in her body. Made her chest pound, her throat close, her palms sweat, her knees buckle. She thought maybe even her toes quivered.

Did *he* notice? Did *everyone*? Vikk presented himself like a magnificent statue come to life. He called himself a filmmaker. No, he was a god. A warrior. Had he always been that tall and broad-shouldered? It seemed like the suit was molded to him specifically. She wanted to explore every—

The crystal elevator dinged as it reached the fourth floor.

Priorities, Mara. Now was not the time to let her thoughts run in *that* direction. So she focused on what was right in front of her. They had been given a literal royal welcome. They were living in a gorgeous palace apartment on an alien planet.

She felt rested and clean. Her clothes were amazingly soft and hugged her body perfectly with zero digging into her belly.

Most of all, she wasn't bogged down with stress, headaches, or the never-ending pile of student papers to grade.

An adorable Finley skipped out of the elevator. She looked happy and healthy. Mara didn't know if it was the food or the air or the prospect of tomorrow's medical appointment, but Mara could not deny that her daughter was exhibiting more energy than she had in years.

Vikk touched Mara's back and she had to take a quick breath. "You look nice tonight," he said in a low voice. While there was humor in his tone, the heat of his fingertips reached her core, fanning out like a mini radiator.

It was his touch. It was magnetic. Mara *had* to break contact or she'd disintegrate into lava.

"Thank you." She stepped out of the elevator and put distance between them in the hallway. "I like your suit."

He let out a low chuckle just as Areola, who was up ahead, said something in Vraitheian. From her tone and the way Areola marched forward, Mara figured it was something along the lines of, "Hurry. We must not be late."

Mara squinted at the queen's assistant's backside. Areola's hair looked like a very bright, white rectangle. Hairstyles on Vraithe were interesting.

With some inner rejoicing, Vikk let Mara walk ahead of him as they entered the queen's room of business, which led to the balcony. Mara *had* reacted to him. Granted, her next reaction had been to stand as far away from him as possible, but he wasn't worried. She wasn't used to a heartstring connection.

Humans were familiar with something called *lust*, which was a similar manifestation of a Vraitheian heartstring match, though not as pure. It contained an urge to press yourself against the other. A promise of joining. Of explosive release.

But with lust, humans could part ways with no ramifications. A heartstring connection was solid. It lasted forever.

*If it was severed...* Vikk thought with some trepidation. Well, he didn't want to consider the scenarios as he studied the delicate tendrils of hair curling on back of Mara's neck.

Mara felt his eyes on her as Areola motioned for her to enter the balcony. She didn't mind the smoldering looks he aimed at her, but he had to know she didn't intend to remain on Vraithe long enough to pursue a romantic fling, no matter how appetizing the main platter. Besides, he probably wasn't serious about it, either.

*Focus, Mara,* she thought just as the beautiful scene before her stole her breath.

"Whoa!" Finley said as she came to stand beside her at the stone rail. Her fingertips pressed the smooth surface.

The sky was a silky mauve color while milky ribbons marbled the edge of a nearby land spherule, which contained a mountain-silhouetted horizon. A gentle breeze brought with it hints of honeysuckle and lavender and other fragrances she'd never be able to identify.

A thousand lights shone up from the meadow below as a throng of people milled about. Stirring notes of string music—violins, cellos—reached their ears just as a small commotion beneath the balcony caught her attention. She couldn't lean too much or else she'd fall over, but she thought she glimpsed two very large papier-mâché heads.

But before Mara could point them out to Finley, she turned and found herself in an intense staring contest with a woman standing in the balcony's corner. This must be Queen Uska. She was a tall, regal woman, with long, silver-white hair, onyx eyes, and a golden-sheen glow to her skin. She wore a pink robe with embedded crystals at the hems and collar. The kindness etched in Queen Uska's face was not just visible, it was palpable—there was texture, perhaps even a hidden meaning, in that welcoming smile.

It had been an incredibly long time since Mara felt like she was among trusted friends and family. As a foster child, then in the military, Calix and Finley had been her only family. With her military career cut short and Calix out of the picture, now it was just Mara and Finley against the world. She could always count on her best friend, Hannah Atholms, but Hannah was still in the military and not always readily available at the drop of a hat.

Strange how Mara had never articulated that before. Probably because she was always in constant survival mode.

But now, on this balcony, as Finley pointed at every little thing she saw, Mara's mind was spinning, hoping to make sense of what Queen Uska's smile meant, what this celebration was supposed to represent, and how it might all come crashing down on her at any moment.

Outside of the scandalous pictures she'd seen online this morning, Queen Uska wasn't sure what to expect when Vikkolo and Areola delivered her guests to her. She was already stationed on the fourth-floor balcony connected to her room of business.

The evening sky was morphing into her favorite scene as rays of mauve and pink streaked overhead. The sun was setting just as hundreds of torches bloomed the life in the meadow below. In the quiet she could hear the faint sounds of the waterfall.

So far everything was going according to plan. Lights hung from trees as well as from Taloncourt's outer walls. The light reached the edge of the water's reflective surface. After the joust, the royal band would strike up a few cords while serenading the fireworks display. The hum glow of fairies and the delightful notes of prism birds settled Uska's nerves.

It wasn't often she was on edge. Vikkolo's guests changed all that. Was it only yesterday she'd learned of their existence? And today? Today was a new day. She could only look to the future, not at the past.

She stayed in the shadows as the entourage entered the balcony. A little chamber within her heartstring, the one that had been dormant for so long, quivered. What was her soul trying to communicate? Danger? Concern?

Grumpy, yet faithful, Areola wore her emotions as clear as day. Her oldest friend did not like the turn of events. It disrupted the status quo. Tonight, after the ceremony, Uska would bring a bowl of ribalberries to Areola's suite as a peace offering. The tart treats always cheered her.

Vikkolo, decked out in his usual business attire, was a tall and commanding presence. It was a good thing his rumpled appearance from earlier had been a temporary occurrence. Perhaps Uska was a touch vain, because for a very short amount of time, as she imagined his disheveled profile on a future Vraitheian royal painting, she had seriously contemplated removing him as her heir.

Then their guests came into view. Uska was not known for her ability to judge human flesh, but from all appearances, Mara was an attractive woman. Tall, statuesque, with firm muscle density. She was a pale peach shade, with mostly delicate features, light brown eyes, thin eyebrows, a slim nose. A strong Vraitheian wind might buff it all away. While Mara did not possess age nodules along her forehead, she knew from the magazine subscriptions she received from the Earth's Found Treasures store that humans were born with flat, ugly foreheads. A shame, really.

However, that said, she understood the direction of Vikkolo's feelings. No Vraitheian, to her knowledge, had stirred such a reaction in him before.

Whether or not the human returned those feelings was beyond her scope of understanding.

The younger Earthling, Finley, was tough to read due to her sickly hue. Dr. Smindle had not exaggerated when describing the child's putrid aura. It was as if her combined illnesses could not make up their mind on what aura color to present, so all were meshed together.

Vikkolo had been right in bringing the child here for medical treatment. Though what that meant for the child's future was a mystery. Even if Vraitheian medicine helped, if the source of her illness stemmed from Earth, she might need to make recurring visits. This in itself was not an irregular thing. Many Earth leaders reached out to Vraithe's diplomats stationed across the planet for medical portalport visas.

Unless Uska was mistaken, it would be the outcome of the girl's health—diagnosis or no diagnosis—that would direct the trajectory of Vikkolo and Mara's situation.

Satisfied for the moment, she smiled as a startled Mara met her gaze.

"Welcome to Taloncourt," Uska said. "The joust is my way of saying 'thank you' for assisting Vikkolo with the script."

Mara's face took on a confused expression. Uska looked to Vikkolo for support. Since she rarely spoke with Earthlings, she did not possess great command of their language. She'd said everything in her native language.

Vikk crossed to his aunt, bowing in greeting. If he hadn't been daydreaming about Mara, he should have anticipated needing to interpret Uska's words.

"Queen Uska says, 'Welcome to Taloncourt'," he told Mara.

In the middle section of the balcony, Areola was readying the microphone that would be used to broadcast the joust's play-by-play. Finley was helping thread the cable while pointing at things and asking questions. "And," Vikk continued his aunt's translation, "that the joust is in honor of your memoir."

"Thank you," Mara said. "I am very honored by your welcome. Finley and I are excited about the joust. It should be a lot of fun." Vikk translated this to his aunt, who bowed in acknowledgement.

"Tell Areola to begin," Queen Uska said to Vikk. "Before it gets too dark."

Vikk did so. With Areola and Finley in the middle of the balcony and his aunt in her normal corner, Vikk, approached Mara. "May I escort you? I happen to know that the best seat in the house is in *that* corner."

"The shadowy, empty corner?" Mara asked with amusement.

Vikk winked. "My intentions are honorable."

She appeared to have another retort at the ready, but said, "In that case, lead the way."

She placed her arm in his. Little sizzles seemed to run along his skin in invisible sparks. If she felt anything, she didn't let on as they came to stand on the balcony's far corner. Queen Uska watched. Areola watched. Let them. He didn't give a damn.

Warm air tickled Vikk's nose as he detected hints of her orange shampoo. It felt good to be this close to her. Innocently touching. Inhaling her essence. Experiencing this moment with her while Finley found excitement with Areola. There was a sudden hush below after Areola made her announcement.

She felt the moment he leaned down. In his low rumble voice, she shivered as Vikk translated into her ear, "'Tonight we have a spectacular treat for you, a special Taloncourt presentation of Queen Uska's favorite scene from *Fighting Against Her Struggle*, with guest announcer Finley Eldress.'"

"Vikk, it's called *Fighting for Her: A Soldier's Struggle*."

"I know," he said as everyone cheered. "We don't have a Vraitheian word for *soldier*."

That made sense. Vraitheians were a peaceful people. In the lull, while the commotion below the balcony set themselves to rights, Mara allowed herself to lean against Vikk's broad chest. He was solid. Safe. In that moment it felt right.

Mara didn't want to analyze everything to death. She didn't mind taking risks, but in what world did leaning against a strong man mean taking a risk? She couldn't deny that there was heat between them. Her belly burned merely thinking about touching his skin, about him touching her.

His arm slid across her shoulders, tucking her against him, and she let out a soft, satisfying sigh. It was a comfortable stance to watch the show unfold.

With resounding cheers and jeers, two very large figures emerged from beneath the balcony. It was difficult to assess their size, but if Mara had to guess, the characters, which had papier-mâché heads and papier-mâché horse bodies, were about twenty feet tall. Small groups of Vraitheians, huddled under the horse parts, controlled different parts, to include their jousting lance. There must have been an inner pole to keep the head upright.

"They put this together in a day?" she asked. The materials did not look firm, like maybe some of it had not yet dried.

Vikk chuckled lightly, as if laughing at an inside joke. His lips briefly contacted her ear, which did all sorts of things to her insides.

"I believe there was something of a scramble. I'd say my aunt's theater group assembled it in the last hour."

Areola made her announcement first before handing the microphone to Finley, who said, "Good-General Mara Eldress faces her bitterest foe, Enemy-General Calix, for control of the kingdom of Earth."

Mara decided not to say anything about the mistranslation. *I am just going to enjoy this bizarre joust-play.*

In truth, as the characters got into position—one on the left side of the field and the other on the right side—she couldn't tell who was who. The heads, which were a dark metallic gold color, looked nearly identical. Each character had overly dramatized grimaced expressions. The eyebrows were drawn at angry slants. Mouths were flat and straight. She noticed multiple bumps across the foreheads.

She heard Finley's next announcement. "Angry about losing his twatsizzle, Enemy-General Calix challenges Good-General Mara Eldress to a death joust."

The words "death joust" echoed in the distance. The crowd oooh'd and ahhhh'd. She felt Vikk's chuckle rumble in her back.

Nope. She wasn't going to say anything.

The band's music whipped up into a high crescendo while drums stationed beneath the balcony roared to life. The jousting lances lowered, each one pointing at the other, the tension high. She had to admit it was a menacing scene. The beating drums caused the floor to vibrate beneath her feet, sending the waves through her. For a brief moment, Mara had a worrying knot in her stomach. She shook her head in disbelief.

A large bang echoed across the field. Mara, who still often experienced flashbacks when hearing loud noises, involuntarily jerked into Vikk's arms.

"I've got you," he murmured reassuringly as she slowly relaxed her tense muscles.

He held her tight as the two characters before them dashed forward as best they could.

Mara found herself letting out a shaky laugh. Shakespeare this was not. She didn't know how four or five people could run in unison with zero visibility, while also trying to control different parts of a papier-mâché contraption.

Both characters fell before reaching each other.

Raucous laughter came from every corner as Good-General Mara Eldress and Enemy-General Calix comically righted themselves. The heads, however, were now turned the wrong way and one horse had lost a leg.

Mara wished she had a camera to capture the nonsensical scene playing out in the brilliant star-filled evening.

Areola said something into the microphone, who then said something into Finley's ear. Finley's version came out as, "But then Earth's gravity levels disrupted the atmosphere of struggle."

Clever, Mara thought as the characters charged. The crowd was shouting words and Vikk told her, "They are trying to give the characters directions."

After the tumbles, the actors beneath the horse bodies were charging the wrong way.

Finally, after following the shouted directions, the characters collided in a less than spectacular way. One bounced back and fell just as the jousting lance of the other pierced its papery shell.

Cheers and a smattering of jeers erupted. The band kicked off a jaunty tune and throngs of couples started dancing in the meadow.

Mara watched for a few minutes, thinking more might happen, but it appeared that organized events were now complete as ad hoc dancing commenced.

"So...who won?" she asked Vikk.

She was still in his arms. Queen Uska's corner was empty. Finley was helping Areola pack up the announcer's setup while fireworks exploded in the night sky. Her eyes landed on the edge of the land spherule, and it didn't terrify her, not while she was with him.

It was a long moment before he answered. "I did."

Finley was doing her best to not look at Mom and Mr. Stravdas. She might be a homeschooled kid with no friends and no life, but she knew what it looked like when two people *liked* each other. And from the way they were leaning into each other, gazing up into the flashing fireworks, they *really* liked each other.

Finley couldn't remember a single instance where Mom had ever even looked twice at a guy.

Mr. Stravdas seemed really awesome and nice, and Finley had a feeling he'd be really good for Mom. The big issue, of course, was that Mr. Stravdas was an alien. She knew that most long-distance relationships had their challenges. How do you make it work with someone who lives on another planet?

Areola tapped her shoulder. "CeCe is annoying at you below."

At first Finley was confused but then realized Areola meant *yelling*, not *annoying*. She leaned over the railing and spotted CeCe jumping up and down, waving a papier-mâché horse leg at her. There was a sheen of sweat on CeCe's face.

"Were you in one of the horses?" Finley called down.

"Yes! Come hang out with me and my friends. Our bruised egos need soothing."

Her heart leapt into her throat. "For real?"

"For real!"

Finley ran to her mom. "CeCe's invited me to hang out with her. Can I, please?"

Through reflective fireworks overhead, Finley spotted the hesitation in Mom's face. She'd be worried about her. Worried she'd faint or get too tired. Except Finley felt wonderful.

"I don't know, honey."

"I never get to do anything," Finley said, frowning. She knew it wasn't a fair thing to say. It wasn't that Mom kept her from doing things, it was because her health always made things difficult to do. "I promise not to stay out late."

Mom sighed.

"CeCe will look out for her," Mr. Stravdas said. "In fact, they all will."

"All right, Finley, but promise me you'll be careful."

"I promise!" Finley jumped.

"And don't stay out too late."

"I won't!"

"Don't stray far from CeCe."

"Mom!" Finley flew to the railing again and yelled down to CeCe, "I'll be right there."

Mr. Stravdas chuckled. He said something to Areola who then said, "I'll escort her downstairs."

Finley gave a quick wave to Mom before following Areola out into the hallway and to the crystal elevator. From Mom's worried expression, you'd think she was being kidnapped by aliens or something.

Mara watched her daughter skip through the queen's room of business. Vraithe agreed with Finley. What would it say about her as a mother if she took her back to Earth, only for Finley to get sick again? That she'd willingly do that to her only child?

They'd been here for only a matter of hours. Nothing was certain. Mara didn't even know what the Vraitheian medical team was going to discover tomorrow. She looked up at Vikk. He'd been great through everything thus far. Sweet. Generous. Kind. She'd be lying if she didn't admit to wanting him.

They were alone on the balcony and it had been a few minutes since the last of the fireworks had shot off. She leaned against the railing and looked out into the landscape. Smoky firework shadows hung in the sky. She could still smell the sulfur in the air. In the distance she heard the lapping of water.

"I hope I can wipe the worry off your face," Vikk said. "Finley will be fine. CeCe's core group of friends are dependable and trustworthy."

Vikk matched her by leaning against the railing. They were close but not touching, not like before.

"I believe you. I'm actually thrilled that she's feeling well enough to hang out with others." She turned to look at his profile. She must be getting tired—here, in the shadows, she thought she saw tiny bumps above his eyebrows. "I think Vraithe is good for her. Is that normal, for humans to respond well here?"

He turned and they were now facing each other. "I believe that to be the case. Given who my aunt is, I have it on pretty good authority that Vraithe treats humans with rare medical cases or impossible-to-treat diseases throughout the year."

"There are so many who are sick and dying, though."

"I know what you're thinking, Mara. Vraithe does not possess the antidote for every illness. Our DNA is different. What works for us does not always work on humans. Some treatment might injure or kill you. However, several of our vaccines and treatments have proven to work well for both our species. We have always passed that knowledge onto Earth's leaders through authorized channels. Mostly, we possess the technology to isolate and detect illnesses. That's what our medical staff will be doing tomorrow at Finley's appointment."

"Meaning that even if you can discover what's wrong, you may not be able to treat it?"

Vikk nodded. "That is possible. I certainly hope for a more positive outcome but I do not wish to give you false hope, either." They were silent for a moment. Prism birds chirruped while prairie beetles and fairies flew about, their little tails all aglow. "Listen, I'd like to continue our conversation, but I don't want to do it here."

"In Taloncourt?"

His eyes danced. "No. On my aunt's balcony. She's been spying on us this whole time. In fact, I wouldn't be surprised if many secret eyes are on us right now."

# NINE

Mara tried not to feel apprehensive as Vikk escorted her to his apartment. She wanted to be back in her own suite before Finley returned. She figured she'd have an hour or so, which was plenty of time to discuss tomorrow's plans with Vikk.

It didn't matter that her insides tingled at the thought of something *more* happening between them. The fact that she *thought* something might happen had her agreeing that it would be best to discuss things in his room as opposed to hers. The last thing she wanted was for Finley to walk in on them.

The twelfth-floor hallway was dimly lit as they entered what Vikk called the Swest Wing. The Vraithe language possessed mashable directions beyond north, south, east, and west. Swest meant *southwest,* which seemed incredibly efficient to her. This part of Taloncourt was not as ostentatious. The hallway was not as ornate. Mara had an impression that this part of the palace was unused, like an attic.

She wondered why Vikk lived here instead of the grander part of Taloncourt. Perhaps he liked his privacy. Couldn't blame him there.

Small sconces lit the hallway as she studied his tapered backside. His shoulders had always seemed wide but when he pushed open the door to his suite, he occupied the entire doorway. It had to be a trick of the light.

"Welcome to my humble abode," Vikk said in a husky voice, gesturing for her to enter first. He closed the door and was silent as she took stock of his suite.

His rooms were tasteful but simple. The plain furniture worked for the space, for the man. The main chamber was his room of business. His desk, which appeared to be well-used, was stacked with papers that looked to be printed manuscripts. Behind the desk, a wall full of books gave the space a warm feeling. Mara could never be uncomfortable around books.

On the other side of the room a round table with four chairs was situated in front of the glass doors that led to his own balcony. Would she see the lake and the mountains from this view, or something different? Other cities? Mountains? What else was on Vraithe?

Mara peeked into the connecting rooms—the bathroom, then his bedroom, which was consumed by a bed massive enough to fit him. She turned to face him, to say something humorous, and was startled when she looked up.

He seemed to hold his breath in that moment.

Mara wasn't looking at the Vikk she'd come to know. Oh, it was clearly him, but different. The light was *not* playing tricks on her and it wasn't just his shoulders.

The main thing she noticed was that he was several inches taller. At five foot eleven, Mara wasn't a short woman, but even *she* could tell the difference between six foot two and six feet six, and Vikk was now six foot six by her estimation.

His skin tone had always been rich, but now, in this room, looking up at him, his hue had altered. His skin was a blue-gray shade, like steel-blue. Ten nodules rose out of his forehead, just above dark, thick eyebrows.

Mara backed away ever so slightly. She wasn't afraid. She knew that he'd never hurt her. Not in a million years.

No, she was confused. Had he done something to alter his appearance?

"Mara?" Vikk asked gently, reaching out slowly with one hand. Her insides heated as she met his unblinking onyx eyes. She felt the passion in those orbs. She read the worry in them, too. *Accept me. Love me. Touch me*, he seemed to be saying.

She thought about closing the distance between them, but she already didn't have a clear head, and wasn't willing to risk it. Better to be honest.

"I don't understand what's happening right now, Vikk," Mara said. She'd never had to deal with a man whose appearance changed drastically in the course of one day.

Vikk knew that the next few minutes could alter the course of their future. He had to be careful. He could not scare her, not that he would ever want to do that, but if he handled this badly, her perception of him might backfire.

"Shall we sit?" Vikk indicated the table on the far side of the room. Mara's eyes followed his large hand as he pointed. She nodded, but her steps were wooden as she walked slowly across the room.

Once they were sitting across from each other, he said, "I'm not entirely sure how you are perceiving me right now, but the first thing I want you to know is that you are not going crazy. Your eyes are not deceiving you."

He heard her quick release of air. "That's good to know—I wasn't sure if I was high on psychedelics or just imagining things. I drank Dr. Smindle's tonic this afternoon, after my shower," she said with a laugh. "I was beginning to regret that. So you are telling me that you're..." Mara trailed off.

"A steel-blue alien god? Yes."
She grinned at that.

Mara relaxed instantly. If he was joking about it, then she should be less worried about the whole thing. Sure, it wasn't every day you came across a statuesque man who made your pulse race, but it also wasn't every day you found yourself staying in a marble palace on an alien planet.

It wasn't about how he looked; it was about how he made her feel.

*Just take it one fact at a time, Mara.*

"I was thinking *ocean-blue*, but yes, I think steel-blue is a more accurate description. But a god, Vikk?" She smirked as she leaned back in the chair. She took him in, the way he sat there under her inspection, ready for her words, her questions, to correct her misconceptions. He'd probably strip if she asked. Mara could tell that he wanted to be an open book. "We'll see about that. What about the ridges on your forehead?"

"Klaums are hereditary. Some are bumps, like mine, others are like tiny twigs. Some do not have any klaums at all."

"Why do you have them? Do they serve a bigger purpose?"

"Why do you have freckles or moles or two nostrils?" he asked with a chuckle. "Because it is how you are formed. Vraitheians have klaums. It is how we are formed. For comparison to Earthlings, think of them as beauty marks. The bigger or the more abundant, the more attractive."

Mara nodded. She could understand that. "Why did you look human at first?"

"It's called a glamour veil. While on Earth, think of it like a coating the portal puts on us—humans see us as human. No big deal. But once a human travels through the portal, the glamour veil deteriorates. In the beginning, you see what you expected to see. So you saw the 'human Vikk Stravdas', but now that the veil has faded, you see the real me."

"What else is different?"

She saw his black eyebrow rise. He knew what she meant and she liked his growing smile.

"Shall I show you?" Within seconds he'd stood, removed his suit jacket, and unbuttoned the top of his shirt. She saw a wide span of muscled steel-blue flesh contrasted against the brilliant white of his tailored shirt. Mara noticed that the locket he had been wearing the night previous was now gone. "What do humans say, *A picture is worth a thousand words?*"

"That's not necessary, Vikk."

He grinned as he paused, working the buttons. He retook his chair and left his shirt as is. Mara desperately wanted to turn on an air conditioner. "Would most Vraitheians consider you attractive?"

He thought about that. "Average attractiveness, if I'm being honest, Mara."

Mara blinked in disbelief. *Average? No way.* If he had wings, she'd think him an archangel.

"To me, however," Vikk continued, "I desire to only be attractive to my heartstring mate." His hands moved to his chest, like he was searching for the missing locket. "It is more about what's on the inside than the outside. I have no interest in what others think of my appearance."

Mara felt a pinch in her chest, like a balloon deflating. Hope seemed to fade away.

The way he said it, all casual-like, made her think that he was talking about someone specific, a Vraitheian, his heartstring mate.

She realized she barely knew Vikk Stravdas. Perhaps Dessa didn't know that he already had a mate here in Taloncourt. That didn't excuse the way he'd been making eyes at her, but it was possible he'd not declared himself to this mate and that he was dallying with her. Mara cleared her throat, desperate to change the subject.

"You were wearing a locket last night. I have noticed that many here wear the exact same piece of jewelry."

Vikk sensed the second her demeanor changed. He wasn't sure what he'd said but whatever it was, it was wrong. Should he have not play-acted in removing his clothing?

He had hoped they might grow closer tonight, that he might be able to touch her, even if briefly on her hand or elbow or shoulder, with the affection of the heartstring quivering in his chest, but it was not yet to be. The truth was, he just wasn't sure how she felt, and until then, he could not press his suit.

Vikk pressed his hand against his chest, felt the absence of the locket. It felt good to have removed it. His heartstring connection to Mara was stronger than ever.

"The lockets are made from a specific meteorite called Casetti. Many years ago we discovered that the Casetti metal was a rare emotional blocker. Once melted and encased in a different Vraitheian metal, the same kind we use for the portalpods, it prevents a false heartstring connection."

"I'm not sure I fully understand."

"Vraitheians mate for life," he said, his heart thumping loudly in his chest. How could she not hear it? "When wearing the locket, a Vraitheian can enjoy casual sexual encounters without feeling a false heartstring connection. But once a true heartstring connection is formed, we no longer need to wear it."

"That seems like a useful thing to wear," Mara said, briefly glancing at his chest, then back up to his eyes.

Vikk tried not to frown. Did she understand that he'd removed it for her? That he'd all but confessed his undying love and devotion? Her expression did not alter. Humans and

Vraitheians expressed affection differently. She did not seem to understand what his statement meant, which made sense. Vikk needed to tamper his expectations.

He couldn't allow his heart to shatter in front of Mara, so he thought it might be a good idea to redirect the conversation. "Finley's glamour veil faded this afternoon. She saw the real me and didn't panic."

"She didn't breathe a word, but I'm glad she didn't. I might have freaked out, otherwise. Sometimes the fear of the unknown is much worse than the actual truth."

"You seem to have some experience with that, don't you, Mara?"

She nodded. "A little, but it's not something I'm ready to discuss tonight. I am glad that I can see the real you. Clarity and honesty are important to me." Mara paused and Vikk wondered if she was deciding on what to say next. "I'd like to get a better idea of what tomorrow looks like."

It was then then he knew that tonight would not go as he had hoped.

"Of course. After breakfast, we will take the portal to the medical facility where Finley will undergo a series of tests, scans, and evaluations. It won't take very long, but the results will take a few days, at a minimum. Once the tests are completed, Finley will be free to hang out with CeCe and her friends while you and I go downstairs to the studio. I want you to meet the actors, see a few scenes. Then we'll work together on the script. It is mostly the conclusion I need help with."

"Sounds pretty straightforward." Mara stood so Vikk did, too. She was a tall woman, yet still he towered over her. Some of her hair had come out of the bun. His fingers burned to tuck one strand of hair behind her ear. He wanted to brush a kiss upon her forehead. He felt that she'd welcome it, maybe even lean into it, maybe even surrender into the connection. Except, when she reached his door, she opened it, yawned, and said,

"Today has felt like one *really* long Saturday. We can only stay a few days."

She looked exhausted, which made sense. One Vraitheian day was the equivalent to two and a half Earth Days. It was already Monday on Earth.

Not trusting his voice, his words came out as little more than a whisper. "I understand," he said.

Mara looked up at him expectantly when he whispered, "I understand. Vraitheian days are long." She felt the warmth of his breath, the scent of something sweet, like wine.

She had the feeling he wanted to say more, but was holding back for some reason. They hadn't moved from his doorway. She brushed her fingers against his and felt the electric shock send delightful shivers up her arm.

Mara heard his intake of breath and her own blood seemed to thicken and throb. Would every touch do that? What would intimate touches do? Probably kill her, she thought with a wry smile. Best to not think about it. Vikk had a heartstring mate somewhere, and now that he wasn't wearing his locket, any interest he'd been displaying toward her must be only a casual attraction; he said as much tonight.

She dropped her fingers. It would never work out.

"I'll find my own way back to my suite. Goodnight, Vikk."

In a weird kind of way, as she walked next to CeCe and her friends, Finley felt like a wolf cub from a fairytale. Instead of sitting at home, watching her favorite sitcom on television, Finley was inventing her own adventure with CeCe Banks on the gentle, though fractured planet of Vraithe.

No conflicts. No battles.

Their biggest worry had been on which snacks to bring with them to the lake. The foods they mentioned were unknown to Finley, but they looked like berries and nuts, so she helped herself when a boy named Serstene offered them to her.

Serstene was a few inches taller than her with gold eyes, blue hair, and copper skin. She could just make out the tiny ridges dotted along his brow bone. She wondered if that meant he was young or inexperienced.

There were two moons in the vermillion sky. The bigger one was lilac purple whereas the smaller one was turquoise blue due to all the gemstones on it, or so CeCe told her when she asked. "We can take a portal trip to it, if you want." Sadly, Finley didn't think she'd be here long enough for long distance portal trips, but she just replied with, "Maybe."

Against the outline of the sky, Finley saw the tops of a mountain range in a faraway land spherule.

They'd all been to Earth multiple times due to mandatory school field trips, which Finley found funny. Serstene, like CeCe, wanted to act on Broadway. He'd been telling her all about how they'd performed their best under the papier-mâché horse, but that it had been tough with only an hour's practice. "CeCe was like a school matron, bossing us around like little kids," Serstene said in a voice that was at times a baritone and at times a bit high and scratchy. "It's no wonder we lost."

"She *is* pretty famous on Earth," Finley said in CeCe's defense, to which everyone laughed and started to tease CeCe.

"Don't listen to them, Finley," CeCe said as she popped a few berries in her mouth. She wore a cheeky expression. A glowing bug flew right in front of her face and she swatted it way. "Prairie beetles are so annoying! Anyway, my cousins wish they had it as good as me on Earth."

"*I* wish I had it as good as you on Earth," Finley said with some honesty.

CeCe put her arm around her shoulders. "But that's why you're here, right? To get a diagnosis?"

Serstene asked, "So it's not just about the heir's script?"

"Serstene Rozen!" CeCe warned.

"What, we're not allowed to ask?"

"What do you mean, 'the heir'?" Finley asked.

CeCe let go of Finley, ran toward Serstene, and playfully shoved him to the ground. A plume of glowing bugs wafted up from the patch of grass where he fell.

"That's what I meant, 'the heir' part." He just rolled over and laughed and CeCe waited for Finley to catch up.

She still had a lot of energy, but not as much as she'd had before they started walking toward the lake. She was worried about getting too close to the water's edge. Stretches of music reached her ears. They walked past all the dancers, some of whom were kissing, their bodies pressed really close together.

"Who's the heir?" Finley asked.

"Vikk, whom you call Mr. Stravdas, is the heir to Talon-court. No big deal. Queen Uska could change her mind at any time and name any other Stravdas as her heir. Like, for instance, CeCe here could be named heir."

"Decline," CeCe blurted out happily. She continued to chase the glowing beetles. "I'd skip town and live on Earth forever, just like Qoral did. She left ages ago and never returned."

"Qoral was queen Uska's daughter," Serstene explained to Finley. "The original heir. Since it seems unlikely that Qoral will ever return, Vikk is locked in, unless he does something stupid."

Finley asked, "Would someone fight him for it?"

"No way," Serstene said. "Vraitheian civilization is well past the warring stage. If we want to learn about war, we simply take the portal to Earth."

Finley let that knowledge sink in her brain for a little bit, glad there was no judgment in Serstene's tone.

A few moments later they reached the lake. In the darkness she couldn't tell what color the water would be. Was it pink because of the pink sky? She liked the idea of pink water. It just seemed pleasant.

She could hear the water falling over the edge but she couldn't hear it landing on anything. "How far does the water go?" she asked Serstene. "It is a bottomless pit?"

"No," he said. "We've engineered a portal for the water. Thirty feet below the edge, the water goes through a portal that redirects it to a different portal that replenishes the spring beneath the lake."

Finley smiled. "Like a looped waterfall?"

"Exactly. As a fragmented planet, we do our best to not waste water. So, how long do you think you'll be staying at Taloncourt?" Serstene asked.

He said it nonchalantly, like it didn't matter to him, yet Finley knew differently. He sat down beside her on the lake's rocky shore. CeCe was carrying a bug in her hand and chasing one of her youngest cousins with it.

Finley picked up a shiny stone. Mr. Stravdas had mentioned that gemstones were as common as Earth rocks. What might she be holding right now? An emerald? A blue diamond, like the one from the movie *Titanic*? She played with it in her hand, tracing its edges.

"I'm not sure," she explained. "A few days, I think. I'm supposed to see the medical team tomorrow."

Serstene tossed gems in the lake. They made thunking sounds.

"What's wrong with you?" he asked.

Finley appreciated that he wasn't shy about asking direct questions. She felt that sometimes people were too polite to ask questions or make honest comments. What usually happened was no one really talked to each other. You never made true friends, people who knew you, who'd stand up for you.

Perhaps that was her loneliness talking. For the longest time it had been just her and Mom.

"We're not sure, to be honest. The doctors think it's something called CFS, or chronic fatigue syndrome. I've been sick for going on two years now, but really, I think I've probably been sick my whole life. I get these really bad headaches sometimes, like my head is going to split in half. I have to manage my activity level so that I don't overexert myself. If I do, I can't get out of bed for days. Certain foods make my insides twist in agony. CFS is sometimes a catch-all for a collection of symptoms that doctors can't explain or cure."

"Do they think you're making it up?" Finley held her breath. By him asking that, did *he* think she was making it up? He stole a glance at her. He must have sensed she was unsure of how to answer, or to even answer. "I'm not saying that's what I believe."

"No one has outright said that. A few doctors said it might be psychosomatic, where the body acts like it is ill even if there are no underlying issues. It's like they're waiting for me to magically feel better."

"And Vikk thinks our medical team can help?"

Finley nodded in agreement. "But that's not the main reason we are on Vraithe. Mr. Stravdas wants Mom's help with the movie script for her book, and offered Vraithe's medical services in exchange. She didn't really want to do it. In fact, she thought he was lying about being from another planet—I mean, it does sound kind of crazy. Well, for humans, at least. I've pinched myself at least a hundred times today wondering if I'm going to wake up in my bed back home and find that this was all just a dream."

"I hope that doesn't happen," Serstene said with just enough seriousness that Finley did a double take. He wasn't making a joke at her expense, was he?

CeCe ran back to them, out of breath and laughing. "Want to go swimming?" she asked them.

"I can't," Finley said with some reluctance. "I'm getting tired. I don't think you'd want me to drown."

"Yeah, that'd be harsh!"

"I can take you back to the palace," Serstene offered.

Finley looked expectantly at CeCe. She'd promised not to stray far from her.

CeCe seemed to know what she was asking. "I have to round up the others first," she said, "and they aren't ready to go inside. It's like they are allergic to bedtime. Probably best if Serstene walks back with you."

"Okay. I'll see you tomorrow then."

"Night kiddo," CeCe said, mussing up her hair. She flicked Serstene on the forehead and he muttered, "Ow!"

"CeCe has a lot of energy," Serstene said after they'd started walking back.

Since they were facing the biggest and brightest moon, Finley was able to see his face in the moonlight. As he looked at her, she saw a lot of concern in his eyes. She saw something else there, too. Romance?

She hoped that they were friends, because if they were friends it might lead into kissing. Finley decided she was not opposed to kissing Serstene.

Walking side by side, his hand brushed up against her hand. Lightning bolts shot up her arm. It was warm and exciting, and made her heart beat really fast. It seemed to reboot her brain, too. By the way he snatched his hand back, he felt it too.

"What was that?" she asked. Her voice, which had a catch in it, like she was out of breath, came out as the barest whisper.

"Electric connections happen sometimes," Serstene said. "I wonder..." He trailed off, turning to face her. The moon was now behind him, casting him in a romantic silhouette. "May I?" he asked. He closed the distance between them.

Finley's breathing stuttered. "May you what?"

"Kiss you?"

A jolt of nervous energy made her belly flip. It's just butter-flies, she told herself.

Finley closed her eyes, leaned forward, and pressed her lips to his. Worlds flashed before her eyes. From the top of her skull to the tips of her toes, electricity flowed through her like a constant current, and she knew—*knew* beyond a single doubt—that Serstene wasn't kissing her just to see what it was like to kiss a human girl.

No, he *liked* her.

The kiss was a chaste one, and only lasted mere seconds, but she had never experienced anything as sweet, or as exciting, as what that brief contact created within her.

Serstene stepped back and his lips lifted into a wide smile. "Wow," he gushed.

Serstene had never felt anything like it in his life. Granted, he was only sixteen and never so much as liked a girl before. Finley was different. Sweet. There was some fragility about her that initiated his desire to take care of her. Not that he wanted her to be ill or weak. Only that he wanted to be by her side through it all.

He hoped that Vraitheian medicine helped her, even if that meant she went back to Earth and he never saw her again. It would break his heart. This much he knew. That kiss activated something he'd only heard his older relatives discuss—his heart-strings.

Serstene had never felt so much activity in his chest before. It was going wild, like a newly activated machine. He'd only just received his Vraitheian black locket last year. If his connection to Finley was *this* strong while wearing it, how would he feel had he left it behind? Would his chest crack open to let his heartstrings fling out and envelope Finley?

"I know," Finley said in the moonlight. "Wow." There was a dreamy quality to her voice.

He liked her light-colored hair; her dark yet iridescent eyes played tricks on him. Something glimmered on her chest. A necklace of some sort. Did humans have their own version of a Vraitheian black locket?

Serstene gently lifted the oblong metal disks, turning them in his fingers. "What is this?"

"They're called military dog tags. They were my mom's—she had to wear them when she was in the army."

His eyebrows scrunched together, so it must have been obvious that he was confused.

Finley continued, "I was always worried about her. You see, her job was to stop bombs from, well, exploding. If something ever happened to her, the military could use the dog tags to identify"—Finley stopped to take a shaky breath and Serstene felt her shiver—"to identify her remains. Mom still suffers because of it but her military career continues to be a significant part of her identity. Mom hasn't always had the easiest life and she's worked hard to improve things. So, I wear her dog tags because I'm proud of her."

"You love your mom a lot, don't you?"

"More than anything. She's the best mom in the entire universe."

Serstene compared human parents against Vraitheian parents. Vraitheian parents were somewhat more detached from their offspring.

"I believe you." Serstene looked at the moon's placement in the sky before hugging Finley. "It is getting late. I don't want your mom to worry."

Finley nodded. "And she will worry, if I'm out too late." As they entered the brightly lit palace and stepped into the crystal elevator, Finley's face reanimated like she'd remembered something. She pressed the button for the twelfth floor. "Oh. I've been meaning to ask someone about a word from tonight's joust. What does *twatsizzle* mean?"

Serstene nearly choked on his tongue.

Finley laughed at him. "I'm being serious. What does it mean?"

"You should probably ask Vikk that question."

"I thought we were friends."

The elevator dinged and the door glided open. "We are."

Finley stepped out into the twelfth-floor landing but kept her arm over the door so that it wouldn't close. His heart leapt around his ribcage like a fluttering prism bird.

Finley knew she had Serstene trapped. She would keep them there all night it that's what it took.

"Tell me," she said.

His handsome face turned a different shade of copper and she had to wonder if he was blushing. Twatsizzle must be a bad word here.

"Fine, but remember, you forced me. Twatsizzle is another word for penis."

Finley stumbled back, a gurgle of laughter building. First, the portalpod was right in front of a huge green graffiti penis, and now this.

The elevator door closed. As it closed, she heard Serstene say, "I'll come find you tomorrow!"

# TEN

Finley hadn't yet made it back to their suite when Mara entered. Even though she was flat-out exhausted, her watch told her only about an hour has passed since leaving Vikk's room and wandering the twelfth floor, searching for their bejeweled door amongst a dozen bejeweled doors.

As if thinking about her conjured her, Finley rushed into the room, breathless, a bright expression on her face. Finley leaned against the door in much the same manner a lovelorn character did in the movies. She even sighed.

"Someone had an enjoyable night," Mara said with a chuckle. She had just finished up in the refreshing chamber and donned a pair of clean pajamas, and was sitting at the desk at the far end of the room, brushing the tangles from her hair. It wasn't often she saw her daughter in such a mood.

"Everyone here is just so nice."

Mara smiled. Finley smelled like wildflowers and the beach. "You're a nice kid to get to know."

Finley pushed away from the door to rummage through the clothing CeCe had left for them. She extracted a long T-shirt and soft shorts.

"It's different here, though," Finley said. "On Earth, no one cares about anyone. Here, I feel special. Like I belong, or something. How is it that even possible?"

"To feel a stronger connection to the people of an alien planet versus those on your home planet?" It wasn't such a strange question, really, the more that Mara thought about it. Deep in her core, she detected an unbreakable connection to Vikk, she just wasn't sure how or why.

As Mom asked the question, Finley went into the refreshing chamber to wash her face and get changed. When she emerged, she said, "Well, yeah. I feel like I have a connection to my new friends."

"In the world of literature, that's called a paradox."

Finley rolled her eyes.

"Not now, Professor Mom. This is real life, not fiction."

Mom laughed. "No one would believe it, though, would they? Like, no one would believe that we traveled through a space portal? Or that Vikk and CeCe are actually blue-hued aliens with odd bumps on their heads?"

"So you saw him for real? CeCe said that once the glamour veil faded you'd see the real them, the real Vraitheians."

"Does their appearance frighten you?" Mom asked.

"Oh no!" Finley blushed as she recalled Serstene's handsome face, his gentle kiss, the way she felt around him, protected and loved. "I mean, it seems like I've known them all my life."

Mara smiled a knowing smile. "I know what you mean." She kissed her daughter's forehead as she scrambled under the covers. She reminded her of their schedule for the next day, to which a sleepy Finley murmured, "Mmmk."

*Young love is a buoy*, Mara thought. Heartbreak might be inevitable, but it would be the same if they were on Earth. Whoever had captured Finley's heart had to be a special soul, Earthling or Vraitheian. She would have the sweetest of dreams tonight.

Mara went into the second bedroom, turned off the lights, and slid into the plush bed. She pushed thoughts of Vikk from her mind. Mara couldn't afford her own heartbreak. She had a daughter to take care of and a life to get back to on Earth, even if that life wasn't as fulfilling as she'd have liked it to be.

Hours later, in the corner of the room, next to the backpack Mara had left on the desk, her phone lit up like a Christmas Tree, but the buzzing wasn't loud enough to wake her.

It was a brand-new, wet-behind-the-ears navy lieutenant ten hours into his twelve-hour shift operating a 24/7 classified watch floor in a bunker beneath Cheyenne Mountain who finally noticed the red-tag alert. At first, Vice Admiral Cheryl Clayton dismissed the young officer's spot report. It wasn't often they received such alerts, but when she opened his encrypted email and read the details, it quickly became apparent that it was important for two reasons.

One, it would trigger significant media attention.

And two, the source of the red-tag alert meant she would have to notify the Space Force combatant commander.

Certain soldiers had specific protocols marked against their records. The Vice Admiral typed in several authenticator passwords into a standalone terminal in the corner of her office and reviewed the electronic records in question.

The records, which very much existed, were annotated in red: *Do Not Confirm Existence.*

Because Vraithe's premier medical facility was located on a land spherule on the other side of the planet, the portal trip took a few seconds longer than the portal hop from the portal-port terminal to Taloncourt. Mara's stomach plummeted. It felt as if she'd jumped from a skyscraper, but just before she would have hit the ground, her foot made contact with the connecting portal exit. She stepped onto the platform as right as rain.

"I will *never* get to used to that," she said once her heart had climbed out of her throat.

Finley appeared next, and then Vikk, who was dressed in faded jeans and a light gray T-shirt. Mara had a difficult time not sneaking glances at him.

Now that her glamour veil was gone, she could admire his strong figure, his chiseled facial features, the way his vibrant steel-blue skin glowed in the sun, and his dark-as-night eyes. Yes, he was an alien, and yet she didn't see him that way. She pondered what lay beneath the clothes. He must be glorious.

*Stop looking!*

Mara kept her face expressionless lest she give her thoughts away.

It had to be just another day for Vikk. Finley looked windswept, her cheeks were reddish, and her eyes were bright, as if she'd just finished a thrilling rollercoaster ride and was demanding to go again.

Vikk hadn't been wrong about the medical facility—it was state-of-the-art. Made of reflective blue glass and stainless-steel beams, the building rose regal and tall, like a monument.

"A medical representative will escort us to the correct suite," Vikk said as they walked through an arched entryway and a clerk at the check-in counter scanned in the badge lanyards Vikk had given them the previous day. Everything was clean and pristine—even the windows were spot-free—and Mara had a worrying thought that they were bringing in unnecessary germs.

"It is a self-cleaning facility," Vikk added, as if reading her thoughts. Now that she considered it, Mara had to wonder if Vraitheians had the skill of mind reading. She'd have to ask.

For Finley, the next several events happened in a blur. A bald Vraitheian with purplish-pink skin and amethyst eyes named Dr. Keiji Vuzmuc met them and whisked them up a fast elevator and into an eerily quiet white room the size of a basketball court. It was filled with all sorts of machines, some of which were as big as tanks.

They were going to test her blood, scan her with five different scanners, and conduct vision and hearing exams as well. "Think of it as an annual wellness check," Dr. Vuzmuc told her. "Except all the tests take roughly one hour versus weeks upon weeks on Earth."

"Have you ever been to Earth?" Finley asked because their accent was so spot-on. Mom and Mr. Stravdas were outside, waiting, while she was sitting in a chair. Dr. Vuzmuc was asking a ton of medical history questions, which were being automatically transcribed onto a slim tablet.

A technician was drawing her blood while another gave her a cup labeled with her name that she'd need to urinate in. Thankfully they didn't have to watch her do that.

Dr. Vuzmuc smiled. "Yes. For years. I trained at Johns Hopkins before taking up residence in Washington, DC. I've worked in emergency departments, family medicine, prison medicine, and once, to round out my education, as an elementary school nurse. Young human children are adorable but menacing. They like to bite and kick!"

Finley laughed. "I am a human child and can confirm." Dr. Vuzmuc's face took on an alarmed expression. "I've grown out of that phase, though."

"Excellent news, Finley, for I do not care to be bitten. These days, my specialty is in human medicine. When Earthlings travel to Vraithe for medical treatment, I am their doctor. When I am working on Earth, I am an attending physician at Capitol Children's Hospital in Washington, DC, too. All right," they said. "We've collected enough blood and I've entered your medical history into the system. Take the cup into the refreshing chamber and fill it at least halfway."

Finley did as she was bid, returned, and surrendered the cup to the waiting technician.

"Hmmm," Dr. Vuzmuc said, staring at their medical tablet as they stood next to a large machine. The doctor's eyebrows were all scrunched up, like something wasn't working.

Finley's stomach dropped. "What's wrong?"

Dr. Vuzmuc glanced up. Their face morphed into a gentle smile. The doctor's face softened.

"Nothing to worry about, Finley, just a technical glitch. I'm pinging Earth's medical servers. I have privileged access, which allows me to request medical records from Earth. However, at the moment, I'm getting an 'access denied'. Probably due to a solar flare or some such nuisance. I'll try again later." Dr. Vuzmuc pointed toward the large machine beside them and Finley's nervousness tripled as she bent over to look inside the tunnel-like tube of the patient table. "Ready? It's scanner time. Tell me, are you claustrophobic?"

Even if she was—and she wasn't sure—Finley wasn't going to let it affect her.

"Let's do this." She was here to get answers, once and for all.

In the waiting room, sitting on a comfortable couch, Vikk wanted to take Mara's mind off of whatever she thought was transpiring inside the medical office. He got her a cup of coffee from the cafeteria, which appeared to greatly improve her spirits, before digging out the script for *Fighting Against Her Struggle* from his satchel.

"Here," he said, handing a thin tablet to her.

Her hair was pulled back into a ponytail and she wore a white T-shirt, jean leggings, and brown ballet flats. It was a casual outfit seen on thousands of women, yet on Mara he couldn't tear his eyes away.

Vikk had dreamed last night that she let him brush her hair. Just that, nothing else. Soft feathery strokes, murmurs in her ear, a tickle of fingers on her nape. He woke sweating and incredibly erect. There was no rule that said a Vraitheian could not pleasure themselves. Long-term sexual relationships were usually confined to heartstring unions, but it was not a requirement. Self-pleasure would never equal a true union, or so he heard, but this morning, in the darkness of the wee hours, as brilliant stars winked at him in the night sky, he stroked himself hard, fast, and furious until he cried out Mara's name.

He'd never been so relieved to be tucked away in an isolated part of the twelfth floor where no one could hear him. If Dr. Smindle happened to overhear, Vikk chuckled at the thought of the good doctor prescribing a healing tonic for such outbursts.

"I won't be able to read it," Mara said, bringing him to the present. She pointed at the text. "It is in Vraitheian."

There was a quiet inflection in her voice. It might have

been because she was nervous about Finley's tests, but he couldn't ignore the suspicion that she was displeased by something he said or did last night. Her aura was black, which usually meant sexual arousal, yet her demeanor was not representative of that shade.

Vikk didn't often "read" humans on Vraithe. He supposed it was possible his ability to read her here was not as strong as it was on Earth. Mara would almost certainly be feeling so many emotions and sensations on an alien planet that detecting *one* single aura trait might be near to impossible.

"Press the translate button in the upper left and toggle down to English."

Mara snorted at Vikk, but he looked too eager to tease, so she did as instructed. "English translated into Vraitheian translated into English." Mara smiled at him. "I cannot wait to see the final result."

"It won't be perfect, but it should give you a gist of the script."

She read the opening scene.

INT. GOOD-GENERAL MARA ELDRESS'S HOUSE - REFRESHING CHAMBER - EVENING

Good-General Mara Eldress has stepped from shower. Clothes gone. Water drippies down skin. She hears smoobing sound from somewhere in the house.

GOOD-GENERAL MARA ELDRESS
(smoobed)
Hello?

With right hand, she picks up sword next to the sink. Exits the refreshing chamber to investigate.

Mara stopped there and closed her eyes. "What does *smoobing* mean?"

"I think the word *concerning* might be close."

She nodded and counted to ten. When she reached ten, she kept going until she reached twenty. Mara thought through this. Okay, so in the film, her character heard a concerning sound. She was *smoobed*, or concerned.

In reality, her memoir opened with her waking up from a coma in Landstuhl Regional Medical Center, the US Army's elite medical center in Landstuhl, Germany. She'd survived two concurrent IED blasts. Due to the swelling in her brain, doctors decided it would be best to put her in a medically induced coma until the swelling subsided.

She had no memory of the blasts or the three weeks she was in a coma.

Mara tried to view her memoir from a Vraitheian's point of view, a society with no wars or military conflicts. The idea of an IED blast or a medically induced coma might not translate well for them. But then again, Vikk's script had introduced a sword. Unless *sword* meant something entirely different here, like *soap*. Good-General Mara Eldress grabbed *soap* to investigate a concerning sound.

Mara let out a deep breath. When she opened her eyes, Vikk seemed to be distracted by something in his hand. It looked like a phone, but not an Earth one. It was a glossy black metallic device that appeared to be made from the same material as the portalpods.

"Everything all right?" she asked.

"Dessa sent me a few notes," he said, switching it off and putting it in his back pocket. "I'll check it later. Anyway..." He lifted his eyebrows. "What did you think of the opening?"

"It certainly starts off with a bang, Vikk. But," she added somewhat carefully, "I can see now why you wanted my help."

She leaned in far enough to bump her shoulder against his. It was her way of showing camaraderie, that they were in this together. The script. Finley's tests. Mara recalled how Vikk talked about a heartstring mate. They needed to set boundaries. There was no denying the looks he had been casting her way, but it couldn't be a fling. For her, it had to be serious or nothing, and with Finley's health on the line, establishing a fling with Vikk—and it ending badly—might derail their ability to come back to Vraithe should Finley need further medical intervention. She had to keep Finley's needs above her own.

"Business partners, right?" Mara asked.

His expression was incredibly unreadable in that moment. "Absolutely. I hope we can be friends, too. Don't you want that?"

Vikk held his breath, waiting for her to answer.

"I don't want things to get complicated," Mara said, tapping the lanyard. "This can't be forever, you know. We have lives on Earth. I have a job that I love, school board be damned." She muttered the last part under her breath. "We can give you a few days but soon winter break will be over. So far, Finley seems to be thriving here and I will keep an open mind about the script." She held out her hand. "Deal?"

What Vikk mostly heard was, *We have lives away from here, away from you.* Areola's prediction was fast coming true. *"You are headed for heartbreak, Vikkolo Stravdas."*

He felt his heartstrings retract. It was a protective mechanism. Curl in, hibernate, wait for one who could thaw them. Vikk didn't want to give up, but for it to be a true heartstring union, the tender feelings had to be reciprocated.

Finley emerged at that moment. Her thin frame was a little wobbly on her feet, but she looked upbeat and ready to conquer the universe. Thinking about to how he'd originally presented the idea to Mara, his deal had been that he'd get Finley into Vraithe's medical facility if Mara assisted with the script.

That was the deal.

The deal she'd agreed to.

There had never been a deal that suggested they would become lovers or heartstring mates or even friends.

In order to keep Mara in his life, Vikk would have to keep things professional, no matter how much it crushed everything within him.

He shook her hand. "Deal."

To Mara's surprise, Taloncourt's film studio was located in the palace's vast basement levels. Near the entrance, there were viewing rooms with reclining chairs and a large projection screen. "This is where Queen Uska and her party watch movies," Vikk said. His voice was businesslike. He seemed pleased to bring them to his studio, but ever since they'd shook hands at the medical facility, agreeing to a professional-only relationship, his body language was definitely on the stiff side.

Mara found herself disappointed, but it was what she signed up for and couldn't blame him.

Mara peeked inside the room Vikk had just indicated. It was dark yet inviting. Mara grinned at a long-ago memory of kissing a boy in high school while sitting in the back row of the local movie theater. If she were being honest, she'd have to admit that it was not so much kissing and more or less fumbling and teeth bumping.

Vikk continued the tour down a well furbished hallway.

"It definitely resembles movie theaters from back home," Mara said as she admired the crimson velvet walls, decorative sconces, and movie posters with titles like *Disaster From Zone 10*, which had an exploding planet on it, and *Juicy Swizzletarts Steal Hearts*, which appeared to be an extremely sensual film that might delve into the realm of pornography, if Mara wasn't mistaken by the open legs displayed on the poster. "Is that a va—?"

"Swizzletart?" Vikk asked in a matter-of-fact tone. "Yes."

"And is this—?" Mara placed her finger on the poster, right at the tip of the protruding double-pronged organ.

"A twatsizzle? Yes." Vikk did not look even remotely uncomfortable. In fact, he kept walking and pointing out some of the larger theaters, as if he'd shown them nothing more significant than a water fountain.

She had to know more. Choking back a laugh, she asked, "Are these accurate representations?"

Mara glanced at Finley. She'd hung back but her daughter's face was bright red. Mara wasn't a prude and had had "The Talk" with Finley when she was twelve, but to see what she thought was alien genitals displayed out in the open like that was not something they were prepared for.

Vraitheians did not appear to be uptight about sexual content. Using context alone, Mara felt certain she could surmise what a swizzletart and a twatsizzle were.

He stopped, turned, and studied the poster. Then he grinned. "There is *some* artistic license present in those particular posters." Vikk then pointed out the concession stand, which, at the moment was dark and empty, as well as the door to the wardrobe chamber. "CeCe will probably be in there, Finley, if you want to go look for her. I promised her a role in the movie."

"Awesome, Mr. Stravdas, thanks!" Finley said while chewing on something called naglewruts, small pieces of fruit, like a date with a nut in the middle. Mara didn't think she cared much about the studio itself, but the promise of hanging out with someone closer to her own age had to be infinitely more appealing than a tour of dark, unused rooms. "Can I, Mom?"

Mara tilted her head, as if thinking long and hard about the request. Finley all but growled at this delay tactic. Now her hyper-alert expression seemed to be screaming, *Please don't subject me to any more alien sex posters.* Winking, Mara said,

"How about, I'll see you at dinnertime, kiddo. Have fun making new friends."

"Thank God," Finley mouthed before disappearing into the wardrobe chamber.

Vikk watched the petite Finley all but sprint away from them. No, sprint was too strong a word. *Shuffled.* She shuffled quickly.

He chuckled after her, remembering that Dessa had told him that many Earthling societies were staunchly opposed to any discussion or visualization of sexual intimacy. Which was interesting considering there was a lucrative business on Earth that catered to those who wanted to read or watch human sexual intimacy. Having watched some of it himself, he saw the appeal. The human form was beautiful.

Why hide that you desired it?

"What's so funny?" Mara asked conversationally. She'd come to stand next to him and was peering at the closed wardrobe door, same as him. He could hear a chorus of voices from within the wardrobe chamber. Everyone inside must be welcoming Finley. It warmed his heart that Mara and her daughter were instantly liked by everyone.

"I was thinking about the conundrum of sex, Mara." She quirked an eyebrow as he led them farther into the film studio. Side by side they walked down the wide hallway. "*Human* sex," he said, to clarify.

Mara nearly swallowed her tongue. Of all the things she thought he might say, it was not *that.* "How so?"

"Humans pretend that they do not like to watch sexual activity, yet it is prevalent in your movies, television shows, and fiction. I was just wondering about that. I know different societies have different values and rules, but it does seem strange to me that something as fundamental as intercourse would be shunned from main view."

Mara didn't have an easy answer for him. "Intercourse is usually an act done in private between two adults. We have war on our planet, and it is very much out in the open—even the violent aspects of it. Sex, for us, is a human-to-human connection, conducted behind closed doors. On Vraithe, you do not have war, but sexual connections seem to be out in the open for you. I'm not sure there's a parallel there, but I think it has to do with birth, life, and death, and how they are so intertwined."

Vikk opened a door that led to a sound stage with lights and cameras. At any minute it might fill with actors, stagehands, and production assistants. Now, though, it was empty. Mara had never been on a movie set before.

Their footsteps echoed in the cavernous space. The set was designed to look like a house. Mara noticed a bedroom, a kitchen, and then a room that might be meant to resemble a military office. There were swords and a shelf filled with uniforms.

Vikk stopped in front of the camera and inspected it. "That makes sense," he said after fiddling with the camera and turning to look at her. "And yet your actors perform sex in movies."

"It's not *real* sex," Mara said. "It is acting. They are only pretending to have sex." He gave her a confused look. "There are physical barriers between the actors when they are being filmed."

Vikk's expression shifted into one that said, *Oh, now I understand.* "You have very good actors on your planet," he said with a smile. "Here, sex is not acted out. It is for real."

"You mean...?"

"Copulation shown in our movies is considered educational. Vraitheians generally mate for life with their heartstring mate, but we make certain allowances for entertainment. For instance, if I were to remove all my clothing, it would be to educate you on my anatomy."

Mara let out a shaky breath. "Wouldn't your heartstring mate get upset?" She accidentally backed into a chair that fell over before she could quickly set it to rights. This soundstage was beginning to feel mighty warm.

"As my business partner..." He took off his gray T-shirt. Vikk's wide steel-blue chest was smooth and covered with dark tattoos. Mara was going to hyperventilate. "Who is helping me with the script..." He removed his jeans, revealing black boxers over massive thighs and an even bigger bulge at the apex. No, it was *now* that she was going to hyperventilate. "Because the act is not simulated in my film, you'll need to fully understand Vraitheian physiology when comparing the script against each scene."

His fingers dipped to his waistband, flirting dangerously. Mara swallowed hard. She was one spark away from combustion. God, there was even a bed ten feet away.

Vikk was dying.

Literally dying to touch her. Her aura was as black as the portal. One touch and she would explode in his arms. Mara would attack him and he'd let her. Let her have her fill. Her way. He wanted to gorge himself inside her silky chamber, filling and stretching her. He wanted to capture her every moan on his tongue, press his body atop hers and never get up.

He wanted her eyes to consume him, to explore him. He couldn't remember the last time he was this aroused. Mara wanted him. He saw the truth in her eyes. And he wanted it to be *him* she saw first—not one of his actors.

But he also read her hesitation. *It was an act done in private,* she'd said. They had all the privacy they needed—she didn't know it, but the soundstage would remain empty until he pressed a button next to the camera.

"Shall I?" he asked huskily. He barely recognized his own voice.

She nodded and that was all the encouragement he needed.

# ELEVEN

Mara didn't move. Didn't breathe. Didn't think. She felt lust wash over her. The desire to see him, the real him, *all* of him, burned deep in her core.

"Yes... Yes, I want to see, but we can...*not* do anything," Mara whispered. Was her face red? It felt red.

He seemed relieved by her words, like she'd given him a gift.

In a blur, his boxers were off and Mara's heart imploded. She couldn't just zero in on his crotch, not right away, so she looked up to focus on the top of his head, his dark eyes and kiss-able mouth. She admired his shoulders, the wide span of his chest and how it narrowed into a firm waist with a visible eight pack.

He was hairless everywhere, to include *there*. Mara could avoid it no longer. It was calling her like a beacon.

Between his massive thighs hung an impressive cock. It was erect but it wasn't sticking straight out, either. The outer skin looked soft, the girth pliable, like it might give in ever-so-slightly if she squeezed it. On the sides, there seemed to be a dark line that started at the base of the shaft that ran lengthwise to the tip, then went over the tip, and then down the other side.

Vikk must have noticed her inspection of that part. She gasped when reached down and used his fingers to part his cock. It wasn't just one shaft. Vraitheian cocks were really two cocks in one.

Mara was drenched thinking about what that might mean when having sex with a Vraitheian. No, not just any Vraitheian. Vikk. Sex with Vikk.

Standing there, observing him, she was torturing herself.

Was this just academic to him? Educational? Every neuron in her body was wildly crashing into each other. Brain cells were exploding. Her core was throbbing and the heat of her, the part of her that wanted him inside of her, was hot and achy, like she needed to feel all of him in her, or she might expire.

"You are beautiful," she said hoarsely before clearing her throat. He smiled, completing this perfect picture. "Could we..." She paused, swallowed, took a steadying breath. She grabbed the back of a chair for support. "Begin the rehearsal now? I'm sure your actors are eager to get started."

She tore her gaze away and studied the camera track bolted to the concrete floor. Mara heard him chuckle as he dressed. A moment later, he pressed a button on some sort of intercom and instructed the actors to get ready for the opening scene.

Everything that had just happened seemed so matter of fact to Vikk, like it meant nothing. Except, she thought, he *was* erect. Mara kept telling herself to *just be cool*, but how the hell was she going to be able to recover from *that*?

Backstage, Finley was making herself useful by fetching certain outfits and props for CeCe and the other actors while making eyes at Serstene. He was a rookie prop master, or so he said. He pointed toward one of the wooden swords.

"I painted it," he said with pride in his voice and Finley had to agree that it did look like a sword. A bright pink sword with inlaid rubies on the metallic cross-guard bar, which was the part of the sword that stopped the holder's hand from sliding onto the sharp blade.

Since it was made of wood, it wouldn't really matter, but without it, it would have just been a pink stick. Serstene was running around, so they didn't have much of a chance to chat, but he did suggest that they hang out after rehearsal.

"Did everything go all right with your medical testing today?" he asked a while later. He was carrying bags of red liquid that might be movie-prop blood.

"I think so," she said. Finley was mostly happy to be in a wide-open space and not confined in medical scanners. She shivered just thinking about having to lie still inside that narrow tube. Thankfully it hadn't last too long. "The doctor said it would take a few days to analyze everything."

Someone called Serstene's name, so he had to run along.

A few minutes later CeCe entered backstage. "Hey Finley-bug," CeCe said cheerfully. Finley beamed at the new nickname, watching as CeCe donned her outfit. Her role was that of a military officer. A *sexy* military officer, for some reason.

"CeCe, I wanted to ask you something," Finley said. "This is going to be a film version of my mom's book, right?" CeCe nodded as she buttoned the top. It was incredibly tight, which caused CeCe's small breasts to morph into ample cleavage. "The thing is," Finley continued, "we do not use swords anymore. At least not in combat. We only use ceremonial swords for funerals and retirements."

CeCe shrugged, obviously preoccupied. She was now in front of a brightly lit mirror, applying bright silver mascara and orange lipstick. People were running around now that Mr. Stravdas had called for first scene.

"Films are always open to interpretation, Finley. I wouldn't think too hard on it." Finley felt the older girl's eyes on her, so she looked at her reflection in the mirror. "In fact, Finley-bug, it might be best to not think of it as your mom's book at all. I have a feeling my cousins, Dessa and Vikk, have botched the translation by human's standards. But for us Vraitheians, we do *love* a good military romp."

Finley frowned. "The thing is, CeCe, Mom's book isn't a... a...*romp*."

CeCe paused, a slight panic dusting her nerves. She didn't want Finley to become upset. Damn Vikk for not explaining things.

"You know, Finley, it might be best for you to stay backstage." CeCe said, remembering how, when she started acting on Earth, it had surprised her that all intimate scenes were simulated—that there was *no* actual touching of genitals. When on Earth, you have to play by the rules. But here on Vraithe...

"Why?" the younger girl asked.

CeCe knew Finley to be a smart young lady, but since she was a human and had not grown up with Vraitheian films, which were not shy about depicting all aspects of Vraitheian sex, she was worried that Finley would end up highly shocked by the scene they were shooting today—especially since two of the characters happened to represent her parents.

CeCe stopped applying her makeup and squatted down to Finley's height. "Some of the scenes might be disturbing to you."

Finley crossed her arms and huffed. "I'm not a baby, you know. I'm fifteen."

"No, I know. On Vraithe, a fifteen-year-old is nearly an adult. By sixteen you can decide to live on Earth or move out of your parents' house. If you wanted to take the portal to the amethyst moon to hike the Zilverine Mountain trail, no one here could or would stop you. But," she said while gently squeezing Finley's thin shoulders, "in this instance, I think I have to be upfront and honest with you." CeCe took a fortifying breath and spat out, "Today we're rehearsing the scene where your mom cuts off your dad's penis."

CeCe stood up with a start. There, she'd said it. No turning back now.

Finley stumbled backward as if CeCe had struck her. "Excuse me?"

"You heard me. Now, is that something you really want to see?"

"Good God, no. Why would I *ever* want to see that? And why would she do that?" Then, quietly, almost to herself, she whispered, "Would Mom do that?"

The girl seemed to think long and hard on that question, like maybe she was wondering if her mom had actually cut off her dad's penis in real life. Because CeCe hadn't read the English version of the book, she wasn't sure either way. It probably hadn't happened, but it wasn't like it had never happened before.

"Sorry to spring it on you, Finley-bug. I thought it was best to just let you know. That particular scene in the book is a big debate amongst Vraitheians. There are fans who think your mom did Enemy-General Calix dirty. I don't disagree, but it makes for good drama, don't you think?"

Finley hoped that her penetrating glare could cut through skin and bone.

CeCe wisely retreated. "You know what, don't answer that," CeCe said, hands up, backing away, a grim smile on her face. "I've got to run on stage. You can hang out in the prop room if you want. They set up the catering table near there, which means Serstene won't be too far away."

With that, CeCe winked and disappeared through an open door that led to the main stage. There was still a bustle of activity happening backstage, but without CeCe, Finley knew she'd get bored. And she wasn't about to watch the rehearsal, not after what she'd just learned.

Finley meandered toward the prop room, wondering if she'd see Serstene. She also wondered what snacks might be available. Better to think about food than...than...well, severed penises.

It was already Wednesday back on Earth, and Dessa had sent so many texts to Vikk on her Vraitheian device that her fingers had gone numb. *Why the hell isn't he responding?* He was either having incredible heartstring sex with Mara, or he was dead. There could be no other situation to keep him from responding to *this*.

Sitting in her car across from Mara's house, Dessa took video as police officers entered the premises. Last night on the local news, Dessa watched in horror as the anchors talked about how a local high school teacher and her daughter were missing.

The anchor teased, *"Foul play or a simple misunderstanding? We will bring you updates as we receive them. We will speak to the distraught ex-husband tonight, at eleven."*

The police, now milling about with brown paper bags, were evidently collecting evidence. Early this morning, Dr. Brady, the principal at Riley High School, called Dessa. "You were possibly the last one to see Mara Eldress," Dr. Brady said over the phone. "The police would like to speak with you, to see if you have any clues to their whereabouts."

"I can do that, but our conversation was about novels," Dessa shared at the time. "And I've never met her daughter, Finley." Dessa hadn't even known Mara had a daughter. For the longest time, she'd thought Finley was a cat. Dessa was embarrassed about that.

Dessa checked the time. She was due at the police station in an hour to give a statement.

She then sent another text to Vikk and waited helplessly for him to respond.

Vikk's communications device continued to vibrate even after he shut it off. The only times that occurred were when Queen Uska sent text after text, demanding a new book because she'd just finished the last one he'd given her, or when Dessa was spamming him with a million pictures of snow.

There were only so many images of white fluff he could take before he just lost interest. *I get it Dessa, there is a lot of it. Every tree looks the same to me.*

So he felt safe in ignoring the constant barrage of vibrating. He was more interested in Mara's expression as she watched the rehearsal on one of the main screens. The screen jumped from camera to camera to follow the action, without her having to figure out where to look.

She sat a few feet away, looking adorable in a pair of over-sized headphones. His heart thumped at recalling her reaction to him as he stripped. She wasn't immune to him, thank the rising goddesses. He saw that she was nibbling on her finger-nails, skimming the script. She wouldn't understand what the actors were saying during the actual rehearsal since everything spoken was said in Vraitheian, but if she followed along with the script, he felt certain she would understand the meaning. After all, it was *her* story.

In the translation, there was *some* ambiguity in how she severed Enemy-General Calix's twatsizzle, which meant there were hordes of readers who wanted to see it accurately portrayed in the film. However, depending on who you asked, many of the readers questioned whether or not it had occurred at all, and if it did, why wasn't *Mara* the "enemy-general"? Severing a twatsizzle was on the extreme edge of the extreme.

Vikk hoped that Mara would shed some light once she'd seen the rehearsal. After they received her guidance, he could continue filming the rest of the movie. Everything hinged on this scene.

Mara, for her part, was feeling too many emotions to focus on the screen before her. Vikk was just too close. She'd bitten her thumbnail down to the quick and was working on the other thumbnail when she spotted the word twatsizzle in the script. She rolled her eyes. If the opening scene had her naked, perhaps she came across a very handsome man and together they decided to get down and dirty. None of that had appeared in her memoir, but from what Vikk said, Vraitheians appeared to like a lot of sex in their movies.

The screen before her came to life and someone yelled, "Eeeeee, Loxtel!" which Mara thought was the equivalent of, "And...action!" A long-limbed, nude, female actor—the one playing Good-General Mara Eldress—stepped out of a shower.

Mara studied the actor playing her character. Her skin was purple-hued with a lot of tattoos. She wore her black hair short and possessed matching eyebrows and piercing pink eyes. She had firm breasts with gold areolas, a slim waist, and wide hips.

Instead of a cock, the apex had a dark purple slit with light pink flesh that flared out like petals.

That must be a swizzletart, Mara thought.

She then noticed a black locket around the actor's neck, which resembled the locket Vikk had worn when trying to convince them to travel to Vraithe with him.

Mara followed the action with the script.

"Hello?" her character said after hearing a crashing sound from within the house. From the stage, Mara heard moans of pleasure just as Good-General Mara Eldress picked up a bright pink sword that happened to be propped up next to the shower stall. The camera zoomed in on her character's heart-shaped bottom and the little beads of water that ran down in shimmering rivulets.

From the close-up, through the gap in her thighs, you could see the light pink fleshy petals as she sauntered out of the room.

Mara had a difficult time catching her breath. Should she or shouldn't she be aroused right now? She was very confused.

The camera cut next to the bedroom. Two figures were on the bed. The top figure, who was straddling a robust, silver Vraitheian who Mara was not familiar with, was clearly CeCe. She was wearing a military uniform and was deftly undoing one button at a time. Looking at the script, Mara knew the dialogue read, "Oh, Calix. What if your spouse comes home early?"

As CeCe's character cooed these words, she removed her top to reveal tattoos on her shoulders and a pair of perky, cerulean-blue breasts. She, too, wore a black locket. Large silver hands snaked up to cup her breasts, tweaking her orange nipples in his fingers. Suddenly, CeCe's character was flipped over, face down, and her trousers were whisked off. The camera panned to her exposed, pulsing cunt and her pert anus bud.

Mara blinked and shot a glance at Vikk. He was staring at her, a business-like smile on his face. Feeling slightly off-center, she turned back to the screen. This was *very* explicit, and CeCe was his *cousin*.

The masculine voice of Calix's character said, "I must taste you first, Drill Sergeant Ashley."

"Oh, yes please, General Calix," CeCe moaned as Calix's character practically tore off his own clothing, revealing an incredibly muscled body. The camera first focused on his strong back and the way the lighting played on his silver skin.

Panning down, it captured his tight buttocks, his anus, and his testicles, all exposed. His thick cock hung low and heavy, glistening from base to tip, as it bounced up to smack Drill Sergeant Ashley's core.

There was a loud moan—Mara wasn't sure who made the sound—just before the scene cut to another camera, which was a close-up of Good-General Mara's face, her eyebrows furrowed in concentration as she moved like a naked stealth ninja through what had to be a mansion. The camera focused briefly on her lips, the way her tongue flicked out.

*Why hasn't she found them yet?* Mara wondered. Were they even in the same house?

Absently she was mimicking her character's tongue movement. In the background the camera shifted to reveal family portraits and military-esque photos where Mara's character was carrying a sword. It then swirled to the sword in her hand. No surprise there, it was the same sword.

Mara was beginning to get the hang of watching the screen and glancing at the script—sort of like bootleg closed captioning. The next camera jump was back to the couple, but now from a profile view. Drill Sergeant Ashley was still face down, though she was facing the camera. *That orange lipstick looks really good on CeCe,* Mara thought.

Her ass was high and angled for Enemy-General Calix's cock. Mara noticed that he wore an identical black locket around his neck. They clearly took heartstring connections seriously.

His chest was glorious, though now that Mara had someone to compare it to, Vikk's chest was far superior. Calix's character's silver skin glowed like an avenging angel. His wide hands were on CeCe's hips as his cock hovered at her entrance.

"Don't keep me waiting," her character said as she wiggled her cunt at him. The bed squeaked loudly. Calix's glistening cock plunged into CeCe's quivering slit. She screamed out with intense pleasure—Mara saw the sheer joy on her face—as Calix's character's large cock buried itself inside her, all the way to the hilt.

Mara was no expert, but given his robust girth, she figured it had to be nine or ten inches long. He was crying out, "Ashley, oh Ashley, my heart, my heart!" as he pulled out and slid in again, over and over, with slick, slurping noises as her cunt sucked him back in each time.

His cock separated then, to which CeCe's character begged, "Yes, please, please, please," as the lower cock sluiced against CeCe's swollen dark blue clit before pat-pat-patting it.

*Could he control its movements?*

The little smacking pops matched the rhythm of CeCe's "Yes! Yes! Yes!" and "Harder! Harder! Harder" until the lower cock was swinging down and back up again harder and faster.

Seconds later, he was shifting positions, and in the blur he was lying face up and CeCe's character was riding him. From the camera angle you could see one cock entering her cunt and the other one standing ridged against her clit. CeCe's character was performing a see-sawing motion where the cock in her cunt would slide in and out while the front cock slivered side to side, curling in like a tongue before rapidly smacking that ever-growing clit. It was the size of a thumb, at least, Mara guessed.

Just then, the camera switched to show Good-General

Mara's progress. From the angle, she was in the hallway leading to the bedroom. The shadows silhouetted on the hall wall clearly showed a woman riding a man. Good-General Mara could hear the pleasurable sounds emanating from the room and, in surprising fashion, she appeared to be turned on. As she crept closer to the room, the camera shifted to her backside, from her calves to her buttocks, revealing her glistening cunt petals and a stream of milky liquid slowly rolling down her inner leg.

Back in the bedroom, Calix's character was now on top of a face-up CeCe. Her breasts jiggled as the two cocks, now back as one, plowed her cunt with vigor. A pink shimmer slicked his shaft with each withdrawal and Mara surmised that CeCe had legit climaxed. Her body quivered as the camera zoomed in. Her skin was dewy with sweat and Mara didn't think she'd ever seen a more attractive person in her life than CeCe in that moment, the way her body accepted his cock, and loved it, and wanted more and more and more, begging with each word uttered from her pillow-soft lips.

As Good-General Mara entered the room, Calix's character let out a guttural cry with his release. The room vibrated as he swiftly removed his cock from CeCe's swollen cunt, stroked himself in a tight fist, and ejaculated in two silver streams all over CeCe's breasts, abdomen, and her juicy opening.

"How dare you betray me, Calix," Good-General Mara said with stark clarity.

The way she was carrying the sword, the bulbous pommel below the grip was angled against her wet slit, and the viewer was left to wonder if she'd rubbed herself against it while listening to them fuck.

CeCe's character screamed with alarm, rolling off the bed while Calix's character tried to explain himself to Good-General Mara. That character was having none of it. In another blur of movement, and clever camera work, the next image was of Good-General Mara's sword swinging down to sever Calix's cock from his body.

Red blood spurted everywhere.

"Eeeeeeee, Yhackt!"

*And, cut!*

# TWELVE

Vikk turned to witness Mara's raw reaction. Her aura was copper tinged with several black rings. Strong, strong violence.

Her mood was pretty clear: *Mara wanted to kill him.* They must have translated the scene wrong. Very wrong.

Best if he kept his distance and waited to see what happened next.

Mara sat stock-still, stunned that a memoir about her time in the military, her injuries, and how she navigated the military medical system, could have been translated into an erotic femme fatale film about a wronged woman who cut off her cheating husband's penis.

She rubbed her face, her eyes, the back of her neck. At least she was no longer aroused. She was the opposite of aroused. Mara shuddered. Not that she needed any confirmation, but she was glad to know that severed penises did not do it for her.

The actors were donning robes and offering a critique of

each other's performances. No one appeared to be worked up or aroused. It was just another day at the office for them. Mara had no issues with sex or sex work. But this wasn't the premise of her book. None of this ever happened.

"So," Vikk said from his producer's chair. He'd been studying her. "We'd like to get that last part right. Does Good-General Mara Eldress *mast...master...*uh, I can never pronounce that word correctly."

"Masturbate?" Mara asked quietly.

"Yes!" Relief appeared to flood his face. "Does she do that with the sword's bulbous pommel? Also, does Good-General Mara sever Calix's twatsizzle before or after he climaxes? There are many who have read that scene in the book and claim that there is *no* dismemberment. We want to get it right. It happens to be one of the biggest debates on Vraithe right now."

Mara just starred at Vikk.

How could she even respond to such a question?

It did explain the *Team Good-General Mara Eldress* and the *Team Enemy-General Calix* signs from the portalport exit. There was no fixing this. The only solution was to feign ignorance, burn it all down, pack up and go home.

*Laugh or cry or scream into the nether?*

"Vikk," Mara said in a clear voice, the one she used in her classroom. "None of that is in my memoir. Not a single line. Not one of those scenes has ever existed outside of your translation. I have never met anyone named Drill Sergeant Ashley. Jesus, who even came up with that name? It's too on the nose! There is zero fucking in the book. Zero. How did you even—" She stopped, biting her tongue.

Mara had an audience. CeCe, Logea, the fabulous Vraitheian who played Calix, and Jagert, the purple-pink goddess who played the part of Good-General Mara, had turned to look at her. All three were wearing identical black lockets. Now that she understood the purpose of the lockets, it made sense that they would be wearing them during intimate scenes.

"No, Vikk." Mara sighed, speaking quietly. "Good-General Mara Eldress does not masturbate with swords, nor does she sever Enemy-General Calix's twatsizzle."

Vikk looked so relieved that it suddenly occurred to Mara that he might have been worried she was capable of such an act.

*Why invite someone who cuts off penises to your planet?*

He clapped his hands together. "Excellent, we can remove that part of the script." Vikk said something to someone scribbling into a notebook. Then he turned back to his actors. "CeCe, Logea, Jagert, will you be ready to film it tomorrow, after a fresh script read-through after first meal?"

"Can do, cousin," CeCe said, taking a sip of water. "Though Serstene will be disappointed about the lack of blood. He made buckets of it earlier today."

Logea, who was dabbing his body with a towel, nodded and said, "Happy to, Vikk," with a British accent. Jagert, who seemed the silent type, said something in Vraitheian that sounded like an affirmative.

Mara stood, a move she learned from Dr. Brady, the principal at Riley High School. "Vikk, I'd like to find Finley and leave now."

As Dessa walked out of the police station, someone thrust a microphone in her face. "Are you friends with Mara Eldress and her daughter? Can you give a statement on their whereabouts? What was the last thing you two spoke about?"

The reporters acted like vultures, ready to pounce on her and tear off all her flesh. Dessa wasn't about to play the media's game.

Dessa stayed quiet, pulled her winter coat's hood over her head, and averted her eyes. She heard the clicking of cameras as her boots crunched in the snow. The sun was shining but it was still freezing outside. Dessa's main focus was to not slip on any hidden black ice as she entered her car.

Through the window, another reporter yelled, "Can you tell us if the school board's decision to ban one of her chosen books has anything to do with her disappearance?" while another asked, "Have you been in contact with Calix Eldress?" A third demanded, "As the librarian at Riley High School, do you agree with the school board's decision to ban the book, *The Curse of Mathilda's Sorrow?*"

Dessa fingers positively itched to roll down her window to address the last question. *The Curse of Mathilda's Sorrow* was a brilliant piece of fiction that deserved to be on everyone's bookshelf. Instead, the school board were acting like petulant children by banning a novella they hadn't even read. If they had, they would have been weeping, not banning it. The one good thing that had come about this was that the literary world was learning more about the novella in question and was on its way to becoming a national bestseller.

Headlines read: *Teacher goes missing after school board bans book chosen for assignment. Related or is it a coincidence? We'll have a full report at the six o'clock news hour.*

Fuming, Dessa did her best to not mow down the reporters as she drove out of the police parking lot. Dessa needed to get home—to Vraithe—as soon as possible. There would be no way to contain what she'd just learned from the police.

"Was she upset about the school board's decision?" the police sergeant had asked moments ago while she sat inside the police station.

"Mara did not express her opinion on the matter, but *I'd* like to go on the record and say it was a bullshit move on their part. Here," Dessa expertly slid a book across the desk. "I brought you a copy."

The police sergeant glanced down at the book's dark cover. He did not seem all that impressed. He was probably a true crime reader.

"Did she give any indication she was leaving the area when you spoke on Friday after school?"

"We did not discuss plans. We discussed books."

"Why?"

*Because I'm a librarian and Mara is an English teacher, dumbass.*

"Because I'm a librarian and Mara is an English teacher."

"Were you aware that Ms. Eldress was under financial distress? That she might have been upset about her memoir's failure?"

*It is not a failure on Vraithe.*

"No."

"Were you aware that Calix Eldress, Ms. Eldress's ex-husband, was getting remarried?"

*Without a penis?*

"No."

"Were you aware that Mr. Eldress was planning to sue for full custody of their minor daughter, Finley Eldress?"

*Finley is not a cat.*

"No."

"Are you aware of any abuse in the home?"

*Does my brother kidnapping them count?*

"No."

"Last question. Are you familiar with the term, 'Stolen Valor'?" When Dessa shook her head, the police sergeant continued. His bulldog face was offensively angry. "It is a term used when someone pretends to have served in the military when they haven't. Now, I'm not saying Ms. Eldress did or did *not* serve in the armed forces, but the department of defense happens to be declining all knowledge of your friend. Thoughts?"

*Mara Eldress has more honor in her pinky finger than you do in your entire body, mister.*

"Perhaps you spelled her name wrong. Try again."

His lips went flat. "Thank you for your time, Ms. Strab-doz," the police sergeant said, butchering her last name as he handed over a business card. "If you think of anything else, or if Ms. Eldress contacts you, please call me. My cell phone is written on the back."

He'd given her a look of interest, as if she'd ever give him the time of day after insulting Mara's character.

Once Dessa was home and away from prying eyes, she logged into her Vraitheian device to see if Vikk deigned to respond. Nothing. She let out a string of Vraitheian curse words. She sent another text with what the police were asking. After that, she booked a portal reservation time. The first slot she could get was at 7:01:01 tonight.

Dessa just hoped she wasn't too late to contain the damage brewing here on Earth.

Mara's anger was solid. It lapped up against Vikk's skin like crashing waves. His heart sank. She wanted to leave. Leave him. Leave Vraithe.

"What about our deal?" Vikk asked, masking his disappointment. Moments ago he'd all but growled at his actors and they vanished from the set. CeCe would know to keep Finley occupied and away for a while. Now, it was just the two of them, Vikk and Mara, with a gulf of anger and disappointment flowing between them like an engorged river. He didn't want her to leave. Not when he knew that he'd walk over glass for her. "You agreed to stay and help me with the script if Finley received medical treatment."

Vikk had her there. She couldn't argue with the knowledge that they wouldn't receive Finley's results for several days. Plus, Finley was happy here. Healthier. The conflict inside Mara burned and ached and pulled at her from multiple directions.

Her reaction and attraction for Vikk made everything that much more frustrating. She wanted to fuck him. She also wanted to see him suffer.

Mara swirled and glared at him. "This isn't a film based on my book, Vikk. It is as simple as that. How can I even help you if it doesn't even remotely resemble my memoir? And," she said with a harsh laugh, "it wasn't even that good of a memoir. No one on Earth read it. I poured my heart and soul into it, and no one cared." She tried to mask the hitch in her throat. *No one cared.* "I wouldn't be surprised if those who did buy it bought it for fireplace kindling."

Vikk wasn't sure what that meant but he sure as hell wasn't fooled. Feelings of failure hurt Mara. It hurt her deeply, which meant he had to find a way to heal that hurt. As her mate—even if she didn't *know* he was her mate—it was still his duty to support her in every way possible.

They were too far apart. He needed to comfort her. He wanted to be a solid presence for Mara and the only way he knew how to do that was physically. To hold her. Protect her. Place himself in front of all her obstacles to blunt the impact of those forces.

He closed the distance between them. Mara stood her

ground. He could tell she wasn't one to back down, not when he could feel the emotion emanating from her.

"Then pour your heart and soul into me, Mara."

He put his hands on her shoulders. The electricity that flowed through his body forced his senses to waken. From his head to his toes, and especially his cock. There was a pleasurable jolt there. He wanted to cover her, comfort her. His heartstrings were going wild.

And yes, he wanted to fuck her, but more than anything, he wanted her to want to fuck him.

"What did you say?" she whispered.

*Pour my heart and soul into him?*

Mara wasn't good at that. She'd attempted it once, with Calix, and everything crashed and burned around her. Could she trust the connection with Vikk? She wanted this, wanted to give in, to feel *something*.

Vikk had to know his effect on her. Did he feel the same? He must, or why else would he remove his locket? Wouldn't he be wearing it if he wanted to *prevent* a false heartstring connection? Did it matter that she was human?

When he embraced her, Mara felt a strong bolt of energy enter her entire body. If she weren't secure in his arms she might have been flung across the room.

She was warm all over. Her belly flipped and her core, that deep part of her that needed him, ached and flared red hot.

The tension, which had always been present between them, was now a physical presence, like a force field. She'd never felt this kind of pull toward anyone in her life. It was a compulsion, a need, a desire that could not be turned on or off with a switch. It was just there. Present.

"I beg of you, tell me you want me," Vikk breathed out, his voice raw and scratchy.

He leaned down to inhale against her neck; the spicy, aroused scent of her did something to him. Some primal feeling rose up from his groin to his brain.

He felt Mara shiver in his arms. He'd lick every inch of her if she let him. He pressed himself against her. She moaned slightly. His cock throbbed angrily against his jeans, wanting out, wanting to be in her hands, in her. Could she feel it against her belly? Now that she knew his size, it was impossible to hide it.

He whispered hoarsely, "Even if it is a lie, Mara. Tell me you want me."

Dear God, Mara thought, how could she even resist him? Even if she hated him, and she didn't, she'd be powerless to resist the chemistry that had been building between them since that first handshake outside the school.

Even if he was destined for a Vraitheian mate at some point in the future, she would not lie.

"Of course I want you," Mara said with heat, which was all he needed. Vikk pressed his hungry lips to hers and she all but melted into his embrace. His lips were greedy, demanding, seeking to take everything she would offer, and then some.

Slanting, Vikk deepened the kiss. His tongue parted her lips. Mara met him halfway, moaning into his mouth. She couldn't breathe, but when a gorgeous being like Vikk Stravdas was making love to her mouth, did she even need to breathe to survive?

He lifted her then, his mouth hungrily consuming hers. He

let out grunts that flipped Mara's belly. Mara wrapped her long legs around his tapered waist and returned each kiss with so much enthusiasm she felt like a sex goddess. She could feel his throbbing erection against her bottom now.

My God, what would he feel like inside her? No matter how wet and aroused she was, it would take time to get used to his size. Would she come quickly, or would he tease her long enough to draw out an explosive climax? No matter which, Mara knew it would be good. It would be better than good. It would be earth-shattering.

Vikk needed more. He'd positively expire if he could not get closer to Mara. His fevered skin needed to touch hers. It was as if her moans were entering his bloodstream, driving him wild, uncontrollable. Vikk had never experienced anything like this. Yes, he'd been intimate with others before, but he'd always worn his locket. His unbridled feelings for Mara and the way his body responded to her was a whole different league. A different universe.

They couldn't just stand there. When Mara started nibbling at his neck his heart skipped a beat and he nearly ripped off every stitch of clothing from both their bodies. His hips arched, his cocks instinctively seeking an entrance to Mara's hot, wet cunt.

Vikk needed to slow down. His brain warned him that he was going too fast, that he needed to make this good for her. He refused to fuck her standing up. Mara deserved a proper fucking—the kind of fucking where the bed broke beneath them.

He carried her up a set of stairs to one of the unused sets, where there was a bedroom with a large bed.

"I need more," he said in-between kisses. "I need to taste all of you." Chairs, cameras, and other props fell over with nary a thought as he shoved them aside. He didn't care if he broke every single one.

In his arms, Mara vampirically bit at his neck, wanting more than just his tongue in her mouth. The only way to do that was with less clothing and a bed. Hell, she'd settle for a couch. And, if pressed, she'd probably be fine fucking him on the cold floor if that was the only surface available.

"Fuck me, Vikk. I need you in me."

She attacked his lips and felt her own begin to bruise. She didn't care. She squeezed her legs around him, which pressed her core against torso. If she bounced a little, she'd be able to rub her clit against the fabric between them. He growled into her mouth and she loved it. She loved the primal part of him taking control.

Mara saw that they were in a bedroom. She glanced at the bed and her stomach flipped with joy. It appeared to be big enough *and* sturdy enough to accommodate the lusty activity that was about to happen on it. She had a feeling that Vikk would not go easy on her, which was good because she wanted all of him.

"I refuse to rush this part, Mara," Vikk said as he placed her down on her feet. With swift movements, he removed her top and bra. His steel-blue fingers roamed over her light peach skin, from her lips to her clavicle, to each breast. He drank her in. The way his eyes fell on her made her feel sexy, brazen.

Mara closed her eyes to savor the exquisite feeling of his hands on her, the combined roughness and gentleness of his movements despite his huge size, the way his strong fingers pinched her dusky pink nipples.

"Beautiful," he murmured right before his head bent down.

Vikk's mouth captured a nipple, sucking on it, as his other hand tweaked her other nipple.

"Oh, that feels amazing, Vikk," Mara exhaled as her pulse raced. She gulped for air as she watched the progress of his mouth leaving a trail of hot, wet kisses on her skin. Her own hands had a mind of their own when they automatically crashed into his hair, pulling his dark strands loose from the nape of his neck.

Vikk was an inch away from climaxing all over himself. Mara's skin was a sweet nectar against his tongue, his taste buds tingling. From the moment of their first meeting, he'd known Mara would be delectable, but he had only dared to dream of holding her in his arms, his tongue roaming over velvety skin.

His hands trailed lower and lower until they were unfastening her pants, which came off easily.

He didn't remove her panties, though. If he had, he might have embarrassed himself by exploding right then and there. Mara, looking down at him with lust-pupiled eyes, protested, but he gave her a wicked grin that promised debauchery.

Truth was, Vikk needed a barrier between his mouth and her wet core so he could maintain *some* semblance of control. Even if that barrier was the skimpiest piece of fabric that left nothing to the imagination. Her skin was smooth and glorious. He wanted to bathe her just to get to touch every part of her, every fold, and every curve. Her breasts were small but perfect, the nipples pert cland eager for attention.

Her panties, which were soaked through, were pale pink in color. Vikk could see the outline of her pubic mound and labia lips. He fancied he could even see it quivering, swelling with desire. He looked up at her and witnessed the heated arousal in her face, which silently demanded, *Lick my pussy already.*

If he moved the fabric an inch to the side he would be able to see her inner lips. The urge to bury his face in her cunt sent zaps of electricity through his body. He was about to get up close and personal with Mara's delicious cunt. Would her honeyed juices drip onto his tongue?

Her scent was murdering him. He could smell her. Her desire *for him*. Her heat. Her pulsing core. It was as if invisible tendrils had enveloped him, invading his senses. The way her body begged for his touch, the skim of his fingers, the press of his lips, the flick of his tongue. The thought of pushing his cocks inside her made him want to faint, it would be so good, so tight.

Of course, the carnal part of his mind wanted to fuck her fast and hard, that was a given, but his heartstrings checked this. His heartstrings would always be the voice of reason.

*Not now, Vikk,* it said, *and certainly not for your first time with your mate.* The length and girth of his cocks would require time and effort.

Vikk, still on his knees, leaned back ever-so-slightly, and chuckled. "Oh, how I am going to tease you, Mara Eldress."

Mara gave him a saucy smile. She liked his playful side, though she could tell he was trying to rein in his desire or else he might go feral. While she didn't want him to lose control, she enjoyed the fact that she caused that reaction in a man so sexy he could possess anyone, man or woman, with the crook of a finger.

"Tease away, Vikk Stravdas." Her voice was husky, breathless.

She stepped forward, which put her pussy in line with his lips. Then, grabbing his hair to lock him in place, she pressed her wet pussy against his mouth, grinding her sensitive nub with just enough friction to cause cascading pleasure ribbons to flare up like flames.

If a deep, guttural growl could be erotic, his was. She felt the vibration stretch deep into her core. When she pulled away, his lips were glistening with her juices. His expression was priceless, primitive. If she ended up suffocating him with her cunt, he'd probably die happy.

She did it again, and this time his tongue slid out to stroke her clit through her wet panties. Mara cried out, legs buckling. She continued to grind herself against him, hips moving rhythmically. His movements matched. At this rate, with the way her pleasure was building at such a rapid rate, Mara knew she would not last long.

Vikk must have sensed this because he detached himself from her, rose up to his full height, and picked her up like she weighed nothing before placing her on the bed. Mara automatically spread her legs, enjoying this brazen side of herself. She felt like the most beautiful bird of paradise showcasing her forbidden wares.

*Come hither,* her eyes told him as she arched her back, lifting her hips enticingly.

He growled again, his eyes flashing unbridled desire. Through her panties, he buried his nose to sniff her essence before his entire mouth covered her. With his tongue, he lapped her clit, the silky wet fabric adding a source of friction that was almost too much to bear.

Mara's hips bucked up as ripples of ecstasy crashed through her. She felt delirious. Wanton. Ready to beg for more. Just as she was about to, he pulled her panties off, exposing all of her to his hungry eyes.

Vikk was going to faint. He just knew it. With Mara's cunt

revealed to him, his eyes consumed her delicate flesh, the trimmed hair guarding her womanly entrance. Mara's ripples and petals were glorious. She reacted beautifully when he licked her topmost nubbin, and he did so now, over and over, but instead of her panties acting as a barrier, his tongue lavished her scorching core.

Her hands were in his hair, threading, pulling, yanking. He'd be lucky if he had any hair left after this encounter, he thought with a smile. Her moans activated a carnal switch in him where all he wanted to do was possess every part of her, her heart, her soul, her cunt. He'd gladly offer his all in return. Vikk's longer-than-human Vraitheian tongue swirled and lashed lower to enter her passage.

As his tongue snaked thickly inside, her hips bucked, her screams deafening his ears. Mara's inner muscles squeezed around his tongue. The pleasure center in Vikk's brain was duly rewarded. His cocks were so hard it was almost painful— he'd never been so aroused in his life.

He covered her mound entirely as he tongue-fucked her. Her erratic pulse throbbed against his mouth and tongue as he drank up everything she offered. He kept his hands on her even though his cock was protesting, wanting out of his trousers, begging to be touched. If he removed that one final barrier, he'd lose every ounce of self-control.

He loved her scent, her taste—sweet and juicy, like the most decadent dessert. He had a front row seat in witnessing her vertical ascent toward a crushing climax. He pulled back and replaced his tongue with a finger. She bucked again, panting incoherently for more.

When she looked at him, her eyes were wild, her hair a tussled mess. No soul could have been more alluring to him than Mara. Her legs and knees dug into him, pressing for purchase, for stability when everything inside her must have felt like turbulent flames.

Vikk slipped in two fingers, then three. Her cunt was wet, greedy. Could she accept him? Oh, the thought of sliding inside her, watching her slick juices coat his swollen cocks, sent erratic shivers down his spine. He broke out in a sweat. No, this was about her, not him.

His tongue vigorously circled her clit. His drenched fingers slid in and out of her velvety slit. His only thought was to maintain a consistent depth and rhythm. The slight slurping sound as his fingers fucked her made him breathless, edging him toward some oblivion he'd never experience before.

She kept crying, "Oh, God. Oh, God," over and over as her hips arched up to meet his fingers.

Mara was on the verge of bursting in half. There was the Mara *before* Vikk went down on her with that long, marvelous tongue, and then there was a Mara *after*. There was no reconciling the two. Her thighs squeezed his head as her breathing became shallower and shallower. In a moment of clarity, she wondered: Can *he* breathe?

Probably not. Oxygen was overrated.

She'd never wanted—or needed—a climax more in her life, and Vikk seemed determined to give it to her.

Her entire body felt as if it were being subsumed by lava. The bed squeaked as she rocked with him, her aching pussy clenching his long fingers, her clit bathed by his wide, rough tongue. It was like a dream come true. Vikk seemed to know what she liked without her having to voice a single word. She'd made a nest of his hair, pulling and tugging him into her cunt, as if they'd join by osmosis. Her fingers roamed over the bumps on his forehead, which appeared to give him pleasure. She wanted all of him in her, wanted to feel his sweaty weight on her, wanted to feel him thrusting inside her, his heavy breathing at her ear tumbling in words of love, the promise of many tomorrows.

Vikk turned her on like she'd never been turned on before. If he'd offered a contract to sign over her soul, she would have signed it in a heartbeat, ramifications be damned.

His fingers were lovemaking experts, his tongue a tenured professor of pleasure. Every sexual sensation was building inside her, a crescendo of desire peaking at the highest mountaintop, the tension deep in her core threatening to burst into scattered flames. The moans he rumbled into her flesh were music to her ears. Higher and higher she went.

In her peripheral vision, Mara imagined a shadow lurking at the edge of the bedroom. She wanted to point, to call out *Intruder! Voyeur!* but in that same moment, waves of pleasure foamed in from some unknown abyss. Her vision clouded as she reached her highest peak and coherent thought evaporated into thin air.

Her core burst, radiating sparks of hedonistic flames. Mara screamed, not caring if all of Vraithe heard.

Lightning pulsed round her core. A sea of stars crashed in from Vikk's fingers, his tongue, spreading, spreading, wave after wave, as several long climatic shocks electrified her body. Her hips arched up one last time, accepting the pleasure that washed over her as she crashed back to the land of the living.

Gently, Vikk removed his fingers and cupped his entire mouth over her sex.

His tongue slipped inside, swirling, which felt amazing, as he feasted on the abundance of her climatic juices. He groaned into her, sending ripples of aftershocks through her. She moaned out again as he licked her clean. Satiated, she wore a contented smile as he looked at her, the promise of more in his eyes.

When he pulled away suddenly, Mara protested, but it was only so that he could remove his pants.

Then, there in the corner, she saw the shadow move and she froze. Vikk must have noticed the change in her body language because he said, "If you're not comfortable we can stop."

"No, it's not that," Mara said quickly. She was intensely worried that Finley had witnessed everything. "Who's there? Come out."

Vikk jerked his head to the front of the room.

Thankfully the shadow did not belong to Finley.

With an embarrassed expression on her face, CeCe came into view. Vikk looked ready to snap at her.

"I am very sorry to interrupt this," CeCe said. She was looking at Vikk, who was still wearing his pants, but they were unzipped and seconds away from being yanked off. "It's just that Dessa keeps calling. Seems like there's an emergency on Earth."

"Since when do we care about Earth?" Vikk asked through clenched teeth.

Mara sat up, still in a climatic daze. "Wait, what's going on?" Mara was conscious that she was naked, but she was grateful that CeCe wasn't staring at her.

"You both will care about this. Mara and Finley have been declared missing. The police are searching for them, and"—CeCe paused, which made the hairs on Mara's arms stand up— "Calix is talking to anyone who will listen. It's not good."

# THIRTEEN

CeCe truly had no desire to step into her cousin's love den. Granted, it wasn't exactly his style to fuck his visitors on set, but perhaps Mara got his juices flowing. Far be it for her to criticize. In fact, as she watched Vikk devour Mara's swizzletart like a man on the verge of starvation, she didn't blame him for his eagerness.

Mara was a hottie, no doubt. She looked wild lying there on the bed, legs spread, her hair fanned out around her head, dewy from the heat pulsing from her core. Vikk looked at home with his head buried between Mara's quivering folds.

CeCe was mostly shocked that Vikk wasn't yet naked and thrusting himself inside her. He appeared to be controlling his impulses.

Vikk had always been selective with his partners, but truth be told, he hadn't had many partners, at least, none that she remembered. He was older than her by a dozen years, so who knew who he'd fucked before CeCe was aware of such things. Casual sex wasn't taboo on Vraithe. Talking about sex was like discussing what you ate for dinner the night before, though she had to admit that Vikk was more private than most.

As she watched, CeCe decided it would be better to wait until Mara climaxed, rather than upset them both with her interruption. Vikk's anger she could take any day. But she liked Mara a lot and didn't want to hurt her feelings. Besides, Mara looked like she needed a good release. CeCe felt something like pride that she'd found it with a Vraitheian and not a human.

Now, as Mara got herself to rights by dressing, and as Vikk's scowl grew from worse to less worse, CeCe noticed one particular fact more than anything else: he wasn't wearing his locket. She'd never seen him without it.

CeCe's eyes darted between Vikk and Mara as realization dawned on her. This wasn't some fling for Vikk. This was big. Like the biggest of big.

He was literally declaring himself to Mara. Any Vraitheian who looked at him would realize that immediately. But did Mara know? Would Vikk tell her the significance? CeCe had her doubts.

CeCe would have teased her cousin about it, but she sensed it would not be welcome when there were more pressing matters to contend with.

Mara surprised herself by not feeling ashamed of what CeCe must have witnessed. Indeed, less than an hour ago, she'd had a front row seat when CeCe and Logea went at it on camera. Mara put on her clothes, but stuffed her wet panties in a pocket.

"What is Calix saying?" Mara asked after she pulled her hair out of her face and up into a bun. She'd never known Calix to be vindictive, but how did he even know that she and Finley were not at home? It wasn't like he lived nearby. He lived five states away, and happily avoided them the same way she and Finley avoided him.

"It might be best if you watch the video Dessa sent," CeCe said, before handing over the communications device to Mara. Vikk, who was now back in his shirt, stood beside her, his hand at her back.

Mara pressed play.

The video was from the local six o'clock news. The anchor looked into the camera and said, "And now onto a developing story we first brought you last night. Local Riley High School English teacher, Mara Eldress, and her fifteen-year-old, home-schooled daughter, Finley Eldress, are missing." Mara's official school photo was up on the screen. "Mara was last seen on Friday when school let out. Very few individuals have seen or met Finley, which leaves officials with more questions than answers."

The display switched to a video of a police officer. The banner beneath him read, Police Chief Vargus. "We're looking at all avenues into their disappearance. We do not know if it was voluntary or by force." Then the video showed police entering Mara's house, with police officers clearly carrying out items in brown paper bags. "It doesn't seem like they took much with them but also nothing seems to be disturbed inside the residence either."

The video switched back to the anchor. "We spoke with Ms. Eldress's ex-husband, Calix Eldress." Mara's blood ran cold when she saw Calix on the screen, talking to an unseen reporter in the dark, right in front of her house. "I just want my little girl back. I texted Finley on Friday that I would be picking her up on Monday. Abigail and I are getting married, and we want nothing more than for Finley to be in our wedding. Sadly, Finley never returned my texts. I'm not even sure she got them. It wouldn't surprise me if Mara found out I was getting remarried and took Finley someplace I wouldn't know about."

Mara could not stomach another word. She paused the

video and sank onto the bed. "Calix all but said I kidnapped Finley to avoid acknowledging that he was getting remarried."

Vikk placed a gentle hand on her shoulder. "Did you know?"

She shot him an accusatory glance. "No, of course not. Calix is free to do as he wishes. He can get married a dozen times if he wants, I don't care. If Finley knew, she didn't tell me. I would have been fine with her going to the wedding, but it's just like him to not keep me informed of his plans."

Mara's brain rewound. The news report said Calix had come on *Monday* to pick up Finley. They left Boston on Saturday and had been in Vraithe one day. Today was Sunday. *How could the report say they'd been missing since Monday?* "When was this news report, CeCe? It's made to sound like Finley and I have been missing for days, except it's only Sunday. Monday hasn't come yet."

Vikk opened his mouth to answer, but CeCe spoke first.

"On Earth, it's already Wednesday night," CeCe answered matter of fact. "One Vraitheian day equals two-and-a-half Earth Days. I though you knew."

CeCe threw a questioning look at Vikk. In RMO, she asked him, *"You didn't tell her about the time differential, did you?"*

In RMO he responded, *"I was going to get around to it eventually. It never occurred to me that she'd be reported missing. Schools are on a two-week break. Dessa told me it was Earthling vacation time, something about celebrating one of their gods with gifts and food."*

Mara watched Vikk and CeCe talk with their eyes. More

likely, they were communicating through some other means. Either way, the stalled silence was deafening. She witnessed the jockeying back and forth, except nothing audible came out of their mouths.

"Can you please have your discussion where I can understand it?" Mara asked. She didn't care if she sounded snappish. "Earth thinks I'm missing. My ex-husband is ruining my reputation, and the two of you are having some cute conversation in your heads. Frankly, I find it insulting."

CeCe had the grace to look admonished, her glittery cerulean cheeks taking on a darker glow.

"Sorry, Mara," Vikk said. He sat beside her, placing his hand on her thigh. "I meant to tell you about the time differential—for us it's nothing more than an interesting tidbit, like trivia. It never occurred to me that it would factor into something this serious. What CeCe said is correct. Earth days advance quicker than Vraithe. Our rotation is slower. So, for each day on Vraithe, two-and-a-half days pass on Earth."

CeCe's eyebrows went up. It appeared she had an idea. "When you go back, just tell Enemy-General Calix that you've been visiting family. It's not like it's unusual to visit family at Christmas, right? I mean, *we* don't celebrate Christmas, why would we, but how crazy could it be that you're not home?"

"I'm an only child, CeCe," Mara said, "and both of my parents are dead. Calix knows I have no family to visit. Other than an occasional trip to see Command Sergeant Major Hannah Atholms, a good friend of mine who is still active-duty army, Finley and I don't do much traveling. She gets sick on long car rides, and you can forget plane flights. The drive from Baltimore to Massachusetts is usually a seven-hour drive—it takes us three days. If Calix was planning to pick her up on Monday, that means his wedding is on Friday or Saturday. He wouldn't want Finley to get sick in his car, so he would have built in enough time to pick her up and drive back to Baltimore."

As Vikk listened to Mara explain her situation with Finley's dad, he worried that maybe Mara wasn't thrilled about her ex-husband remarrying. Was it because she still harbored feelings for Calix, or because she was anxious about Calix wanting more time with Finley once he'd remarried? Even in the short of amount of time he'd known Finley, Vikk felt a strange sort of kinship with the little urchin. He'd hate it if he never got to see her again.

Or was Vikk's worry more about some insecurity within himself? He shook the cobwebs from his head. *None* of this was about him. It was about Mara and Finley and the predicament they found themselves back on Earth.

Then it dawned on him. "Oh no," he groaned.

"What is it?" Mara asked.

"My device has been vibrating since this morning, but I turned it off because I wanted to focus on Finley's medical appointments and the film's rehearsal."

In a matter of seconds, Vikk switched it on and a dozen texts and missed calls popped on his screen. All were from Dessa and were various worded messages that said, "Call me" and "Where are you?" and "Calix's now on the scene" and "I just left the police station, please call me" to the last, "Vikk the shit just hit the fan. It's bad. CALL ME!"

"Call her, Vikk!" Mara said with eyes blazing. "Call her now. Something more could have happened."

Vikk pressed several buttons until Dessa's face appeared on the screen.

"Finally," Dessa muttered. She was at the portal station in Boston. "Seriously, I figured you were dead or fu—" She stopped and peered closer into her device. She must have noticed that Mara and CeCe were both with him. "Never mind what I thought, dear brother," she finished with a tinkle of nervous laughter. Vikk knew what her other thought was and his little sister was not that far off. "Hi CeCe, hi Mara!"

"Hi Dessa," Mara said but with less bubbliness than Dessa's cheerful voice. "CeCe just filled us in. What is the latest?"

"It's probably better if I push the most recent news segment. It's gaining national attention, Mara, just so you know."

Mara steeled herself for something even more horrible. When the video came through, it was slightly pixelated. She supposed that the Vraitheian version of the internet might have issues picking up video that had been sent through space. When it fully loaded, it turned out to be from one of those national headline news stations that focused on missing or dead women. Mara groaned. She recognized Patti Stoltz, the program's Southern-spoken host.

"We've got a mystery here tonight, folks. Mara Eldress. I want you to remember that name and this face. She's pretty ain't she? She's an English teacher up in Massachusetts. Except she wasn't always a teacher. Oh, no folks, she was in the army for fifteen years. She even wrote a book about her experiences."

Patti Stoltz held up Mara's memoir. "And now this army veteran turned English teacher is missing. And it isn't just her, folks, her fifteen-year-old daughter is missing, too. Finley Eldress. She's been chronically ill for several years. Are you following me? Let's try to connect the dots, shall we? Is there something in Sergeant Eldress's memoir that the military didn't like? What if they wanted to gag her? Sergeant Eldress suffered not one but two—two!—IED injuries that ended her military career. Was she bitter about it?"

The camera angle changed, as Patti turned to a new theory. "Or, how about this. Guess what folks? There's an ex-husband, Calix Eldress. He's getting remarried this week and was supposed to pick up Finley on Monday. They weren't home. No one's seen them since Friday. He thinks Mara Eldress was angry about his upcoming nuptials, that he was suing for custody. Here on the Stoltz Program, we've got questions. Loads of them, folks. Was she angry about her ex's wedding? Did she snap under the mountain of pressure of raising a chronically ill child? Or, what if...and it's a big what if...what if the army didn't like what she wrote in her memoir? But here's a zany tidbit, the army won't even confirm she served in the military. What's up with that? What happened to vet Mom? Maybe the answers are in here."

She waved the book again before pointing at the camera. "More after the break."

The video went to commercial, which was when Dessa came back on the screen. "What did I say? Pretty bad, huh?"

"Jesus," Mara said under her breath.

If Patti Stoltz was on the case, Mara knew her name would be on everyone's lips before the end of the week. Her heart was in her throat. She'd worked so hard on improving their lives, of starting over. It felt like everything was suddenly slipping through her fingers. She couldn't think or speak, but she knew that she and Finley needed to return to Earth, if no other reason than to quell rumors.

When Mara looked up, she saw Finley standing at the edge of the set. From the look on her face, she'd been there for a few minutes, which meant she heard everything from the Stoltz Program.

"Come on out, Finley," Mara called out to her.

Finley shuffled into the bedroom set and went to Mom. Tears stained Finley's pale cheeks. Everyone was looking at her. She was embarrassed because she thought she looked like a crying baby.

"I'm so sorry, Mom," she said through hiccups. She was tired, hungry, and mad at herself. She was so stupid sometimes. "I didn't mean to get you in trouble."

"I know you didn't," Mom said in her gentle voice. No matter what, Mom always loved her. "And I'm not in trouble. Come here, sweetie."

Finley threw herself into her mom's outstretched hands, the one place she always felt loved and secured, even if she was too old to be held.

She'd heard everything Patti Stoltz had said. But she'd heard more than that. She overheard Mom, CeCe and Mr. Stravdas discuss the time differential. If Finley had known that they'd be here longer than a couple of days, she would have said something to Mom.

"Did your dad tell you about the wedding?"

Finley leaned back and nodded. She hadn't told Mom about the wedding. Not that she thought Mom cared. No, Mom would have insisted on Finley going. She would have wanted Finley to have a good time. She felt horrible. Mom wiped away the tears staining her face. When she could talk, Finley said, "He told me not to tell you, that he was going to call you and tell you himself."

Mom frowned at that. She was going to say something when the Vraitheian device chirped. Mr. Stravdas clicked on it. It was his sister, Dessa Stravdas. "Vikk," Dessa said through the device. "Since you're now aware of the situation, I'll stay here on Earth to keep an eye on things. Send me a note when you know Mara and Finley's return time."

With that, the screen went dark.

Mara held her daughter, stroking her hair. She didn't like that Calix had asked Finley to keep secrets from her.

"I know we probably have to return, Mom, but I really like it here."

Mara smoothed down her daughter's flyaway hair. "I know you do, kiddo. So do I." She looked over Finley's head and into Vikk's concerned eyes. He was mostly unreadable to her right now. Did he want her to go? Or to stay? It wasn't as if she could stay forever but she still wanted to know how he felt.

They'd gone from lava-hot to arctic-cold with this news. It was on both their sides. Oh, there was still chemistry, sizzling in the air between them. But with her daughter in her arms and a situation developing on Earth, Mara knew she couldn't sit immobile for long.

She might be a teacher now, but for many years she was a soldier, an explosives ordinance disposal soldier, deployed to chaotic regions around the world. Words could hurt but they couldn't kill, not really, not in the way Calix thought they might. If anything, he was hurting his chances at reconnecting with Finley more than he was injuring Mara. Mara would be fine. Finley...not so much.

"I think a solid night's sleep is in order," Mara said. She wanted some space to think, to figure things out. Then to Vikk, she added, "It might be best if we depart in the morning." Before their lovemaking session she was already determined to leave; she'd even said as much. But why did it hurt even more to say it now? "That will put us returning, what, Thursday night on Earth?"

Vikk swallowed hard as she spoke of leaving in the morning. What if she decided never to return? What if she refused to see him if he visited? Would his heartstrings shrivel and die?

"Thursday evening, yes." He kept his voice neutral.

"When you get Finley's medical results, will you send them to us? Perhaps there will be an Earth medicine or remedy for her condition." It occurred to him that she said nothing about returning to Vraithe for medical treatment. Was their time at an end? Did their lovemaking mean nothing, then?

He looked at Finley. Her eyes were closed as she nestled in as close as possible to Mara. Even though the child had been crying, she'd never looked so healthy. There was something about Vraithe that agreed with Finley's health.

"I promise I will find a way to get you whatever you need, Mara."

She gave him a simple smile that blew him away. She was so beautiful and he wasn't thinking that just because he was still covered in her silky scent.

"We'll head upstairs now." With the film studio being located in Taloncourt's basements, their room was literally an elevator ride away.

He looked around before he touched her arm. CeCe had disappeared at some point, so it was just the two of them, not counting Finley, who seemed to have fallen asleep. "Can I check in on you later tonight?"

Mara's expression conveyed that she understood his meaning but she shook her head.

"Finley feels guilty about all of this, even though it's not her fault. I need to be with her all night in case she wakes up in a panic. We'll see you in the morning. I appreciate whatever portal reservation time you can get for us."

As Mara carried Finley off the set and out of the theater, Vikk sat on the edge of the bed, staring straight ahead at nothing.

He'd never felt more alone in his life.

Mara kept her emotions in check as she entered the brightly lit, bejeweled elevator. Finley, snuggled in and snoring lightly, was sound asleep in her arms. She was slightly heavier than she remembered, as if she'd gained a few pounds over the last two days on Vraithe. That was a good sign—it was not very easy for Finley to gain the weight she needed to maintain a healthy size for her age.

There were dark circles under her daughter's eyes. Poor thing. If Mara had to guess, she figured Finley had been toting around guilt since they'd left Earth, carrying it like a piece of luggage. Naturally, Finley could not have anticipated the time differential, and she wasn't calculating second and third order effects of Calix driving up to get her only to find them both missing.

The elevator dinged. She stepped onto the twelfth floor and made for their room. "Almost there," she said to a sleeping Finley.

Mara did not blame her, nor was she angry about it, though it was virtually impossible *not* to focus inward on the quagmire they'd be stepping into once they returned to Earth. How was she going to explain their absence? After searching her house, the police would have known they had not packed for a trip and it was only a matter of time before they found her truck in Boston. She'd be grateful if they hadn't found it already. If they had, the police probably would have impounded it, which meant they would not have a vehicle to drive home in.

Claiming they'd been abducted by aliens would only hasten her trip to a hospital's mental ward.

She could already envision Calix's smug face somehow finding fault with Mara as he lectured her on how to raise their daughter, as if he wasn't the one who left them for one of his personal trainers.

When they'd first met, as soldiers at Fort Bragg, North Carolina, Mara had been swayed and dazzled by him, swept away by his handsome face and charismatic charm. She'd fallen head over heels in a matter of weeks. It hadn't taken long for those feelings to evaporate, but by then they were married and Mara was already pregnant with Finley.

As strange as it seemed, it was as if she'd seen through his veneer after Finley was born. Calix whined that she should spend more time with him, demanded that *he* deserved more of Mara's attention. It seemed odd to Mara that Calix was jealous of a newborn baby, but still she felt compelled to make it work.

It was around the time she'd been injured that Calix began to think of a career beyond the military. He had already left the service, but was still in peak condition with an interest in fitness and nutrition. He truly walked the walk when it came to physical fitness and eating clean. He'd show any stranger his washboard abs in under a second if they feigned a remote interest in the topic.

Mara herself had never been much swayed by his business acumen, but people had come out in droves to fund his nutrition business when he was getting it off the ground—he'd always had a penchant for schmoozing people out of money. She hadn't kept track, but from all appearances, Calix's nutritional shake and vitamin business was doing well enough that he'd purchased a very nice McMansion in Baltimore. She didn't know who Abigail was, but one of Calix's previous girlfriends was a former Miss Virginia.

Mara's biggest problem with Calix was that he'd been a poor father to Finley while Mara was deployed. He resented having to take care of his own child. While Mara was still in the military and deployed overseas, it killed her every time a crying Finley called her long distance from their neighbor's house because Calix had dumped her there so he could go do "adult" things.

Calix had always treated Finley like a burden, so it was a surprise to Mara that he would claim he had filed for custody. Was he preening for the cameras to make it seem like he was the *good* parent in this equation? Would everyone believe it? They might since she wasn't there to contradict his message.

Sighing, Mara shifted Finley in her arms and opened the door to their luxurious apartment.

As the door swung open, she was startled to see a tall, thin figure standing in the middle of the room. Her bright silver-gray hair and regal bearing gave her away almost instantly.

Queen Uska.

"Hello," Mara said.

The queen did not reply. She stood there in a long, flowing turquoise robe. The color was so vibrant it put the chamber's dark green color scheme to shame. Now that the glamour veil had faded, Mara could see her true form. She was a very tall individual with long arms and fingers. Her skin was the color of gold that glimmered inside the room's glittery opulence.

Nodules honored her forehead. Two thin lines the size of narrow twigs started at the top of her nose and spread out to form a V on her tall forehead. There were tiny pearls etched at the tops of both. Her eyes were like chips of black diamonds, shiny yet deep and cavernous, as if she'd seen worlds come and go in her lifetime.

As the queen turned toward her, her placid expression turned darker.

Mara shivered. Uska's deep frown worried her, and she feared she had somehow offended Vraithe's ruling monarch.

# Fourteen

Uska watched the human enter her daughter's former room. Mara was not much to look at—not a vibrant color inherent anywhere in her features. Beige skin, plain hair, unremarkable eyebrows above ordinary eyes. Not that Mara was unattractive, but Uska would not have minded an orchid purple or even a light lavender complexion on her.

There was a weariness hanging over Mara's head. An aura encapsulated with worry, regret, longing. Uska also detected the scent of sex on her. So Vikkolo had left his mark on the human? What mark had Mara left on him?

If she were being honest with herself, Uska was not entirely surprised by this. Vikkolo, while private, had a mind of his own. He had not sought his queen's approval, which was something she admired in her prime relative. Vraitheians were a peaceful race, but that didn't mean that there weren't those who tried to curry favor with her by providing gossip, or delicacies, or a newly translated novel.

As it stood, one such individual had already reported that Vikkolo had removed his Vraitheian black locket. The implications were clear: Vikkolo was declaring to all of Vraithe his affection for the human, Mara.

"I believe I may have startled you," Uska said in rough English as Mara closed the door quietly behind her before transferring Finley to the unmade bed.

"Only a little," Mara said without preamble, pulling the blanket over her daughter's sleeping figure.

Uska studied the sickly child. Her aura had improved in the days since her arrival, yet the putrid shade had not fully dissipated. Doctor Smindle was correct: Vraithe air and food appeared to be having a positive influence on the child, but there was more yet to do. Some mystery hung about the child's illness, and Uska had opinions of her own, but until the test results came back from the medical clinic, she would conjecture no further.

But this was not why she'd chosen to talk to Mara Eldress alone.

Uska inclined her head toward Mara. "We Vraitheians do not enjoy scandals."

Mara's eyes went wide as she said this. Standing beside the bed, next to her child, the light was behind the human woman. It illuminated her athletic build, her confident stance. Uska was not an expert in human flesh. She did not know if Mara was important or considered a prime specimen on her home planet. She'd met Earthling monarchs, presidents, and prime ministers who exuded power and authority. Those Earthlings had demanded every privilege under the Vraitheian suns.

And yet Uska had let none of them stay in this room.

Everyone at Taloncourt wondered at Uska's willingness to share Qoral's apartment with these humans. The reason—a deep and ancient instinct that told Uska this human would become important to her—was one she planned to hold close to her chest. For the time being, Uska was pleased to see the room being used by worthy individuals.

Mara surprised her by letting out a light, musical laugh. "You would not enjoy Earth, then, Queen Uska. Scandals abound there. You will be pleased to learn that we are leaving soon. In the morning, hopefully."

Uska narrowed her eyes and shot a glance at Finley's sleeping form. This was sudden. *Pleased?* No, not at all. She'd come up to discuss Vikk changing the twatsizzle scene and the scandal the change would cause; but now, with this news, Uska needed to know how Vikkolo felt about their departure. Would he even tell her? Had Mara rejected his declaration?

"*Before* we learn of the child's medical diagnosis?"

Mara was confused. Didn't the queen want her to leave? By "scandal" wasn't Queen Uska referring to her situation on Earth?

Then it occurred to her. Perhaps the queen did not approve of the Vraitheian heir dating a human. There would be issues with future heirs, not that Mara could have more children given the emergency hysterectomy she had after the IED blasts. Even so, she wasn't sure if humans and Vraitheians could even procreate. She'd not given it much consideration, but now that she had given it a tiny amount of thought, it was probably a good thing that they were departing.

The last thing Mara wanted to do was impact Vikk's future role as king.

Her face briefly turned red. The future king of Vraithe had gone down on her like a man on the verge of starvation.

Mara cleared her throat.

"There are things on Earth that require my attention, Queen Uska. Finley's father has reported us missing. We need to return as soon as possible before the authorities charge me with kidnapping my own child. Vikk will contact me with Finley's results."

"I see." There was a long pause. Mara was beginning to wonder if the queen would say more, when she finally continued. "Before you go, I will host a dinner in your honor, Good-General Mara Eldress. There will be dancing, food, wine, and games for the younger set."

The queen appeared to look out the windows. "*Plenty* of time to plan such a party for tonight."

Mara was touched by her generosity. There was a lot of daylight left—more than enough, now that Mara understood that days here were twice as long as an Earth day.

"I beg that you will not go to any trouble on our account. I should be thanking *you* for your kindness and for agreeing to help with Finley's medical mystery. Vikk and CeCe have both been wonderful to Finley. They have been very kind to me, as well."

Queen Uska gave her a knowing look, one that suggested she was fully aware of her relationship with Vikk. Well, relationship was too strong a word. Connection. Her *connection* with Vikk.

Her heart pinched then. There was no hope. No hope of a future for them. His home was here. Their life was on Earth. Why attempt such a galactic, long-distance relationship?

The queen made for the door. "I will hold it in your honor, regardless. I hope that you and Finley will join us."

With that, the queen let herself out of the room.

Back on Earth, Calix was enjoying an old-fashioned at the bar at The Godfrey Hotel Boston, his phone buzzing nonstop. The police wanted to know if he'd heard from Mara or Finley since their last conversation, while several of Mara's friends from her military days somehow got ahold of his number to ask if they could do anything to help.

*Screw them all*, he thought, as he deleted their messages.

News stations were calling him as well, wanting to book him for short segments. He forwarded these messages to Jasmine, his executive assistant. He knew things were headed toward primetime when the mainstream media started contacting him for interviews.

"Book CNN first," he wrote in a text to Jasmine. The low-lit bar was mostly quiet given the recent snowstorm. The soft hum of conversations mixed with overhead music. "And avoid Patti Stoltz's program at all costs." *That woman ate husbands for breakfast.* She always made a point to ask about alimony or child support, like that had to do with anything. Calix had no desire to answer questions on those toxic subjects, not if he wanted to look like the good parent right now.

*He* needed to be the one to establish the narrative that Mara had violated that precious trust as a wife and as a mother. *He* was so worried that she'd succumbed to stress and financial hardship. His pending nuptials must have been a trigger for her. He cared for Mara, of course, and wanted nothing but the best for her, even if that meant jail time. Was Mara poisoning their daughter to gain attention? He had his suspicions. All he wanted was to get his daughter back so that he could take her to a specialist, which was something he'd been begging Mara to do for years.

His fiancé, Abigail, was naturally distraught at having to postpone their wedding ceremony. *People* magazine had even commented on one of her social media posts about everything, so she was riding high on that notoriety.

His nutrition business was attracting new clients, as well. In short, Mara's disappearance was good for business. And the ace in Calix's hand was that he'd truly had nothing to do with their disappearance, so he could wave away all the naysayers online who wanted to point fingers at him like he was some deranged ex-husband. He wasn't exactly a fan of the online chatter.

There seemed to be two divided camps—one on Mara's side and one on his side. Someone had even started a podcast on the case. The two hosts were doing a close read of her memoir, looking for secret clues. Weird, but whatever.

Did he think they were really missing and in danger? No. He presumed they were vacationing in some cabin with little or no internet capability. Mara was a writer at heart, a stupid aspiration in his opinion. He could see her wanting to go somewhere to write her next book, even though it would probably turn out to be a dud like the first one. He chuckled at that. Chances were good that Finley had never received his text messages about the wedding in the first place.

He had no personal beef with Mara, but hey, any publicity was good publicity.

However, *one* friend in particular worried him. Army Command Sergeant Major Hannah Atholms had left him a long voicemail.

"Hi, Calix," her message began. "You may not remember me. I'm Mara's former boss. We were deployed together. Mara isn't one to just disappear; she's very 'steady-state' if you know what I mean. This all feels wrong, and I'm not liking how the press is depicting Mara right now. Listen, I'm now stationed at Ft. Drum, New York. I can be in Boston in under six hours. Please call me back to let me know how I can help."

If anyone was going to ruin all his plans, it would be Command Sergeant Major Atholms. She would paint Mara in a positive light. The soldier possessed rank, prestige, and military authority. And, if he remembered correctly, she had been awarded the Bronze Star, too. A hero on the battlefield. It would be difficult to go against someone so highly thought of.

He finished his old-fashioned when Jasmine texted. He

was scheduled for a virtual segment with CNN in an hour. Calix paid for his drink and left the bar, studying his reflection in a hallway mirror on his way by. His handsome, chiseled face stared back at him. He smoothed down his short, dark hair and finger-groomed one eyebrow. *You'll do nicely, Calix Eldress.*

With a smile on his face, he went upstairs to his room to get ready for the interview.

There was one request Jasmine Ramona had *not* passed on to Calix. Patti Stoltz's producer had asked for a photo of Mr. Eldress's daughter, Finley. "Could they produce a recent photo of father and daughter together?"

Jasmine was intelligent enough to read between the lines.

Scrambling, Jasmine searched for and found Finley's social media profile to see if she had *any* photos of Mr. Eldress on there. Scrolling, she found *plenty* of photos of Finley and her mother together, but none that contained Mr. Eldress.

Doing as her boss instructed, Jasmine ignored the request, logged of her work laptop, and went home to a family she loved enough to showcase on her own social media posts.

Mara was grateful for the quiet chamber. With Finley still asleep, she could be free with her thoughts. A bubble bath in the refreshing chamber sounded like something that might calm the anxiety roiling in the pit of her stomach. She started the tap and drizzled in healthy dose of orange soap. It started foaming immediately.

The crisp essence of orange filled the room and Mara, stripping off her clothes and leaving them in a pile on the floor, took a long, deep breath as she stepped into the tub and submerged herself in water hot enough to melt away muscle knots.

What kind of shit storm would they be walking into tomorrow when they took the portal home? Would she be arrested? What would happen to Finley? Did Calix really want full custody, or was he merely talking through his ass in order to look like a doting father who'd been wronged by the system?

Patti Stoltz had already coined a moniker: *Vet Mom.*

Her eyes stung. Mara had always been so stoic. She never complained about anything. She'd kept her nose clean while in the foster system, she'd been a good soldier, *and* she was a great mother. *Vet Mom.* It wasn't a good sign when your entire life was reduced to two syllables.

Would Mara even have a job after winter break? She hadn't done a single thing wrong and yet she felt guilty. As a teacher, she wasn't supposed to bring negative attention to the school district. The school board wasn't happy with her choice of books, and given that she was a new teacher, she was still under a three-year probationary period.

Mara could arrive home, produce a healthy Finley Eldress, clear her name, and still be released from her teaching contract. Then what? Write another book no one would read?

With the tub now full, she turned off the tap, sat back, and starred at the gold-foiled ceiling.

Here she was sitting in a bathroom full of precious jewels that held no more value than rocks on Vraithe but would make her a wealthy woman on Earth. She laughed even as a tear leaked from her eye. *Oh, the irony of feeling sorry for myself while taking a bubble bath in a royal suite on the top floor of a palace. Poor me.*

No one would believe it and Mara wasn't about to wrench out the emeralds and diamonds decorating the base of the toilet. She could take a picture, though—*if* her phone still had power. In the other room she heard Finley shift in the bed.

Then she heard the lightest ding, like the ding of a text coming from a muffled phone buried in a backpack.

Was she imagining it? A phantom ding? Was it even possible to receive texts from Earth? Mara grabbed an oversize towel off a nearby hook, wrapped it around herself, and tiptoed into the bedroom.

The backpack was still on the table where she'd left it after their arrival. It never occurred to her that their smartphones would work on a planet ten thousand lightyears away from the nearest cellphone tower.

And yet, after rummaging through crushed granola bars, Finley's journal, her work laptop, a stack of her student's essays, a first aid kit, and one random sock, Mara extracted her phone and saw that she had more than two hundred unread texts, and more than seventy missed calls and voicemails.

Dumbfounded, Mara sat down in an armchair, not caring if her wet hair dripped onto the cushion below. There were texts from Calix. He casually mentioned picking up Finley ahead of his wedding. When she hadn't responded to that text, his messages had become increasingly annoyed. "Why aren't you texting me back?" and "Don't be a bitch about this, Mara."

As for the missed phone calls, she recognized Calix's number and the main line for Riley High School. That must have been Dr. Brady trying to reach her. Other numbers were unknown to her. There was really only one person she hoped to hear from. Command Sergeant Major Hannah Atholms. Her military sister-in-arms and the one person, besides Finley, who cared if she lived or died.

Mara pressed play on Hannah's latest voicemail.

"Mara," Hannah's clear voice said, "I'm starting to get concerned, my friend. I'm about three hours away from your house and I'm fully prepared for jail time *and* a dishonorable discharge from the military if I find out that Calix's had anything to do with your disappearance. For the love of all the gray hairs I've sprouted overnight, please call me back!"

Mara smiled. Hannah had their back. But, almost as instantly, Mara's stomach clenched. It was still bad, very bad. She kept hearing Patti Stoltz's voice saying "Vet Mom" over and over.

She felt hot all over and heard a pounding in her head before she realized it was merely someone knocking at the door.

"Earth to Mom," Finley said in a groggy voice from the doorway. Her mom had been so distracted by her phone that she hadn't heard someone knocking at the door for a solid minute.

Finley recognized Hant Anna's commanding voice immediately. She was Mom's best friend in the entire world. If Hant Anna was on their side, then Finley felt that everything would work out. Maybe that meant they could stay longer.

Mom paused the voicemail. "Sorry about that, sweetie." She held up her phone. "It's just that our phones *work* here. How crazy is that?"

It surprised Finley to learn that their phones actually worked on Vraithe. If she'd known, she would have been taking pictures left and right. She really wanted to take a selfie with Serstene, especially if they were leaving in the morning. Who knew when she'd see him again, if ever?

When she opened the door, it was no surprise that the knocker turned out to be a concerned-looking Mr. Stravdas. It was pretty obvious that he and Mom needed to work through their feelings. "Just one moment, Mr. Stravdas," she said, leaving him in the hallway and turning back to her mom. "It's Mr. Stravdas. Should I let him in?"

Her mom looked down at the towel wrapped around her, and shook her head. "Let me get dressed first."

She disappeared into the refreshing chamber and returned a couple of minutes later, tying a flowery, ankle-length silk robe around her waist. Her shoulder-length brown hair was still wet and she was in the process of finger-combing it around her ears. "Okay, you can let Vikk inside now."

Vikk waited in the darkened hallway for Finley to open the door again. Thankfully, it was only a couple of minutes before she did, a slightly sheepish expression on her face.

"Mom's dressed, so you can come in now, Mr. Stravdas," she said, stepping aside to admit him. "Should I get lost?"

Finley's expression was hopeful, like maybe she *wanted* to get lost. Vikk wasn't blind to the fact that she and Serstene had become close.

"No," he said. "What I need to say should be heard by you both."

Finley looked like she'd just woken up. Her clothes hung at a sideways slant, like she'd shifted in the bed but her clothes hadn't shifted with her, and her epic bedhead would give Medusa a run for her money. Vikk mussed the top of her head and was pleased when she smiled up at him. He'd come to really adore Mara's daughter.

Mara, who stood near the entrance to the refreshing chamber, was a vision. Attired in an amethyst moon flower robe, she looked refreshed and alert. Her phone was in her hand and given its lit screen, she'd clearly discovered that she could receive messages.

"Why didn't you tell us that our phones worked on Vraithe?" It was Finley who asked this question. Her tone wasn't exactly accusatory, but neither was it conversational. It seemed to suggest that he'd been withholding information. Vikk couldn't blame her.

"I apologize for that," he said as he walked further into the orange blossom-scented room. From that point forward he would forever associate the fragrance with Mara. "You are the first humans I've brought with me through the portal. In all honesty, it never occurred to me to alert you to things like the time differential or that you'd be able to receive messages on your phones."

Finley was typing into her phone. "Except it seems like I can't send a return text," she said with a frown.

"The portal is the activator," Vikk explained. "You can receive texts and voicemails because your device traveled from Earth to Vraithe. However, because your device has not yet traveled through the portal *back* to Earth, that tunnel has not yet been activated for your specific device."

"Meaning that when we go home," Mara said with her arms folded over her chest, "the portal will have fully activated a two-way communication tunnel?"

Vikk tried not to flinch when Mara stressed the word *home*. It felt exclusionary. He was excluded from her vision of what *home* meant to her.

"Correct," he said.

Without his locket, his chest felt open and vulnerable. Not that Mara knew it or understood his actions, but he'd all but offered his heart. The thing was, if he said something *now*, it would come across as a ploy or manipulation.

For a man who had wanted for nothing for his entire life, who never had to work for anything, Vikk hadn't experienced heartbreak until now. Mara's aura was presenting a stand-off hue. She did not like to be pressured or pressed into action.

It was then that he realized that in order for Mara to fully love someone, she also had to trust them. Lust and desire were one thing, but *trust*...oh, that was on an entirely different level.

His withholding information, however unintentional, left open the possibility that he could not be trusted. It hurt, but he acknowledged it was his own fault and he had to live with the consequences.

Until she trusted him, Mara was wearing her own version of a Vraitheian black locket that prevented her heartstrings from fully embracing his.

Mara watched the emotions flash across his face. Vikk was coming to some sort of realization. "That's good to know," she said. "Once you learn of Finley's medical diagnosis, we'll be able to communicate that way."

He paused before nodding. "Dr. Keiji Vuzmuc assured me they would know within a few days. That's why I came by. I know you're anxious to return home. I was able to secure a last-minute portal reservation for the two of you after the queen's dinner tonight. You might remember Werlaun, the gray suit steward who escorted us from Earth. She owed me a favor and agreed to be your escort back to Earth tonight."

Mara read between the lines and understood that he would not be joining them. They needed to go home, and it had to be as soon as possible, yet she was disappointed that he would not be returning to Earth with them.

Perhaps it was for the best. Hannah would take one look at the two of them and know immediately something was going on. Their relationship would be difficult to explain and frankly, given everything else that was going on, Mara didn't think she'd be able to do it justice.

Without warning, Finley burst into tears. She yelled at Vikk, "You just can't wait to get rid of us, can you?"

Pain flitted across his face. "Finley, not at all," Vikk began, but Mara knew that Finley didn't hear him. Finley bolted for the door and ran out of the chamber before Mara could call her back.

She and Vikk stood there in silence, looking at the open door and not at each other. Strange how only hours ago they couldn't have been closer, blazing together in a cocoon of heat. Now, barely five feet apart, it felt like the universe was widening the gulf between them.

In a matter of hours, five feet would expand into a distance of ten thousand light years.

Mara knew that Finley would either go to CeCe or Serstene, either of whom would bring her back to the palace for the dinner. Sometimes you had to let someone go so that they could come to terms with the inevitable.

She ached to reach out to Vikk, to touch his arm, something to let him know she wasn't lost forever, but before she could, he moved toward the door.

Maybe Vikk was letting them go. It was the right thing to do, and Mara knew that the sooner they returned to Earth, the quicker she'd be able to douse the dumpster fire Calix had lit. With that on her mind, she'd never be able to devote the right kind of energy to building something with Vikk.

Vikk reached the door, then turned to her. "Please tell Finley I'm sorry, I didn't mean to upset her."

"I will. She's been happy and healthy here. I don't blame her for not wanting to go back. She's most likely worried about becoming ill again, and I cannot return to Earth without her. The authorities will assume foul play. It's a no-win situation."

"Then stay."

The longing in his voice slayed her. It turned her world upside-down before depositing her in a heap of her own confusing emotions. She basked in those feelings for a long moment before reality walked in. *He* didn't get to do that. She shouldn't be the one to give up everything. The military had wrecked her. Calix took everything from her.

Just this once, Mara needed someone in her corner. Someone to fight for *her*.

"Would *you* stay on Earth?" she asked instead.

When Vikk didn't respond after a long pause, Mara had her answer.

# FIFTEEN

Finley didn't know where she was going, only that CeCe's chambers were on the fourth floor. She flew from door to door, knocking on so many and making a ruckus, that several doors opened to investigate the noise.

Down the shadowy hallway, a figure in robes glided around the corner.

"Ah, it is child of Earth," said the figure in unsure English. Finley recognized the willowy silhouette of Dr. Smindle. Her voice was soft, almost nervous. As she came closer, Finley took an automatic step backward. She wasn't scared. The doctor happened to be carrying a tray of various colored-liquid-filled tubes. "My wants communications with child of Earth to impart portal scan."

It took Finley several seconds to understand what Dr. Smindle was trying to say. "So word has already gotten out? I'm sure Mr. Stravdas will give us our portal tickets tonight."

Dr. Thoss Smindle furrowed the klaums on her forehead

while trying to decipher the child's words. *Gotten out?* She was unsure what that meant. What did the portal ticket have to do with the Earth child's portal scan? She thought to herself: *Is the child ill or is she upset?*

Then, as she inspected her tray of tonics, Dr. Smindle thought: *I'm sure I can brew a tonic for that.*

Her visualization of various tonic ingredients was disrupted when the child of Earth jerked her head upright and yelled, "Of course I'm upset, but I don't want a stupid tonic! I want the adults in my life to work things out and not just walk away."

Shocked, the doctor asked, "Did child of Earth just—?"

Just then another voice interrupted the conversation. "Finley-bug, is that you I hear yelling?" CeCe asked from her open doorway.

"Oh, thank God," breathed the child.

After she watched the child of Earth run down the hallway, Dr. Smindle made her way to the queen's room of business. This was a new development.

Finley ran faster than she'd ever ran before. Which meant she didn't slow down when she crashed into CeCe, wrapping her arms around the elder girl's waist like she was a life raft.

They stumbled backward and were saved by a sturdy railing that opened up to the grand ballroom below.

"What's wrong?" CeCe asked as she held Finley tight.

"Mom says we're leaving tonight, and I don't want to go," Finley said through the catch in her throat. She hated the way she looked and sounded when crying. It was like her body refused to obey her, as if she was an alien even to herself.

Four floors down, Finley witnessed a bunch of peopling milling about, setting up buffet tables. Queen Uska was there, too, her regal figure placing chairs at dining tables. Everyone seemed to pitch in on Vraithe. Not even the queen was immune from palace chores.

CeCe ran her hand over her hair, smoothing down her static-prone locks. CeCe wasn't much taller than Finley, but there was still a world of difference between a fifteen-year-old girl and a nineteen-year-old woman. "Listen, Finley-bug, I'll be back on Earth soon, too. You're just a portal trip away. There's a minor portal in New York City. Promise me that you'll come visit me. Heck, come stay for the summer. We will be sophisticated in the city."

At that, Finley stopped crying. *Her, sophisticated?*

"Really, you want me to visit you? In New York City? Where you're famous?"

CeCe smiled down at her. "And here I thought that we were best buds. If you don't want to come..."

Finley shook her head furiously. "No, I *want* to come. I'll be there. I'm sure Mom will let me." Well, she wasn't so sure, but Finley was hopeful.

"Well, that's a relief," CeCe said with animated flare, playing up her job as an actress. "I was beginning to think you thought I stunk to high heaven."

"No, never!" Finley said through a laugh that turned into a hiccup.

Together they looked down at the almost set up ballroom. "True to her word, Queen Uska said this would be an intimate dinner. Correct me if I am wrong, but I spot only five tables."

"But why use the ballroom?" Finley asked. She spotted Serstene. He was pushing something that looked suspiciously like a cotton candy machine. "It almost looks like she's setting up a carnival."

She heard CeCe's chuckle before she felt CeCe's pointed stare, silver eyebrows knitted together. "My aunt is really going all out for you and your mom." Finley saw the quizzical expression etched into CeCe's features. "I wonder why."

Finley was just as curious.

"I'm not sure either. She's been very nice to us, though. Everyone has been."

"Even Areola?"

"Yes, even Areola," Finley said with a chuckle at saying the name out loud, "even though I can tell she *wants* to be ornery. I imagine she's nice to us because Queen Uska wished for it."

"Not much gets by you, Finley. What did Dr. Smindle want?"

Finley rolled her eyes. "Something about a portal scan and brewing me a special tonic."

"Dr. Smindle is incredibly shy but she's a wizard at brewing one-of-a-kind tonics. Years ago, my dear mother complained that my father's sneezes were too loud, and wouldn't you know it, Dr. Smindle brewed two tonics. One for my father, to soften his sneezes, and one for my mother, to trick her brain into not hearing it."

"I've been meaning to ask, where *are* your parents?"

"They have been cruising the stars for three years now, visiting all the celestial landmarks. It is a common thing to do once their secondary relatives—what Earth calls *children*—are adults. Mom and Dad are having a good time. They are constantly blowing up my phone with pictures."

"Very cool," she said while also thinking, *It must be nice to have parents who got along and loved one another.*

CeCe must have sensed the direction of Finley's thoughts because her thoughtful expression brightened when she said, "Why don't you go downstairs and help Serstene. I promise not to tell anyone if you happen to eat some cotton candy before the main meal."

✧✧✧

Sitting in her parked car across from Mara's house, Dessa put her phone away and bristled. She'd just finished watching a clip of Calix's interview with CNN. What an asshole. How dare he suggest that Mara was secretly poisoning Finley for attention. If looks could kill, her phone would have so many cracks in it right now.

Calix was, by all accounts, very handsome and charismatic. Put a military uniform on him and she understood why Mara fell for him all those years ago. That said, there was something mean about him. Calix's entire persona felt made-up. It was like his face had been put together from various male facial parts cut out of magazines. His mouth irritated her, his eyes were like chips of hard-packed dirt, his forehead reminded her of plastic Tupperware, and, even though Dessa was not violent, his square jaw begged to be punched.

All said, he knew how to work with what he had. His expressions were calculated to elicit specific reactions. He looked *just* disheveled enough—rolled-up sleeves, five o'clock shadow—to suggest he'd been out in the cold physically searching for their bodies in the snow. His voice was like an overdose of honey. Calix poured it on thick and had the anchor eating out of his palm. By the time the interview concluded, a clueless viewer would have sympathized with Calix. He was just a father fighting an institution rigged against him. His last words were, "I just want my Finley back."

The interview aired last night, and other stations had picked it up and ran with it, airing clips and sound bites all through the day. The "Vet Mom" story had also been on recycle ever since it had aired. As Dessa sat in her car a block away from Mara's house, no one seemed to notice her, which was good considering local news stations had been filming updated news segments since yesterday in Mara's driveway.

Dessa called and left voicemails with each station, offering her perspective on Mara's character. As of yet, none had bothered to return her call. It was like they only wanted one side—Calix's side—since his version of events were sensational. She was just the crazy librarian who wanted airtime to bash the school board. Dessa had to admit, they weren't necessarily wrong in that assessment.

Was Dessa petty enough to purchase and mail a copy of *The Curse of Mathilda's Sorrow* to every member of the school board? Yes. Yes, she was.

Not all of the news clips were negative. There was a heartwarming story where a large group of Riley high school students banded together to read *The Curse of Mathilda's Sorrow* as a form of solidarity until Ms. Eldress was found safe and sound.

Mara and Finley could not get home fast enough. She'd eaten through all her book money for the month. Thankfully, Vikk had texted to let her know that he'd been able to secure an emergency portal reservation for them. Given the time differential, it would still be several more hours before they arrived at the Boston main portal.

The question of the century was: What excuse could Mara give for their sudden disappearance?

Vraitheians followed a certain protocol when bringing humans to Vraithe. Excuses and reasons were built into the plan—decoy airline tickets, mentioning to family members that they'd be driving cross-country, or just "going off the grid" for a week or two to unwind.

But things were different with Mara. Vikk hadn't been thinking straight when he'd decided to abduct her. Dessa suspected that, at first, his goal was not to disappoint Queen Uska. Their aunt was obsessed with all things Earthling military, which made sense since Qoral had left Vraithe because she wanted to join the military herself. Privately, Dessa suspected that Queen Uska was searching for her long-lost daughter.

Vikk, on the other hand, after meeting Mara, had immediately begun to funnel his decision-making processes through his heartstrings. Dessa wasn't mad about it. She *knew* they'd be a great match. Dessa would not be surprised if Vikk elected to give up everything, even his right to the throne, to be with her. How might the queen react to that? Truth was, there was something very special about Mara.

Too bad Calix had to show up at the wrong time to complicate things.

With things now quiet outside Mara's house, Dessa let out a wide yawn and decided she could finally head home. The threat of more snow hung heavy in the air and she did not want her Mini Cooper to get trapped in place. She'd run out of gas and turn into an icy Popsicle. But before she pulled out of her cozy parking spot, a huge Ford F-150 Raptor guzzled up the residential street and swung into Mara's driveway.

The driver, a nimble woman wearing an unzipped cold weather parka, jumped down seconds later.

She was a tall, erect, authoritative figure that literally screamed, "Follow me into war." Her aura was one of self-assurance and determination. Dessa decided she did not want to mess with someone whose truck could flatten hers as if it were a Matchbox car. She hoped to the amethyst moon goddess that the woman was one of Mara's military friends and not someone doing Calix's dirty work.

Dessa nestled back into her seat and decided to stay just a little bit longer to find out.

When Mara entered Taloncourt's ballroom, she did not know what to expect. Just the word "ballroom" conjured up elegant images of couples dancing, a live orchestra, the clinking of champagne glasses, and formal-attired guests reciting stilted speeches written on napkins.

This was not that scene.

For one thing, there was screaming.

Children were running around playing games of catch and tag. There was an actual playground on the far end of the ball-room, complete with Vraitheian's version of monkey bars, slides, climbing walls, and tire swings.

There was a track-free train circling the space. Young children and teenagers alike were jumping on and off at will, with nary a concern for skinned knees or busted chins. Mara saw Finley in the mix. She and a boy—Serstene, if she wasn't mistaken—were sitting in the train's last compartment, sharing smiles and secrets. At least she wasn't as upset as she was earlier.

Wearing shorts and a T-shirt, Finley looked so healthy. It was like she'd just come in from the beach, complete with salt-sprayed, wind-tangled hair, glowing cheeks, and an envy-worthy suntan.

To be young and in love. As the train passed her location, it tooted its horn, which made Mara laugh. She smelled cotton candy, roasted nuts, and other, savory dishes akin to fried chicken or corndogs.

The smile on her face was not indicative of her true feelings. Mara was sad they were leaving. Finley had found young love. In equal measures, young love was worth its weight in gold *and* in heartache. It was a rite of passage every young person had to endure. For better or worse, every boy Finley met for a very long time would be measured against Serstene, whether she realized it or not.

There was a stage to the right of the dinner tables. It was long and wide and probably meant for stage plays instead of live bands, though, at the moment, a group of musicians were playing a fun, jaunty ditty that would appeal to, and compete with, noisy children.

Then it occurred to her. This was not a going-away party for Mara. It was a party for Finley.

Tears threatening, Mara had to take a second to process this before she could move farther into the ballroom. At the moment, no one seemed to have noticed her.

But delay she could not. After dinner, Vikk would escort them to the portalport with passage back to Boston. She had already packed their belongings, including the clothing and suitcase CeCe had given them. Since they were leaving right from dinner, her backpack was slung over one of her shoulders, she was pulling the suitcase behind her with one hand, and she was carrying their winter coats over her other arm.

Mara knew that Hannah had already made it to the town of Riley. She'd texted as soon as she pulled into her driveway. "Had to be sure you weren't here, Mara. For culpability purposes I cannot disclose my plans once I am face-to-face with Calix, but suffice to say he will not be happy to see me. If you get this text and do not want the privilege of bailing me from jail tonight, please text me back, Mara. I'm being serious."

Mara could easily picture Hannah and her ginormous Raptor truck gunning through the streets of Riley, calling out Calix's name using her truck's built-in speaker system. As *the* command sergeant major of an army division consisting of fifteen thousand soldiers, she had a truck that commanded attention.

Mara *wished* that she could text back. As much as she'd like to see Calix tuck tail and run back to whatever hideous man cave he'd crawled out from, Mara did not want Hannah to jeopardize her twenty-five-year military career. Calix was not worth it.

Across the ballroom, Mara spotted Queen Uska at the buffet table, serving food. Children were lined up, plates in hand, as she selected items for them. Mara's first order of business was to thank her for putting together such an amazing carnival. She was just heading in that direction when someone called out her name. Turning, she spotted CeCe at a face-painting station, beckoning to her.

"How about a going-away gift?" she asked, holding up a precision-tip paintbrush. CeCe's face was covered with stars, hearts, and snakes. Mara laughed. "Flusterline, orbel, or a gifendobe?"

"A what, or a what, or a what?"

CeCe grinned. "Right! Ok, do you want me to paint a snake, a star, or an amethyst moon flower?"

"The amethyst moon flower sounds enticing," she said, getting caught up in the festivities.

"You got it."

Moments later, CeCe held a mirror up to Mara's face.

Mara studied the amethyst moon flower, a mixture of pink and purple petals, that covered the apple of her left cheek. CeCe had many talents. "It's very pretty," she said with a smile.

"Yes, you are," CeCe smoothly interjected with a wink.

Mara studied the rest of her reflection. She seemed bright-eyed and rested. Her skin was dewy and radiant, as if she'd had a professional facial. Vraithe had been good for Finley, but it definitely agreed with her, too.

She left CeCe's station and made her way to the buffet table before realizing Queen Uska was no longer attending these duties. Instead, Dr. Vuzmuc handed her a plate.

"Most of this evening's menu is meant for the children's palates," they said with a smile, "but I think you will enjoy them. Since I spend half my time on Earth, I can easily tell you the Earth equivalent, if there is one. Vraithe have a vegan diet."

After loading her plate with Vraithe versions of fries, crackers, candied nuts, and teal-colored broccoli-like mini trees, Dr. Vuzmuc asked if they could join her.

"Of course," Mara said without hesitation.

She was hopeful that the doctor would have news of Finley's results. She nibbled on all the foods and found them simple but delicious. The nuts and broccoli-like vegetables were satisfyingly crunchy.

"I cannot stay long since I must complete an errand for the queen, but I wanted to ask: Does Finley have a regular doctor? What clinic do you take her to?"

"We are still within the military medical system. Finley sees a doctor at the local military hospital. Why do you ask?"

"I've had difficulty accessing her health records to get a full medical history, but that would explain it. I am confident we will have Finley's results tomorrow. I know you are leaving tonight, but my team will get word to you as soon as possible."

Nodding, Mara said, "Thank you Dr. Vuzmuc."

They reached across the table to place their hands on top of Mara's. "We will figure it out together, Mara. Finley is a delightful child. I have a professional interest in seeing her happy and healthy, no matter what the results tell us."

"Thank you." Mara couldn't make heads or tails if Dr. Vuzmuc felt positive or negative about Finley's pending results, but before she could ask for clarification, the doctor looked at their timepiece, stood, bowed, and exited the ballroom through a side door.

Vikk watched and waited his turn. He'd been checking the time, willing it to slow down. Instead, the clock laughed at him with each passing minute that depleted his time with Mara and rushed its hand toward the moment when he would escort them to the portalport.

He watched as Keiji talked to Mara, then left through the ballroom's back entrance. Vikk was aware of the queen's errand for Keiji, though he had his doubts of it working as flawlessly as his aunt predicted.

The time differential between Earth and Vraithe *could* work in their favor, but Vikk worried they'd executed their part too late.

"Never doubt my wisdom, Vikkolo," Queen Uska said from her room of business less than an hour ago. "I calculate Keiji will arrive at the Boston portal with enough time to move Mara's truck and get back to the portal to greet them before they arrive."

"If Earth's authorities catch on," Vikk had said, furiously running a hand through his hair, "all is lost. I won't be there to help them figure things out."

Queen Uska merely smiled at that. "No, Vikkolo. I have been observing Good General Mara Eldress very closely. She does not require your assistance. She will know what to do once presented with options."

At the time, Vikk's mind focused on the word "options." He wanted her to choose him. *Choose him over Earth?* He knew it would be a long shot.

Now, however, as he watched her fidget with the food on her plate, he approached her. "Hello," he said. "I like your amethyst moon flower."

She smiled up at him. It was an honest smile, one without heavy thought or the weight of the world pressing in around her. In a matter of days, she'd traveled to an entirely new planet, met people she'd consider aliens even though everyone here considered *her* the alien, all while disrupting her entire life back on Earth.

Vikk was responsible for all of it.

"Thanks," she said, rubbing the back of her neck. He acknowledged that he towered over her, especially while she was sitting.

"We have a little bit of time before I have to take you and

Finley to the portalport. Would you care to take a stroll through Taloncourt's gardens? They are lovely in the moonlight."

Mara took him in. He was dressed casually in loose-fitting jeans and a faded T-shirt that might have been a shade of coral at some point in its life. Now, though, it was a snug, dusty-pink shirt that accentuated his muscular chest, shoulders, and arms.

She knew that beneath his shirt she'd see swirls of dark tattoos. In fact, through the faded fabric, she thought she saw a shadowy glimmer of them.

"Yes, that sounds nice."

Mara welcomed the idea of spending a few quiet moments with him. Perhaps they could part on good terms. She would not make promises, but she would not rebuff kisses.

His wide smile melted the beating organ thumping away at her ribcage like a prisoner attempting to slip through jail cell bars.

The sky was an amethyst blanket of shimmering stars. The moon rose high, illuminating the glimmering jewels embedded in Taloncourt's sable walls. One did not need a lantern on a night like this.

Vikk's hand clasped hers and she looked up into his moonlit face. Mara wanted to trace the lines of his face, over his eyebrows, his cheeks, his full lips.

Instead, she squeezed his hand. Mara was not a teenager, so why did her belly fill with butterflies?

Children chased blinking bugs in the distant meadow. The hum and chirrup of birds gave a gentle sense of vibration once she and Vikk entered the palace's garden path. It was a maze of sorts, complete with tall shrubs and arched trellises decorated with cascading flowers giving off scents of amber and honey.

Along this path they were alone. The laughter and screams

of the children at play were well off in the distance and for all intents and purposes they were on a distant planet, hidden from all prying eyes except the moon's single, piercing gaze.

It felt like anything was possible under the amethyst moon.

"What prize awaits us in the middle?" Mara asked. "A water fountain?"

"It depends on what your heart desires," he answered. She thought he was teasing her, but he continued his story. "Vraitheian myth is that every garden has a soul. Finding the center is not the ultimate goal. The garden is curious about which paths you take to get there."

"So, it's the journey that's important?"

She could feel Vikk's smile. "Yes. If you are too eager, your prize might be a meager jar of bugs. If you are thoughtful and deliberate, you might be rewarded with a moon orb. Apparently, the center of the garden changes every night."

"What exactly is a moon orb?" Mara felt herself to be in some sort of trance. Oh, she was in control of her mind and her body, but for the moment she had let go of worry and obligation. She felt safe and comforted, as if someone she loved was telling her a bedtime story right before she fell asleep.

"Well, legend is that a moon orb is a token to allow the bearer to make a wish. Through some agreement, the garden and the amethyst moon will have concluded that you deserve to make a wish."

"Must you make the wish right then and there?"

Mara was envisioning a moon orb as a large, iridescent pearl.

"Some stories say yes, you must make your wish as soon as you are given your reward. Other versions say you can hold on to your moon orb forever, and wait until your dying breath to wish for just one more day."

As they turned down a new row, Mara's thoughts first went to Finley. If given the power of a wish, Mara would instantly wish for her daughter's good health. It was a no-brainer. "Does it matter who the wish bearer is?"

"Are you asking if only native Vraitheians are permitted? It is a valid question, one that I do not know the answer to. I've never attempted to win a wish." He leaned down to ask in her ear, "Shall we try? We have a little bit of time."

She looked into his moonlit face. While there was a hint of promise in his voice, Vikk stood as still as a marble statue. Mara thought about the future. Would she see him again? Was this their last night together?

Was she not entitled to some guilt-free pleasure before she returned to Earth to face the consequences waiting her there?

Mara Eldress had always played by the rules.

She remembered the way his glorious body looked naked. The way he went down on her, the bone-crushing orgasm that flooded her body.

Perhaps, just this one time, she would do what *she* wanted.

"It wouldn't hurt to add a moon orb to my collection," she said, leaning into him. "Lead the way."

# SIXTEEN

As they walked side-by-side, Vikk was reassured by the way Mara held his hand. Strong, secure, steady. Her hair glowed in the purple moonlight. Her eyes were like sparking gems as she viewed the garden's treasured blooms.

He wanted to make her last night on Vraithe meaningful.

In all his life, he'd never once felt the need for romantic reassurance. Not because he was confident in his abilities to keep his mate happy. Rather, it was because he was mostly inexperienced in all things romance. Before, his black locket had always prevented his heartstrings from becoming too attached.

His hand automatically went to his chest. Without the locket, he felt raw and emotional. Vulnerable to heartbreak.

"Do you bring all your girlfriends here?" Mara asked. He detected the smile in her voice. There was a hint of coyness, too. She was teasing him and he liked it.

"In all honesty, no. I haven't thought of the garden in years. Young lovers discovering themselves often come here, and find secret alcoves to experiment away from prying eyes." He grew thoughtful. "In our language, the term 'moon orb' is sometimes a euphemism for sexual awakening."

The more Vikk thought about it, the more he felt the term applied to him, too. Sure, his eyes had been *open* for forty years, but had he ever been more *awake* than he was now, with Mara?

As they turned corners, went under heady-bloomed trellises, and stepped over mini bridges with trickling water underneath, Vikk felt as if he'd been holding his breath for all those years.

Had flowers ever smelled so sweet? Had the moon glow ever been this bright? Had his body ever tingled and ached and desired and demanded this much? Had one simple touch sent him over the edge?

Without his locket, he felt the powerful force of their connection. Even if he never touched her, kissed her, made love to her, the connection alone was enough to power a lifetime of joy.

"I think I hear water," Mara said.

Hands still interlaced, she picked up their pace, and he happily let her lead. As they rounded the last corner, the garden opened. In the center was a black jade water fountain. Lights shone from beneath the water, casting dancing shadows on the nearby bench.

The ground was a soft blue blanket where tiny insects blinked on and off. Vikk did not see any other entry or exit from the center, except the way they'd come. Provided no one entered the garden after them, they would not be interrupted.

He looked at Mara, reading her aura, which matched his feelings exactly, and felt a quickening low in his belly. Heat rising, he considered the possibilities. They didn't have all the time in the world, but they had enough.

Vikk led her to the bench and sat.

But instead of sitting beside him, Mara surprised him by straddling his lap and crushed her lips to his.

Delightful shivers ran down her spine when Vikk moaned into her mouth. His pebbled tongue found hers before deepening the kiss.

His strong arms ensnared her, pulling her into him. Mara felt his heat, his energy, his pulsing cock.

Or rather, his *cocks*. Plural.

Her core pulsed at the thought of sliding down on his cocks, opening herself to him, taking, giving, demanding every last fiber of his being. Heat flared through her body. His kisses were long and slow, but greedy, and his mouth captured her whispered moans of pleasure.

Mara wasn't afraid of being loud.

As hot as she felt, their embrace did not feel frantic or rushed. Through their clothes, she gyrated against his bulging erection, enjoying the sensation of rough fabric rubbing against her most sensitive parts.

"I would like to finish what we started earlier," Mara murmured, her voice soft, quiet.

"Me, too," Vikk said, nipping at her ear and neck. He pulled off his shirt before removing Mara's shirt and bra.

She pressed her bare skin against his smooth chest. Her breasts were heavy, achy, as her nipples hardened from the combination of his touch and the cool evening air.

His skin was strong and muscular beneath her fingertips. His large hands roamed across her shoulders and lower back, kneading, skimming, his gentle fingers running along the outer portion of her breasts.

Vikk lifted her to a standing position, then removed his pants to reveal himself to her. Muscles rippling, he stood before her like a Greek god. His erection was impossibly thick, the tips glistening.

"See what you do to me?" he said in a husky voice that

drenched her. Her pussy pulsed and ached. She wanted to be stretched from the inside out by his combined cocks.

His hand went around the base of his cocks. Squeezing, liquid dribbled from both tips, which he used to lubricate himself.

An erotic surge went through Mara. She was jealous of his hand.

She felt the urge to fall to her knees, to catch his essence with an outstretched tongue and open mouth. Oh, she'd never be able to take him fully in her mouth, but she would be an eager participant. Mara pictured him ruthlessly fucking her mouth, his cocks sliding past her teeth, down her throat, as his balls slapped the underside of her chin.

A grin spread across his face. Just this once she *hoped* he could read her mind.

But no, that would not be tonight.

Tonight was one of exploration.

Mara stepped out of her pants, and removed her panties.

"You are magnificently beautiful, Mara Eldress."

"Ditto, Vikk Stravdas. I want you to sit on the bench," she instructed.

He sat, legs spread. As he sat, watching her, he continued to spread his essence up and down the length of his cocks. A slow hand job. With his girth and size, Mara needed all the lubrication possible. She wanted *all* of him inside her.

She climbed onto his lap, her knees on the cold bench, and slid her clit against the length of his scorchingly hot cocks. Vikk groaned in pleasure, and intense desire rippled out from her core, up her belly, into her chest.

His hands came to her hips.

"Do you like that?" he asked.

When Mara said yes against his lips, he cupped her ass to pull her closer.

Her hips rocked gently against him, a slight up and down

movement, over and over, as her wet pussy lips rubbed against the underside of his slick cocks. She was so turned on, even her inner thighs were sticky with their combined juices.

"I need more," she moaned.

"I don't want to hurt you."

"As long I control the speed and depth, you won't."

Mara rose up, angled closer, and hovered over the pulsing tips of his cocks. There was a moment of weightlessness. Collectively, they held their breath and it as if like time stopped. They were the only souls alive in that moment.

When his tip touched her opening, heat throbbed within her core.

Gently, oh so gently, Mara sank down. His tips slid in, stretching, seeking, before she rose a little only to sink down further, inch by inch. His mouth found hers and she could tell that Vikk was restraining himself, holding back from thrusting upward.

Her leg muscles twitched each time she rose and descended. Mara held onto his neck for dear life, his hands on her hips kept her steady.

She could not speak, so she let her body take over. The primal need within her knew what to do, knew how much of him she could withstand. In the glow of purple moonlight, a sense of hedonism flared out from their joining as she fucked him.

Here, in this magical garden, it felt natural for lovemaking to be soft, slow, measured. It was pleasurable and, at first, painful, the deeper she took him. Once Mara adjusted to his girth, pain gave way to waves of rapturous pleasure. Within a matter of minutes, Mara was sliding up and down three-quarters of his cocks. His breathy gasps each time she sank down made her heart race.

✧✧✧

Lips pressed against Mara's neck, Vikk said, "You have no idea how bad I want to thrust deep into you, but I can tell it is hurting you."

Mara smiled. "It's not you, but the bench. The concrete under my knees..."

Vikk did not like the idea of Mara being hurt in any way during their lovemaking. "I have an idea." He stood and lifted her with him. He was still inside her and he felt her squeeze her inner muscles against his pulsing girth. "Put your legs around my waist."

When he sat back down on the bench, Vikk was careful not to jolt Mara or to thrust up, lest he go too deep by accident.

He put his hands beneath her bottom and lifted her slowly up and down his cock. Pleasure exploded deep within his balls as Mara's slick heat scorched around his cocks.

"Oh, my God!" she gasped into his mouth, her teeth nibbling his bottom lip. Her hands were pulling at his neck and shoulders. "Oh, fuck, that's amazing."

Vikk was slow and steady with his pace and before long she was taking his full length. Mara's face was etched with pleasure, her mouth open, little sighs escaping. His chest clinched with pleasure, with love, with joy.

They were both drenched with sweat. He could fuck her like this all night.

Then he lifted her, allowing his two cocks to separate.

As he lowered her, one cock reentered her quivering cunt. The second cock slid semi-firmly against her inner folds and sensitive clit.

Mara cried out in so much pleasure that she thought she might black out.

He lifted her again, rejoined his two cocks, and her pussy swallowed *all* of him.

Mara groaned. "Fuck, that feels amazing."

Could a woman die from too much pleasure? She enjoyed the fact that he was carrying all her weight. The pleasure his cocks were giving her was one for the memory books. She'd never felt so full, so wet, so aroused.

Looking down, she watched their joining bodies as he lifted her again. When he separated his cocks, she saw the front cock sluice against her clit while the inner one slid nice and long inside her. She'd never been fucked so good.

"Keep doing it that way," she said, panting, her slick skin against his. While their movements were not out of control, both were panting and breathing heavily.

Her core pulsed wildly, the intensity building higher and higher. She didn't know how long he could continue to lift all of her weight up and down, but she wasn't far away from a massive climax.

And when the tip of the outer cock started to gently smack her clit, sparks of pleasure radiated from her center. She saw stars, and swore she was going to die at any moment. Just pass out from the sheer ecstasy shooting through her body.

Vikk's breathing came out frantic, uncontrolled. His eyes were dark and expressive. Lust and something more, something *deeper*, stared back at her. Mara pushed aside any thought of his heartstring mate. She wanted to believe that he felt the same way about her that she did for him.

Building and building, fibers uncoiled deep within her core. Warmth spread, hotter and hotter, until the blood flowing through her veins had transformed to molten lava. Her mouth crashed to Vikk's as he relentlessly fucked her. Everything burst within her, and all thought evaporated even as her body continued to accept Vikk's beautiful cocks.

"I'm coming, Vikk. Fuck. Fuck." She let out a guttural cry,

her head snapping back. Shooting stars blazed in the night sky and she wasn't sure if she'd imagined them or if it was real.

Mara's body shook and quivered, the climax extending for the longest time, until she was spent, exhausted.

Her climax gushed from her, coating his cocks, and he slipped easily in and out with quicker movements. His breathing was hot and heavy in her ear, his murmured Vraitheian words foreign to her, though their meaning was perfectly clear.

He picked her up and lay her on the soft grass. Vikk nestled himself between her thighs, his cocks pushing against her abused but satisfied pussy, and her legs spread wide for him.

She wanted his weight pressing down on her. She wanted his thrusts and grunts. He entered her quickly, without resistance, like a man on fire.

"Oh, Mara. *My* Mara," he moaned, burying himself deep within her, thrusting over and over, punishingly. His face was in her neck, biting, sucking, leaving ownership marks all the way down to her breasts.

Mara watched as he rose up slightly. She lifted her hips and watched the full length of him pumping inside her. He was thick, engorged, his body vibrating with unreleased tension. His thrusts became shorter, quicker, his shoulders taut, his face one of blended ecstasy and agony.

Deep within her, she felt him swell in size, stretching her like she'd never been stretched before.

His grunts filled the air as his body jerked. Heat radiated from his cocks as he spurted deep, hot, and heavy inside her. It was fire, delicious fire meant to consume, to own, to define, to claim. He'd just done all of that to her.

Mara welcomed it with open arms.

Stars blinked in the amethyst night and a breeze blanketed the garden, cooling their fevered skin. Vikk placed the gentlest of kisses on Mara's lips before he rolled over and pulled her close to him.

Together they lay on the grass, legs intertwined, drinking in heavenly stars, sharing their last moments together, in a magical garden that could make dreams and wishes come true.

Keiji Vuzmuc knew their way around human vehicles, including trucks. However, after arriving at the Boston portal-port terminal, and locating and warming up Mara's truck, the confirmation message Keiji sent to Queen Uska, ended with, "I was not informed it would be a manual transmission."

Keiji had no illusions the queen would respond, and she did not. She had asked for a favor and Keiji would not refuse the queen over a minor difficulty.

Before leaving the lot, Keiji placed a technological black-out device on the dashboard. The device would block traffic sensors, toll cameras, and even cell phones from capturing images of Mara's truck. That done, Keiji switched over to a human watch, calculated that the local Earth time was ten o'clock on Thursday morning, and got on the road.

It would be a long drive—at least seven and a half hours—to Washington, DC.

Serstene still could not believe that Finley would be leaving shortly. Oh, he'd known she would return to Earth at some point, but he figured he'd have more time than *this*. More than a matter of *days*. Hours, really. And now, with Finley clutching his arm as they walked outside the palace and into the breezy meadow, with a guide of glowing beetles and the mournful harmony of two lake larks, he looked up at the amethyst moon and groaned.

"What?" Finley asked. Her voice had taken on a dreamy quality, one that Serstene liked, but she shifted and he could tell she looked up into the sky, too. She let out a little sigh. It made him think she was dreaming about him and not about returning to Earth. Returning to her real life.

Returning to other people that did not include *him*.

He hadn't meant to make his groan audible. He didn't want her to see him upset. But then he thought more about that sentiment. Why not? Why shouldn't she know how he felt? There was no law against that. He pulled her in close. It wasn't cold out, not in the least, not with the warm fragrance of moon water lilies bathing them, but she nestled in just the same.

"I wish you didn't have to leave," he said softly. His heart-strings pinched. Would it always feel this way? The pinch? The hurt? The longing for Finley's touch, even if by accident, even if it was just her little pinky finger brushing up against his? This was agony.

They walked slowly in the direction of the reflective lake, where they'd bonded just the night prior. Was it only one day ago? It felt like eons. Being near Finley meant time moved both slowly and way too fast at the same time. How was that even possible? He'd never find that happy medium, would he?

Finley was thrilled with Serstene's words. "I wish I didn't either, but I have to."

Earlier, when they'd sat at the back of the kiddie train, she'd explained the situation to him. Serstene had a vague understanding that her mom would be in trouble if she went back to Earth without her, that authorities would think she'd done something terrible to her own daughter.

"Like what?" he'd asked.

She'd sensed the confusion in his words. "They'd probably think she murdered me or something," Finley had whispered since there were little kids around, not that any of them would really understand her English. She had her doubts that Vraitheian five-year-olds could comprehend the meaning behind the English word "murder."

Now, though, as she pressed herself against Serstene's firm form and gazed up at the plethora of shooting stars darting in front of the vast purple moon hanging low in the sky, and breathed in the warm floral scent tickling her senses, the idea of leaving him behind in a matter of hours felt like she was murdering herself. That she was cutting her heart out of her own chest, because that's what it felt like to leave the person your heart beats for ten thousand light years away.

When they reached the lake, they sat. "When will you return?" Serstene asked, kissing her temple.

Finley felt his breath on her ear, felt the rapid beating of his heart when she wrapped herself in his arms. She was small, but felt protected in his embrace.

The gentle waves lapped against the sparkling gemstone bank, where emeralds and diamonds reflected the moonlight alongside her beat-up canvas shoes. Finley imagined their huddled silhouettes outlined against the giant moon, how someone looking at them from behind would not hear the heartache thudding in her chest, how the low, melodic tone of the lake larks seemed to echo their feelings.

There was a pause before Finley responded, and for a moment Serstene almost stopped breathing, his hopes all but dashed.

"Hopefully soon," she said finally. She told him about a

thing called "Spring Break" and how she hoped her mom would let her return then. There was so much he didn't understand, not truly, about Earth's holidays and the school schedule. He'd barely passed his Earth anthropology class last year.

Finley shifted in his arms and a second later he spotted her Earth phone. He smiled for the photo and made her promise to send him a copy. She made a joke about texting him a hundred times a day, which, in his mind, seemed perfectly reasonable.

Serstene held her tight, knowing that in a matter of minutes they'd trudge back to the palace, that he'd watch her step through the portal, that he'd keep himself together up until she was out of his sight.

And after that, after she was gone, he didn't know what he'd do. Exist? He supposed he'd just exist until he could hold her in his arms again.

As Uska witnessed the development of two very important relationships from her fourth-floor balcony, her dearest friend *and* part-time antagonist, Areola came to stand beside her. The light from within her room of business barely reached the edge of the balcony, but cast enough illumination for Uska to see that the large klaums on Areola's forehead were furrowed with concern.

"Do you plan to interfere, Uska?" Areola's voice was deep and rich. There was a thread of warning, too, which, if Uska was being honest with herself, was not unwarranted.

"Interfere?" Uska asked softly, turning to address her friend. Areola's squat profile was studious in nature. Uska thought about what Dr. Smindle had just told her, that Finley might have *heard* her inner thoughts. Had Areola guessed? "Not in the way you think. I have no wish to repeat my past action."

"I am pleased to know you learned from your mistake," was Areola's simple, though devastating reply.

How long had she been waiting to say that line? Thirty years?

"I deserve that," Uska said. There was a slight tremble in her voice and Areola, not insensible to the feelings of others, placed a reassuring hand atop her own.

Side-by-side, the queen and her chief attendant watched as Finley and her young beau, Serstene Rozen, forged a direct path toward the palace's south entrance. Glowing prairie beetles briefly illuminated their faces as the pair navigated the meadow's grassy stalks.

Uska observed how the young sweethearts moved quickly while still seeming reluctant about it. Their coupling brought back a memory of the blossoming romance between Qoral and Boheerim. They had been about the same age. By itself, it was not painful, as young love was always brimming with joy, but in the years since, the memory had warped into a sad reminder of what was not to be. How Qoral should be standing beside her now in preparation for becoming ruler. Oh, her nephew would do a magnificent job, especially with a worthy mate at his side, but she wished things had turned out differently.

Still, the pang of regret and the roots of shame were buried deep in Uska's long-dormant heartstrings, heartstrings that, as of late, had slowly started to thaw.

To the left of the palace, Vikkolo and Mara emerged from the garden maze. Uska zeroed in on how they were holding hands, the warm nature of their body language, how their pace was anything but determined. By her estimation, they had mere minutes to reach the palace's portal. Vikkolo was cutting it close, but she knew he would not sabotage Mara and Finley's return.

Her nephew had too much honor for that, and there was too much at stake.

Areola, for her part, knew that Uska was not telling her everything. She watched her friend, the steady queen, and studied the direction of her gaze, which was mostly focused on Finley and Serstene. There was more going on than Uska was letting on. Areola had an inkling, but was wise enough to not ask. She did not want to ruin this quiet and reflective moment.

Her queen and dearest friend seemed to be learning a personal lesson that Areola was loath to interrupt. Uska had said she would not interfere, and Areola would have to trust that.

She was very patient, more patient than the queen deserved.

Below, the two couples met. All four then proceeded toward the palace's portal and were soon out of sight.

Uska sighed deeply, her hand on her chest. "Invite Serstene's parents to tea tomorrow," she said. "I should like to get to know them better."

Areola nodded, but hid her smile.

# Seventeen

As she escorted the quartet to Taloncourt's portal, Werlaun was having an out-of-body experience. No one was talking and, for some reason, she felt it was her responsibly to break the tension.

The queen's heir accompanied them, but only to Taloncourt's portal. Per the queen's orders, Stravdas was not authorized to enter. The fourth member of the party, young Serstene Rozen, who hailed from a lower branch of the queen's family, would also remain behind.

"Nice night," Werlaun said conversationally, even though no one bothered to respond. "I've never seen a more vibrant moon." She felt silly when she realized she'd pointed toward the sky. *Where else would the moon be?* she thought.

She chanced a glance over her shoulder. All four of them looked lovesick. She rolled her eyes. She was not the romantic type—her heartstrings were content as they were, thank you very much. When she looked up at that wholesome, lavender moon, she did not see love or romance or quivering heartstrings, no, she envisioned her dream vocation: a chef on an orbital cruise.

True to her word, she did not tell a soul that she was escorting Good-General Mara Eldress back to Earth. Even so, rumors were swirling that the Good-General was unhappy with Taloncourt's version of her book, that she disapproved of the final version of the twatsizzle scene, and that she could not wait to leave Vraithe. Word was that the film was being pulled from production. It was such a scandal. Why else would she leave at an unseemly hour after the portal had already closed for the day?

Werlaun itched to tell someone, anyone, but she'd kept her device offline the entire time. A heroic feat, for sure.

"Don't start the portal sequence just yet."

Werlaun jumped in surprise. It was Stravdas who spoke, his voice clipped and gruff. He looked downright prepared to tackle anyone who got in his way.

Her arm was already extended toward the portal, poised to scan the special mission visa valid for three passengers and three passengers *only*: herself, the Good-General, and the young human.

Werlaun dropped her arm and stepped away. She knew that the queen had refused to grant Stravdas's portal visa. That must explain his outburst.

"Five minutes, please," Stravdas all but begged after she inspected her timepiece.

Mara watched as their escort bowed and said, "I will let you say your goodbyes," before stepping to the side to afford them some semblance of privacy. The portal, which Mara had expected to be silvery and swirly, was just an empty wall. She assumed that it had to be activated, which must have been what Werlaun was about to do.

Glints from the amethyst moon slanted across the

portal's rounded Romanesque arches. Parts of the carved symbology were highlighted. Even though the Vraitheian words were foreign to her, she tried to memorize the shape of the patterns. She had hoped to avoid looking at Vikk at all, worried that she'd become emotional, that tears might come.

Part of her wanted to stay, but until her situation on Earth was resolved, her Earth-bound life must be her focus.

The garden was their goodbye, Mara thought, as her stomach flipped. After their lovemaking, he'd gently cleaned her with fountain water. She'd made a joke, asked if there'd been a moon orb. He shook his head but offered a sweet smile, saying his wish had already come true.

Mara had no ready answer for that.

She did not want to part on bad terms. She could not live here full time, not with Calix making her life a living hell, and even though his eyes told her he cared for her very much, as the queen's heir, Vikk had made it clear he could not live on Earth full-time.

An impasse, so to speak, made all the more painful when he suddenly pulled her into a full-body hug, his arms wrapped tightly around her. It was like he wanted her without fully committing.

That's how it felt, at least. Casual relationships might be normal on Vraithe, but Mara couldn't accept anything less than a full commitment.

"Will you let me know when you've made it back?" Vikk asked once he set her down. His voice was tight, raw, as he stepped away.

"I will."

A clammy hand slipped into hers. Mara looked down into her daughter's forlorn face. "I'm ready, Mom." Finley's voice was small yet stoic. She knew what was at stake. Serstene had already started back toward the palace. Yes, his shoulders were slumped over, but sometimes quick goodbyes were the best anyone could manage.

"Me, too," Mara said with a gentle smile. She squeezed her daughter's hand reassuringly. She wished she could tell Finley she'd see Serstene again, but Mara refused to make promises she could not keep. "We are ready, Werlaun."

Vikk watched helplessly as Werlaun activated the portal sequence.

His heartstrings reached for Mara. He wished he had more time. He wished that he told her how the felt, but to do so right now, in this moment, would have come across as selfish.

It felt as if part of him died when Mara and Finley stepped through the portico. Shadows covered their forms and he had to squint to see them.

He stood there in silence, his jaw clenched, though his mind roared as the portal swirled into action. A blast of silver illuminated the terminal, etching his retinas with their darkened silhouettes. Vikk thought Mara looked back, but it was too bright to know for sure.

Then the abyss that welcomed them took their essence away from him. His chest caved, his mind went blank, and his desire to live all but vanished.

Mara's stomach summersaulted and her chest felt as if it might crack open and unravel, as if parts and pieces of her might float away, never to be recaptured. Even though she'd gone through a handful of portals since coming to Vraithe, the tumultuous feeling warring inside her had absolutely *nothing* to do with her body floundering for the few seconds it took before her foot found solid purchase as they stepped through at the portalport, and *everything* to do with Vikk's parting expression.

He'd looked as if he was attending a funeral. Whose, though? Theirs or his?

Once they were all through, Werlaun deactivated the local portal and beckoned them to follow. "We must move with quickness."

The mostly dark portalport building loomed ahead, the bright moon lighting their path. A gentle breeze carried with it the scent of warm flowers as well as the jovial notes of music and singing. Mara searched for the origin. In the distance, one of the land spherules was lit up like an amusement park. Too bad that was not their destination. Her chest squeezed again.

Finley crushed her hand. "Everything is going to be okay, Good-General Mara Eldress," Finley said with a twinkle in her eye.

Mara let out a short burst of laughter that echoed in the stillness. Werlaun, who was speed walking ahead of them, spun around with alarm, ready to launch into action.

"We're coming, Werlaun," Mara said, then to placate the steward, added, "with quickness."

As they entered the portalport and passed by empty booths and swiveling book racks filled up with her memoir, Mara wondered when her daughter had become such a grownup? Finley had always been levelheaded—having to make your voice heard at dozens of doctor's appointments did that to a person—but her childlike features now bore a layer of maturity. Mara wasn't eager for her daughter to grow up.

*Be a child for a little bit longer, please.*

It wasn't fair to wish that, she knew. Her daughter was growing up, and to try to prevent that would do more harm than good.

The portalport terminal was clean, almost antiseptic, and

their footsteps squeaked on the polished floor. Up ahead someone called to Werlaun, who sprinted up the portalpod dais. Keys were produced to activate the portalpod and within seconds the pod hissed open. Werlaun's worried facial expressions were both comical and meaningful. Finley pointed at a countdown clock. They did not have time to dawdle. Every minute they delayed meant Calix had that much more time to ruin Mara's reputation.

"At least we know what to expect this time," Mara said as she and Finley buckled themselves into side-by-side chairs. The pod was cold and dim but not unwelcoming in nature. The seats were comfortable, and for those who stayed awake during transport, small porthole windows offered an outside view of outer space.

Werlaun pressed a series holographic buttons and the pod whistled, buzzed, and hissed into action. Within seconds Mara felt the numbing effects wash over her. She let it happen this time. There was no fighting it.

She'd have plenty fighting to do once she landed back on Earth.

Until then, as the sleepiness pushed in, she let her mind drift back to her time with Vikk, the warmth and heat of his gaze, the scorching trail of his fingers, the way their bodies molded together perfectly, how she felt safe and protected in his arms.

But more than any of that she felt like she belonged—not just with him, but on Vraithe, as if there were an unseen familial connection. That was all she'd ever wanted, right? A family. To belong.

Keiji Vuzmuc rarely thought much about Earthling travel or the time differential between Vraithe and Earth, but in this particular instance, as Keiji drove from Boston to Washington, DC., it was the only thing they thought about.

The queen had been certain their plan would work. Keiji shook their head after downing a fourth cup of coffee. Queen Uska had not been to Earth in decades, and she most certainly had not had to drive a rattle-prone pickup truck going south on Interstate 95.

If Keiji's brain did not melt due to the over-consumption of caffeine, the traffic congestion on I-95 would certainly finish the job.

Nevertheless, Keiji was in the service of the Vraitheian Queen.

While a necessary part of their civilization, human roads were not conducive for long-distance travel done quickly. However, because time passed faster on Earth than it did on Vraithe, it gave Keiji the additional hours needed to get to the Capitol Children's Hospital, leave Mara's truck in a parking garage, and make the necessary admittance arrangements.

Command Sergeant Major Hannah Atholms knew how to surveil and inspect a building for threats or clues. She'd been doing such things on and off the battlefield for decades, usually by detecting anomalies or anything that might detonate. Hannah wasn't too worried about anything detonating at Mara's place.

As plain as it was, Mara's house was a minefield of information. Within five minutes of searching the perimeter and letting herself inside—Mara had mailed her a spare key when she rented the place—Hannah could easily rattle off Mara and Finley's normal daily schedule, the last meal they'd eaten, their activities and habits. She could distinguish between the house's normal state and what the police had done, too. Thankfully they had not wrecked the place.

Hannah could also tell that either Mara or Finley had packed a small bag, perhaps for a day trip, and that there had been *zero* coercion in their disappearance. Sure, the house was in something of a mess—books were everywhere, Mara was clearly grading English assignments, and given the paints and a canvas easel in Finley's room, one of Finley's treatments was in the form of art therapy—but Hannah detected no signs of forced entry or a rushed exit. The police probably tried to make a bigger deal out of the pizza in the fridge, like maybe it showed evidence of a struggle, but Hannah surmised that one of them had merely dropped the box.

When Mara and Finley left, they had gone of their own accord. No amount of upside-down pizza boxes would tell her otherwise.

Hannah knew soldiers. They were her life's business. She knew when they were doing well, and when they were not. Mara was no longer a soldier, but she still had the mindset of one. Mara's fridge and pantry were full, which meant they had not planned for a long trip, but it also meant that she wasn't planning to harm either herself or her daughter. People did not go grocery shopping before ending it all.

All of this also meant that Mara's ex-husband, Calix, was not to blame here.

Oh, that irked her to no end. If anyone deserved to be throttled, it was Calix Eldress, especially after his last interview. How dare he insinuate such things about Mara? There were plenty of places Hannah could stash his body with no one the wiser. Daydreams for another time.

"Where are you, Mara?" Hannah muttered as she locked up the house. None of this was like Mara. It was like she'd fallen off the face of the Earth. "And why aren't you picking up your phone?"

Standing on the small porch, Hannah zipped up her parka and surveilled the view. The sky was gray and overcast, nearby yards displayed holiday decorations, and the streets were filled with mounds of snow.

That's when she spotted the tangerine Mini Cooper idling one block away. A few seconds later it pulled away from the curb. Hannah took stock of the driver, a tiny blond woman, who briefly made eye contact with her as she drove by.

*Finally*, Hannah rejoiced. *An anomaly.*

Adrenaline filling her body, she jumped into her truck. It was time to go get some answers.

Finley felt groggy and jet-lagged when she cracked her eyes open. Her limbs were thick and heavy and didn't seem to want to obey her commands. The pod rattled ever so slightly. It was moving slowly on a track, with a series of high-pitched metallic screeches that pinched her ears.

Turning, she saw that Mom was still asleep, head down, mouth gaping open.

"The return for Earthlings is jumbling," Werlaun said, speaking in English, "because you are traveling forward in time and your Earthling clock is confused." Werlaun smiled at her. "At least I think that is the reason. Vraitheians do not have clocks in our bodies so I am not really sure."

Looking through the little porthole, Finley caught glimpses of the dank Boston basement. The secret lair. The severely muted colors. They were definitely back on Earth.

"We do not rush dismount on the return," Werlaun said.

"Glad to know you don't just push us out." Finley let out a soft laugh. It was funny to imagine a literal clock with tiny ticking hands in your body. "How come I can see the portal contraptions?" She leaned over, peering further into the portal station. There were several unattended portal daises with darkened, stationary pods. "When we came the first time, we saw nothing but walls." *Walls with giant green graffiti penises.*

Werlaun nodded as the pod came to a stop. "Earthlings always ask." She stood and straightened her gray uniform. Finley had the impression the steward was about to launch into a lengthy speech. "The act of traveling through the portal unlocks an ocular mind block."

Finley waited for more but it did not come. She recalled that Mr. Stravdas had said something similar when they were entering the portal for the first time. "Meaning...now that I *know* about the portal, I can see it?" Finley guessed.

Werlaun smiled and said, "Knowing about it is one thing, but you have to have traveled through it, too. That's what ultimately unlocks the block."

"That makes sense. Do you know what time it is, on Earth?"

Werlaun's palm hovered over a holographic button and the dots and dashes on the holographic clock transformed into English. *Thursday, December 22nd, 11:11 a.m.* Finley did the math in her head. They'd spent all of Saturday and Sunday on Vraithe. If each day on Vraithe was two and a half days on Earth, then she and Mom had been gone for five Earth days. Her heart began to race. What had she done?

Her face flamed hot with shame. If only she'd texted Dad back and told him not to come, that she didn't want to go to the wedding, none of this would have happened. They could have spent a few more days on Vraithe, happy and carefree. She'd messed up so bad. It was her fault that Mom was in trouble. What if they put Mom in jail? What if she had to live with Dad?

Was Finley a selfish person, like Dad? All he cared about was prestige, status, and money. Did he even care about her? She'd checked her phone before they left Vraithe, and other than Dad sending her an *"I'm at your Mom's hop in let's go"* text and later a *"did your Mom put you up to this?"* message, there was nothing else.

No *"I hope you're doing OK"* or *"I am worried about you"* or even *"Just let me know you're safe."*

In contrast, Finley thought about Mr. Stravdas. She'd only known him a handful of days, but she'd bet a million dollars that he'd be super worried about her if he thought she went missing. Mr. Stravdas would actually *do* something to help find them. He would never appear on television pretending to be a victim.

Maybe she was being too hard on Dad. What if he just didn't know how to show how he felt? Like maybe he was stunted, emotionally. Finley considered that for a moment and realized she was deceiving herself. Either Dad did not care that she was missing, or he knew they weren't really missing and was using the situation to gain a national spotlight.

Both explanations were terrible.

Werlaun watched the child with interest. So many thoughts and feelings were flitting across the girl's face and aura circles. It must be exhausting to be an Earthling. So many feelings and emotions. Werlaun could almost hear the thoughts brewing in the child's head, as if perhaps Earthlings had their own form of RMO.

*How do they keep it all straight?*

Next to the girl, Good-General Mara Eldress stirred into wakefulness. Werlaun's instructions were not to activate her device until both Good-General Mara Eldress and Finley Eldress were alert. Everything from this point forward would be up to the Good-General. The queen's heir had been adamant on that front.

Werlaun was not brainless. She knew what this was all about. Stravdas was worried about keeping possession of his twatsizzle. But no one ever wanted to know Werlaun's thoughts on anything, so she kept them to herself.

She activated her device, sent the message as she'd been told, and waited for her next set of instructions.

Keiji Vuzmuc had just made it to the parking garage on the north side of the hospital campus and completed the admittance paperwork when Werlaun's message came through.

Mara and Finley had arrived the main portal in Boston.

Keiji checked the time. *This might work.*

Keiji kept a vehicle in the same garage and drove to a mini-portal located deep in the heart of Rock Creek Park.

Keiji replied to the steward's text: "Ten minutes out."

Mara assumed she'd battled an entire army while she slept. She felt combative, angry when she spotted Werlaun standing before her, a large holographic clock between them. So it was true: the world thought they'd been missing for five days.

*Vet Mom.*

Mara's mouth tasted like she'd been chewing on thin strips of metal. What other allegations had Calix accused her of by now? Kidnapping, murder, how about espionage?

"Mom," Finley said in singsong fashion, "we're back on Earth, safe and sound."

Mara opened her eyes and groaned. "Safe and sound, my foot. Why does it feel like we crash landed?"

To herself she asked, *Why does it feel like my chest is empty?*

"Werlaun says it is because our internal clocks are messed up. We've traveled into the future and our bodies are confused."

Werlaun held up a hand like a student in one of her classes. "Yes, Werlaun?" Mara asked with a wry grin while trying to rub feeling back into her chest.

"I apologize, but I forgot to mention the gravitational variance," Werlaun said. Her device dinged and she glanced down for a brief second before continuing. "Earth's gravity is two percent denser than on Vraithe. That is why you feel like boulders."

*Well, that was one way to put it,* Mara thought.

Mara looked at Finley and together they burst out laughing. "Thank you, Werlaun," Mara said as she wiped a few tears from her eyes. "I needed a good laugh. But," she said as she unbuckled her lap belt, "it is time to face the music."

"What music?" Werlaun asked, tilting her head from side to side. "I hear no music."

"It's an Earthling expression," Finley answered. "Can you open the pod? We'd like to dismount now."

When Werlaun failed to move, an uneasy feeling began to build in the pit of Mara's stomach. It wasn't physical danger, of that she was certain. Mara could take down Werlaun in a split second. No, the uneasy feeling was apprehension, the not knowing. Whatever Mara thought was going to happen next— i.e., get out of the pod, find her truck, and drive home and confront Calix—was not the real plan.

From what she could tell through the small porthole window, they were in the Boston terminal—she recognized the dank basement as they one they'd departed from. But instead of answering, the steward was studying her device, like she was awaiting orders.

Like she was *stalling*.

Mara didn't like the thought of not being in control of the

situation. And while no matter how she sliced it, she was not in control of much right now. She still wanted choices, even if they were limited in nature. So what was Werlaun waiting on?

"Werlaun?" Mara said, standing. She walked through the holographic clock and stood before the steward. "Who are you communicating with?"

"Taloncourt, of course," Werlaun said innocently. "The queen's heir says to tell you that Dr. Vuzmuc will meet you shortly."

Mara sat back down, her mind racing, her heart pounding. "What does Dr. Vuzmuc have to do with anything?" Pausing, she added, "Did Vikk say that Finley's results came in?"

Werlaun appeared to be stunned by the question. "I am just an escort, Good-General Mara Eldress. I operate the portalpods. You will need to ask Dr. Vuzmuc."

Eliza Brady valued tidiness, prompt attendance, and good manners. Even so, after educating thousands of students over the course of forty years, she had developed a measure of patience and leniency. No one could expect tidiness, promptness, or perfect manners from children.

However, the person standing unannounced at her doorstep at eleven in the morning during winter break was not a child, but a full-grown adult with the manners of a child. Calix Eldress, dressed like he was going to a boardroom and not looming on her porch, stood there, harassing his ex-wife's current employer. Dr. Brady resisted the urge to wave away the overpowering waft of his cologne that stung her eyes. What was wrong with the man? Did he really think he could go on national television and all but accuse Mara Eldress of deliberately causing her daughter's illness and then show up at her doorstep this morning as if visiting her was a normal occurrence? Bad manners, for sure.

"Listen, Dr. Brady," he said, pivoting smoothly when she refused to allow him inside, "I fully understand if you regret hiring Mara. I should have warned others about her unattractive qualities, but I didn't want to prejudice anyone against her. But I must say, I really admire your willingness to give her a shot when so many turned her down."

His expression conveyed just the right amount of concern, confidence, and confidentiality. *See how I'm trusting you with these inside secrets?* his sparkling dark eyes seemed to say. "I'm just here to help, to make everything better. For you, for me, for her. Mostly for her, of course."

Eliza had heard every trick and excuse in the book. Children thought were clever that way. She'd encountered a hundred of Calix Eldress's ilk throughout the years.

"Please leave," Eliza said with no emotion. Oh, he was clearly handsome and charming in that fake sort of way, but his ruthlessness shone through like the blinking bright red light of a fire alarm. If she were Mara, she'd disappear to get away from this man, too. "You are not welcome here."

Calix wanted to laugh in her face but instead he tried a new tactic on the old biddy. He nodded at her like he understood her sentiments. He even rubbed his eyes, which wasn't *all* for show. He'd hoped he could get someone to say something negative about Mara, just one person, but so far, no joy.

"I know this is a trying time, Dr. Brady, and I won't keep you. I just want you to know you can trust me. Has Mara contacted you? Did she say anything to you the last time you spoke? Even the smallest of details could help break the case. Disappearing the way she did is very concerning, but it's not necessarily out of the blue. She's done this before, sadly. Finley isn't healthy. I'm not sure if Mara ever mentioned our daughter to you. She liked to keep her hidden away at home, out of sight, if you catch my drift. If you know anything, you have a responsibility to tell the authorities."

Calix watched as the biddy's thin lips flattened even further. "The only drift I'm catching is the foul stench of your bad manners, Mr. Eldress," she said. "If you thought you could come here and besmirch one of my most promising teachers, you have a valuable lesson to learn, young man. You and your plastic face, your designer clothes, your practiced words carry no weight with me. As far as I am concerned, Mara is on a two-week vacation and you are disturbing my peace. Now if you will excuse me, my tea is getting cold."

With that, the ancient principal slammed the door in his face. Foul stench? Bad manners? Of all the nerve.

Calix knew the odds; *he*, the ex-husband, could not be the sole person accusing her. That was never a good look. There had to be *other* sources or else the media would sniff out alternate conclusions.

He hopped back in the toasty warm rental car and looked at his phone. Jasmine had sent him two texts. One was a Patti Stolz's news article. She'd done some digging, which had painted him in a not-so-flattering light. Thankfully, they'd used his professional photo for the article. Good-looking men always got a pass. Sure, he had his detractors, but his supporters far outweighed the naysayers.

Calix grinned. *Doesn't matter what they say about me. I had nothing to do with it.* He'd always come away innocent.

The second text was a link to a *Publisher's Weekly* feed update. National coverage of Mara's disappearance had generated heightened interest in her memoir. It had moved nine thousand units in the last two days alone. *Fighting for Her: A Soldier's Struggle* had become a #1 *New York Times* bestseller in the Nonfiction category and landed as the #9 bestseller in the Top Ten Overall.

Cursing, Calix crushed his phone in his hand. Bits and pieces of it fell to the driver's side footwell and he wiped his bloody hand on a microfiber towel he found in the glove box. He was too angry to feel any pain.

Good things were meant to happen to *him*, not Mara. He was the exceptional son of a distinguished and decorated army general. Mara was an orphaned guttersnipe. In no universe should she beat him.

He backed out of the principal's driveway.

*Where the hell are you, Mara?*

Calix's purpose had suddenly changed. The longer Mara was missing, the more interest her memoir would generate, and he couldn't have that.

No, now the goal was to actually find her and convince the world she was a fraud.

# EIGHTEEN

Vikk paced the carpet of his aunt's room of business, tracing a well-worn path between her desk and the balcony doors. He could not appreciate the inky sky or the serenading melody of a million insects humming in perfect unison. Not with his aunt's onyx eyes silently watching him, judging him.

Not with Mara gone.

To say that he was a hot mess was an understatement.

Having Mara so far away was eating away at his heart, his soul. His very essence was evaporating into thin air. The tug on his heartstrings was stretched almost to capacity, and he feared at any moment they would spread too taut, too thin, and snap. If that happened, he'd be a shell of himself.

No, that wasn't right. He was already a shell of himself. If his heartstrings detached, he'd expire. It was as simple as that. Mara was the oxygen for his lungs, the retinas for his eyesight, the joy in his mind.

Without her, Vikk had no reason to breathe, to see, to experience happiness. He felt hot and cold and clammy all over.

Beads of sweat trickled down his temples, his clothes clung to his skin, and he shivered.

He ran a hand through his hair, tangling it in the process. They'd been gone only for a few hours.

Mere hours.

*Goddess above*, he swore through clenched teeth. He thought he was made of sterner stuff. But that was before he met Mara.

"Aunt," Vikk said in a rough voice. There was no way he'd survive a lifetime of this torture. How had he made it to the age of forty without ever feeling lovesick? "If you care for me, unlock my portal visa. Grant me passage."

Uska followed her nephew's movements with clock-like precision. She suspected he was on the verge of figuring things out. She was an old, wise Vraitheian and had seen this play out before, with others.

Vikkolo had to come to a decision.

There would be a moment when his mind and his heartstrings would merge and his way forward would become clear. A true heartstring connection was for a lifetime, but the heartstrings alone could not be in full control. The Vraitheian's mind must be in agreement, and Vikkolo, her dear, prime relative, could not yet see his path.

He must quiet his heartstrings and listen to his mind.

Uska smiled as he continued to pace—stomp, really—around her room of business.

And since he was her business at the present, she stayed put, watching, observing.

"You may leave Vraithe at any time, Vikkolo," Uska said. "Every adult Vraitheian has that right."

Her prime relative jerked his head in her direction. "I am

aware of my rights, Aunt." His black eyes flickered darkly. *Such intensity,* Uska thought. "Do not mistake which portal visa I am asking for."

Vikkolo had always had it so easy, too easy, really. As her heir, his path had been mapped for him after Qoral ran away. And though Vikkolo had never rejected or resented his role, Uska could never tell if his whole heart was in it. He would become Vraitheian ruler because she and fourteen other prefects all agreed it was his destiny. However, Vraitheians enjoyed long lives, and Uska could easily be expected to rule for decades longer. It wasn't as if she was expected to immediately step down.

Besides, other options had recently come to light.

When Qoral had abdicated, many presumed that Uska had invalidated her portal visa, that she'd denied Qoral the chance of returning. The rumors were wrong—she'd never taken any such action against Qoral or Boheerim. Their portal visa was valid to this day. She renewed it annually.

Uska did not enjoy playing politics or matchmaker. She did not *need* Vikkolo to take over at the present, but she was curious to see what her heir would do if she placed an obstacle in his path.

"As I said, Vikkolo," Uska said, watching him closely. He vibrated with so much pent-up energy he could have been mistaken for a shooting star. "You have full permission to travel to Earth. I have no intention of preventing that, nor would I. However, at this time, I have revoked your return visa. Should you go, I believe you understand the ramifications."

Uska let that hang in the air.

Her nephew's mouth opened and closed several times. He most definitely wanted to give her a piece of his mind, and what a song it would be. In the end, he wisely decided not to say anything. Instead, he pivoted on his heel, exited her room of business, and slammed the door behind him.

Uska sat back in her chair, amused.

She could not predict the future, nor would she want to. She liked surprises. She hoped that Vikkolo did not disappoint her.

As Dessa drove away from Mara's house, she wasn't at first aware that she was being followed. In hindsight, she acknowledged that she should have noticed such things. The truck was, after all, the size of a bus, very loud, and literally right behind her. In her defense, she was a high school librarian, not a detective.

After several turns in and around a snow-filled Riley Township, and as she carefully proceeded to head toward the main portal in Boston, Dessa decided to check out the true crime podcast—*Where is Mara?*—that was doing a deep dive into Mara's memoir. The podcasters had come up with two possible theories on Mara's disappearance: one was that the military wanted to gag Mara, and Finley was simply a victim of circumstance.

The other theory, to Dessa's delight, was that Mara and Finley had been abducted by aliens.

Each episode was short, fifteen to twenty minutes long, and by episode three, Dessa realized she'd done a terrible job in accurately translating Mara's memoir. There were no swords, no severed twatsizzles, no lengthy sex-filled battles to correct atmospheric gravitational disturbances.

*What boring lives humans lead,* she thought to herself as she started episode four. Instead, with her Vraitheian translation, Dessa had elected to add in dangerous sword fights and erotically charged sex scenes.

In truth, Dessa was not very familiar with the Earthling military or its terminology, so in her rush to translate it, she skipped over many parts while reading it, which meant she'd confused the name "Finley" with "feline." She felt bad about that part.

However, the longer she listened to the podcast, the more it became astoundingly clear that she owed Mara an apology. Dessa had massively misunderstood Mara's military medical retirement, her traumatic brain injury, and her and her daughter's journey toward healing, education, and starting over in a new town with a new job.

That said, Dessa found solace in the fact that even with her mistranslation, Calix still ended up as Enemy-General Calix. No matter which planet he lived on, he'd not be welcome.

Her other comfort was that without her translation—er, *mis*translation—Vikk would never have adapted the book for a Taloncourt feature film, and he would not have asked Mara to help him with the script. Once all the facts were taken into consideration, Dessa felt that *no* blame could be attached to her and that everyone should be thanking her.

She'd just started on the fifth episode as she pulled into a parking lot near the Old State House building. With her attention fully on the podcast, she crossed the lot and opened the doorway to the stairwell that lead to the secret basement next to the East Boston Tunnel station.

When the door didn't close behind her, Dessa removed her earbuds, turned, and saw the shadow in the doorway.

The figure slowly advanced while Dessa stood still, waiting with bated breath. Step. Step. Step.

There was a thudding against her chest, pressing hard against her Vraitheian black locket, telling her to pay attention. She recognized the parka, the boots, the lean figure. Closer and closer she came. Dessa breathed her in. She smelled like the majestic Zilverine Mountain forest after a rain. Mature. Solid. Real. Dependable.

Deep down, Dessa had known the stranger would follow

her after they'd locked eyes back at Mara's house. The age difference might be an issue, but some things were meant to be.

Mara did not like how it felt like she was standing on the edge of a cliff. She'd feel more secure about her situation if Vikk were standing beside her. Not because he'd keep her from falling over the edge, but that they could fall over together. Live or die, win or fail, as long as you were with those who loved you, who had your back, you never truly died, you never truly failed. You learned. You grew. Your heart expanded because you could trust yourself to let others in. To trust others. To love again.

At the moment, a dull ache throbbed behind her eyes, and she felt like a book with half the pages torn out. She didn't know how this story was going to end.

She'd refused to look at her phone, or clips of news, or social media. She entrusted Finley to be the keeper of the phones for the time being.

They'd convinced Werlaun to let them outside of the portalpod, but because the portal had a plethora of stewards on hand, they were not permitted to leave the portal station.

Additionally, because everyone seemed to know who Mara Eldress was—she'd overheard, "Is that Good-General Mara Eldress?" whispered numerous times now—they'd acquired an audience, with Werlaun only too happy to translate questions, comments, and answers.

"You should be a public relations representative," Finley said to Werlaun, to which Werlaun, her brows furrowed, asked, "Are public relations representatives chefs on Starfleet cruise lines?"

This led into a fevered conversation about Earthling cruise

lines, where Werlaun seemed to question her entire existence and future career path.

Now that Mara was accustomed to Vraitheian citizens, she perceived them as they were, and not through a glamour veil. If someone appeared to look human, she knew they were, in fact, human. Throngs of individuals came and went. Pods arrived and departed with extreme precision. Various announcements were made, all of which were in Vraitheian. But all in all, the portalport still had the look and feel of a dank and dark, though well-functioning, airport.

Finley watched her mother closely. She was looking for signs of stress, a migraine, of extreme fatigue, and was pleased to see that Mom was handling things fairly well.

Of course, things were not ideal. They were being detained in a secret alien lair, but—if you did not count Mom's book groupies—they were not being harassed. One of the stewards had kindly provided refreshments and offered them a place to sit while they awaited Dr. Vuzmuc, who was traveling on the queen's emergency visa.

Finley had no qualms with being the "keeper of the phones."

On the bright side, she'd sent the photo to Serstene, who replied back right away.

On the not-so-bright side, Dad had appeared on additional news stations while the more sensational prime-time cable show, *Patti Stoltz Program*, trotted out an alleged murder-for-hire theory while also stating that military sources would neither confirm or deny that either of her parents had ever served in the military. The last clip she watched showed Mom's former literary agent making the morning news rounds to discuss how he'd always believed in Mom's memoir, which was apparently a bestseller now. Go figure.

Mom practically pounced when Dr. Vuzmuc, who was breathing heavily, as if they'd flown all the way from Vraithe, stepped out of a nearby pod.

"Hello Mara, Finley," the doctor said with a magnanimous bow. "I arrived as soon as humanly possible, and I mean that quite literally."

Finley felt a ping of disappointment when it became apparent that Mr. Stravdas was not with Dr. Vuzmuc. While Mom was stealthy about it, she ever-so-slightly craned her neck to see if Mr. Stravdas was behind the doctor, and her expression gently crumpled before she resumed her normal stoic expression.

"Please tell me you have legitimate information and are not here to babysit us," Mom said, gesturing toward the crowd of fans and stewards. "It's lost its appeal."

Dr. Vuzmuc nodded. "I would have discussed the queen's plan on Vraithe, but we were not sure if the timing of it all would work out, due to the time differential. You might not remember, but when we first met, I mentioned that I maintain a doctoral residence at the Capitol Children's Hospital, in Washington, DC. When I left Vraithe last night, I came here, collected your truck, and drove many hours and six coffee cups' worth to the hospital. By the by, you should really think about asking a professional to examine your struts and steering alignment. Most atrocious, Mara."

Mara was about to confront the good doctor on taking her truck without permission, but Dr. Vuzmuc gave her such a stern, almost parental look, as if expecting a response to their last statement, that Mara, who was too tired for any of this, sighed and said, "Rest assured, as soon as my schedule permits —and as soon as I understand *why* you took my truck and left it five states away—I will take it to the mechanic. Please continue... if it is no trouble."

"Yes, of course, thank you, Mara," Dr. Vuzmuc said. "Only moments ago, I boarded a mini-portal near the hospital and came here, straight away. I apologize for keeping you waiting. Now, as I understand it, you have been reported as missing for several days here on Earth. Vikk, with the queen's blessing, suggested that if I parked your truck in the hospital's parking garage and backdated Finley's admittance date to last Saturday, then it would appear that she has been in Washington, DC., as my patient, the entire time. Which would mean you—"

"Are not missing," Finley cut in.

"Affirmative," Dr. Vuzmuc said with a wide smile.

"That's..." Mara was astounded. It was a far better plan than she had whipped up in her head, which was to go straight to the police, produce a not-dead-slash-not-kidnapped Finley, and claim they'd been at a cabin so that she could draft her next book. "Vikk thought of this? He didn't say anything about it to me."

Worry stole across Dr. Vuzmuc's amethyst face. "If this plan is unsatisfactory, you are not obligated to accept. You are free to proceed at your own direction. After Vikk consulted the queen, she spoke with me, and I readily agreed to my part of the plan. Because we did not know if it would come together, the queen did not want to raise false hope."

"No, no, it's a great plan," Mara said. She turned to Finley, who looked up from her phone just then. Was she texting Serstene? Letting him know that she missed him and couldn't wait to see him again? "What do you think? Will it solve our problems?"

Mara watched as a full spectrum of emotions flashed in the depths of Finley's eyes.

*No, it will not solve all of our problems, but it solves a major one.*

"I think it's our only option," Finley said, before smiling. "It's like a plot from a novel."

"Thank goodness," Dr. Vuzmuc breathed out. Mara guessed that the good doctor had been very worried she'd say no. They looked at their time piece. "We should take the next transport pod. The lunch hour at the hospital is a busy one, and if we get there before the next shift begins, we can slip in unnoticed."

Werlaun acted like a bouncer by parting right through Mara's groupies, directed their small group to the portal dais, then used the queen's royal visa to activate it for the next sequence. A dark black metal pod arrived with a flurry of wind and screeching brakes.

Mara wondered if this was like speeding on the highway. You could do it, but was it safe?

The pod hissed open, and the departure clock countdown materialized. They had just stepped into the pod as an eruption of shouts came from the portalport's main entrance. Looking back, Mara spotted Dessa Stravdas—rather, she believed it to be Dessa since it was her likeness, but instead of a tiny human, she saw a tiny, silver-hued Vraitheian with glittery silver hair piled on top of her head. What Mara mostly recognized was her ginormous puffy purple coat.

Mara heard someone call her name.

"Who is that?" Dr. Vuzmuc ducked to peer out through the pod's opening.

Mara casually said, "It's just Dessa."

"Um, Mom," Finley said at the same time, peering through the pod's small window. "Is that Hant Anna?"

"Hannah?" Mara asked incredulously, scanning the commotion. There was too much movement to see clearly. "There's no way—"

And *that's* when a shocked Mara saw her best friend, Hannah Atholms, a muscular and athletic, five foot, ten inch–

tall career soldier, being tackled and brought down at the steps of the pod's dais by the minuscule Dessa Stravdas.

"Werlaun, wait," Mara called out. "I know her. She's my best friend, Hannah Atholms. Can she come with us?"

"Absolutely not. No visa, no entrance, Good-General Mara Eldress. We try to not liquidate humans." Werlaun looked back at her from the control panel. "On purpose."

"Gross," Finley said with a little shudder.

The pod's countdown clock reached zero, the door hissed closed, and Mara and Finley were automatically locked into the pod's chairs. Seconds later the entire unit hurtled through one of Earth's planetary connected warp tunnels.

Vikk's chest was going numb. There wasn't much time before his heartstrings turned dormant, but he refused to don the Vraitheian black locket that would preserve his heartstrings. For Vikk, it was Mara forever, or no one.

At some point within the last ten minutes, Dr. Thoss Smindle had left behind a special tonic at his doorstep. "To enhance the numbing," her note read. The shy doctor wasn't known for her accurate predictions, but Vikk wasn't exactly keeping his emotions in check. It had to be incredibly apparent to others how he was feeling.

Vikk poured the bubbly tonic down the sink. He appreciated Dr. Smindle's concern, but he'd rather feel something—pain, torture, agony—than nothing at all.

He was doing a terrible job of scheduling his portal departure reservation and packing his belongings, while simultaneously maintaining text message strings on two different devices—his Earth smartphone and his Vraitheian device.

Thankfully, Finley replied when he asked if they'd made it back to Earth safely and if Dr. Vuzmuc had located them. He'd sent the note to Mara at first, but when he didn't hear back within what he felt was a reasonable time—he must have waited at least ten seconds—he'd reached out to Finley.

He could not have been more relieved that they'd accepted Dr. Vuzmuc's offer. He hoped Mara and Finley knew that they'd not just claimed his heart, but everyone's. News had already begun to spread about their situation on Earth. Queen Uska had even declared that Mara and Finley were being issued permanent visas to travel to and from Vraithe whenever they wanted.

That didn't sting at all. Vikk had zero problems with this arrangement. He threw clothing, toiletries, a large case of gems, and several other items into an oversized duffel bag. He'd happily wait for them on Earth whenever they visited Vraithe. He'd watch movies, bake pies, and learn Earthling languages.

Dessa, on the other hand, was doing her utmost damnedest to kill him. Vikk was trying to understand his dear sister's texts, and how Mara's best friend Hannah Atholms had found Dessa, followed her, and had gained admittance into the portalport entrance. One of those things, sure. Two, maybe he could see it happening. But all *three* events were permitted to occur under Dessa's watch?

Nope. Vikk did not buy it for one second, but his mind was not clear enough to solve the puzzle.

He rubbed his chest, cinched the duffel bag closed, left his suite, and made his way to the portalport.

Goodbye Taloncourt.

Goodbye Vraithe.

*Hello to the rest of my life.*

Disbelieving her own eyes, Hannah watched Mara and Finley, along with a woman wearing a starched gray suit and a very tall person dressed in a doctor's white coat, disappear into thin air. Just...poof!

"Have I died?" Hannah wheezed. She was face down on the scuffed, concrete floor. This was embarrassing because it wasn't even that hard of a tackle. But maybe she'd hit her head. "Is this hell?"

"What did you say?" the voice behind her ear asked.

Why did it have to be such a pleasing voice? Hannah wondered. She never let such things get to her.

Confusion *was* one of the first signs of a concussion.

Hannah tried to shift but the weight on her back was not budging. Granted, it was not a heavy weight. The young woman who clobbered her was the size of a poodle, but somehow possessed the obstinate strength of a sled dog.

Hannah ran through scenarios in her head. The crowd around their prone forms started to dissipate. She'd found the exit, several possible weapons, and was taking stock of her petite detainer. Except Hannah didn't want to move. Not really. This in itself was alarming

"Perhaps if you got off my back, we could talk facing each other. It might make hearing the words coming from my mouth somewhat easier."

Dear Lord, why did she say it *that* way?

The poodle on top of her shifted. Hannah sprung up, pivoted, and faced her foe. Right off the bat Hannah realized there had to be a good twenty years' age difference between them. The cute woman before her was a tiny thing, all bright and shiny, like an over-enthused dental hygienist.

*There was nothing exciting about teeth.*

"I know all about words, thank you," the young woman drawled in the most fascinating accent she'd ever heard. Where in the world was she from? There was a tinge of defiance in her animated face, too. Such a contradiction. "Words are my life. I am a librarian."

"I'm afraid to see what you'd do if someone failed to return a book. Firing squad? Guillotine?"

"Both, of course, *and* a late fee."

Hannah grinned at that, but she'd never let herself get distracted by a pretty woman with a dazzling smile and dark piercing eyes. Hannah took a step forward and the space between them contained bottled-up energy, like the charged air before a bolt of lightning struck its target.

*Step away,* Hannah told herself, only to immediately ignore her own advice.

"You're going to tell me what kind of place this is and where my friend and her daughter went."

That defiant look returned, but there was a slight softening in the woman's shoulders.

Hannah knew she'd get the information she needed.

# NINETEEN

Crushing the cell phone had been a bad idea, Calix realized as he made his way back to the Godfrey Hotel in Boston. He hadn't done something like that in a while, but that old biddy'd really set him off. Now he had no immediate way to reach Jasmine to ask for updates, or call Abigail to tell her to hold lunch until he arrived. Both knew the sheer mountain of stress he'd been operating under lately. They'd be fine.

He stopped off at a cell phone store and attempted to win over the salesclerk by saying his dog chewed on it. "That's on you man," the clerk said with zero compassion while extracting the sim card and placing it in a brand-new phone. "Sounds like you need to feed your dog better."

Perhaps the citizens of Boston were not easily charmed, Calix thought, as he left and drove past the Old State House. He texted instructions to Abigail—it wasn't like she ate much to begin with—before calling Jasmine's line. His assistant didn't pick up. She'd lasted longer than most of his assistants, but maybe it was time to rethink Jasmine's employment status.

Calix was scowling at his screen just as an enormous,

gunmetal-gray Ford F-150 Raptor pulled out of the parking lot and cut him off.

His eyes narrowed into chips. He'd recognize that truck, that personalized license plate, those Army bumper stickers *anywhere*.

Command Sergeant Major Hannah Atholms.

So, she'd arrived, as threatened. Calix's knuckles went white as he griped the steering wheel. She was the one woman who seemed to instantly loathe him when they'd met fifteen years ago. It wasn't lost on him that she'd been the one who'd poisoned Mara against him.

Then again, Atholms *was* a literal bloodhound. She'd sniff out Mara's hiding place with her eyes closed.

Calix relaxed his grip. Perhaps this was fate.

All he had to do was follow her.

Mara wasn't sure how Dr. Vuzmuc had managed it. The next several minutes were a blur of activity as the doctor whisked them from the Rock Creek Park mini-portal to the hospital. Slipping in through a back entrance, Dr. Vuzmuc escorted them up a freight elevator, down a hallway painted with cheerful murals, past a nurse's stationed identified as "Elephant Station 3," and into a corner patient room.

The room was outfitted with a hospital bed, a sleeper sofa, a stack of pillows, a desk with a roll-out chair, and a mounted television tuned to the Cartoon Network.

With Mara's personal medical history, she'd all but blocked from her memory her many trips to the emergency department, various military doctors and specialists, and too many nurse-line phone calls to count. With Finley, however, the pediatric wings of most hospitals did what they could to make children feel comfortable and welcome.

Mara felt the urge to discuss these past experiences with Vikk, to hear a comforting voice, to know that he was in her corner, but he wasn't here, so Mara pushed him from her thoughts. She needed to be present for Finley. Her own feelings would have to take second place. Once Calix's psychological storm here on Earth had quelled, she'd take stock of herself.

Staying quiet near the door, Keiji hung back to observe both mother and daughter. "I hope the room is to your liking," Keiji said to Finley.

From the window, Finley turned her head. She looked exhausted, deflated.

"It is, thank you Dr. Vuzmuc," Finley said. "It looks comfortable—and it's kinda neat that we're so close to the Capitol." Finley moved to the bed and plugged in the cell phones. "Both phones are dead, Mom."

"I'm surprised they lasted as long as they did," Mara said. Keiji knew that Finley had been texting Serstene almost nonstop, and suppressed a smile at Mara's oblique reference. "Dr. Vuzmuc, how long do you think we'll need to stay?"

*Excellent question,* Keiji thought.

"It depends on Finley's results," they said.

The queen had her thoughts on the situation, though Keiji was not required to adopt the queen's opinion. Keiji was at liberty to form their own medical conclusion. "Perhaps through the weekend. I anticipate getting her results tonight or tomorrow morning."

"In that case, we should make the space look lived-in," Mara said as she inspected the very clean room.

She spoke in a very can-do attitude, as if she was trying to avoid her true feelings. But Keiji agreed that Mara was right;

with one glance, no one would believe that Mara and Finley had been here a full week.

Finley, zapped from the whirlwind trip and longing to be alone with her own thoughts, kicked off her shoes and climbed into the bed, intending to shut her eyes for a brief moment. Her eyes fluttered as she watched Mom retrieve her laptop from the backpack and plug it into the outlet near the sleeper sofa.

As she drifted off, she heard Mom and Dr. Vuzmuc speaking in low tones as they discussed logistics and how the doctor had already posted a full medical workup to her file. "Because I took samples while on Vraithe, I can pull those records over quite easily," Dr. Vuzmuc was saying. "In a very short amount of time, I will back date those actions within the hospital's system."

"And no one will question it?" Mom asked.

"Not the records, per se, but the nurses and orderlies assigned to this floor will know you haven't been in this room the entire week—but that's not to say you have not been assigned to another floor."

After that, their voices blurred in her mind and Finley tuned out the rest of their conversation.

Maybe things would look better, feel better, after resting. Finley wanted to be able to reconcile the fact that she had a mother willing to sacrifice a chance at love and happiness to take care of her, against the knowledge that her father was taking advantage of the situation for his own personal gain. She curled on her side, skin sweaty, stomach clenching.

Which of the two would she turn into? The selfless one or the selfish one? Why did it feel like she was at war with herself?

When Finley woke, dusk had settled outside. She'd slept longer than she had intended. A fluttering of snow flurries flew past dark windows. The winter wind cut around the building's outside corners, emitting a low groan, like that of a moaning ghost. The only light in the room was from the television, which was tuned to an old black and white film where a man was running in the streets. Mom was lying on the couch, under a thin blanket. Finley couldn't tell if she was asleep or not.

"Is it Christmas Eve, Mom?" Finley croaked. Her mouth was so dry it tasted like saltines. She looked over to see if there was a cup of water on the bedside table and was relieved to find one filled to the brim with mostly melted ice cubes.

The room was less tidy than what she had remembered. The suitcase was on the chair, unzipped, overflowing with the clothes CeCe had given them. Food wrappers were in the trash can, and a small stack of books and a pile of papers were on the floor, near Mom, who stirred at her voice. Mom must have been grading papers. The counter along the far wall contained a vase of get-well flowers, a basket of goodies, and, of all things, a small printer.

"Not 'til tomorrow, honey." Mom must have sensed the direction of her thoughts because she added, "They are from the doctor. The printer, too."

"Oh."

Finley focused on herself. There was an intravenous line hooked to her arm and she heard the soft sounds of electronic hums, chirps, and beeps. A pulse oximeter was clamped over her index finger.

For an alarming second, Finley feared she'd dreamt everything. The portal. Vraithe. Mr. Stravdas. Serstene. CeCe Banks. Finley felt hot all over and her eyes burned as the tears streamed down her face.

*No, please be real. Please be real.*

Her heart racing, Mara rushed to her daughter's side. She'd been studying Finley when she heard the accelerating beeps accompanying Finley's skyrocketing pulse. Thankfully, her other readings looked fine, at least for the moment.

"I'm here, sweetie," Mara said in a soft, practiced voice. "Let me know what you're feeling and we'll deal with it together. You're not alone. Never alone."

"How long have I been here?" Finley asked in a tiny voice, shivering.

When Mara said, "Just a few hours," Finley's heart rate began to slow.

Mara had an inkling of what was bothering her daughter. She spread another blanket over her. "You fell asleep pretty much the minute we got here. Dr. Vuzmuc and a few nurses have been in and out, checking on you. Dinner's not for another hour, but I can grab something for you, if you're hungry."

"It's just...that I thought it was all a dream," Finley whispered, her eyes wet with tears. "That I'd been here for a week. That Vraithe was a figment of my imagination."

"You miss it, don't you?"

Finley nodded.

"Me, too," Mara said. "It felt like..." She trailed off.

"Like home?"

Mara smiled sadly. She'd never truly felt welcomed anywhere like that. She experienced some of that feeling while she served in the Army, and she'd hoped to feel that way with the teachers at Riley High School. But Vraithe had been different, special.

"Yeah, like we belonged." Her eyes burned with unshed tears. Swallowing a lump in her throat, Mara added, "But, sweetie, please understand that we can't just leave Earth for good. Vikk, Queen Uska, and Dr. Vuzmuc helped us this time, but it won't always be so simple. Look at what your dad is putting us through. I never like to talk bad about Calix, but he's not been very kind to us this week. I cannot take the high road and ignore it. It's my job to protect you. I never thought I'd have to say this, but it also means I have to protect you from your own father, as bad as that sounds."

"About that"—Finley hesitated—"have you seen the news articles and the interviews?"

Mara could tell that Finley was nervous about asking, but it was a valid question. "Yes," she said with a soft sigh. "As much as I wanted to, I couldn't ignore that, either."

The fact that he'd accused her of poisoning their daughter for attention while forcefully preventing Finley from attending Calix's wedding was every cable news anchor's wet dream. With zero evidence to back it up, the networks seemed to be running with it nonstop. Patti Stoltz, in one of her last clips, was so emphatic that Calix had chopped up their bodies and dumped them into the Mystic River that Mara feared the anchor was two commercial breaks away from having a stroke.

On the positive side, she'd also discovered interviews with several of her students, who were reading *The Curse of Mathilda's Sorrow* in her honor, and one with Dr. Brady, who, after detailing what a talented writer Mara was, hypothesized that Ms. Eldress was in a cabin somewhere, writing her next book.

Mara continued. "Things are not as bad as they seem, Finley, I promise. Calix can be very charming—*alarmingly* charming—and he has this ridiculously easy way of getting others to do his bidding—but in this instance, I do not think he realizes how much of a fool he's been. Because of his actions, my memoir is actually climbing the charts." Mara smiled. "That has to injure his pride."

Privately, Mara suspected that, out of everything, *that* would be the thing to really set him off. Because he'd had nothing to do with their disappearance, he wasn't truly worried for their safety. Calix knew she was a good mother and would never jeopardize Finley's health. It was all about notoriety for him. Because he was safe—safe from actual prosecution.

However, once the profits of his efforts benefitted someone else—namely, Mara—he'd take it as a personal insult. *That's* when he would become unpredictable and erratic. She'd already had a word about it with Dr. Vuzmuc, who said they'd notify hospital security.

"Did your literary agent contact you?" Finley asked.

"Former agent," Mara corrected. "And yes, he sent me a note, which I have yet to reply to. He hopes that wherever I am, that I'm hard at work on my next book. Too bad for him my response will be, 'Sadly, our interests no longer align, but I wish you continued success in the future.'"

"Karma," Finley said with a grin. "I love it. Maybe a tall, handsome man will come by, wanting to turn your next book into a film."

"I think one film experience is enough for me, thanks," Mara said. She couldn't help but chuckle at that, even if it stung her heart, which was something of a blessing since her chest cavity was alternating between numbness and a crushing weight since they'd departed Vraithe. Maybe she should ask Dr. Vuzmuc's opinion on it.

As Finley got out of bed to use the restroom, dragging the IV stand with her, Mara thought about the sparse texts she and Vikk had exchanged.

*"Did you make it back safely?"* Vikk had texted. *"Did Keiji meet up with you?"*

*"Yes,"* she'd written back hours later, once her phone had charged. Now that they'd traveled back through the portal, their phones could communicate with Vraitheian devices. *"Thank you for assisting us. It was a very good solution."*

*"I miss you,"* he texted only moments ago.

*I miss you, too,* her fingers itched to type out.

But Mara did not reply. It hurt too much.

Instead, she'd texted Hannah, told her that they were safe, sent her the address, and that she'd explain everything when she got here. Hannah, ever the brief and direct command sergeant major that she was, merely wrote, "Already en route."

Mara had to think about that for a second. Assuming Hannah was still with Dessa, and if Dessa was in on the plan, it meant they were traveling together. Would they get along? Or was Dessa talking Hannah's ear off already? She wished Vikk were here so she could discuss it with him, to get his thoughts, to hear him laugh.

Mara shook her head. Focus on the here and now. She cleared her throat as Finley shuffled back to the bed. "Are you feeling better about everything, sweetie?"

"Yeah, thanks Mom." Mara tucked the covers around Finley. "I'm sorry that Dad's being shitty."

"Language, young lady."

A tap came at the door and Dr. Vuzmuc stepped inside, a tray in hand.

"Who's hungry?" the doctor asked.

Mara knew it was not normal for physicians to bring meals to their patients, but Dr. Vuzmuc explained to the staff that Finley was under their special care and that they'd take care of a majority of her and Mara's needs. Even their very names were marked private and password-protected in the medical system.

One or two of the nurses had apparently taken offense, but Dr. Vuzmuc was a well-respected physician.

With all their precautions, Mara knew it would not take long for folks to start making connections.

As the prime relative and heir of Vraithe's queen, Vikk never thought he'd encounter anything other than cooperation from the portal stewards. But he'd just landed at the main

North American portal in Boston, Massachusetts, and one of the gray suits was refusing to answer his question.

"Don't make me ask again," Vikk said in Vraitheian. "I am not in a good mood."

He'd texted *"I miss you"* to Mara and she had yet to respond.

This was what despair felt like, he was sure of it. A black hole. A hollow heart.

"As I said, Stravdas," said the gray suit steward named Aurguren, "I am not at liberty to discuss where Dr. Vuzmuc escorted the queen's royal visa passport travelers."

The problem for Vikk, well, *one* of his problems, was that he wasn't sure which children's hospital Keiji worked at while on Earth. When he searched on his Earthling phone, the results were in the hundreds, and he wasn't about to guess. And even though Keiji had mentioned the location several times, he hadn't been listening closely to that part of the conversation.

The portal population had thinned out for the time being, but he'd already heard about Dessa tackling the giant human woman before they'd up and left together. Aurguren was more than willing to talk about *that*.

"You do know who I am, right?" Vikk asked. He hated that he was resorting to these tactics.

Aurguren was nonplused. Damn him.

"You are Stravdas," Aurguren said, "which means I am fully aware of Taloncourt's hierarchy. However, your visa does not reflect your status. You are not traveling on a royal visa, which means you are not traveling under the queen's protection, which means I am not at liberty to impart the knowledge you seek."

"If you say 'which means' one more time, I am going to snap," Vikk growled. Vraitheians were not violent by nature, but his blood was beginning to boil.

At that moment, one of the local mini-portalpods arrived. Werlaun, and *only* Werlaun, exited.

*She's just returned from somewhere.*

Vikk never thought he'd be happy to see Werlaun again.

"Werlaun," Vikk yelled as he jogged toward her.

Werlaun, unused to someone calling for her, especially in a joyful tone, stopped in her tracks, surprised to see Stravdas running toward her. Thankfully, he did not appear to be upset with her. She'd kept to her orders. She had not told a soul who she was with or where she'd taken them. In fact, she'd been offline for so long her friends were worried she'd died.

Werlaun felt like she was deserving of a medal for her honorable service to the queen.

Stravdas towered over her, taking the steps two at a time, and joined her on the dais.

He had a wild look about him, like he'd challenged a bear to a wrestling match and wanted to get out of it. It was clear Stravdas wanted something, Werlaun just didn't know what it was or why *she* was the individual he had identified to gain it.

Mostly she wished he'd smooth his hair back. It was in shambles.

All of his emoting was giving her a headache. She'd happily wear *two* Vraitheian black lockets to keep from ever feeling the way he looked.

"Good afternoon, Stravdas."

"Where," Stravdas breathed out, "did you take them?"

Oh, this was a trick, wasn't it? He was trying to test her.

"Of whom do you speak, Stravdas?"

He growled at her. She'd never seen him look so beastly.

"Of whom you damn well know. Mara and Finley. Keiji

escorted them to a children's hospital. Which children's hospital? And why are there so many of them on Earth?"

Werlaun paused. This didn't sound like a test. Unless it was a test meant to not sound like a test but was a test. This was becoming confusing.

She'd been accused of overthinking things in the past.

"How is it you do not know?" Werlaun asked.

Stravdas showed her his Earth phone. The map displayed hundreds of red pins. "I don't know which one. I am asking for your help, Werlaun." When she didn't respond right away, he added, "Name your price. Nothing is too high."

She was going to joke and ask for *three* Vraitheian black lockets but then she realized he was being serious. This was Werlaun's shot at her dream. She squared her shoulders and took on a professional tone.

"What do you know about the apprenticeship program on the Starfleet cruise lines?"

Patti Stoltz's producer slid a piece of paper across the anchor's desk as the sound technician pinned the microphone to the front of her blouse.

Patti was due to tape a teaser segment in five minutes, so the sound stage was in the final phases of assembly. It wasn't unheard of for her producer, a former celebrity paparazzi, to obtain late-breaking information. The gal had a ton of insider sources.

She glanced at Glenda's note. "What's this?"

She was about to go on-air to allude to a full-on military coverup. No one on God's green Earth could produce Mara or Calix's military records. Was the couple involved in counterintelligence? Were they bona fide spies, but now retired and reenacting a cold war on their marriage? The department of defense had resoundingly refused to confirm or deny either had ever served in the military.

Patti was loath to abandon her theory on Calix having murdered his ex-wife and daughter. She could not deny that they were getting a lot of viewer traction with the alleged chopped-up bodies theory. It didn't hurt that Calix Eldress possessed movie-star good looks. There was something about a handsome killer that was enticing and repulsive. He was every woman's dream and nightmare, combined, but that wouldn't stop thousands of women from writing fan mail once he was in prison.

She'd angle for an exclusive with him.

Still, as she read Glenda's sparse note, Patti raised one eyebrow. This better be good.

"Why do you want me to fly to a children's hospital?"

Glenda merely smiled her trademark Cheshire grin and walked away.

After conducting a once-over for Finley's checkup, and asking a series of questions, a few things were becoming clear to Keiji—though they thought it best to not verbalize these impressions until the child's results from Vraithe were received. Her vital signs, however, were all within normal ranges.

Her aura, however, told a different story. Human medicine could not decode everything. Sometimes, instinct, intuition, and of course, the Vraitheian's ability to decipher auras, supplemented Keiji's medical recommendations.

Upon arrival, Keiji had submitted another request for Finley's medical records, this time through the Children's National transmittal network. They'd finally received a heavily redacted version, which Keiji studied with interest. For each annotated visit, both Finley's attending physician and her diagnosis had been blacked out. The mystery was coming together.

On paper, Finley Eldress was a healthy child. She had access to education, medical care, fresh air, and quality food. She lived in stable housing and, setting aside the girl's father, possessed a loving parent. But that did not tell the full story, because her body's output was not simply a one-for-one product of her input. Consuming a well-balanced diet did not always equate a perfectly functioning digestive track.

In the dim room, as a cartoon played on the television, Keiji watched the pair, observed the love and affection between parent and child, the easy way they communicated with one another. Trust. There was trust there.

All of Finley's obvious needs were being met, yet there was what Keiji called a "combative imbalance" within her system. It wasn't enough that Finley did not feel well; her body was actively fighting her, which made it difficult for human doctors to pinpoint its origin. Her aura was so putrid in color that it nearly filled the hospital room. Keiji believed they understood the source, but feared the solution was beyond their control, or capability.

Thankfully Finley had a reliable parent to help her navigate.

Keiji saw Mara's resilience, her determined mouth, her focused eyes. She was a parent who was solely concentrating on her child. Mara's aura was rather dire, one they'd rarely seen on a human before. It was misty, almost like a cloud with wispy tendrils that might evaporate at any moment. If she wasn't careful, it might prove terminal.

Mara, a woman caught between two worlds, was developing a hollow heart.

No amount of medicine, human or otherwise, could resolve that.

# TWENTY

"And that's why Vikk removed his Vraitheian black locket," Dessa said in conclusion. "They're as good as married." She was a passenger in the biggest vehicle she'd ever been inside as Hannah drove them south to Washington, DC. It was really nice to see over the tops of other cars on the highway. Driving a Mini Cooper never afforded her such a grand view.

Hannah, who had remained fairly quiet with the exception of a few clarifying questions here and there, briefly glanced her way before returning her attention to the road. Granted, Dessa hadn't exactly explained everything in chronological order, and it was something of a rambling three-hour story, so perhaps she'd been wise to remain silent.

Dessa was surprised that Mara's very good military friend seemed to believe her. Well, perhaps *believe* was too strong a word. *Humored* her was more like it.

"Married, huh?" Hannah asked. Dessa detected the skepticism in her voice.

Humans were too cynical by half, and this one, whom she'd come to understand was an important leader within the Earthling military system, wore a very cynical expression. It hadn't left her face since they departed Boston nearly four hours ago.

"Well, okay, not *technically* married," Dessa clarified. "Naturally, a Vraitheian bonding ceremony is required and of course Mara would have to agree to it."

"Naturally," Hannah murmured instead of inquiring about the exquisite bonding properties of the Vraitheian black locket. Dessa *really* wanted to go into the intricate details of a Vraitheian bonding ceremony.

"It's romantic."

"Are you always this animated? You don't have to bounce in the seat, you know. My truck has really good suspension, so I know you're doing it yourself."

Dessa felt a blush prickle her face. So maybe Hannah didn't believe her. Should Dessa just sink into her puffy coat and pretend to fall asleep?

"I'm just really excited to see Mara again."

*I'm just really excited to be near you.*

"Plus, I've eaten most of the red licorice."

*I've eaten all of it.*

"Would you like the rest?"

*The bag is empty so please say no.*

The candy would absolutely wreck her system for a day or two, but the waxy, sugary sticks were just too good for Dessa to ignore. At home she had an entire cupboard full of them. Taloncourt's palace doctor regularly shipped her a special tonic to counteract their effects. Good ole Dr. Smindle. Such an enabler.

"It's fine," Hannah said, barely looking at the bag. She studied the rearview mirror before adjusting the windshield wiper frequency. Snow was falling faster. The milky moon was low in the darkening sky, which cast a pallid mood on the white-dusted landscape. "I don't eat much candy, to be honest."

"I'm confused. When I asked if you wanted a snack from

the convenience store, you said 'yes.' You even offered to turn the truck around."

Dessa watched as a suddenly nervous Hannah rubbed the back of her neck. Her aura was an embarrassed hue, like she didn't want to admit to something. "It seemed like it was important to you, so..."

"Oh."

*Oh.*

"Is your brother, Vikk, a lot like you?"

"Oh goodness, no! He's as tall as a mountain and as stubborn as one, too," Dessa said with a laugh. "Vikk is stoic to a fault, always duty-bound, and incredibly private. He's literally the future ruler of Vraithe, so it's not like he can become a party animal." She paused. "That doesn't make him sound like a fun partner for Mara, does it?"

Hannah drank from her coffee cup. "Mara has been let down by a number of people in her life," she answered in a guarded tone, which suggested she wasn't willing to discuss how she knew this information. "She's one of the most honorable and trustworthy people I know. A partner who is fun sounds great and all, but what she needs is someone who is loving, loyal, faithful, and unwavering in their support. That someone will need to put Mara and Finley ahead of their own needs."

"Vikk cares a great deal about Mara and Finley."

"Of that, I have no doubt, Dessa," Hannah said. "But think about it: if your brother is the future monarch, or whatever you call it where you're from, then that means he probably won't be able to be that person for Mara. He'll have a country to run."

"A planet."

Hannah blinked a few times. "Right," Hannah drawled out. "A planet."

✦✦✦

For a few moments there, Hannah had forgotten that the sparkly woman in her passenger seat was claiming to be from another planet. She couldn't ignore the fact that she'd seen, with her own two eyes, Mara, Finley, and two other individuals, one who looked like a bellhop and other who resembled a doctor, disappear into thin air back in Boston. How they'd gotten to Washington, DC., in such quick time was a mystery. Jet? Teleportation? Thankfully, Mara'd finally returned her texts. She'd have answers—real answers, not some crazy alien abduction-slash-romance story—soon.

Then again, Hannah had witnessed interesting, almost unbelievable things during her twenty-five-year military career. Superhuman soldiers. Communications that delved into near telepathy. The ability to sway and influence the actions of others.

Calix Eldress was like that.

He could make almost anyone do his bidding, including Mara. Mara, who had grown up in the foster care system, had been no match for Calix's charm offensive and love-bombing tactics, but once Finley came along, and Mara no longer put Calix first, he showed his true colors. Thankfully Mara saw the truth, but by then they were married, and it was too late to easily dissolve things. She'd spent every moment after that detangling herself from Calix's tentacles.

Hannah glanced in her rearview mirror again. His SUV was still following them. She wasn't sure *how* he'd found her, probably sheer luck, but did he really think she wouldn't recognize him?

If Calix knew where they were going, he wouldn't be following her so closely; he would have zipped around her right off the bat. Apprehension tingled along her spine. Hannah felt certain they were all headed toward a showdown.

"I know it's a lot to take in," Dessa said, cutting into her thoughts. "I don't blame you for not believing me."

Hannah desperately wanted this Vikk guy to be good for her best friend. Dessa gave off good vibes, though she was a bit eccentric.

She shrugged. "It's not everyday someone tells me my best friend has fallen in love with an alien prince from an alien planet, where wearing a specific necklace allows everyone to engage in casual sex, but removing it binds you to your soulmate for life—but if the soulmate rejects his heartstrings, then the alien prince develops something called a *hollow heart,* which petrifies his ability to ever love again."

"So you *were* paying attention?" Dessa said, throwing her a bright smile, which caused Hannah's heart to skip a beat.

Hannah chastised herself. *You're a forty-five-year-old woman, Hannah, not a teenager.*

"Let's say all of that is true; what are their options? An intergalactic long-distance relationship? That does not seem like workable plan."

"I agree." Dessa's expression turned contemplative. "The way I see it, there are two options: Mara and Finley permanently relocate to Vraithe or Vikk abdicates the throne to live here on Earth."

"Both options sound pretty monumental."

"What is love, if not monumental?"

Vikk's appearance was anything but royal when he finally disembarked from a portalpod in the Washington, DC., area. He was rumpled, hungry, and jet-lagged. A trip that should have taken mere minutes took hours because Werlaun insisted on his meeting with the director of Vraithe's Starfleet cruise line before she would give him the information he needed.

"You realize this is extortion, right?" Vikk seethed after agreeing to her terms. Though, what choice did he have?

Werlaun was young and inexperienced, but she was determined to get what she wanted, and, to his surprise, what she wanted was to become a galaxy-renowned chef.

"It is not extortion if you benefit from our agreement, Stravdas," Werlaun pointed out as they transported to a portalport located on Vraithe's amethyst moon and the home base of the Starfleet cruise line. As Werlaun was still traveling on the queen's royal visa, but he was not, Werlaun was wise enough not to mention the discrepancy when she declared only herself as she typed in their travel coordinates.

Given Vikk's close relation to Queen Uska, he would not require a prescheduled meeting with the Starfleet's director. And, indeed, the director was only too willing to meet with them. During the brief conversation, Werlaun rattled off her professional opinions on food and nutrition, hypothetical dish pairings, and explained several food creations she'd developed on her own. Impressed with Werlaun's ideas, creativity, and enthusiasm, the director enrolled her into the next apprenticeship program cohort.

Giddy, Werlaun thanked Vikk all the way back to the portalport. "This is the best day of my life," she said, sighing in complete happiness.

"I just stood beside you, Werlaun," Vikk said. He wished he could call Mara to inform her of his crazy excursion with Werlaun. Mara would get a kick out of it. "You did all the work."

"Well," Werlaun said, giving him what Finley would definitely call *side-eye*, "some of us have to work hard to achieve our dreams." Clicking noises were coming from the portalpod's control screen. Werlaun was reestablishing their Earth-bound coordinates and arranging for an arrival time.

He jerked his head and glared at her. "What do you mean by that?"

"Not everyone has it easy like you, Stravdas. You are the

queen's heir. You've probably never had to work hard to achieve your dreams."

The portalpod launched off the amethyst moon and zipped through a portal tunnel. Vikk looked out at Vraithe through the porthole. With his next blink, the fractured planet was already behind them. Far way stars and galaxies dotted the inky landscape.

He wanted to argue with Werlaun, to tell her that she was wrong, that he most certainly worked hard for his dreams, but he came away with two conclusions: one, she was right, he did not work very hard at achieving his dreams, because two, that up until recently, he had no dreams of his own.

He'd always lived his life as the next ruler of Vraithe. Why aspire, or hope, for something different? It wasn't exactly what he wanted, but it was his duty. He had never asked himself, "Do I want to be the next ruler of Vraithe?" because there never been an event, or an obstacle, placed in his path that had caused him to question his future.

Not until now.

Not until Mara.

Werlaun seemed to sense a change in him. Her snide tone evolved to one of curiosity, perhaps even pity. "You do have dreams and aspirations, right, Stravdas?"

Vikk put his head in his hands. How did one answer that? A question so deep, so personal, that, once answered, it revealed a truth you didn't know existed before that very moment. Had it been building? Had it been just under the interior of his skin, hiding in his heart, waiting for someone to scratch at the surface of his mind?

When the portalpod arrived at the portal closest to the children's hospital, Werlaun gave him the final directions, thanked him for his help with the Starfleet apprenticeship, and wished him luck.

Vikk exited the pod but didn't immediately leave the dais.

"I do have dreams, Werlaun," he said. "Your dreams are written in the stars. Mine...well, my dreams are right here, on Earth. My success, however, is not certain. But you helped me realize something, and for that, I thank you. Goodbye."

Jasmine's boyfriend joked that she was too invested in her boss's antics. He wasn't wrong. She'd set up various keyword searches that crawled the web and sent hourly aggregate emails with the results.

Too bad she'd signed a nondisclosure agreement upon being hired. Otherwise, she would have agreed to every interview request that came her way.

"Former boss," Jasmine said as they put the finishing touches on the small Christmas tree in their small Baltimore apartment. They'd spend all the next day at her parent's house, opening presents and eating a big Christmas Eve dinner, but tonight it was just the two of them, snug and cozy, each with a glass of red, just like she liked. She'd worry about a new job after the holidays.

"I emailed him and Abigail my resignation letter earlier today," she continued. "I have no interest in being connected to Calix Eldress when the shit hits the fan. He's either a murdering scumbag or he's using the situation to his personal advantage. I blocked all their numbers and email addresses."

She apparently hadn't blocked *all* their numbers. Moments ago, Abigail had texted her from her personal phone, *"Do you know why Calix is driving south? Can you believe he stranded me in Boston? The nerve. Book me on the next flight to Balti-more, Jasmine."*

Jasmine did not book the next flight.

Between Calix and Abigail, Abigail *was* the nicer one, but not by much. Abigail's family was loaded; the heiress would be just fine without the support of an executive assistant who struggled financially.

Just then, Jasmine's phone made a *synth* sound, signaling that she'd received an updated aggregate email. Out of habit, she scrolled through the list. The story hyperlinks were the normal assortment of murder-for-hire, alien abduction, literary hoaxes, and kidnapping theories. Jasmine ignored them. Those had all been reported to death. A small scattering was about the school board's book-banning decision, though that theory, which was less sensational, had lost media appeal.

But a developing story from NBC4, a Washington, DC., news affiliate, caught her attention.

*"Anonymous sources report Vet Mom and missing daughter spotted at local children's hospital."*

Well, that explained why Calix had abandoned Abigail and suddenly headed south. Probably to save face and orchestrate some new explanation.

Jasmine put down the phone, poured herself another glass of wine, turned off the lights to take in the full effect of their Christmas lights, and snuggled up against her boyfriend on the couch. He kissed the top of her head and she sighed contently. Sure, they lived in a cardboard-sized apartment, drank cheap wine, and slept under two blankets to keep from turning on the heat, but they were happy.

That's what really mattered, right?

Uska was reading Finley's medical results when a call from Dr. Keiji Vuzmuc lit up the screen on the video device on her desk of business. It was not a surprise call—she'd all but ordered the doctor to call her immediately.

"Good day, my queen."

The doctor appeared to be in their office at the children's

hospital. They were still wearing their medical coat, which was a nice contrast against the doctor's amethyst skin. The rest of the room was horrid, with bland white panels, and a square Earthling calendar tacked to the wall. Humans and their drive for deadlines and timetables. None of it made any sense to Uska, but she understood that Dr. Vuzmuc, while on Earth, had to accede to humanity's inane quirks.

"Hello, doctor," Uska said evenly.

She was doing her best to keep every muscle in her face neutral, and her heart rate and breathing in check, lest she betray any emotion. No one needed to know how she was feeling. She'd just left Vikkolo's suite. There, on top of the dresser, on full display, was his locket along with a handwritten note that read, "I forfeit all inheritances."

She'd smiled when she read it. Her prime relative had never coveted the crown, which, among many other superior merits, made him infinitely qualified to rule. If he had desired power and complete authority, Uska would have stripped him long ago and appointed another. As it stood, she had time to decide. She wished Vikkolo were here, wanted to ask his opinion, but she was alone, her dear prime relative was finally following his own destiny and not one she'd appointed for him.

Of course, Keiji's report could change everything.

Uska's destiny would be revealed in Keiji's report.

"I'm reading your report now, Keiji," she said evenly. "When did you begin to suspect that Finley was part Vraitheian?"

Uska herself had felt an immediate connection with the young girl on meeting the child, as if they were kin long separated by time and distance and an ocean of fear and regret.

"Almost right away, my queen."

"And you did not share your thoughts with your queen?"

The doctor paused before answering. It was not a heated

question. Uska was curious by nature. She wanted to know everything.

"Opinions are not scientific. I chose caution over speed."

"What else did you observe, Keiji?"

"Finley's human aura was scattered, as if it was short-circuiting and compensating for it, making it larger than life. That is not human-like. Her medical records with the department of defense were difficult to obtain and, once received, were heavily redacted. I take this to mean she is enrolled in the military's secret extraterrestrial program. You know as well as I do that the Earthling military has its way of keeping tabs on Vraitheian citizens who join their ranks. Apparently, this also applies to Vraitheian offspring, which I find distressing. Finley is a child, not a member of the armed forces."

Uska had to agree with the doctor on that last assessment. If the Earthling military was already keeping tabs on Finley, she would always be under scrutiny and observation, and tracked. What else might they do? There were treaties between Vraithe and Earth. Things had always been peaceful between them, but that did not mean it would always be that way.

"And your results confirm her Vraitheian status?"

"Correct. I ran a DNA algorithm scan. Separating human and Vraitheian DNA sequences is an arduous process. This is what we were waiting on. Finley's results confirm she contains Vraithe DNA."

Uska closed her eyes before she asked her next question. "How much?"

"Fifty percent." It was as Uska suspected, hoped. A number higher or lower would have invalidated everything. "One of Finley's parents is human and the other—"

"Is full Vraitheian." Uska's heartstrings skipped many beats. They'd been dormant for so long. It was by choice. She'd all but destroyed her Vraitheian black locket after Qoral fled. Heartstrings were not just for romantic love. They also formed a tethered connection to close kin—direct kin—which could be passed down as an heirloom.

"Did you run her sample through our database? Is Finley my—" A slight spasm twitched the edge of her mouth. She was too afraid to vocalize the full question.

"She is, my queen."

With fifty-five years of nursing under her belt, twenty of which had been at the Capitol Children's Hospital, Nurse Ogilvy thought she'd seen it all on the nights she staffed the reception counter. But she was not prepared for the sudden influx of visitors, nor the notoriety of those they wanted to see.

She put down the historical romance novel she'd been reading to observe the odd couple walk in.

A tall, commanding woman with short black hair, and a small, petite woman with bright white hair, entered together. It was like looking at a thundercloud standing next to a sparkly rainbow. The pair could not be more different, yet Nurse Ogilvy sensed they'd fit well together, opposites attracting and all that. She had a sixth sense about those things.

"Good evening," the thundercloud said. There was a zing about the tall woman, as if she was full of energy but wasn't ready to release it, like a fine wine refusing to be uncorked. Nurse Ogilvy wasn't sure if the rainbow standing beside her was the cause, or if she was nervous about being in a hospital. Even the most stoic of visitors were afraid of hospitals and doctors. She'd once drawn blood from a beefy wrestler only to have him fall in a dead faint at her feet. "We are here to see Mara and Finley Eldress."

"Spell the last name," Nurse Ogilvy said, and typed it in as it was dictated to her, but then it dawned on her.

Wait a minute. She *knew* those names. She'd been

watching Patti Stoltz nearly every night talking about chopped-up bodies and military cover-ups. She just loved the way Patti's red bob emphatically jounced as her Southern accent dramatically enunciated the wrongdoings of the alleged murderous husbands of missing pretty wives. The Patti Stoltz wig was a popular Halloween accessory.

And Patti's current obsession was right on target...that sexy murderous husband, Calix Eldress. Hell yes, Nurse Ogilvy would let him murder her pus—

Just then a bedraggled man rushed through the main visitor doors, huffing and puffing like a bystander who'd accidentally been roped into a marathon-in-progress and had just found a way to exit the race.

"Vikk!" the sparkly rainbow squeaked out as she spun around and spotted him. "Dear goddess, did you...*crawl* here?"

The sparkly rainbow had a point, Nurse Ogilvy mused. Vikk was a nice drink of water, though currently a bit roughed-up. The marathon analogy no longer worked. No, he'd been battling a patch-wearing villain hellbent on stalling his journey.

Nurse Ogilvy studied him. This Vikk fellow had a romance hero's "just come to his senses" vibe and was entering the part of the novel where he groveled for forgiveness to restore the heroine's affection. Put this man in a kilt. She was down for that—she was a sucker for a good grovel, though she would have preferred he have a scar run across some part of his face to compliment his long, disheveled, chestnut-brown hair.

Vikk, not the least bit aware of the nurse's romantic musings, was extremely relieved to see Dessa. As he'd rushed to the hospital, he was so worried he'd go in through the wrong entrance and waste more time running around in circles.

His lips tugged into a quick smile. He'd update Dessa later.

"Let's just say I had to take a few detours before I could get here."

His sister, from what he understood, had all but forced Mara's best friend to drive her here. *All good?* he asked using RMO. Dessa gave him a thumbs-up, which was answer enough —the ginormous grin on Dessa's face needed no further explanation.

"Why does it look like you're carrying everything you own?" the tall woman beside Dessa asked. She squared off against him, arms crossed, one eyebrow cocked. She had to be nearly six feet tall, with a frame—and a voice—meant for combat.

"Because I *am* carrying everything I own," Vikk answered, shifting the bulging duffel bag to his other shoulder before extending his hand to her. "You must be Hannah. I'm Vikk Stravdas, Dessa's brother and Mara's...friend."

Hannah took his hand in a firm grip. "I am Hannah Atholms." She paused as she assessed him. "I suppose we'll see about that last statement."

Ouch, but deserved.

"So," Dessa said, gesturing at the duffel, "that means you—"

"Left Vraithe? Yes." He let out a long breath. It felt good to say it. It was already real, but saying it out loud made it an undisputed truth.

"And our aunt knows?" Dessa's bright eyebrows furrowed like tiny caterpillars.

Vikk let out a short laugh. "She wasn't mad about it. I think she wanted me to go. Aunt Uska has something brewing up her sleeve."

"Doesn't she always," Dessa said. She skipped toward him, reaching up to fix his hair, but he swatted her away like a gnat. She gave him a little pout. "Just trying to clean you up before Mara lays eyes on your atrocious state."

"Listen." The nurse cleared her throat. "Sorry to disrupt

your weird family reunion but in case you didn't notice, this isn't a banquet hall. Take your conversation outside."

"Sorry," Dessa said.

Vikk looked over the counter to see the nurse's nametag. "Can we go up to see Mara and Finley Eldress, Mrs. Ogilvy?" Curiously, she had a peculiar aura. It was in equal parts annoyed and aroused. The first made sense, the second, well, he was at a loss to understand.

"It's Ms. Ogilvy," she cooed at him.

*Oh.* That explained a few things. For a split second he was speechless. Beside him, Dessa snickered while Hannah muttered, "You've got to be kidding."

"*Ms.* Ogilvy," Vikk corrected, using his smoothest voice. He noticed that the reception desk had elephants-wearing-stethoscopes statues as part of the decor. "I like the elephants."

"Don't use that voice on me, young man," the nurse said through thin lips. "You three are playing a prank on me, trying to use that poor woman's name and her daughter as some sort of cruel joke. I'll have you remember that this is a children's hospital."

Hannah had had enough. She'd rather deal with a brigade of green recruits who didn't know their ass from their teeth. While Vikk's flirting with the nurse might help them in the long run, this was stupid and she was losing her patience.

Hannah put her hands on the counter. "We know she's here," Hannah said in her utmost authoritative voice.

The nurse faltered ever so slightly, but not enough to satisfy Hannah, because as Nurse Ogilvy came to a standing position, her expression hardened into a "try me" mode.

Hannah did not want to get arrested when she was so close to finding Mara and Finley. She'd been worried sick for the last five days, and she trusted no one until she saw both with her own eyes. "Ma'am, Mara texted me her room number. It's 321. We'll go upstairs, you can return to your novel, and we can all pretend that this never happened."

"One, we have no patients with that name," Nurse Ogilvy said. "I searched. Two, even if we did, only two visitors are allowed at a time." She pointed at a sign on the counter, as if a piece of paper somehow explained their dilemma. "Now I am going to have to ask you to leave or I will call security."

The nurse's eyes jerked to the far corner of the reception area. "And you," the nurse shouted to a shadowy corner "need to stop lurking and come out. Acting like you got some invisibility cloak. Don't pretend I don't see you."

Hannah swiveled, her hackles rising.

"What is it?" Dessa asked her, coming to stand right beside her. Why was her tiny presence so reassuring?

Hannah noticed that Vikk took a sudden interest in the interaction between her and his sister. Not that it mattered in the moment. She'd sized him up when he first fumbled into the hospital. Vikk was tall and strong, but that's not what kept her from challenging him. No, he was like a dragon who'd just discovered someone had stolen his treasure hoard. Hannah was wise enough to stay out of his way.

"My guess is Calix has slipped in," she muttered. "We need to get upstairs right now."

"Are you saying Calix is *here?*" Vikk asked, dropping the duffel and sprinting across the lobby, inspecting every corner. He was fast, faster than anyone Hannah had ever seen.

"He followed us from Boston," Hannah added.

Dessa asked, "Why didn't you tell me?"

"What would you have done?" Hannah asked even as she admired Dessa's desire to protect Mara.

"I would have thrown licorice sticks at him from the back window."

It was on the tip of her tongue to remind Dessa that she'd eaten all the red licorice, but that would have revealed she'd been intently aware of her passenger's actions during the drive.

"The lobby is empty," Vikk said through gritted teeth.

"Wait just one moment." The nurse's tone had shifted dramatically. "Are you implying that the husband is *here?*" You'd think they'd just admitted her favorite celebrity was on the premises. "In my hospital?" she whispered wistfully.

"I thought you said Mara and Finley were not patients here?" Dessa asked.

The nurse quickly bunched her lips. She'd been caught, not that she'd ever admit it, Hannah thought. "All of you need to leave." Nurse Ogilvy's voice was like an immovable object.

An instant later, everything changed.

Just as the nurse picked up her phone to call for support, the front door slid open. A lithe woman, who walked like the world was meant to part for her, sashayed her way into the reception area.

As if on cue, Nurse Ogilvy's mouth hung open in stupefied shock. A heartbeat later, she fainted, taking the entire phone box and cord with her.

The newcomer's expression was eagle-eyed, her fiery red bob defining, and her projected persona one of ambition, determination, and ferocity. The cameraman following her would carefully edit out the fact that she'd puncture your beating heart with the heel of her Louboutins if it meant she got the inside scoop.

Hannah knew things were about to go from bad to worse when Patti Stoltz waltzed onto the scene.

# TWENTY-ONE

"I think you are going to have to repeat all of that, Dr. Vuzmuc," Mara said after sitting down on the pullout sofa. Her knees were weak, her mind was utterly confused, and it was difficult to swallow the large lump forming in the back of her throat. In fact, the room was closing in on her. The edges of her vision were shrinking, the corners fading to black.

*Just breathe, Mara.*

Leaning over, she inhaled several deep breathes, releasing them slowly. She practiced her counting.

Mara had had no way to prepare for the doctor's statement when they came into the room, closed the door, and said, "We are in unprecedented waters," before launching into the most insane diagnosis she'd ever heard in her life.

Finley did not seem to be having as difficult a time in processing the doctor's words.

"I'm Vraitheian?" she all but squealed joyfully. "Mom! Did you hear? I'm Vraitheian!"

"*Half* Vraitheian," Dr. Vuzmuc clarified in their even tone.

Oh, Mara had clued in on that part, too, after the doctor

said it the first time. She could not tell if the doctor was pleased or displeased with this information.

"Does this mean I'll get better?"

Even Mara held her breath at the question.

"Not necessarily." Dr. Vuzmuc seemed to choose their words carefully. "I want to manage expectations. I believe we now understand *why* you are experiencing issues, but there is no cure, Finley. You are caught between two worlds. As I said, we are in uncharted waters here. For example, human puberty takes between two to five years. Vraitheian puberty is usually a twelve-year process, and we are not what you might call fertile until our mid-twenties. That's just one example of how your human developmental cycle is at odds with the Vraitheian version. Your hypothalamus is waging war with itself by pumping either too much or too little hormones into your system as it seeks to regulate."

As Mara listened intently to every word Dr. Vuzmuc said, she watched her daughter. Finley seemed to be taking it all in much better than she was herself.

"Your scans," Dr. Vuzmuc continued, "indicate that your gut flora are causing a significant amount of inflammation. This affects everything—from your energy levels, to how regular your digestive system is, to getting your body to absorb the nutrients it needs to fuel your body. Adding food, water, and other nutrients from Vraithe to your diet might assist in alleviating this inflammation and offset some of your symptoms. Dr. Smindle, Taloncourt's physician, has a very good program for this. She sends nutritional care packages to several Vraitheians who make Earth their home."

"Even a little bit of improvement sounds appealing to me, Dr. Vuzmuc," Finley said. There were tears in her eyes. "Just knowing what the issue is, is such a relief. It validates that I've not been making it up. What about the headaches? Sometimes it feels like my skull wants to implode."

"My assessment is that it is due to the partial development of the Vraitheian receptive mind orbit—which we call the 'RMO'. Vraitheians can communicate with one another with their minds through telepathy. It is one of our seven senses."

Finley let out a sigh. "That would be cool if it didn't hurt so much. Can I turn it off?"

Mara had seen RMO in practice when CeCe and Vikk were "talking" with their minds after CeCe showed her the videos from Earth. Mara recalled that it made her feel unwelcome and alienated from the conversation.

"Once it is fully developed, yes, RMO can be switched on and off, like a light switch," Dr. Vuzmuc said. "It can take some practice, but I think in time you will be able to turn it off."

"Are there..." Finley hesitated. "Are there others like me?"

Dr. Vuzmuc's expression softened. "I don't have a good answer, but it is a fair question. Vraitheians have been regularly visiting Earth for over one hundred years. Do I think there are others who are part-human and part-Vraitheian? Yes, the odds are high."

"You don't keep track?" Mara asked. From her time in the military, she was so used to everything being monitored and recorded that it seemed highly irregular that Vraithe would not at least be curious.

Dr. Vuzmuc shook their head. "Not that I am aware of."

"Mom?" Finley asked, sliding off her bed and coming over to sit down next to her on the small sofa. "Are you all right?" Finley took her hand. "I know it's a lot to take in, but now we know why doctors here could never figure it out."

"I'm all right, kiddo," Mara said, squeezing her hand reassuringly. "You're right, it is a lot. You're so strong, Finley. I appreciate how well you are accepting everything."

The problem for Mara was that everything was becoming so real, it was unraveling everything she'd always thought was real right before her eyes. Yes, they'd been on an alien planet, and she now knew for an absolute fact that intelligent life existed beyond Earth. The glamour veil had dissipated. When she looked at Dr. Vuzmuc, sometimes Mara still saw a human form, but mostly she saw their Vraitheian form.

Strange how none of it had felt real until now, in this moment, as she learned her daughter was half...alien.

Then again, *was* Dr. Vuzmuc's diagnosis accurate? Could she get a second opinion? She felt a hysterical laugh bubble up. A second opinion from whom?

There was really one question on Mara's mind, one she'd been trying to ignore.

If Finley was half Vraitheian, that meant one of her parents was full Vraitheian.

But *which* parent?

The ringing in her ears rose to a fevered pitch. The room was getting smaller and smaller.

Mara was an orphan. A foster care child. She'd never known her parents. Never had a family tree or extended relatives who mailed her birthday cards or ugly sweaters for Christmas.

Was she the child of Vraitheians who'd not been able to keep her for some reason? Who hadn't wanted her? Had something happened to them?

As a child, she'd always wondered about her parents, but as she grew up and learned firsthand just how unfair the world was, Mara had let go of that trauma. Or rather, she'd buried it. Deep down she knew that it wasn't really gone. It hadn't just vanished into thin air. But she supposed she'd been doing an adequate job of hiding from it.

But now, after hearing Dr. Vuzmuc's words, it all came crashing down on her.

The abandonment.

The fear of not being enough.

The desire to be absolutely perfect, so those who were in her life did not reject her.

For a few days, while on Vraithe, and with Vikk, Mara had felt a sense of calm and belonging she'd never felt before.

She missed it. She missed Vikk.

Finley, still sitting on the pullout sofa, watched her mom suffer in silence.

*That's who Mom is: a silent, suffering warrior, who takes care of everyone else before she addresses her own needs.*

Finley remembered Mom after she'd been injured on the battlefield—memory loss, confusion, dizziness, outbursts of uncontrollable sadness mixed with anger. Dad had been useless at the time, so ten-year-old Finley had to keep track of her mom's medical appointments and therapy sessions.

Granted, this wasn't the same thing as a combat injury, but Finley still wanted to help her. To fight for Mom. To make decisions.

"This is good news, Mom." Finley said. "Don't you see? It explains why Vraithe felt like home to us. If I'm part Vraitheian, then that must mean you are, too." Finley glanced at the doctor's purple-pink face and saw the uncertainty written in their furrowed klaum nodules. "Right, Dr. Vuzmuc?"

"We do not know which parent, Finley. I did not collect any samples from your mother. I can, but the analysis will take several days, just like your tests did."

"I'm too light-headed to let you draw blood, Dr. Vuzmuc," Mara said weakly. "No offense."

Dr. Vuzmuc smiled at her. "None taken, Mara. While I do not know which of your parents is Vraitheian, Finley, we do know the Vraitheian family tree from which you are descended."

Mara's heart was in her throat. The lump returned in triplicate. Why did this feel monumental, that everything would change even further after learning this information? She chewed on a thumbnail.

"The Stravdas line," Dr. Vuzmuc said without any buildup or preamble. "Queen Uska is your great-grandparent, Finley."

Mara heard Finley's sharp breath as she locked her hand in a death grip.

"Who else knows?" Mara asked.

"Queen Uska is aware. I believe she is pleased with the news."

Had the queen known all along? Or suspected? Is that why she allowed them to use Qoral's suites while they stayed at the palace?

Was Qoral *her* mother?

The room started to spin.

Mara desperately wanted to talk to someone about this, someone knowledgeable, someone she could trust with feelings that boiled just below the surface like lava threatening to erupt. Dr. Vuzmuc, who was very nice, was not that person.

And Finley, well, Finley was her daughter, and should not be saddled with her mother's emotional insecurities. This was big news for both of them. Vikk was that person for her. She should have convinced him to come with them.

She should have tried harder.

Finley had to concentrate, to tell her lungs to breathe, her brain to think, her heart to beat, her eyelids to blink. Sure, Mom was beside her. Dr. Vuzmuc was standing in front of her. The television was on. It was very dark outside. The wind was howling. But she saw none of it. Heard none of it.

*The Stravdas line.*

Royalty.

Her great-grandmother was a queen.

Did that make her a princess?

Did that mean she was part of a bigger family?

When the door behind Dr. Vuzmuc creaked open, Finley didn't notice. Not really.

When the shadow leaned against the doorframe, it reminded her of Mr. Stravdas in his Vraitheian form. Tall, broad-shouldered, with visible klaums on his forehead.

She felt the smile forming on her face as she started to rise, saying, "Mr. Stravdas! You won't believe what—" Her words broke off and she sank back to the sofa once the figure came into the room.

Even Mom stiffened.

The man was tall. He was broad-shouldered. He had klaums on his forehead. Finley noted the metallic teal of his skin, his dark slate-gray eyes. He looked like he'd lived on Vraithe his whole life, except she knew he had not. She knew without a doubt he'd never stepped foot on the planet.

"Dad?" Finley asked.

"Calix?" Mom said at the same time.

Even as a child, Calix Eldress knew he was special. Rules never seemed to apply to him. His parents, both military officers, rose quickly in rank due to their athletic prowess, their excellent strategic and operational thinking, and their ability to get others to do their bidding. He'd taken after his parents in looks, ability, and skill.

As an adult, no one could deny him. No one *wanted* to deny him.

Women came easy. So did money.

He was wickedly intelligent, funny when it suited him, ruthless when he needed to be, but it was all crafted with charm and polished sophistication. It wasn't a production, per se, but his natural persona. In short, things just came easy to him.

So when he slipped into the hospital unnoticed at the exact time he needed to learn Mara's exact whereabouts, Hannah Atholms, that loud mouth who thought she could outsmart him just happened to say "Room 321."

*Thanks, Command Sergeant Major Atholms. Such a good soldier, following the orders of her betters.*

As he walked down hallways with elephant murals and entered a stairwell, it irked the shit out of him to learn that Mara had been here the entire time. He'd lose face with the media. He didn't like looking bad. His business might take a dip in sales. They'd take one sniff of the situation, grant saint status to Mara, while painting him as the negligent dad who couldn't care less—hadn't even *known*—that his own child had been admitted to a children's hospital a week ago.

Calix saw the headlines already: *Delinquent Dad tries to marry fashion heiress while sick daughter is in the hospital*, and *Vet Mom fights for ill daughter while Deadbeat Dad sucks up to the camera.*

So what if he'd accused Mara of kidnapping Finley?

Patti Stoltz had been claiming he'd all but butchered the both of them. He was just waiting for her to speculate he'd used chainsaws for the job, to make it even more sensational. Early on, he'd appreciated Patti's devotion to such outlandish fabrications, but when she'd moved on to some ridiculous narrative that he and Mara were military spies, she'd lost all credibility in his eyes. Sure, he'd would have been fine had she speculated *he* was the spy—he would have gladly accepted a James Bond-like moniker —but to add Mara, a foster kid mutt, into the mix? Yeah, no.

Calix decided the best course of action was to keep running with the theory that Mara had been poisoning their daughter for years. Why else would they be in the hospital six states away from where they lived? To throw authorities off the scent.

Of course, the hospital *was* less than an hour from Baltimore, which was where he and Abigail lived. Those with half a brain cell might conjecture that Mara had chosen a hospital close to Calix so that he might be able to visit.

Damn you, Mara.

The third floor was quiet. The hallway lights were dimmed and the reception desk, decorated with elephant doctors and colorful balloons, was unmanned. A room to the side appeared to be lounge of some sort, with a television, couches, and vending machines. Calix heard a small hum of conversation from that direction, but no one glanced his way as he passed.

When he reached Room 321, at the end of the hallway, the door was shut, but he heard several distinct voices behind it. He tried the handle, and the door quietly swung open.

He scanned the room. Finley and Mara were sitting on a sofa against the far wall. A tall, bald doctor happened to be standing a few feet to the side, clipboard in hand. Flowers decorated the counter. Half-eaten food containers filled the side table, with empty cartons in the waste receptacle near the door. By the stack of paper near the foot of the pullout sofa, it looked like Mara had been grading school essays.

It was clear they'd been here a while.

All eyes zoomed to him, which, if he were being honest, he was used to. People did tend to admire him. But this felt different. The air was heavy and suffocating, as if he'd entered a box with a ticking time bomb where a smoke grenade had gone off early.

It was perplexing.

For a split second Finley seemed overjoyed to see him, which was, well, bewildering. Never in the course of her life had Finley been excited to see him. Even when she was a baby, with big, round, unblinking brown eyes, she'd viewed him with distrust. It was like Finley had actually understood when he'd complained her mom was spending too much time with her, so she shouldn't blame him for wanting to give her away to a very nice couple he'd just met.

Finley's excitement was followed by her calling him "Mr. Stravdas."

Who the fuck was Mr. Stravdas? And why would Finley be excited to see this person?

She'd grown taller, her hair was longer, though stringy. He grimaced as he took stock of her sallow complexion. How old was she again? Fourteen, fifteen? Jesus, child, eat a carrot. Stand in the sunshine. It had been a year or so since he'd last seen her, before Mara moved to take that stupid teaching job. Not that he really cared, but he'd still challenged Mara in family court, just to put a thorn in her side. In the end the judge had asked Finley what she wanted, and that was that.

Now, as he watched Finley's face fall when she realized he was not this Mr. Stravdas person, he was surprised to see that her expression morphed into something else, something like shock, like she was seeing a ghost.

"Sorry to disappoint you, Finley," Calix said, coming farther into the room.

Instinct told him he was walking into a storm, that he should turn tail and escape while he could, but he was nothing if not cocky and self-assured. Puffing his chest, he turned to the doctor. Best to go ahead and take control.

"I'm Calix Eldress," he said. "That's my missing daughter,

Finley Eldress, and unless you want lawsuit in your hands, I suggest you contact the authorities right away."

Patti Stoltz could already feel the prestigious weight of the Pulitzer Prize for Journalism in her hands. Thank-you speeches were already being written in her head when she encountered the small group of jackasses standing at the children's hospital reception desk, including the one who fainted. Awe, thanks for that, darling. Must be a regular viewer.

Within seconds, Patti had already dismissed the blond short-stack and the tall, tousled man who looked like he'd developed a last-minute epiphany to climb to the top of a mountain in a business suit and loafers. Dumb idea, sure, but, upon further inspection, Patti wouldn't kick him out of bed. She wouldn't even make him shower. He had an unkempt Viggo Mortensen vibe.

It was the fourth member of that party that drew Patti's interest.

She'd been doing some digging on Mara Eldress. Found a few photos online. Several photos contained a Xena Warrior babe. Tall, jet-black hair, unsmiling, biceps for days, looked like she could kill you in three moves or less. Patti had asked Glenda to sniff out the details and Glenda, as usual, was right on the money.

Standing before her was one Command Sergeant Major Hannah Atholms.

Talk about prestige, honor, and bravery. The soldier was a living, breathing recruitment poster in the flesh, one who might challenge a young man to an arm-wrestling content. Win, congrats, you're enlisted. Lose, sucks for you buddy, you're enlisted.

Patti's panties grew damp at the thought of mind-jousting with this top-rated soldier. She loved a good adversary.

"You two head upstairs," Sergeant Atholms told the other two while staring daggers right into Patti's soul. "I'll deal with her."

"What about the nurse?" short-stack asked in an undecided tone. She and unkempt Viggo looked eager to run away, but empathy held them back. Cute but boring, like bland meals from a kid's menu.

Patti's laugh was just husky enough to be both sexy and condescending. "We're in a hospital. Page a doctor."

"Just go," Atholms said. "I've got it from here."

Patti's lips curled as they ran down the hallway.

It was just Patti and Xena Warrior babe.

And Patti's trusted cameraman.

Keiji stood back and observed Calix Eldress. The *real* Calix Eldress. There was a lot of bluster in the man. Now would have been the perfect time to use a magnifying glass, to study the unusual teardrop-shaped klaums on Calix's forehead, but Keiji had left that tool in their office on Vraithe.

"Most interesting," Keiji said instead of addressing Finley's father's statement about calling the authorities.

Keiji doubted the man knew his true appearance. By Vraitheian standards, Calix was well above average in appearance, but this was by no means the same caliber physique he commanded using the glamour veil here on Earth. Keiji had seen the videos. Here on Earth, Calix Eldress was quite the specimen. And because he'd been born on Earth and had never traveled the Vraitheian portal, he would only have seen the glamour veil version of himself.

*Oh, yes,* Keiji thought as they circled him. *There is certainly a draw toward him, an unseen force that causes the eye to focus on him and him alone.* Keiji's inquisitiveness was, of course, medical in nature. It would be quite the honor to dissect his teal layers, to see which version might present itself underneath, Vraitheian or Earthling.

Behind Keiji, Finley's incredulous voice asked, "Like, you're both seeing what I'm seeing, right?"

Medical curiosity aside, it answered the child's Vraitheian parentage. Keiji was old enough to have known Qoral before her abdication. The resemblance was there, especially in the teardrop-shaped klaums and the teal coloring. Calix was, without a doubt, Qoral's son, which made him Queen Uska's grandson.

"Yes," Mara answered. "I see it."

Keiji turned to Mara. "There will be no need for that blood test, Mara."

Mara looked utterly dumbfounded—she'd had one too many surprises today—but she managed to say, "I concur, Dr. Vuzmuc."

"Will *I* develop teal skin?" Finley asked.

"Blood tests? Teal skin? What the hell is going on?" Calix hissed. He smirked at Mara. "And what's with the stupid flower painted on your cheek, Mara?"

Keiji took note of the sneer, that cruel curl of the lip that was nothing like Uska. Sadly, Earth had changed Qoral and Boheerim, changed the way they'd raised their offspring, and not for the better.

"While I doubt my patient is pleased to see you, Calix Eldress—and she is most certainly *not* missing—I must say your entrance was perfectly timed to answer a pressing medical mystery," Keiji said just as their beeper buzzed.

Keiji read the code. The hospital's security had been breached.

Vikk didn't wait for Dessa to catch up.

"Don't worry about me," Dessa said as she entered the stairwell. Vikk detected the sarcasm, but he just didn't care. He was already two floors up. "You go on ahead. I'll hang back and wait for Hannah."

He paused and leaned over the railing. "I think you're barking up the wrong tree, Dessa, but I'm not exactly an expert on any of this."

"Yeah, no kidding," Dessa said with a laugh. "Just tell Mara how you feel."

"That's my plan. Do you think I'm sprinting upstairs for my health?"

"I think you're an idiot. Why are you talking to me when you should be looking for Mara?"

Vikk growled down at his sister. She just laughed at him. "From now on, little sister, you can bring the books to Taloncourt yourself."

"Don't be hasty, Vikk. Let's talk about it first," Dessa called up. She said more but he was no longer listening as he exited the stairwell and sprinted down the hallway. The numbness in his chest cavity began to lessen. He was closing the distance between him and his beloved.

*Mara, I'm on my way.*

It almost felt like he could breathe again.

Mara was rendered speechless as she observed her ex-husband. Calix's physical appearance flickered, alternating between his human form—tall, handsome, with a chiseled jaw, and a very cut physique—to his Vraitheian form. She understood why Finley mistook him for Vikk at first. In the shadows of the door, Calix had mostly presented a silhouetted outline.

Calix's true from was impressive. His sparkling gray eyes were startlingly brilliant beneath a strong brow bone set with several klaums on each side. He was at least four or five inches taller than his human form and the teal coloring visible on his hands, arms, and face was a beautiful hue.

His striking shoulders, tapered waist, and strong legs would make a personal trainer weep tears of joy. Mara could not lie. One thing about Calix, he was and would always be a handsome man on either planet. It was his insides that ruined the package. Thankfully, in the years since their rushed wedding, Mara had become immune to him.

"He doesn't know, does he?" Finley whispered. "Like, he has no idea he's really from...?" She seemed reluctant to say the rest out loud.

"I believe he's totally in the dark," Mara whispered in reply. "Doubtful his parents told him."

But it explained so much, Mara thought. His athleticism. His charm. Everyone who met him felt that invisible string that tugged them toward him. They wanted to get to know him. Wanted to please him. Wanted to be the object of his attention, his desires and affection. It was why people like Patti Stoltz glommed onto him with damn near obsession. They didn't even have to meet him in person to feel captivated.

It was quite shocking to realize that Calix was the grandson of a queen. He was anything but regal.

Strangely, Mara was not fearful. In fact, she felt like she could breathe fully and deeply for the first time in ages.

She thought that once she'd come face-to-face with Calix, she'd feel his rage. Instead, he seemed more confused than angry. They were all looking at him like *he* was the freak in the room. For someone so used to adoration, that had to be disorientating for him.

Dr. Vuzmuc was inspecting Calix as if he were a horse for sale, even going as far as pulling out a tape measure and asking doctor-type questions, like, "How tall would you say you are? And your weight? When and where were you born?"

Of course, Mara was not surprised when Calix refused to answer any questions.

"What kind of quack doctor are you?" he snapped. Then he turned on the charm. "Though I do not blame you for wanting to measure me. I *am* a model of perfection. I balance cardio with lifting, and eat only a plant-based diet. I limit all alcohol, don't smoke, and get plenty of sleep."

"No animal products," Dr. Vuzmuc murmured. "How very interesting, though I am not surprised. That may explain your balanced system. Have you ever met someone named Dr. Smindle? Do you take any supplements?"

This was going to be interesting because Calix's successful start-up was a supplemental vitamin business. He'd convinced thousands of subscribers to take his unique blend of supplements to get into top shape.

Except Calix knew it was all a scam. He wouldn't consume his own supplements if you paid him a million dollars.

"Stop trying to doctor me and instead diagnosis my daughter, who, even I can see just by looking at her, is very sick and has been for years." He turned to Finley and Mara. "Finley, it is for your own benefit that I say this in your hearing, as well as the doctor's. I am prepared to prove, in a court of law, that your mom has been consistently poisoning you ever since I filed for divorce."

Mara rolled her eyes. It was just like Calix to lie while coming across as charismatic. Without pausing, he redirected his attention to Dr. Vuzmuc. "I want you to test Finley for all known toxins and fax everything to my attor—"

✦✦✦

"Just stop it, Dad." Finley took several fortifying breaths. She had had enough. She stood, giving Mom a squeeze on her shoulder that was meant to convey, *"I'm good. Don't worry about me."*

Nervous energy and adrenaline coursed through her. With deft fingers, she removed her IV line.

"The only toxic thing in my life is *you*," Finley continued. "You expect everyone to drop their lives the second you show interest, as if we should be grateful for your presence. But I've got news for you: your presence stinks like days'-old garbage."

"How dare you speak to me that way," Dad said. His face had turned a deeper shade of teal and his eyes narrowed into slivered chips. He stepped around Finley like she meant nothing to him, and Finley knew that to be true, so it didn't hurt too bad. If he'd pretended to love her this whole time, maybe Finley's heart would have been crushed, but as it was, she was not surprised that Dad was making this about him and him alone.

She turned as he addressed Mom, looking down at her where she still sat on the sofa. "Is this how you've been raising our daughter, Mara, to become a rude and inconsiderate child who has no respect for her parents?"

"Don't act like you care," Finley said, jumping in before Mom answered him. "You never have, Dad. You are a cheater, a liar, and a manipulator."

"Finley, you're too young to fully underst—"

"I'm fifteen years old, Dad," Finley interrupted him as she wiped at her eyes. "Or did you forget? You know what I *do* understand? I understand that you're selfish. I understand that because we don't pay you an ungodly amount of attention, you act like we're an inconvenience to your existence. I understand that you cheated on Mom when she was recovering from her combat injuries."

Dad looked at Mom like she might save him. When that

didn't happen, he glanced at Dr. Vuzmuc, who was taking furious notes on a clipboard. "Are you writing everything down verbatim?" Dad asked.

"Naturally." Dad took a step toward Dr. Vuzmuc and tried to snatch the clipboard, but the doctor was quicker. The doctor clicked their tongue and pulled the data back. "We don't take what's not ours."

Dad's eyes went wide. He pivoted, looking for an ally. Stammering, he said, "It is clear to me your mom has been misrepresenting the facts." He looked bewildered, as if he were lost in the woods and didn't know up from down. "Listen, kiddo, I had needs your mom was unable to address."

"Screw you, Dad." She was too angry to stop the tears. Finley had to get it out or she would burst. How could she be related to this man? "You're full of excuses, aren't you? It's all about you, you, you. Nothing is ever your fault, right? You'll use any situation to your advantage."

Her muscles were shaking and her head was buzzing as she poked a finger in her dad's chest. She wished she could poke through it, to reveal his termite-infested heart. "You told the press that Mom was hurting me. Like, what part of your brain told you that that was okay?"

He surprised her by taking a step back. She moved forward and kept poking and he kept stepping backward. "Mom might be able to forgive you for that, but I don't think I ever will."

They had reached the open door, and were almost into the hallway. Dad kept trying to interrupt her, but Finley didn't give him a chance. "You are a disappointment to me. Associating with you is incompatible with my health and happiness. I never want to see you again."

A hiccup escaped and the tears streamed down her face. In that moment she came to a conclusion: she was nothing like her father and for that she was thankful.

Behind Calix, a shadow appeared, towering over him.

Standing before her was her second-most favorite person in the universe. From his disheveled state, he looked like he'd been traveling for eons to find them.

"Oh, thank God you came," she whispered, just as the shadow's owner knelt down. She pushed her dad aside and rushed into Mr. Stravdas' open arms.

# Twenty-Two

Mara leaped to her feet. There were not many people on the planet Finley would rush to, certainly not after giving her father a piece of her mind.

Mara knew Hannah was here—she'd received a cryptic text that read, "Slightly delayed. Putting out fires in the lobby." She expected to see Hannah's face appear behind Calix, to hear her voice, but at the moment, Mara's soul trembled.

She hoped, prayed, it might be another.

She dared not whisper his name. She couldn't take the disappointment if she was wrong.

Mara was so proud of her daughter for standing up for herself. She knew that it was something Finley had to do on her own. Had she done the mom-thing, had she jumped in at any time, it would not have had the same impact for Finley's piece of mind.

Besides, it was great to see Calix squirm under Finley's intense scrutiny.

Adding to the zaniness, it had been bizarre to see that Dr. Vuzmuc was more interested in scribbling notes than intervening. Perhaps the good doctor also realized that Calix would not actually harm Finley in any physical sense. To do so would have ruined Calix's chances at media redemption. Calix did not refrain from any sense of duty or honor; no, it was self-preservation.

Calix was a like a cat: he'd always land on his feet, no matter what.

So whose arms had Finley run into? Mara's heart raced wildly as she moved toward the door.

If Vikk hadn't been holding a crying Finley, he would have had more of a physical reaction to seeing an unknown Vraitheian in the hospital corridor.

Except, he wasn't entirely unknown. Within seconds the full force of what he was witnessing, what he'd just heard, punched Vikk in the gut. It was the teardrop klaums that revealed the stranger's identity.

They were roughly the same height and build, though Vikk was pleased to see that he had the greater muscle density of the two.

The Vraitheian before him—one Calix Eldress—had no clue he was the grandson of Vraitheian's longest-reigning monarch, or Vikk's second cousin. If Dessa were behind him, she might have been rendered speechless for once in her life, but she'd decided to wait for Hannah at the stairwell at the other end of the corridor. He wouldn't have minded hearing her immediate thoughts on the situation.

Vikk had caught the tail end of Finley's speech as she admonished her father, a man he'd never met but detested with every fiber of his being. Vikk had seen Calix's interviews. Knew what he looked like. Or, rather, what he *thought* he looked like.

The glamour veil had remained intact in the videos, which was interesting in itself.

"I've got you," he whispered soothingly to Finley. She nodded, squeezing her arms around his neck. "Everything's going to be all right."

All of this, of course, meant that Finley was of Vraitheian descent, which might explain some of the symptoms she'd been experiencing. Relief flooded through him. Not because it was an easy solution, but because it meant they had discovered the circumstances behind her illness, and he knew that was something both Finley and Mara were keen to learn.

"Put my daughter down," the man seethed as he stepped fully into the corridor and glared at Vikk.

Vikk wasn't fooled. He felt the blast of Calix's ice-cold stare. There was a gathering maelstrom in those orbs. He was being sized up like an opponent before a boxing match. Calix, still locked in a glamour veil, would perceive Vikk as a human. And as a human, Vikk was tall and incredibly fit, and not somebody you'd mess with. Calix, who was easy to read, felt a sense of ownership over Finley's existence. It was doubtful Calix actually wanted to hold Finley, but because she was in someone else's arms, because she chose someone over him, Calix's jealousy was on full display.

"I don't think so," Vikk responded calmly. "The young lady has made her choice. I wouldn't try anything if I were you."

On the inside, Vikk was ripping the man to shreds. How could someone be so selfish, so stupid, as to give up this family? What a shameful excuse of a man—whether human or Vraitheian—to not understand the worth of someone like Mara, the joy of a daughter like Finley.

Vikk stilled, holding his spot in case Calix tried anything.

He felt his beloved's presence. His heartbeat regathered, matching hers. She was inside the room, just around the door, just beyond Calix.

"What are you," Calix sneered, "some pretend knight in shining armor? Hoping to save Mara from the big bad monster?" Calix's eyes turned dark as he looked Vikk up and down, taking stock of his disheveled state. "You look like a bum to me."

Vikk stood, lifting Finley and closing the gap between them. "The difference between you and me is that I know Mara doesn't need saving. She can hold her own against whatever the universe throws her way."

Vikk could smell the slight tinge of uneasiness coming off the other man. Not fear precisely, but apprehension of the unknown. Calix must have sensed his otherworldly nature.

"What a load of crock."

"I know you're a little slow, so let me explain it to you," Vikk said. "Mara doesn't need someone to fight her battles *for* her. She never did. If you weren't so self-absorbed you might have picked up on that. Mara deserves someone who is her equal, someone who will fight *with* her." Vikk took another step and Calix backed into the wall. "You applied for the position and were found lacking. Any questions?"

"Mara," Calix called over his shoulder, nostrils flared, fists clenched, "I question the company you keep. Admit it, you were never a good judge of character."

"You're right." Vikk heard her soft laugh, as if she had just come to some realization. "After leaving you, Calix, my ability to measure the quality of the people in my life improved considerably. I have you to thank for that. Now, if you don't mind"—her voice was pleasant, almost saccharine—"you are interrupting Finley's rest. Get the fuck out of our lives."

Hannah had no way of knowing that Nurse Ogilvy would be the one to knock Patti Stoltz off their scent, but by the end,

Hannah could credibly add *Public Relations* to her military resume. Hannah liked to consider herself the strong, silent type except when instructing soldiers. All she had to do was pretend that Stoltz was a wayward soldier and it immediately put her in the right frame of mind to play a war of words with the smooth-talking queen of cable crime news.

Granted, most soldiers were not as polished or cutthroat like Stoltz, but they could be conniving and did anything and everything possible to get out of a scrape. Still, Stoltz could hold her own and then some. At any rate, they were locked in the hospital. She'd heard the main doors snick a moment ago, as soon as the emergency alert went into effect.

Hannah did not know how long they'd remain undisturbed, but for the moment her primary goal was to keep Patti Stoltz and her cameraman from going upstairs.

"Grant me an exclusive, Command Sergeant Major Atholms," the viper news anchor said with an arched grin, "or I'll just attribute whatever I like to you. I doubt your higher-ups in the military would approve of either approach, but if you grant me an exclusive, at least you'll have some sway over what I report."

The expertly tailored anchor sauntered over like the moon hung from her every word. Hannah had to admit Stoltz was attractive in a femme-fatale, Russian-roulette sort of way. If Hannah were the dangerous type, the type of person who cave dived, stole motorcycles, or flirted with crime lords, she'd spar quite delightfully with the devil-spawned anchor.

The problem was, Hannah *was* the dangerous type. She chased it, lived it. She'd been injured in combat. She was a master parachutist. Her hearing was beyond repair, and she wore customized hearing aids behind both ears. Her hips and knees ached constantly as the result of jumping out of eighty-one planes. Soldiering was her life and that was all she knew.

But that was the Hannah before she met a sparkly short-stack alien librarian with a penchant for red licorice and dystopian novels.

"I agree to your terms," Hannah answered with no emotion, which seemed to annoy Stoltz. Did she expect fireworks? Tears? A challenge to fight in hand-to-hand combat?

It was clear Stoltz wanted *something* since she'd been so amused when the nurse fainted in soap opera fashion. But Nurse Ogilvy wasn't out cold. She'd picked herself up, resumed her seat at the reception counter, and was listening with rapt attention.

Seeing her daughter comforted in Vikk's arms was an instant balm for Mara's nerves, her sanity. Her chest thudded as if a happy arrow had hit straight and true. Was this content-ment? Happiness?

She dared to dream. To hope.

For the first time, Mara knew that she and Finley were not alone. It was true they had Hannah, but a best friend—an aunt —was not the same thing as a life partner or a father figure.

Mara barely glanced at Calix as he slunk away with zero fanfare or acknowledgment. There were questions written all over his face. He was dying to know who this man was, what his relationship was to her and Finley. Frankly, Mara didn't give a damn about Calix's state of mind. He didn't deserve another second of her time. He knew he was not wanted, not welcome, and that leaving was in his best interest.

She also knew that Vikk would not erupt in anger or react violently. It wasn't in his nature. Calix didn't know that, though.

She hoped he encountered Hannah on the way downstairs. Hannah wouldn't be as dignified. Mara figured Dessa was also in the hospital. Probably with Hannah.

Watching Calix's receding figure, Mara had a feeling he wouldn't bother her for a long time to come.

Then she turned to face Vikk.

"Hi," Vikk said.

"Hi," Mara said with a smile.

They were still standing in the hallway beneath a flickering florescent bulb. Sometimes Mara saw his human form. From his tousled state, he must have had a rough journey getting here. She couldn't wait to hear all about it. Other times, his shape flickered to his Vraitheian form, and he changed hue and size right before her eyes.

Visually, it was disorienting. Physically, however, she wondered why was it she could breathe easier with him nearby? Why did her heartbeat finally feel steady and true?

Patti wasn't sure if she was being outplayed. When Xena Warrior Babe agreed without negotiating, the hair on the back of Patti's neck prickled. It wasn't often she met anyone she considered her equal, but there was always a first time for everything. She launched into her program intro before introducing her special guest. She wasn't live. Glenda and her wizards would stitch it all together in post-production, but she doubt Xena Warrior Babe knew that.

As her mentor always said, *The best way to keep your viewers guessing was to keep your guests disoriented.* It hadn't failed her yet.

"Sergeant Atholms," Patti said in her anchor voice, "for five days, the world has been looking for your friend and former subordinate, Mara Eldress, and her teenage daughter. Officials within the Department of Defense refuse to corroborate Mara's military service. What can you share with me and the Stoltz Program viewers?"

"Thank you for the opportunity to set the record straight. I am, of course, speaking to you in a personal capacity and not as an official spokesperson for the Department of Defense. I have known Mara Eldress for over twenty years. She was an excellent soldier who served with honor. Unfortunately, Mara was injured in combat and, as a result, was medically retired from active duty. Since then, she received treatment for her injuries, gone back to college, and began a new career as a ninth grade English teacher. It is quite admirable what she's been able to accomplish in a short amount of time."

Patti was bored to death. She wanted Xena Warrior Babe to imbue intrigue, mystery.

*You're building a larger case. This is just one stop of many.*

To maintain her enthusiasm, she envisioned the Pulitzer Prize Board announcing her name.

"Mara Eldress appears to be a very capable woman. Can you address the theory that Mara and her ex-husband, Calix Eldress, are former military spies?"

"There's nothing to address. It's not a real theory."

"You can share your secrets with me, Sergeant," Patti said with a conspiratorial tone, winking at the camera. "You're amongst friends."

What Patti really wanted to do was use her microphone as a pugil-stick against the back of Atholms' head. Why did Xena Warrior Babe have to look so serious, so unflappable?

"I am unable to comment on a theory you invented, Ms. Stoltz."

Patti laughed for the camera. "No doubt the Department of Defense has a wish to keep its secrets safe and sound. You are doing *them* proud, Command Sergeant Major Atholms, but the greater public deserves the truth." Patti had to pivot the conversation. It was like interviewing a mule. "Can you share with me why you're here, at the Capitol Children's Hospital in Washington, DC.?"

"Finley Eldress is receiving specialized care from the excellent physicians here. She was admitted last Saturday and is responding well. I am not at liberty to discuss her illness nor her treatment, but we have every expectation that Finley will thrive due to the exceptional care she is receiving."

Xena Warrior Babe almost cracked a smile as she continued, "Your viewers can learn more in Mara's memoir, *Fighting for Her: A Soldier's Struggle,* where she discusses not only her own frustrations with the military medical system, but also the challenges she's faced in getting a diagnosis for her daughter's chronic illness. Mara selected Capitol Children's Hospital because it was close to Calix Eldress's Baltimore residence. Because they were so immersed in Finley's medical appointments, neither Mara nor Finley were aware of Calix's claims until today."

Now *this* was something Patti could sink her fangs into.

"Shall we go inside?" Vikk suggested in a low voice. A smile tugged on his lips. When Mara didn't answer right away, he added, "It's fine if you want to stay in the corridor."

"You're blocking the door, Mom," Finley whispered in a scratchy voice that was laced with a touch of laughter.

"Oh." She'd been so caught up in starring at Vikk that she forgotten how to operate her legs.

As they went back into the room, Dr. Vuzmuc said, "Ah, Stravdas, I was wondering when you would make an appearance."

The doctor had finished up their notes and was leaning over to pack everything away in a beat-up leather satchel. Mara noticed that their Vraitheian black locket slipped out from under their clothing. Without missing a beat, Dr. Vuzmuc caught it and tucked it back beneath their shirt.

"It's a long story," Vikk said as he deposited Finley onto the bed. She immediately took a long drink from her water cup. With the four of them in the room, the space felt cramped.

The doctor grinned. "It would have to be, to keep you from restoring your heartstring connection." There was an instant pause in the conversation. Dr. Vuzmuc glanced ever so briefly between Mara and Vikk. "I suppose I shouldn't have said anything."

"It's just that..." Vikk said with some trepidation. His eyes flew to Mara's. "It's just that we haven't really discussed it."

Mara looked at Vikk's throat. With the state of his disheveled clothing, it was easy to see he was still not wearing his own locket. Mara picked up on the fact that Dr. Vuzmuc said Vikk had returned to "restore" his heartstring connection. She was becoming more confident that Vikk had meant her all along but was afraid to confess how he felt.

"Discussed what?" Finley asked as she picked up her phone and changed her mind on joining the conversation. "Actually, never mind. I need to update Serstene and CeCe. Do you think they'll have to start calling me Your Royal Highness?" she joked.

"Well." The doctor coughed and made for the door. "I should let you two get caught up. I'm off to order a round of nutritional care packages for Finley from Dr. Smindle. I think with the right amount of tinkering we'll find a good solution for Finley's needs, though"—Dr. Vuzmuc glanced down at a device in their hand—"I should probably respond to hospital security first, considering they've been paging me for twenty minutes. Seems there's a situation in the lobby."

Mara watched the door close and refocused on Vikk. "Hallway?" she asked. Vikk appeared to understand that she needed answers, and that those answers could not be said in front of Finley.

He nodded. "Hallway."

Patti smelled blood in the water. She feasted on such things.

"Are you saying Calix Eldress was aware of their location the entire time, even as he claimed Mara kidnapped Finley as revenge to prevent him from remarrying?"

"I am not in Calix's confidence, nor do I know his rationale, but the hospital *was* chosen with his knowledge."

Looking directly at the camera, Patti said, "It certainly sounds like Calix has some explaining to do."

"He's here, you know," chirruped a voice behind the reception counter. "You can ask him yourself."

Patti observed the elderly nurse. Earlier, she'd dismissed her right out the gate, even with the fainting. It was nice to meet her fans, but she didn't actually want to interact with them. Now, however, it was clear that Nurse—Patti squinted at the name tag—Ogilvy was about to become her new best friend.

"Hey boss," Jerry, her cameraman called out cheerfully. He'd already pointed the camera down the hallway just as a lone figure emerged from an elevator. "Look who I found."

Patti watched the tall, broad-shouldered figure try and fail to open each exit door.

"Jackpot," Patti purred before telling her cameraman, "call Glenda, tell her we're about to go live." Patti felt warm and aroused all over, like a spider approaching its prey just before their panic set in. She wouldn't be satisfied until she caught Calix stranded in a corner, squirming with a camera and a microphone in his face. "And Jerry, if you mess this up, I will feed your corpse to feral pigs."

"Easy-peasy, boss," Jerry said good-naturedly as he made the necessary connections. "I got this."

"Technically," the nurse said, "I'm the one who found him. The reception desk has security monitors."

Patti snapped her head back, intending to order the nurse to keep her damn mouth shut, when she realized their party was down one person.

Hannah Atholms was gone.

"You didn't have to wait for me, Dessa," Hannah said with surprise as she entered the low-lit stairwell. If it wasn't for the bright red Exit sign, which emitted a soft glow on the surroundings, Hannah would have tripped over her.

"What if you needed backup?" Dessa grinned at her own question. Dessa's skillset was mostly on settling disputes and calming others down. She wasn't fast like her brother, nor was she persuasive like other Vraitheians. She liked translating books, happily-ever-afters, and being caught in stairwells with Hannah Atholms.

The last was a recent development.

However, it did not appear that Hannah was in full agreement. She didn't smile like Dessa hoped she would. "I left Calix in Patti Stoltz's destructive hands. She'll do the dirty work for us."

"Why does it feel like you've let him off easy?"

"On the contrary," Hannah said with a slight shake of her head. "Calix values his reputation above everything else. Of course, I'd like to sock him a good one, but he'd be able to spin that in his favor. He'd be the victim and somehow manage to pin it on Mara."

"Which isn't something we want."

"Exactly. Plus, I doubt Mara would want me to jeopardize my career. With Patti Stoltz cornering Calix, he has to face the lies he's been telling the world. Stoltz clearly has a hard-on for him, but she's more interested in elevating her career, not sampling his wares. It couldn't have gone any better if you ask me. Remind me to send flowers to Nurse Ogilvy."

Stumped, Dessa scrunched her eyebrows. "I don't understand. Because she fainted?"

"No, because she saved my ass back there. I was able to sneak away because of her."

"But *I* wanted to save your ass." Dessa couldn't believe she was jealous of the nurse.

Hannah opened her mouth to say something, then stopped. Finally, she said, "It's sweet that you wanted to help me, Dessa, but..." She trailed off.

"But what?"

"I'm not in a good place for something like this"—Hannah motioned between them—"a relationship. Next year, I'll be retiring from the military after serving for twenty-six years. I'm not young like you, Dessa. I don't even know where I plan to live. I'm forty-six years old and you are what, twenty-five?"

Dessa knew she looked young, and the glamour veil didn't help, either. "Do you want human years or Vraitheian years? On Vraithe, I'm thirty years old. On Earth, due to the time differential, I'm closer to seventy."

Hannah sat on a stairwell step. "Are you telling me you're seventy years old, Dessa? You have flawless skin and a youthful appearance."

"Yes." Dessa sat as well. "We age differently."

"Well, that certainly adds another layer of complication." Hannah rubbed her face. "I went from being too old for you to being too young." She chuckled disbelievingly. "It still doesn't change where I was going with the conversation."

Dessa's face dropped, and she studied her hands in her lap, not sure what to say.

"I hope you'll forgive me if I'm assuming there's more going on here than there is," Hannah said. "You're sweet and beautiful and I'm, well, I'm just a broken soldier with a very big truck. I'm not good at relationships. None have ever lasted. You deserve dancing and a whirlwind romantic adventure where someone sweeps you off your feet. My dreams involve getting more than three hours of sleep a night and dulling the constant ache in my hips and knees. What I'm saying is, don't waste your time on me, Dessa."

"I..." Dessa started, but then nodded. She wanted to argue with Hannah, tell her that she was monumentally wrong about all of this. That none of it was a waste. But you couldn't force love. "I understand, Hannah. Thanks for being honest."

Dessa pressed against the locket at her chest, felt it vibrate. Some heartstring connections were not ready to develop. She knew this. She understood this. But knowing it did not take away the mortifying feeling of rejection. She wanted to curl up and hide in a faraway corner. Maybe Hannah wouldn't notice if she sank into her puffy coat. She'd just stay in this spot forever, a permanent fixture in the hospital stairwell.

What made it worse was that Dessa knew Hannah felt something for her. It was clear as day in Hannah's aura. It was there, tangible, like the fibrous tissue between vital organs.

"Thanks for understanding, Dessa."

"For the record, I like your big truck."

Hannah smiled at that. "Maybe when you're seventy-five I'll let you drive it."

"Hey!" Dessa playfully swatted at Hannah's shoulder.

"I hope that we can at least be friends, Dessa, especially if Mara and Vikk are as serious as you make them out to be."

"I'd like that." They stood and began climbing the stairs to the third floor.

"Do you think we've given them enough time?" Hannah asked. "I mean, that's why we haven't left the stairwell, right?"

Dessa's ego took a direct hit. She'd need a full body Band-Aid to staunch the internal bleeding.

She glanced up at Hannah. Her expression was unreadable as she opened the door to the third floor. They really were on different wave lengths, Dessa surmised.

She tried to keep her voice even. "That's exactly right."

# TWENTY-THREE

Mara let Vikk speak first. "I've been a complete idiot, Mara. If I had known my own mind, I would have traveled with you and Finley when you left Vraithe."

"Was someone pressuring you to stay?" During their time on Vraithe, Mara had not met anyone who seemed to try to prevent their pairing. Even the ornery Areola, with her dour face and grumpy mannerisms, eventually appeared to find favor with her.

"No. The moment I removed my Vraitheian black locket, I declared myself to you. Everyone on Vraithe knew."

Realization washed over her. Vikk had removed his locket almost as soon as they'd met.

"*I* didn't know," she said. "You could have said something."

"You're right. I'm sorry," Vikk said, his expression contrite. "In looking back, my motivations were to not distract you from your true purpose in traveling to Vraithe—Finley's health. I believed it would have been unfair of me to place undue expectations on you. While I knew I'd never felt such a powerful heartstring connection before, I couldn't be sure how you felt. I feared it was one-sided."

"It wasn't one-sided," Mara said, "but I appreciate the rationale behind your actions. In hindsight, you did the right thing. I'm the type of person who, for better or worse, needs to make her own decisions free of external influences. And while I know our circumstances and environment impact our decisions, I can be stubborn and sometimes downright obstinate."

"Are you trying to warn me away? Because it's not working, Good-General Mara Eldress." Vikk was smiling now. "I love every part of you—and to me you're absolutely perfect."

The world stopped spinning in that moment. In fact, Mara was sure that gravity had just given up the ghost, because it felt as if her body were in a heavenly state that would float away if she didn't anchor herself firmly on Earth.

Those words, *I love every part of you*, shook her to her core because Mara knew it was not an empty phrase for Vikk. It meant that he accepted her, flaws and all. She wanted to respond in kind, to put words to her feelings, to tell him how her heart expanded with his love, acceptance, and affection, but past experience stalled her. She wasn't equipped for this. Her childhood, her military years, her time with Calix...none of these had prepared her for unconditional love and acceptance.

Vikk seemed to understand. Silently, he wrapped his large arms around her. Mara willingly melted into his embrace.

Kissing the top of her head, he said, "I got so caught up in what I saw as my duty to Vraithe that I forgot the duty to myself and to my heartstring connection—you. It didn't make sense at the time, but I think my aunt placed several obstacles in my path to make me realize I shouldn't feel so duty-bound to Vraithe that I forgot who I was. It was a difficult lesson, but a valuable one. Ever since I was fifteen years old, I have been the queen's heir. I've known most of my life that I would rule the planet."

A sliver of uncertainty crept into the crevices of her mind.

"You don't have to change your destiny for me, Vikk. I

understand you have obligations that prevent you from coming to Earth with any frequency."

As much as she wanted Vikk with her full time, and as much as she wanted him to choose her over Vraithe, Mara wasn't a fool. She wasn't a selfish person. Vraithe's monarchy was set.

"I don't say that to make excuses. I mention it because it was my mindset, one that I've had for several decades. I needed to be knocked off course to see what was right in front of me. I'd been on autopilot. No dreams of my own. No aspirations beyond making films that my aunt might like. Why have dreams when your path is preset for you?"

"What changed?"

"Believe it or not, Werlaun changed my trajectory."

Mara stifled a laugh. Well, *that* took her down a peg. She'd expected to hear her own name.

"Werlaun?" She stepped back to look up into his earnest face. She saw the love, but also the humor in his expression. "This I have to hear."

"*She's* the reason I look like I got lost on the Zilverine Mountain Trail." Mara had to admit he did look a little worse for wear. "The Zilverine Mountains are home to giant, yeti-like bears. At the time, I would have rather faced a yeti bear than Werlaun, but after blackmailing me into helping her obtain an apprenticeship position aboard the Starfleet cruise line—it's a long story—she challenged my way of thinking. She inadvertently put me on the correct path of questioning the differences between my mind and my heart. In that moment, Werlaun was clearly the maestro with me as the novice."

Mara's eyes crinkled. There was so much to unpack in that statement. She wanted to tease him, to congratulate him on *not* facing a Zilverine Mountain yeti-bear. However, after learning more about Werlaun on their trip back to Earth, Mara wasn't at all surprised that the steward had been able to bend Vikk to her will to gain that apprenticeship.

Instead, Mara asked, "What did you learn?"

"My heart was always yours. That I didn't have dreams until I met you. The second I laid eyes on you on the front steps of Riley High School, I was done for. It was like my entire existence had been holding its breath until I entered your orbit. From that moment onward, I knew that all of my possible futures involved you."

"I felt something then, too," Mara admitted. "There was this pull in my chest, like my insides wanted to unravel and grab hold of you. I'd never experienced anything like it." Mara grinned. "Saying it out loud makes it sound like the plot of a horror movie. Honestly, though, at the time, I thought I was having a heart attack."

Vikk's smile widened. "That's your heartstring. No wonder you rushed away that day. While we were together on Vraithe, my heartstrings were communicating with me, but I didn't let my mind process everything correctly. My obligations to my aunt and to Vraithe kept my heart and mind separate. I didn't see a solution because I didn't know how to reconcile my planetary duty with my personal hopes and dreams. After you left, it felt like I was dying inside. Some call it a "hollow heart," where your heartstrings eventually go dormant, never to feel again." He bent down and brushed a kiss on the top of her head. "In a way, I needed the separation to understand what I was feeling, to listen to my heart and my mind, and put everything in unison."

Mara took a long breath and leaned into him again. She felt so content, so full of love and life. She didn't want to think about it ending. Vikk was here now and that's what mattered.

"It was agony being away from you, Vikk. If humans have heartstrings, like you say we do, mine went numb when we left Vraithe. I couldn't feel my chest until you arrived. Now that we both understand what happens when we are apart, we can plan for it."

He squeezed her even tighter. "You're not getting rid of me that easily, my love. I'm here for good...if you'll have me."

"But what about Vraithe? You are its next ruler."

"Not anymore. Ruling Vraithe knowing I'd given up my heartstring connection would make me an infinitely inferior ruler. My life would be empty and meaningless. *Your* life is on Earth. I want to be with you always. I would rather die a thousand deaths than be separated from you again. And before you protest, my aunt is fully aware. I'm quite positive she wanted me to come to this decision."

"You gave it up for me? You would do that?" Mara barely got out the words. He was putting her first? She leaned away, looking up at him.

"I would give up far more, my love, to be worthy of your affection." Vikk paused, studying her face. "And for the record, I will *never* be worthy of your love and affection, but I will do all within my power, day in and day out, to make you and the urchin on the other side of that door happy. Deal?"

"Finley is an urchin, isn't she?"

"True, but that's not the part I'd hoped you'd single out." She felt him shake with suppressed laughter.

"My heart is too full to voice how I truly feel. I accept your deal."

A movement at the far end of the hall caught Mara's attention. Two figures—one tall and statuesque, the other a waifish fairy—were heading their way in a decidedly non-hurrying manner. They'd have company shortly.

"Kiss me before they get here."

When his lips captured hers, Mara allowed herself to become vulnerable to falling in love again. To opening herself to creating a new family, a new bond. One that would not disintegrate, because this time it was real, it was true, and it was hers.

She closed her eyes and sunk further into Vikk's encircled arms.

She knew from that moment forward, Vikk would be by her side no matter what.

As they approached the lovey-dovey couple, Hannah decided that Vikk's looks had improved considerably now that he was in Mara's good graces. Her best friend seemed to bring out his best side. In truth, Hannah had never seen Mara look so content. As long as Vikk supported Mara and Finley through thick and thin, Hannah could rest easy.

And if he didn't, she was only a few hours away to straighten him out.

The part that stood out for Hannah was when Mara's eyes landed on Dessa. It was as if she'd never seen her before, which was odd. She knew they worked at the same high school.

Hannah updated them on Calix, ending with, "Until the hospital gives the all-clear, he's stuck in the lobby with Patti Stoltz and her cameraman. I'm sure the entire encounter will air on her program tonight."

Hannah avoided watching such programs like the plague, but she might make an exception for this one.

"Apparently the fainting nurse played a part, too," Dessa added with a cheeky grin.

Hannah was glad that Dessa wasn't too embarrassed by the conversation from the stairwell. She meant everything she said. It would never work out.

"Piranha news anchors? Fainting nurses? What kind of adventures have you three been having without me?" Mara asked with humor-laced incredulity. "You know what, never mind. I'm going to focus on the fact that Patti Stoltz will flay Calix alive. Or," she added, tilting her head, her voice contemplative, "they'll fall madly in love and create a path of destruction from which the world will never recover."

"Dear God, Mara, don't put that fear in my brain," Hannah said, already imagining the worst. "Stoltz is ambitious enough to eat her own young. Calix doesn't stand a chance." She paused before asking, "Is Finley awake? Can I go in and see her?"

"She might make you bow and address her as Your Royal Highness," Mara joked.

Hannah was confused. "That makes no sense."

"Not only is Finley half-Vraitheian—on Calix's side—she's the great-granddaughter of Vraitheian's ruling monarch," Mara explained. "We've made many discoveries today. One of which is that Finley is a princess."

Had that come from Vikk or Dessa, who claimed to be from an alien planet, Hannah wouldn't have batted an eyelash. Coming from *Mara*, Hannah's first instinct was to place her palm on her friend's forehead to check for a fever.

"Is that a medical diagnosis?" Hannah asked with some befuddlement.

Mara nodded. "In a way, yes. We discovered the source of her symptoms—it's genetic. Things aren't perfect, but they are looking up."

"At least Finley isn't a cat," Vikk added. Hannah saw that there were tears of laughter in his eyes.

"Hey, it was an honest mistake," Dessa said, cheeks burning. "I stand by most of my translations. They are at least"—she seemed to pause to think about it—"eighty percent accurate."

Hannah looked at Mara to get her take on the conversation happening around them. Mara was fully engaged and interacting with them as if they weren't speaking an entirely different language. While yes, *she* was confused, Hannah took it as a good sign that, whatever was going on, Mara was an active and willing participant.

"False! It is zero percent accurate," Mara said with a laugh. "*Fighting for Her: A Soldier's Struggle* is not an erotic thriller, Dessa." Mara turned to Hannah. "All of this probably sounds foreign to you. I'll update you later. For now, feel free to visit with Finley. She'll be excited to see her Hant Anna."

Hannah sensed that Mara and Vikk wanted a few more moments alone. She looked down at the sparkly Dessa. "Do you want to join me in meeting the not-cat Finley?"

Dessa beamed up at her. "I'd love to. You know, I introduced Mara and Vikk. When they perform their bonding ceremony, do you want to be my plus-one? I can secure you a portalport visa."

Hannah knew from their conversation on the drive here that a bonding ceremony was akin to a wedding. "Will it occur on Vraithe?"

"Yes. My aunt will go all out for the celebration. Fireworks, music, jousting."

Hannah's eyebrows rose. She was now intrigued. "You had me at jousting," she said as she opened the door to Finley's room.

From the bed, Finley waved and mouthed, "Hant Anna!"

She was on the phone. It sounded like a conference call. Several voices came through the device at once and Hannah overheard one young male voice emphatically say, "Yes, Your Royal Highness—of course, Your Royal Highness."

"I like your friend, Hannah," Vikk said.

Truthfully, he was glad to have the introduction over with. If anyone was going to object to their union, it would have been the one person Mara trusted above all others.

He wanted to round everyone up and leave the hospital. Until they were all home, safe and sound, with no Calix or Patti Stoltz lurking about, he'd be happier for it. He wasn't worried about keeping them safe. It was that there could be many ears listening in on their conversation.

"I think she likes you, too," Mara answered. "Or, if not, at least she doesn't think you'll boil my bones and drink my broth."

"I didn't know that was an option. Can we go back and redefine our relationship?"

"Not on your life." Mara bunched her eyebrows, a question gathering on her face. "So, about Dessa...this was my first time seeing her Vraitheian appearance and I must say I am surprised. Her pixy human form is very similar to her Vraitheian form. In fact, except for her narrow klaums, I really don't see a difference. You two are related, right?"

He snorted out a laugh. "It's uncanny, isn't it? We may not look related, but she is my sister, through and through."

"It wasn't a concern," Mara clarified. "I was only curious. Also, she mentioned a bonding ceremony...what is that? Will Queen Uska restore your visa?"

"I have a feeling that given Finley's new royal status that my aunt might reconsider my visa status. As to your other question," Vikk said feeling suddenly nervous, "a bonding ceremony is like a dance where the newly bonded couple dances first, before everyone else joins the dance floor."

A dance? No way did she buy that. Mara smirked at him and crossed her arms.

"That doesn't sound like a ceremony that would make you so nervous, Vikk."

"You see, well, on Vraithe," he stammered, "it's not a

dance." Curiously, Mara watched as beads of sweat formed on his forehead. Why would dancing make Vikk anxious? "The newly bonded pair bury their Vraitheian black lockets together before having lusty and vigorous sex in the center of the circle, in front of everyone. After a few moments, other bonded pairs in attendance can join in on the action."

"Are you honestly telling me the Vraitheian bonding ceremony is"—she lowered her voice because they were still standing in the hallway of a children's hospital—"an orgy?"

"Not in the sense that partners are *shared*," Vikk clarified. He wiped his face with a rumpled sleeve. "They have sexual intercourse *nearby*."

"*Like* an orgy?"

Just then another figure approached them in the hallway. Mara was so distracted she didn't notice until they spoke.

"I always cry at bonding ceremonies," Dr. Vuzmuc said conversationally. "Buckets and buckets of tears."

Bewildered, Mara asked, "Does 'tears' mean something else on Vraithe?"

"No, of course not."

"So Vikk is *not* joking?" She was visualizing the scenario in her head and wasn't sure what to make of it.

"Not at all. We take bonding ceremonies very seriously. Don't worry: you *can* control the invitee list, if it makes you more comfortable."

"Thanks," she deadpanned as she refocused on Vikk. "I'll keep that in mind."

He met her gaze but looked bashful. Mara didn't know if she should laugh or cry. "We'll discuss the specifics later. I'm sure we can come up with a different solution. Besides, I don't have a Vraitheian black locket to bury."

Vikk sighed, relieved. For several heartbeats, he'd sincerely feared Mara would freak out. Keiji was not wrong. Bonding ceremonies were emotional, but also a lot of fun. Even though he was no longer his aunt's heir, Taloncourt would still go all out for a royal bonding ceremony, which meant the guest list would be a lot larger than Mara might be comfortable with.

They'd deal with that later.

He was just glad she wasn't revolted at the idea of bonding with him. He felt a little taller with that fact. Jubilant, in fact. His heartstrings were going wild, and he puffed out his chest just as Mara elbowed him.

"Pay attention," she blurted.

He'd missed the first half of what Keiji had said.

Keiji cleared their throat. "As I was saying, I had hoped to inform you that the lobby was clear, but it seems like the news media have converged downstairs and are reporting on Patti Stoltz's interview with Finley's father. It was a bloodbath, metaphorically speaking, of course. Interestingly enough, it appears the night reception nurse, Olivia Ogilvy, assisted him in escaping."

"Same nurse who fainted?" Mara guessed.

"One and the same," Vikk said, shaking his head.

"Calix can be very persuasive." Mara's voice was firm but not bitter. "Women were always falling at his feet."

"Nurse Ogilvy is at least seventy-five years old," Keiji said.

"Go, Nurse Ogilvy." Mara's eyes danced. "Age makes no difference. But seriously, if Patti Stoltz cornered Calix and made him answer his claims, I'm satisfied for the moment."

"You're amazing, Mara," Vikk said, shaking his head. "I'd love it if a meteor fell to Earth and smashed Calix's face. How can you be so calm about everything?"

She appeared to think through her answer before responding.

"I am *not* calm. I have been employing tools to manage my

stress levels constantly since before we left Vraithe. I'm just trying to view things through an objective lens. What's helping the most is that this time around, I'm not alone." She nudged him and he hooked an arm around her shoulders. "I've got all of you."

"Nicely said, Mara. I admire your fortitude and methods." Keiji pivoted to Vikk and said disapprovingly, "Honestly, Stravdas, a meteor? It's best to not invite chaos. Do keep that in mind." Keiji arched one amethyst eyebrow at him.

Was he being admonished?

"It's not like I can summon meteoroids on command."

"Circumstances being as they are," Keiji continued, clearly ignoring him, "I have discussed it with hospital security, as well as the queen, and it is our opinion that an immediate discharge is in order. I have ordered a special car service to transport you to the portal. Be downstairs in the employee basement entrance in thirty minutes. Is this acceptable to you?"

"It sounds like the only option, Dr. Vuzmuc," Mara said. "Thank you for making the arrangements. I hate to ask, but what about my truck? It's also parked downstairs."

The always-stoic Keiji's bony shoulders sagged. Vikk guessed what his aunt had asked and hid a grin behind his hand.

"I know precisely where it is parked," Keiji groused. To Vikk, it looked as if Keiji tried to force a smile but their thin magenta lips twitched instead. "Your truck will be seen to, Mara."

"And we'll see you soon?"

"In a day or two. I will set up a time with you to discuss Finley's records, including her medical records, which are held by the military."

"Thank you"—her voice turned unsteady and her eyes swam with unshed tears—"for everything."

"Glad to be of service." Not one to linger, Keiji saluted and walked away at a brisk rate.

"Such an interesting individual," Mara said. "I can never tell what the doctor is thinking."

"Keiji has always been that way, for as long as I've known them. My aunt trusts Keiji with her life, which means I do, too."

"When you're on Earth, where do you stay?"

"Usually with Dessa or in hotels, if I'm traveling."

"I plan to check with Finley first, but if she's okay with it, do you want to stay with us until we can figure out a future plan? Our place is small, but I'm sure we can pool our resources together to find a bigger house. Now that my memoir is selling well, I should receive a healthy royalty check from the publisher in a few months."

Vikk had some awareness of currency and spending money on Earth. He even had a banking account to deposit the money he received when exchanging Vraithe's gems and diamonds into dollars and euros. He pulled out his Earth phone, opened his banking app, and showed it to Mara.

"Is this enough to get us through the next two months? My duffel is half full of gems if we need them."

Mara looked at the phone, not expecting to see much, and immediately went weak in the knees. Was this a joke? She looked again.

His account balance had over three million dollars. She snapped her eyes to his. He was honestly clueless.

"I think we'll make do, Vikk."

Mara moved to open the door, but Vikk said, "About the bonding ceremony, Mara..."

"Yeah?"

"I don't want to assume anything, but the truth is, my whole body is thrumming with the desire to climb the tallest building to inform the universe that you've claimed my heart and I want to spend the rest of my days with you. But my reward is not yet secure. I also need to know that you choose *me.* That you want to be with me the way I want to be with you."

Even under the hideous flickering florescent light, he was so gorgeous, so sexy, *so* amazing, that it surprised Mara he needed affirmation.

She supposed that even steel-blue gods needed to hear that they were loved.

Mara faced him and tried to assume a serious expression, but failed miserably when she beamed up at him with all the joy her smile could muster.

"Vikk Stravdas, no matter which planet's sun we orbit, I want you next to me forever. I'm happiest when I'm around you. Finley adores you. Hannah has not secretly texted me saying she wants to chuck you from a third-floor window. I'll never forget that Finley ran to you and that you accepted her with no conditions attached. Things won't always be easy, but I promise that with love on our side, we'll make it through everything the universe tosses our way."

"And do you solemnly swear to never cut off my twatsizzle?"

Mara's mouth curved into a wicked smile. "What I swear to do is put it to good use. I seem to recall seeing a poster for *Juicy Swizzletarts Steal Hearts.* Perhaps we can do our own reenactment when we get home."

He nuzzled her neck and growled. "That car service can't get here fast enough."

After playfully swatting his hand away, Mara opened the door and found Hannah and Dessa sitting on either side of Finley. The three of them were chatting with a group of people on Finley's phone. She recognized CeCe and Serstene's voices.

The door snicked closed. Vikk came up behind her and placed an arm across her clavicle, pulling her into him. Mara relaxed against him.

Finley was introducing them to her "Hant Anna." Hannah appeared to take it all in stride. If she was shocked by the alien setting that was likely visible through the phone, Hannah did not let it show on her face. However, Mara noticed that Hannah also glanced quite frequently at Dessa.

Moments later, as they began to pack up the room, Mara was surprised to hear Queen Uska's and Areola's voices through Finley's phone.

Dessa had to do a fair bit of translation. Given her track record, Mara wasn't sure if it was accurate, but the gist of the conversation was communicated back and forth.

When Hannah mouthed, "Her name is *Areola?*" Mara snickered.

From the phone, Areola was crying with happiness as she repeatedly called Finley "Your Royal Highness."

They'd created a monster.

Vikk kissed the top of Mara's head and tears gathered in her eyes. She'd never had this before. The feeling of *belonging*.

The room where they stood contained people who were dear to her, people who loved and cared about her. And on Finley's phone, an entirely new group were now family.

Thank goodness she'd called Vikk's bluff. Otherwise, none of this would have happened. Mara wished she'd given in to Dessa's matchmaking efforts sooner.

As they left the hospital room and made their way to the stairwell and down to the employee basement entrance, Mara overheard snippets of Dessa's conversation with Hannah.

She was explaining the plot of *The Curse of Mathilda's Sorrow*. Dessa confessed she'd become enraptured when the main character transformed into a fire-breathing dragon to prove his undying love for a siren mermaid.

At some point in the future Mara was going to have to sit down with Dessa to discuss the *actual* plot of *The Curse of Mathilda's Sorrow*. There were no dragons or mermaids. Though Hannah, who Mara knew was not a big reader of genre fiction, didn't seem to mind the conversation.

Once in the basement, they parted into two groups. Hannah would never abandon her truck, so she and Dessa were going to take the long way around and drive back to Massachusetts.

Hannah pulled Mara into a hug so tight that she feared her lungs would pop like balloons. "Don't disappear on me again, soldier," Hannah ordered. "Or at least send warning next time."

"WILCO, Command Sergeant Major." Mara smiled. "Thanks for coming to our aid. You've always got my back, Hannah. It means more than you know."

Mara, Finley, and Vikk climbed into the waiting town car. In a matter of minutes, they'd be at the portal, and a few minutes after that they'd be in Boston. Vikk's SUV was parked there, and they'd take it to Mara's house in Riley Township.

"I'm ready to go home," Finley said with a yawn before snuggling up against her side and promptly falling sleep.

"I love you, Mara," Vikk said, leaning over, his lips gently caressing her temple. She felt his heat, the promise of more kisses, of more tomorrows, of a forever.

"I love you, too, Vikk Stravdas."

Finley, mostly asleep, snored softly before adding, "I love you both."

Mara smiled in the darkness.

There was only one thing that remained to make the situation more magnificent. Now that they were back on Earth, Mara could start crafting her battleplan against the school board.

# Epilogue (Abigail)

Abigail Von Grace, one of ten heirs to Von Grace Industries, did not appreciate any form of abandonment.

It didn't matter if it was a flight attendant who failed to come back with her chosen beverage, an executive assistant who refused to respond to texts, or a fiancé—excuse me, *former* fiancé—who ditched her in Boston, Abigail was not one to let bygones be bygones.

When Jasmine abandoned her duties—duties *she'd* been paying for—Abigail called in a few favors. Now she was finally on the tarmac, sitting in a plane bound for Baltimore. She wasn't in first class, but whatever. She could slum it with the poors on a ninety-minute flight.

She'd analyze her Instagram page's statistics while she waited.

Then her phone started blowing up.

Friends, family, strangers, and enemies forwarded clips of some hackneyed cable news talking head.

She'd shrugged at Calix's earlier interviews, the ones where he'd claimed his ex-wife had kidnapped and poisoned their daughter. Yawn. Every family had skeletons in the closet. The

Von Grace family had at least two corpses buried in the concrete foundations of their flagship store on Fifth Avenue.

Really, Calix's past was none of Abigail's business.

Until it affected her personally.

And not just her personally, but her brand. Abigail was a rising nutritionist and fitness expert, and she was *this* close to snagging her first major celebrity as a client.

This new video, however, altered Abigail's mental state to such an extreme degree that she contemplated stabbing her seatmate, who kept hogging the armrest.

Patti Stoltz, a "journalist" and the human equivalent of a Venus fly trap, had cornered Calix in the lobby of a children's hospital. At first, Abigail was confused about the location before she remembered he had a daughter. Calix did not possess dad-vibes and it always slipped her mind he had fathered a child.

Patti Stoltz's voice hounded Calix like a junkyard dog when she asked, "Calix, can you address the allegation that you were previously aware, and consulted, regarding your daughter's admittance into Capitol Children's Hospital a week ago?"

"Who told you that?" Calix said, his eyes darting everywhere but at the camera.

Dark circles and worry lines marred his face. It could just be the lighting, Abigail thought, but it didn't excuse the fact that he looked haggard, like an old man who'd suddenly aged a hundred years.

Super gross. Abigail's last meal threatened to reverse course.

Still, she couldn't look away from this particular car wreck. Patti Stoltz appeared gleeful as she replayed her interview with a woman who could easily win a wrestling match. Then the camera pivoted, following their prey, and catching Calix's backside as he tried every door he came to, clearly looking for a way to escape.

The microphone caught Calix's angry hiss as he muttered, "Hannah Atholms."

"Yes, highly decorated Army Command Sergeant Major Hannah Atholms, Mara's former military supervisor. Thanks for confirming you know her." Calix grunted at that. "So you can understand how it seems a little suspicious that you'd claim Mara kidnapped Finley? I think you even accused your ex-wife of poisoning young Finley? Care to address those claims?"

"Get out of my way." Calix swiveled and bumped into the camera.

He looked feral, unstable, as if he might either turn into a babbling mess or lash out at the lab coat–wearing elephant statue stationed next to him.

Abigail should have bet money on shoving the statue, because a moment later Calix kicked the elephant as if it had killed his father and run away with his mother. Such a Greek tragedy.

"Here's what I think, Calix," Patti said in a deceptively comforting voice. "I think you liked the attention. But it's not always about what *I* think." She peered right into the camera. "Heck, I was convinced you'd hacked them both to death." Patti chuckled like she'd invented a joke. "I like to know what my viewers think. So we ran a Stoltz's viewer poll. Seventy-eight percent of viewers believe you are a lousy father and an unfit father and that you wanted the world to feel sorry for you."

Calix's pitiful face scrunched into an angry red ball.

"Of course, I'm a lousy father," he exploded. "Why wouldn't I be with a weak, sickly, inferior child who clearly did not inherit my genes. I mean, look at me," he boasted like a mixed martial arts fighter taunting his opponent and not like an arrogant idiot insulting a child on national television.

Even Abigail knew that was the wrong thing to do.

Her own father detested her, detested *all* of his kids

between his five wives. Yes, he acted like they were a waste of carbon dioxide–emitting imbeciles, and sure, he had no qualms with letting them know this at various Christmas or Thanksgiving family get-togethers, but Taggert Von Grace would never, ever admit it on camera.

*Have some self-respect, Calix Eldress.*

The video suddenly cut off as an elderly woman rammed into Patti Stoltz and her cameraman as if it were a game of bowling. The last five seconds was audio-only since the frame was stuck on the offender's plump rear end as she said, "Follow me, hunky Calix Eldress, if you want to escape."

The video ended.

Well, Abigail couldn't be associated with a man who had to be rescued by an elderly grandmother. The memes alone would be career suicide.

Before the plane landed in Baltimore, she'd already sent out the necessary emails to remove Calix from their nutritional start-up business. A business that that been funded by Von Grace Industries.

*Don't get mad. Get even.*

She spritzed a refreshing mist over her face, teased her auburn hair, and swiped her signature lip gloss over her pillow-pouting lips. Then she posted a selfie on her Instagram page, captioning it, *"CEO, AVG Fitness, Single and Ready to Mingle."*

# Two Weeks Later

Slants of a New England sunrise peaked through the curtains in their bedroom. Mara stretched and yawned and snuggled closer to the blazingly hot body lying next to her. Some mornings she'd woken slightly confused; she was not used to a naked man sleeping beside her.

She quickly got used to it.

Or rather, her body did.

She went from having no sex to a lot of sex in a short amount of time. She was worried that her bruised inner thighs and the bite marks marring her skin would raise wrong impressions should someone examine her. Thank goodness it was winter, which meant turtleneck sweaters. She didn't know what she was going to do in the summertime now that she'd discovered she had a love of being bitten.

Beside her, Vikk groaned sleepily. An early morning gruff but sexy sigh erupted from his enticingly sinful lips.

*Dear God*, she moaned as she gyrated against him.

Mara felt wetness still coating her thoroughly abused pussy from last night's lusty jousting. She wanted more. Needed more.

She'd fucking die if he did not enter her in the next five seconds.

"Well, good morning, my love," he growled into Mara's ear as she raised a leg and hooked him close.

"Good morning yourself, my sexy alien."

Vikk shifted on top, his cocks slipping easily between her open thighs. Her fingernails scraped his lower back, pulling him as deep as her insides would allow.

Mara gasped aloud but reined it in. She could not be loud, not with Finley down the hallway. Oh, she knew Finley knew. They couldn't always be quiet, but they tried.

His thick cock stretched her beyond the highest pleasure point. She'd gladly sell her soul if it meant he'd ride between her thighs, pushing the boundaries of what she thought was possible.

He all but covered her. When she looked into his sparkling eyes, she saw his Vraitheian form. She loved him no matter how he appeared, but there was something special when she saw his true form and felt his massive weight atop her. Breathing was totally overrated. All she needed was his double cock filling her pussy while his mouth covered hers in deeply satisfying kisses.

Mara couldn't remember a time when she was happier and more satisfied with life. The school board had reversed course on *The Curse of Mathilda's Sorrow* after all the backlash. Her students were really engaged in the classroom.

Calix had all but disappeared. No doubt he was hunkered down due to the scathing reputation he'd gained due to the Patti Stoltz's interview.

Finley's symptoms, while still present, were less severe due to Dr. Smindle's care packages. It would be a series of trial and error, but so far Finley was responding well. It wasn't perfect, but it was progress.

And, with all the encouragement from Dessa, Hannah, Finley, Vikk, and even Dr. Brady, Mara had opened a fresh document and started writing a novel, the plot of which was about how an author's novel bombed on Earth but was a surprise hit on an alien planet. She'd landed a new literary agent who was enthusiastic about her career. Publishers were already fighting over the rights to publish the untitled novel.

It was nice to be fought over. Could life get any sweeter?

It could, she answered herself, as Vikk's head dipped so he could bite her nipples. Ripples of pleasure flared out, red-hot and inextinguishable. Their coupling had to be a five-alarm fire.

Then, she felt herself being tossed around, now facing away from him, as he smoothly entered her from behind. Mara's eyes nearly rolled into the back of her head as Vikk split his cock. With his hands firmly locked on her hips, holding her still, one cock slid deep inside while the other sluiced across her clit.

She arched back like a horny vixen, giving him better access. He grunted in response. Lately he'd caused the top cock to vibrate and Mara all but climaxed five or six times in a row.

Some nights she thought she might literally pass out. Ecstasy really agreed with her.

Ecstasy agreed with him, Vikk thought as he made gentle love to the love of his life. He had no regrets in abdicating the Vraitheian throne. His aunt had not yet announced it, but they had talked and she was prepared to name Finley as heir. Vikk had not yet found a job on Earth, but now that he realized his account contained enough money to take care of them for a while, he mostly spent his days looking for a bigger house for his new family. During his downtime, he discovered a joy of cooking and enjoyed keeping house for Mara and Finley. He knew they were happy because their auras conveyed love, trust, and cheerful dispositions.

Mara was quick to show her love. And what he loved was that she accepted him along with his imperfections and mistranslations.

*And* she was understanding when they had to purchase a new bed frame after their first night together.

Human beds were not engineered for Vraitheian sex.

They'd broken it within a matter of minutes.

Now, nuzzling the back of Mara's neck as her breathing became shallow and her hands more frantic, he smiled as he recalled her burst of surprise laughter, the way she'd thrown back her head, exposing her glorious throat as the bed crashed sideways and they'd tumbled haphazardly to the cold floorboards. It didn't stop their lovemaking. A tangled-haired Mara merely climbed on his lap, cried out, and rode his cocks like her very life depended on it.

Now, however, in the early morning, before Mara got ready for work, before Finley woke up, it was in quiet moments like these, as Mara clutched to him as she peaked, incoherent moans bubbling on her lips, her pussy contracting erratically around his cocks as he climaxed deep inside her, Vikk bit Mara's shoulder and reminded himself that he was the luckiest man in the entire universe.

Vikk's heartstrings quivered as a satiated Mara nestled in the crook of his arm. She mumbled something about it being a Wednesday as she threw a leg over his and caught a catnap before she had to get ready for work.

He gathered her close and smiled.

His heartstrings tethered outward, searching for Mara's essence, seeking acceptance, permission, love. She'd given each freely. This time around he did not have to call back his heartstrings, and knew he never would from this point forward.

# EPILOGUE (FINLEY)

Dear Diary: They found Dad today. I don't blame him for wanting to lay low. His face was everywhere, and not in a good way. Patti Stoltz launched a well-crafted career off her interview with Dad; she has been on all the talk shows to discuss how she suspected Calix Eldress of duplicity long before she cornered him at the hospital last month.

I wish I could say that Dad had flown to a deserted island for a swarthy getaway, but it wasn't anything like that; he had no money after Abigail cut him off from their business. Adding insult to injury, Abigail's notoriety went through the roof and she started dating her new celebrity client.

Not that any of that had to do with Dad's discovery.

It turns out he'd holed up with the same lady who helped him escape. Olivia Ogilvy. She'd lost her job, too, but at seventy-five years young, I guess her retirement income was enough to support her and Dad for a few weeks. He'd probably still be there if they hadn't gotten into an argument. I don't know what they fought about, but by the time the authorities arrived, Olivia was flinging romance novels at him like they were ninja stars, and the police found him huddled beneath a pile of straining breeches and heaving bosoms.

I kind of feel sorry for Dad's reduced state.

Mom says it's okay to feel that way, that I'm allowed to feel my feelings, even if they are confusing and don't make sense. I've gotten used to Mr. Stravdas—I mean, Vikk—living with us. He's like the biggest steel-blue teddy bear with googly eyes only for Mom. It's embarrassing. They are so cute together and I've never seen Mom happier or more content, even when Vikk asks if a stack of one-hundred-dollar bills is enough money to pay for a cup of coffee or when he whips up these amazing meals from scratch.

I think their happiness is contagious. I've been feeling really good lately. Dr. Smindle's care packages seem to be working to lessen my symptoms. I still get bad headaches, and there are days I need to hibernate in my bed with Mom and Vikk taking care of me, but I can feel the difference—I can feel *progress*. And that's enough for now, because I can see the light at the end of the tunnel. I never thought I'd have that.

The queen and I talk almost daily. It's still strange to think of her as my great-grandmother. Our conversations are slow at times due to the language barrier. Sometimes she will holler for Areola, who derails the entire call, and by the end of it, I'm in stitches. All they do is bicker like an old married couple.

Once or twice the queen has hinted that when we visit at Spring Break, she'll be making a big announcement. Considering Vikk abdicated the Vraitheian crown to be with Mom, I have a guess what it might be, but I don't want to take that joy from her. For all I know, I could be totally wrong, and she wants to stage another papier-mâché joust.

I can tell Queen Uska wants to ask me about Dad, about his parents. She's still in mourning at losing Qoral. We found out from the army that she died a long time ago while serving in the military. I suppose it's never easy to learn that you'll never speak to your child again. I'll be here when she's ready to ask and I'll tell her what I know.

As for Serstene...well, let's just say I'm glad no one will ever read my diary but me, otherwise you'd see how bad I'm blushing right now. Serstene is my boyfriend and I like how that sounds. *My boyfriend.* I will see my boyfriend at Spring Break.

I say that out loud a lot while looking at my reflection in the mirror. I've been inspecting my skin for hints of blue, if I see low rise klaums. So far, nothing.

But I can't wait for when I do see them.

# Epilogue (Nurse Ogilvy)

Olivia Ogilvy was an old enough dame and had read enough historical romance novels that employed kidnapping as a romantic device, that she knew when her part in the plot had gone sideways.

Not that she was complaining that the now-bearded Calix Eldress had decided to stay—hide out—in her humble home outside Washington, DC., but it wasn't as much fun as she had anticipated when she'd heroically rescued him from Patti Stoltz.

Patti Stoltz had, at one point, said that Calix was a spy. People had to be looking for him, right? Olivia liked the idea of operating a secret bunker, where spies hid out until the coast was clear. She imagined car chases, military helicopters, and investigative reporters sniffing around the district, trying to catch his scent.

She'd even have settled for a police standoff where he'd barricaded himself in her living room, demanding an audience with the President, twenty bars of gold, and a getaway carriage.

Instead, he'd complained bitterly about losing his house,

job, and reputation all in one night because of the conniving, lying women in his life.

Olivia was ready to sympathize with him until he tried to steal from her. The only type of thief she'd accept in her life was a masked highwayman, not a disgraced man who was trying to sneak out of her house with the professional blender she'd received as a present on her twenty-year employment anniversary.

One must *earn* that blender.

Olivia, seeing red, reached for the first thing that came into contact with her hand, and flung it at him. It was one of her historical romance novels. She looked behind her. Her entire wall was full of romance novels. Hundreds and hundreds of them.

Her pale gray eyes gleamed. Hundreds and hundreds of *weapons*.

The only thing Olivia Ogilvy did faster than read those novels was to throw them at the cur crumpling in her doorway.

Did she have to keep throwing them after the man was down?

No.

But it gave her such immense joy.

It was a true happily ever after.

# Acknowledgments

Writing can be a solo occupation but that does not mean *Claiming the Heart of Vraithe* was a solo endeavor. I have many people to thank. My family encouraged me after I told them in late 2021 that I wanted to write a bonkers romance novel where an author's failed memoir was a huge hit on an alien planet. The idea came to me during my linguistics class while thinking about mistranslations and whatnot, so many thanks to Dr. Busby for an interesting class!

Lyn Worthen, Ron Collins, and Dayle Dermatis were each instrumental in making this novel look as good as it does. Thank you for taking the time to work with me and look over my novel in its various stages.

From day one, my sister Samantha Bontrager has always been my #1 fan and cheerleader. I always know I'm on the right track if she likes the storyline. Trust me, she'll tell me if something is not working. Thank you and I love you dearly!

For those of you who like inside trivia, as I wrote this novel, it was merely called "SF Alien Abduction Romance Novel" until about the 40k word mark. After that, *Claiming the Heart of Vraithe* came into being as the title, and I'm rather happy with it.

Every character, save one, was renamed after I wrote "The End." This is pretty standard for me. So whose name didn't change? Hannah Atholms stayed the same name throughout the novel. You are probably asking yourself, "What was Areola's name before it was changed?" It was Gru'Dela.

Patti Stoltz was a lot of fun to write. She is probably my favorite character to write. You'll see more of her in future volumes. Go ahead and consider her a permanent antagonist.

I'd jump in front of a moving train for Nurse Olivia Ogilvy. What a Dame. What a legend.

More trivia? I did not set out to pair Hannah and Dessa. Those two, once on the page together, had instant chemistry. They completely upended all of my plotting because CeCe was *originally* supposed to be the heroine for Book 2. Back to the drawing board. Hannah and Dessa will be the main characters for Book 2.

What comes next? Well, I hope more bonkers romance! I am coming up with as many zany ideas as I can for Hannah's journey to Vraithe. She's Dessa's +1 for Mara and Vikk's Bonding Ceremony.

Outside of writing the next Vraitheian Alien Romance novel, I continue to write and publish short stories and novellas. I have a few in the pipeline that I cannot disclose at the moment, but I hope you'll keep tabs on my website and my socials to stay up-to-date.

Finally, to my readers: I seriously cannot thank you enough for reading my stories. I am an indie author, so word of mouth and reviews are tremendously helpful in my line of work. As much as I'd love for my novels to become popular on Vraithe, I'd really, really love it if they became popular on Earth.

Until then, happy reading!

# About the Author

A third-generation soldier, Kelly Washington isn't afraid to push boundaries in real life and in her fiction. Regardless the genre—fantasy, science fiction, or romance—her writing style packs a powerful punch by featuring strong and independent, yet flawed, characters. Born into a family of voracious readers, she ignores as many obligations as possible in order to finish reading one more chapter.

Kelly is the author of the Falling for Him military romance trilogy, the four-volume epic fantasy series Reclaimed Souls, the Moira Rothrock novella series (*Unlocking the Devil* and *Sleeping with the Devil*), the stand-alone Freaky Friday-esque military romance novel *Collide Into You*, and the bonkers science fiction romance novel *Claiming the Heart of Vraithe*.

Her short fiction has appeared in *Overheard Magazine, Cutter's Final Cut, spillover mag, Fahmidan Journal, Pulphouse Fiction Magazine, Kaleidotrope, Heart's Kiss*, and multiple *Fiction River* anthologies. Her short story, "The American Flag of Sergeant Hale Schofield" was a 2016 *Year's Best Crime and Mystery* story.

You can find out more about Kelly and her newest releases on her website, www.KellyWashington.com.

www.ingramcontent.com/pod-product-compliance
Lightning Source LLC
Chambersburg PA
CBHW070559300726
48975CB00006B/1639